This book should be returned to any branch of the
Lancashire County Library on or before the date

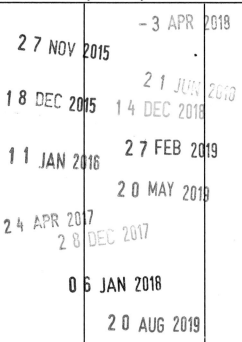

TARA BOND

Beautiful
LIAR

**SIMON &
SCHUSTER**

London · New York · Sydney · Toronto · New Delhi

A CBS COMPANY

First published in Great Britain by Simon & Schuster UK Ltd, 2015
A CBS COMPANY
Copyright © Tara Bond 2015

The right of Tara Bond to be identified as author of this
work has been asserted in accordance with sections 77 and
78 of the Copyright, Designs and Patents Act, 1988.

1 3 5 7 9 10 8 6 4 2

Simon & Schuster UK Ltd
1st Floor
222 Gray's Inn Road
London WC1X 8HB

www.simonandschuster.co.uk

Simon & Schuster Australia, Sydney
Simon & Schuster India, New Delhi

A CIP catalogue record for this book is available from the British Library

Paperback ISBN: 978-1-4711-1160-0
eBook ISBN: 978-1-4711-1161-7

This book is a work of fiction. Names,
characters, places and incidents are either a product of the author's
imagination or are used fictitiously. Any resemblance to actual
people living or dead, events or locales is entirely coincidental.

Typeset by Hewer Text UK Ltd, Edinburgh
Printed and bound in Great Britain by CPI Group (UK) Ltd, Croydon, CR0 4YY

In memory of my lovely, glamorous mummy
Pamela Ann Hyland
15 December 1941 – 6 February 2014
We miss your big smile, generous
nature and love of life

Chapter 1

'You here alone?'

The man didn't look at me as he spoke. He was too busy searching through his wallet. He pulled out three notes to pay for his petrol, and slid them under the small hatch. That was the only way we could take payment after eleven at night, because the shop was locked up as a safety precaution.

Our fingers touched briefly as I took his money, and I recoiled at the clammy feel of his skin. I had to resist the urge to wipe my hand on my overall, and instead busied myself at the till, rifling through the drawer to get his change.

I deliberately hadn't answered his question, and I'd hoped he'd let it go. But then I heard his voice, more insistent this time. 'I said – you here alone?' He glanced at the nametag on my striped overall. 'Nina.'

My heartbeat quickened. There was no one else here, but I didn't want him to know that. Especially since he was the first customer I'd seen since midnight. It was the early hours of Monday morning, and anyone with sense was home in bed, resting up for the busy London week ahead.

I took a deep breath, and turned back to face him. 'Manager's out the back.' I forced myself to meet his gaze. 'I'll get him, if you want.'

The security cameras were out again, so if it came to it, the police would be relying on me to tell them what the man looked like. I searched for a distinguishing feature, but came up with nothing. He was white, middle-aged, and had brown hair and brown eyes. He was also average height and weight – the very definition of nondescript. And the way he'd parked his unmarked white van, I couldn't catch the plates.

The man counted his change with painstaking deliberation, before tucking it into his back pocket. He lifted his eyes to mine and I could tell from the amused look that he knew I was bluffing.

'Shouldn't leave you here alone. Not at this time of night. Young girl like you, it's not safe. You tell your manager that.'

He nodded a goodnight, and then walked away without another word.

I stood watching as he crossed the forecourt and got into his van. It was only once he'd driven off that I realised how tense my body was. I breathed out hard, forcing myself to relax.

It was hard to know what to make of the man. Maybe he was genuinely concerned rather than creepy. Most people thought it was wrong to have a nineteen-year-old female here alone at night, but the late shift paid more than days, and I needed the extra cash.

It was almost 2 a.m., so I forced the man from my mind, and began to go through the process of closing up. I put the meagre takings for the night in the safe out the back, and then shrugged on my jacket, grabbed my bag, and made for the door. I paused for a moment, my nose pressed against the glass as I peered out into the darkness, alert as a gazelle in the Serengeti. I couldn't see anyone lurking in wait, so I flipped the light off. The station plunged into darkness, the forecourt lit only by the fluorescent glow of the sign that loomed out near the road. I pulled open the door and stepped outside.

The smell of petrol hit me along with the cold night air. However long I worked there, I never could get used to the odour. It seemed to get everywhere, seeping into my clothes and skin. After a shift, I'd always spend ages in the shower, scrubbing away, but I still couldn't seem to get rid of it.

I had the huge set of keys for the shop in my hand, the correct ones already picked out for a quick getaway. There were two locks, plus a padlock, and I had the whole process down to thirty seconds. At the end, I gave the padlock chain a quick tug to make sure it was all in place, and then I dropped the keys into my bag and headed off into the night.

As I crossed the darkened forecourt, I stayed on high alert, watching the shadows for movement. It was only once I reached the main road that my heartbeat eased. Most people considered this part of East London to be a no-go area, but I never minded walking home alone at night. Even though Tower Hamlets had notoriously high crime and poverty rates, I'd never had any trouble. I think it's because I managed to give the impression of being pretty tough. Even though I wasn't physically intimidating – only five foot six and naturally slender – in my standard uniform of dark jeans, biker boots and bomber jacket, I didn't look like someone to mess with. Plus with my short dark hair jammed under a beanie hat, I could pass at first glance for a boy.

I set off along East India Dock Road, away from affluent Canary Wharf, and towards less salubrious Plaistow in Newham, where I lived. Usually there were gangs of youths gathered round the kebab shops, but tonight the streets were pretty much deserted. It was late September, there was already frost on the ground, and no one was hanging around outside without good reason.

A couple of girls my age were huddled by the 24-hour convenience store, counting out money for cigarettes. In crotch-skimming dresses, they looked like they were on their way back from clubbing. It was hard not to envy their carefree demeanour. I glanced into the shop as I passed, nodding at the assistant inside. The place was a rip-off, but late at night it was the only way to get the vodka that my mother craved. They'd got to know me far too well over the years.

A sudden blast of sirens broke the silence. Instinctively I looked round, and watched as two fire engines raced by, followed by an ambulance. Five hundred metres ahead, the vehicles turned right, onto my street.

My first thought was: *Oh, Mum. Not again.*

Then I broke into a run.

It took me about ninety seconds to cover the distance. I was breathing hard when I rounded the corner into Hayfield Court, the council estate where we lived. Three soulless tower blocks stretched twenty storeys high around a concrete square. One lone tree stood in the centre, permanently stunted by a lack of sun. I'd just turned thirteen when we moved there – the year my dad died. I'd sobbed my heart out the first time I saw the place. It had seemed such a far cry from the pretty suburban street where we'd lived. But with Dad gone, there'd been no money to pay the mortgage, and a council flat was our only option.

I instinctively looked up to the fifteenth floor of our tower block. Sure enough, there were firemen on the walkway outside my family's flat. I could guess what had happened. This wasn't the first time Mum had fallen into a drunken stupor halfway through a cigarette.

The paramedics were already loading someone into an ambulance, which meant the lift must have been working for once. As I drew closer, I saw that it was Mum on the stretcher. An oxygen mask covered her mouth and nose, for the smoke inhalation, but otherwise she looked unharmed.

She gazed up at me, her large violet eyes sorrowful, her pale blonde curls framing her delicate face. Even after all those years of pounding the bottle, she was still a beautiful woman, the epitome of feminine. I looked nothing like her, and had taken after my father instead – inheriting his square jaw, chocolate-brown hair and eyes, and olive complexion.

'Where the hell's April?' The paramedic looked over in surprise at my harsh voice, but I didn't care. Any sympathy I'd felt for my mum had vanished a long time ago. She'd brought this on herself – had ruined all our lives with her weakness. Sure, it couldn't have been easy to lose her husband, and be left to raise two young daughters alone. But drowning her sorrows hadn't helped matters. She was hell-bent on self-destruction. My sister was another matter . . .

April was only fourteen years old, and she didn't deserve to be caught up in this.

'Where is she?' I said again.

My mother didn't attempt to speak, but her eyes shifted right to a police car. I followed her gaze, and I felt a rush of relief as I saw April standing there in tartan pyjamas, with a brown blanket thrown around her thin shoulders. She was crying loudly, while a young policewoman tried to comfort her.

April must have felt my eyes on her, because she looked up then. Without any thought to her bare feet, she broke free of the policewoman, and ran across the rough concrete to where I stood, hurling herself into my arms.

'Oh God, Nina. I'm so glad you're back.' She sobbed the words against my chest as I held her tight. 'I knew she was bad tonight. I should've stayed awake, but . . .'

But she was fourteen, and needed her sleep. It wasn't fair to expect her to take care of a drunk thirty-nine-year-old woman who should have known better.

I held my sister close, stroking her fair hair. She was the lucky one, who had inherited our mother's looks – although thankfully none of her selfish personality. Outsiders often thought I must resent being the loser in the gene pool lottery, but in truth I was pleased not to have anything in common with our mother.

'Don't you dare start blaming yourself.' It wasn't the first time I'd had to say this. 'None of this is your fault.'

April pulled away, looking up at me with wide, tearful eyes. 'They're going to take me away, aren't they? After this . . .'

She began to cry again.

I could understand her distress. Our social worker had warned us last time that if there was one more incident, April would be placed in a foster home. It was tempting to tell her that she wouldn't be going into care, but I wasn't about to lie to her. Too many broken promises, and you lost your ability to trust. I'd learnt that the hard way. It wasn't fair to take that from April.

I felt a flash of guilt about having gone to work. If only I'd stuck to the day shifts. But we'd needed the extra money, and I'd decided that took priority.

'I'm so sorry, love.' A voice interrupted my self-flagellation. It was our neighbour, Doreen Cooper, a thin, harried mum of five. She'd promised to keep an eye on my mother while I was out. 'I thought she'd gone to bed at midnight. But then the smoke alarm went off . . .'

That was about right. Everyone feeling guilty, apart from the person who should have been – our selfish mother.

I closed my eyes, and wished this whole nightmare would go away.

Chapter 2

'Well, this is quite a mess, isn't it?'

I was sitting in A&E – waiting while the doctors checked April out – when I heard the voice. I looked up to see a short, stout woman in her early fifties, with wild, grey-streaked hair. It was our social worker, Maggie Walker, looking even more dishevelled than usual in an unflattering Paisley dress and long navy cardigan.

'I wondered when you'd turn up.' My voice was hostile. Nothing against Maggie – she'd been fair to us over the years – but her presence here wasn't going to be good for the Baxter family.

Maggie flopped into the chair next to me. 'I thought she was doing better.'

'She was,' I said. 'Sober four months and counting.'

'What set her off this time?'

I rolled my eyes. 'What do you think? She got dumped again.' Since Dad had died, there'd been a revolving door of losers through our lives. Mum moaned about them and fought with them constantly, and then fell to pieces when they left. *You don't understand*, she would tell us. *I need a man. It helps me forget how much I miss your father. I can't stand being alone.*

She often asked me why I didn't have a boyfriend. That was why. Who wanted to be so reliant on another human being that they couldn't cope by themselves?

'So what happens now?' I said. 'To April.'

Maggie sighed, her cheeks puffing out as she shook her head. 'Look, love, I'm not going to lie to you. It's bad this time.'

'Yeah.' I didn't bother to keep the sarcasm out of my voice. 'I kind of guessed that.'

She smiled a little, and then grew serious. 'As of this morning, the court's placed April in foster care. The judge won't make any final decision for a while, but the way things are looking, I think there's a strong chance your mother's parental rights will be removed and your sister will be placed permanently in care until she's eighteen.'

'No.' I was already shaking my head, ignoring the cold, sick feeling in my stomach. 'That can't happen.'

I thought of all the awful statistics about children who'd been in foster care – the high incidence of eating disorders and self-harm. I didn't want that for my sister. In fact, I'd tried to ensure she had as normal an upbringing as possible. I could've gone to university, and left my mum and April to it. But instead I'd chosen to leave school at sixteen and work in a series of minimum-wage jobs, so I could keep our family together.

And now April was going to be taken away from us.

I looked over at Maggie. 'Tell me how to get her back.'

'Very simply, you need to be able to prove that you can give her a safe, stable upbringing.'

'Fair enough,' I said. 'I can do that.'

The social worker pursed her lips. 'Nina, you have to be realistic.' Her voice was gentle – the way it is when someone's delivering news you don't want to hear. 'Right now you don't even have anywhere to live.'

It was true. Weeks of repairs would be needed before the flat was habitable again. Doreen had offered to let me stay on her couch for as long as I needed, but her place was already crowded.

'And your mother needs to get sober,' Maggie went on. 'She needs a more aggressive solution this time. That means rehab—'

'So we'll do that.'

She looked sceptical. 'Come on. You know how long the NHS waiting lists are. The judge will have ruled against you by then. That means twelve weeks at a private facility – which is going to set you back at least ten grand.'

'I'll find a way to get the money. I can stay on a friend's floor—' Even as I said it, I knew how ridiculous it sounded. My work and taking care of my family had never left me time for friends. 'I'll get another job—'

'You've lost your job, too?'

Damn. That last piece of information shouldn't have slipped out.

'I kept being late for shifts.' Dealing with my mother's dramas meant I wasn't the most reliable of workers. When I'd called the manager at the petrol station to tell him that I'd have to miss the morning shift, he'd told me not to bother coming back.

Maggie's grey eyes filled with sympathy. 'Oh sweetheart, be realistic. I know you're tough, but this is too much, even for you.'

'Yeah?' I bristled. 'So you think I should just walk away, is that it? Just forget all about April?'

'No, of course not.' Maggie spoke with exaggerated patience. 'I just think you need to understand what you'd be getting yourself into.'

'Don't worry about me,' I said with far more confidence than I felt. 'I'll do whatever needs to be done.'

Maggie gave me a rueful smile. 'I've no doubt that you will. I'm just not sure you should have to.'

I looked away. I didn't need to be reminded of how hard this would be.

She reached out and squeezed my arm. I turned and saw the concern in her eyes. 'Nina, you can't do this all on your own. Isn't there anyone you can ask for help? A relative or family friend, perhaps?'

'There's no one.' Both sets of grandparents were dead, and my parents were only children, so there were no aunts or uncles around. And my mother had managed to alienate every friend we had over the years with her drinking. 'You of all people should know that.'

Just then, April came out to the waiting room, so there was no more time to talk. She spotted Maggie straight away, and seemed to know immediately what her presence meant. I'd worried that my sister might get upset at the thought of having to go into foster care, but perhaps by then she'd resigned herself to it, because she just gave me a long hug.

'You'll get me out as soon as you can?' she whispered in my ear.

'I will.'

'Promise?'

'I promise.'

Although right then, I had no idea how I was going to keep my word.

After April left, I spent the rest of the day by my mother's bedside. I might have despised the way she behaved, but she was still family, and I needed to make sure she was all right.

It was dark by the time I reached our flat. The emergency services had left and red tape criss-crossed the door, warning against entry, as though it was a crime scene. I quickly checked the walkway. There was no one around, so I ducked under the tape and used my key to let myself in.

The front door opened directly into a combined kitch-en-living-dining area. I stood there for a moment, my shoes sinking into the sodden carpet, and took in the damage. The walls were black from soot and flames; the furniture destroyed by the water and foam used to extinguish the fire. The place was completely uninhabitable.

It was then that the hopelessness of the situation finally hit me.

I had no home and no job. And then to top it off, in order to get April back, I needed to get my mother sober. Maybe that sounded simple enough, but right then it felt as reachable as the moon.

So, feeling like I had no other option, I did something that I knew my mother wouldn't approve of. I took out my phone and called Duncan Noble.

Chapter 3

I spent the night on Doreen's sofa. It was pretty much my only option. Growing up with an alcoholic parent made it difficult to form friendships. Mum's drinking habit was our family's dirty little secret, something that had to be continually covered up, and it was impossible to form meaningful relationships if you were always hiding the truth.

The following morning, just before eleven, I stepped off the Tube at Canary Wharf, London's newest business district. I had fifteen minutes to get to my meeting with Duncan Noble, the multimillionaire owner of luxury leisure group Noble Enterprises.

As I walked through the underground shopping centre to his offices, I tried to ignore the churning in my stomach. I had no idea what kind of reception I was going to get from the man – in fact, quite honestly, I still couldn't believe he'd agreed to see me. My father had worked as his chauffeur for about a decade before he died, and from what I understood, they'd gone from employer and employee to close friends over that time. But still . . . it had been almost six years since I'd last seen Duncan Noble. I'd only called out of desperation the day before because I couldn't think of any other option. But I just hoped I hadn't made a mistake.

Noble Enterprises was located at One Canada Square. It was the tallest skyscraper in the Wharf, fifty storeys high and home to everything from boutique hedge-fund management firms to advertising agencies. I walked into the huge marble lobby and tried not to look as intimidated as I felt. Security checked my bag, and then reception took my name and called up to make sure that I was expected.

Once I was signed in, and had been issued a nametag, I took the lift up forty floors to where Noble Enterprises was based. Now I was there, I felt a flutter of nerves – but there was no turning back. I needed help, and this was the only idea I'd had.

A haughty blonde, who looked only a few years older than me, was there to greet me when I stepped out of the lift. She introduced herself as Pandora Spencer, Duncan Noble's PA. I didn't exactly have much in the way of a wardrobe, so I'd opted for my usual tough-girl look – jeans, T-shirt and biker boots. Next to the well-groomed Pandora, in her tailored black dress and heels, I felt decidedly scruffy.

Pandora must have been of the same opinion, because as her sharp eyes ran over me I could tell she wasn't impressed with what she saw.

'Duncan's ready to see you.' Her voice was clipped and unfriendly, as though I wasn't worth making an effort for. 'So if you'd like to follow me.'

She didn't attempt any small talk as we walked. The workplace was open-plan, but at the sides there were glassed-off offices, which I guessed were for the senior employees. Naturally Duncan Noble had the best of these – a corner office, with floor-to-ceiling windows offering a direct view across the Thames to London's newest landmark, the Shard.

Duncan Noble stood as we entered. Six years on, he hadn't changed much. An attractive man in his late fifties, he had that suave sophistication that made older men like Sean Connery and Pierce Brosnan eternally appealing – from his salt-and-pepper hair to his Italian wool suit and handmade leather shoes.

'Nina.' Duncan didn't smile as he greeted me. In fact, he remained behind his desk, and put out his hand. 'It's been a long time.'

The coolness of his welcome surprised me. I wasn't sure what I'd been expecting – but perhaps a little more exclamation over how much I'd grown up. Wasn't that what usually happened when you saw someone you'd known as a child and were meeting again as an adult? Instead, I got the feeling he really wished I wasn't there.

'Thank you again for seeing me.' I stepped forward and shook his hand, deciding the best way to deal with the situation was to match his formal tone.

He gave a brief nod of acknowledgement. 'So before we start, can Pandora get you a coffee or anything?'

I saw her lips thin at the prospect of having to fetch me a drink, and I have to confess that it was almost enough to make me ask for something. But that would have meant prolonging the meeting, and I frankly wanted to get this over and done with.

'I'm fine, thanks,' I told him.

Pandora retreated from the room before I could change my mind. Once she'd gone, Duncan sat back down in his leather Eames chair, and indicated for me to take the seat opposite.

Once we were both settled, he fixed me with a steely gaze. 'So, Nina.' His tone was brusque and businesslike. 'I presume this isn't a social visit. So why don't you cut to the chase and tell me what the hell you're doing here?'

To be honest, the aggressiveness of his question didn't surprise me. After all, his last interaction with my family hadn't exactly been pleasant.

On the day of my dad's funeral, Duncan had promised to look after our family, and for the first few months, he'd given my mother money and checked in on us all the time. Then one night, I'd woken to the tail end of a huge argument between him and my mother. I'd crept downstairs in time to hear her ordering him out of the house, and telling him never to come near us again.

That was the last I'd seen of him. No wonder he was a little wary about my sudden reappearance in his life.

Luckily, I'd thought through what I wanted to say to him. So I ignored his hostility, and launched into my speech. 'That last night at the house – you said if I was ever in trouble, I should come to you.' He'd spotted me on the stairs when he was leaving, and slipped me his business card before my mother could see.

'I remember.'

'Well, I need your help.'

Given the history between my mum and him, I'd decided it was best not to talk about her part in the story, just in case he refused to help. Instead, I told him that I'd been at university, got myself into some financial difficulty, and had to drop out.

'So how much do you want from me?' he said, once I'd finished speaking.

It took me a second to work out what he was getting at. 'You think I'm here for money?'

His lips curved into a cynical smile. 'It would feel like a safe assumption.'

'God, no!' I didn't want him to think I was a scrounger. 'I just want a job.'

I'd stayed up late the previous night working out the logistics of how I could get us out of this mess. I actually had enough savings to cover Mum's rehab – courtesy of a small inheritance from my father when I turned eighteen, plus I'd saved every penny I could from my jobs over the years. I'd planned to use the cash to help April out with university, but getting my mum sober would have to take precedence.

Unfortunately paying for rehab would pretty much clear me out – which meant I needed a job, and one that paid well. Given the current youth unemployment in London, my chances of securing anything other than minimum wage seemed unlikely. And I didn't have the time for a lengthy interview process. Which made Duncan Noble my best option.

'Well,' he began, and with that one word my heart sank. I could tell he was about to turn me down. 'I applaud you for showing the initiative to come here. But unfortunately I don't think we've got any openings at the moment.' He pulled open the top drawer of his desk, and took out a chequebook and flipped it open. 'However, I'd be more than happy to help you clear your debts. Maybe even pay for you to continue at university—'

I was already on my feet as he picked up his Montblanc pen and started to write.

'I already told you, I don't want your money.' The sharp tone of my voice must have got through to him because he stopped what he was doing and looked up at me. 'I need a job, not charity,' I said more reasonably. After all, he'd been good enough to see me. 'I understand if that's not possible, so thank you for your time. I think it's best if I go.'

I could feel tears of frustration pricking at my eyes, and I turned away quickly, eager to leave before I let myself down by crying. My hand was on the cold stainless-steel handle of the glass door when he said, 'Wait.'

I looked back, and saw that he was frowning at me.

'You're really not going to accept any financial help?' He was looking at me with undisguised disbelief.

'I just want a job.'

He stared at me for a long moment, and I could tell he was debating what to do.

'Before I give you an answer,' he said finally, 'I need you to tell me one thing – does your mother know you're here?'

It wasn't quite the response I'd been expecting. 'No, she doesn't.' To that day, I had no idea what had happened between them – but I could take a good guess. Knowing my mother, she'd probably asked him for an outrageous sum of money, or else she'd made a pass at him . . . 'I didn't think she'd approve.'

I'd hoped he might elaborate – explain what had gone on between them. But instead he said, 'Look, Nina, I'll be honest with you. I admire you for coming here today. I think of myself as a good judge of character, and I suspect you're a conscientious person, like your father. So, as long as you swear to me that your mother won't learn of my involvement in this, then I'm happy to help you.'

I blinked, taken aback. 'I don't understand.'

'I'm saying I'll find you a job in my organisation. As long as you swear to me that your mother will learn nothing of this. So can you do that?'

I realised he was waiting for an answer. 'Yes. Yes, of course.'

'Good. Because now I think about it, I seem to remember we're looking for staff at one of our nightclubs – Destination. You've probably heard of it?'

I hadn't – cool London clubs weren't exactly my scene; I had neither the money nor the time to go to them. But that was the least of my problems. Working in a nightclub wasn't ideal. I couldn't imagine it impressing Social Services. I was meant to be proving that I could provide a stable place for my sister to live in – working unsociable hours around alcohol wasn't going to do that.

But I didn't want to seem ungrateful, and it wasn't like I had any other options, so I swallowed down my disappointment. 'That sounds great. Thank you.'

'My son, Giles, is the club manager. I'll arrange for you to meet him tomorrow afternoon. He'll keep an eye on you.'

I was a bit confused by that. After his initial hostility, he was now tasking someone to look out for me. It was quite a turn around.

I might have dwelt on that longer, but right then the phone rang. Duncan looked at the display, and snatched up the receiver.

'Pandora?' So it was the icy blonde PA. 'What? He's here now?' His eyes flicked to the clock on the wall. 'We were meant to be having a breakfast meeting three hours ago.' I couldn't make out Pandora's response, but whatever it was, Duncan rolled his eyes. Whoever was there, he was clearly irritated by them. 'Tell him to give me five minutes.'

He slammed the phone down, and then turned his attention back to me.

'Well, I think that's everything.' He stood, and I could tell he wanted me to leave. 'Pandora will give you the details for Destination. And as I said, if you need anything else, just ask Giles. He'll look after you.'

'Thank you,' I said. 'For everything.'

He waved a dismissive hand. 'As I said, I'm happy to help you out. It's the least I can do for Jack Baxter's daughter. But I don't want any trouble, especially from your mother. So all I ask is that you keep her out of this.'

He clearly wasn't looking for a response, so I didn't give him one. We shook hands briefly, and I made my way back towards Pandora's desk. As I approached, I saw that she wasn't alone – in fact, the ice queen had melted and was instead giggling up at a tall, well-built young man, who was draped across her desk, looking as though he owned the place.

He was maybe in his early twenties, and he had that aristocratic look about him – with chin-length, dishevelled black hair falling across a perfectly symmetrical face. The high cheekbones, straight nose and porcelain skin might have seemed almost effeminate if he hadn't had a spattering of designer stubble across his chiselled jawline, giving a bad-boy roughness to his looks. I wondered who he was. I'd assumed he'd be someone Duncan was interviewing – but if he was there for a job, he didn't seem too bothered about making a good first impression. Not only was he late, but he only seemed interested in chatting up Duncan's PA.

The man said something I couldn't hear, and Pandora giggled again. They were so engrossed in each other that they clearly had no idea I was there, so I had no choice but to noisily clear my throat.

They both looked up. Pandora scrunched up her small nose, clearly irritated at having her flirtation session disturbed. But it was the stranger who drew me up short. For a second, all I could see was his eyes – they were the palest shade of ice-blue I'd ever seen, and watchful and predatory, like a wolf's. There was something almost unnatural about them. He looked me over with what seemed to be cool disinterest.

'I suppose this means the old man's free.' His voice took me by surprise – I wasn't sure what I'd been expecting, but it wasn't that low, upper-class drawl. And what was it with the derogatory way he'd referred to Duncan Noble as 'the old man'? The stranger turned back to Pandora, who was getting to her feet. 'Don't worry, beautiful. I'll show myself in.'

He stood then, and I could see he was even more physically imposing than I'd realised – at least six foot two, and with a lean, athletic build. But it wasn't just his size that made him stand out. In black fitted trousers, a white pirate shirt and burgundy-velvet jacket, he had that flamboyant look of the Romantic era. He looked even more out of place than me in that corporate environment.

He sauntered over, and as he passed me his ice-blue eyes met mine. There was something in the way he looked at me – an almost penetrating stare that seemed designed to unnerve me. Our gaze held for a second. To my shame, I was the first to look away.

Then he was gone, leaving me alone with a clearly miffed Pandora.

'Well?' she demanded. 'What do you need?'

I forced myself back to the present, and tried to forget about those ice-cold blue eyes.

*　　*　　*

Half an hour later, I stood outside the gates of my sister's school. It was lunch break, and so the pupils were in the playground. April knew to look out for me. At the hospital, I'd whispered that I'd drop by St Mary's, so we didn't have to wait for the official visiting times arranged by our social worker Maggie Walker.

I spotted her easily. She was walking dejectedly, looking tired and pale. I could tell she was fighting the urge to cry.

She ran over to where I was standing. I wanted to hug her, but we had to settle for linking hands through the fence. I quickly asked her how she was getting along – aware that we didn't have much time before she'd need to go in for afternoon classes.

The house she was in wasn't too bad, she told me. The foster parents seemed nice enough, but there were three other kids staying there, and one of the girls looked like she could be trouble. She'd already taken April's lunch money that morning.

I didn't like the sound of that. I told April I'd have a word with Maggie and see what she could suggest. Meanwhile, I searched in my pocket and gave my sister all the money I had on me, and told her to keep it out of view. I also passed her the mobile that I'd managed to rescue from our flat, so we could keep in touch.

April took the cash and phone from me, and hid them away like I'd instructed. But she still didn't look happy.

'I don't want to stay there,' she said.

'I know. Trust me, I'm doing everything I can to get you back.'

From inside the school building, a bell sounded, signalling afternoon registration.

'Oh no.' April's hands tightened on the metal fence that separated us, and she looked up at me in distress. 'I don't want to go yet.'

I could tell she was about to cry, so I placed my right hand on hers, giving her a reassuring squeeze.

'I promise this won't be for long. I'm going to do everything I can to make sure we're back together soon.'

She looked up at me with large, hopeful eyes. 'All of us? Even Mum?'

It took all my effort to force a smile. 'Yeah, Mum too.'

That seemed to reassure her, and she left looking more at ease than before.

I stood and watched until she disappeared inside the school building, aware that I needed to do everything within my power to make this job at Destination work.

Chapter 4

The following afternoon, I got off the Tube at Green Park, the closest stop for Destination. Naturally the nightclub was located in Mayfair, one of the most exclusive areas of London. I walked by the Ritz, and crossed the road, heading down Old Bond Street. My route took me by all the expensive boutiques – Tiffany, Louis Vuitton, Jimmy Choo . . . Beautifully coiffed women emerged from the shops, followed by their drivers, who were laden down with bags. What on earth was I doing here?

After my meeting with Duncan Noble, I'd googled Destination, and now I was even more convinced that it wasn't my kind of place. It was a private members' club, aimed at a young, cool and wealthy crowd. Money and good looks seemed like a prerequisite. To me, it sounded pretentious and elitist, two things I hated. But for now I'd have to make the best of it.

I made my way through the maze of elegant streets until I reached Destination. Like most of the Mayfair nightclubs, it was located in the basement of one of the grand town-houses. The beautiful buildings had once been the London residences of the country's richest people, but now they were embassies, five-star hotels and hedge-fund-manage-ment offices. From the outside, there was no sign, but I followed the directions to the side entrance, where I'd been told to go.

I pressed the intercom.

'Yes?' a clipped voice said.

I confirmed that I was in the right place, and gave my name and reason for being there. A second later, I was buzzed in.

I walked into a small but modern reception area. A cool blonde sat behind a desk. She could have easily been the long-lost twin of Duncan Noble's PA Pandora.

'Take a seat. Giles will be out in a minute,' she said, before returning to her screen.

Behind her, there was a glass-door fridge, filled with bottles of Voss. Clearly I wasn't about to be offered anything, so I settled on the low leather couch and waited.

After five minutes, a tall, slim-built man, who I assumed was Giles Noble, appeared. He was good-looking in a clean-cut, preppy way, with short, sandy hair and a friendly, open face. He wore classic office smart-casual – chinos and a button-down blue shirt, with the sleeves rolled up, as though he'd been having a busy day. He looked like he'd just stepped out of a Ralph Lauren brochure.

'Nina, isn't it?' His cheeks dimpled a little as he smiled at me. 'Giles Noble. Why don't you come through?'

I followed him to his office. He sat at his desk, and indicated for me to take the chair opposite. I'd come across a couple of articles about him in my research on the club, and knew that at just twenty-four years old, he was already considered wildly successful. He was a golden boy, the Oxford-educated heir apparent to Noble Enterprises, who had made Destination the premier nightclub in London. It was safe to say his image fitted his CV.

'So Dad tells me you're looking for work.' He launched straight into the interview without any preamble. 'Tell me – what do you know about the club?'

'Not much, to be honest. I read a bit about it online. But . . .' I attempted a smile. 'It's not exactly the kind of place I hang out in.'

Giles nodded. 'I understand. And that's not a problem. No one expects you to be an expert.'

He launched into a description of the club and what they were trying to achieve. The emphasis, he told me, was on customer service – customers were spending a lot to be there, and they needed everything to be perfect. It was clearly something he felt passionate about, and I couldn't help being impressed.

'You've waited tables before?' he asked, when he'd finished his spiel.

'Yes.' It was one of the many jobs I'd got sacked from because of having to deal with my mother's ongoing dramas. And that had just been a greasy spoon, nowhere in this league. 'But I haven't worked anywhere like this.'

'I wouldn't worry too much about that. I know this place might feel a bit intimidating, but trust me – it's just a club, like any other. You'll be able to handle it.'

'Great . . . Thanks.'

We lapsed into an awkward silence. The formality of the meeting had taken me by surprise. Then, after a moment, Giles took off his glasses, and rubbed the bridge of his nose.

When he looked up at me, he seemed less sure of himself. 'Look . . .' He started and then stopped. He seemed so uncomfortable – I had no idea what he was about to say. I thought at first that he was trying to break it to me that there was no job there for me, but instead he said, 'I just wanted to say that I'm sorry about your father.'

'Oh.' It was the last thing I'd expected him to say. I'd guessed that Duncan Noble would explain who I was, but I didn't think he'd mention my father's death. 'Uh, thanks . . . But it was a long time ago, now.'

'Yes, of course.' He shook his head, clearly annoyed with himself. 'I'm sorry. I probably shouldn't have brought it up. But it's just . . . well, I remember your father from all those years ago. He was often up at Rexley.'

Hearing that name jolted me. Rexley Manor was the Nobles' country estate in Buckinghamshire. It was also where my father had died. He'd driven Duncan Noble there one evening, and was on his way back to London, when his car hit an icy patch, spun out of control and crashed into a tree on a little country lane near the estate. He'd died on impact.

The memory brought an unexpected rush of emotion. I glanced away, blinking back the tears.

'And now I've upset you.' Giles looked distressed. He closed his eyes in self-reprimand. It warmed me to him to see how hard he was struggling to do the right thing. After the formality of the first part of our meeting, it made him seem more human, somehow. 'I just wanted to say that your father was a good man, and he didn't deserve to die the way he did. I'm sure it must have been very hard on you and your family, and so if I can do anything to help you, please let me know.'

'Thank you,' I murmured.

After that, it was back to business. Giles took me through the job – I'd just be bussing glasses at the beginning – and the details of working hours and wages. It was a far more generous hourly rate than I'd been hoping for. Tips were on top, and at a rough calculation it would only take me about six weeks to save enough to put a deposit on a decent flat for us all to live in.

'So when can you start?' Giles said finally.

'Whenever you want me to.'

'How about this evening? Club opens at nine; we need you here from eight. How does that sound?'

'Perfect.'

'Good. We'll get the paperwork sorted now.' He offered me his hand, as though we were shaking on a deal. 'And remember – Dad wants you looked after. So any problems, you come straight to me.'

He flashed me his dazzling smile again, revealing a set of perfect, straight white teeth. I smiled weakly back. To be honest, I felt slightly overwhelmed by all the special treatment. I hadn't expected Duncan Noble to take such an interest in me. I knew he'd got on well with my father, but even I was surprised at his concern for my welfare. I wasn't sure what I thought about Giles looking out for me, but it didn't seem like I had much choice in the matter.

Once I'd filled out the paperwork, it was just before six. It would be a while before the club opened, so I went off to get some dinner.

I found a nearby café, and used some of my money to buy a tea and a cheese and ham toastie. It was ridiculously overpriced, but everywhere round here would be.

I settled at a table in the corner, and sipped at my tea. I had two hours to kill, so I'd brought over some newspapers to browse, but first I sent my sister a text, asking how she was getting along. I'd spoken to our social worker that morning about the girl who'd bullied April, but Maggie Walker hadn't been much help. She'd told me that she could contact the foster parents, and they'd speak to the other girl directly, but cautioned that it might do more harm than good. Basically, if it got that bad, they could move April to another home – but there was no guarantee that that would be any better. It was hard to know what to do for the best. I felt the beginnings of a tension headache, and rubbed my temples to try to relieve it.

After a few minutes, April texted back saying that everything was fine, so I was able to put my concerns about her away for the moment, and concentrate on the evening ahead instead.

By the time I was ready to go, the waitresses were shooting me dirty looks, and I could tell they were impatient to lock up. As I stepped out onto the street, a blast of cold air hit me. It was a shock after the warmth of the café. I stuffed my hands in my pockets, and hurried back over to Destination.

As I drew up to the building, I was surprised to see the transformation from earlier. It had lost its anonymity and now looked like somewhere that housed an exclusive nightclub. Two large bouncers stood by the roped entrance, alongside a stunning Oriental woman with a clipboard and an earpiece. A queue had already begun to form. At the front, a group of four girls were arguing with the doorwoman.

'But we booked a table,' one of the girls insisted.

When Giles had given me a rundown of the club's policies earlier, he'd told me that a handful of non-members were allowed in each night, depending on how busy it was. They had to book a table in advance, but it was at the door staff's discretion to turn them away, 'if they didn't look like they fitted in'. I took that to mean if they didn't look attractive or well-dressed enough. It had taken all my willpower not to roll my eyes at that. I certainly wouldn't have fancied my own chances of getting in.

The group of girls had obviously put on their best clubbing clothes for the evening, but even I could see there was a distinct look of the suburbs about them.

'I'm sorry.' The doorwoman looked impassively at them. 'But we're full tonight.'

The girls finally seemed to realise that there was no point arguing, and I watched them slink off. Part of me felt sorry for them, having their evening ruined like that.

But I also wondered why they'd want to go somewhere so snooty.

I went in via the side entrance, like before. It was much busier than earlier. Then, the back corridors had been empty, but now staff rushed by, gearing up for the night ahead.

Giles came out to meet me. Earlier he'd promised to show me round, but now he looked distracted. He called over a stunning mixed-race girl who had silky-smooth skin the colour of white coffee, and long black hair that fell in soft waves around her face. Giles introduced her as Jasmine Wright.

'Shadow Jas tonight, she'll show you the ropes.' He looked at Jas. 'That all right with you?'

Jas gave him a mock salute. 'Whatever you say, sir,' she said with fake deference.

Giles frowned a little, and retreated back to his office. As soon as he was gone, Jas gave a theatrical sigh. 'Oh, he's so dreamy, isn't he? A bit uptight, but in kind of a command-ing way.'

I was shocked that she was so forthcoming. I could never imagine saying something like that to a total stranger.

'Come on.' She linked her arm through mine. 'We've got half an hour till our shift starts. I want to hear all about you before that.'

She took me through to the staff changing room, and ushered me over to a bench. I wasn't quite sure this was what Giles had had in mind when he'd asked Jas to show me around, but she seemed more interested in chatting. As we sat there, she imparted her life story. She'd grown up on an estate like Hayfield, but in South London, and had never known her dad.

'He went back to Jamaica before Mum even knew about me.'

When she was fifteen, her mother had taken up with a new guy who'd shown a little too much interest in her daughter for her liking.

'Mum threw me out the day I turned sixteen. Happy birthday to me.'

She'd supported herself working in strip clubs. It was obvious that she'd have been good at it. Even in the demure black trousers and tunic, she couldn't disguise her knockout body. She did that for two years until a wealthy punter who'd taken a liking to her got her a job at Destination. She'd been working there a year now.

After twenty minutes, if was safe to say I knew everything possible about Jas.

'And what about you?' she finally asked me. 'What's your story?'

I shrugged non-committally. 'Not much to tell.'

Jas looked at me shrewdly, clearly sensing there was more to it than that. 'You don't say much, do you? That's a good way to be. I tell everyone all my business.'

She didn't seem offended by my reticence. It wasn't anything personal. I'd just learnt a long time ago to keep myself to myself. Back when my mum first started drinking, I'd confided in a girl who I'd thought was my best friend. The next day, my secrets were all round the school. I hadn't made that mistake again.

Jas stopped talking long enough to show me more of the changing room. Even it was plush, with power showers and Molton Brown toiletries. More like something out of an upmarket spa.

She found my locker, which had a uniform hanging inside. There were different outfits depending on your job status. Because I was only clearing tables, the lowest of the low, my uniform was the most simple – tight black trousers and a black tunic on top. Simple, tasteful. I guessed the all-black outfit let us move around inconspicuously, like ninjas.

'It's great working here,' Jas said as I changed. 'There're *so* many fit blokes. And they're loaded, too. I've been out with a couple. We're not *really* meant to – but everyone turns a blind eye as long as you're not up in their face. I've got some great stuff out of it.' She pulled out a necklace from beneath her tunic. 'It's Tiffany. Only silver, but still. It's pretty nice.' She touched her earrings. 'These are from there, too.'

'So – you've actually been out with some of the customers? Like boyfriends?'

'Oh, no. I just sleep with them now and again, and they give me stuff.'

I couldn't conceal my horror. She pulled a face. 'Oh, don't look like that. It's just a bit of fun. And the money means nothing to them.'

A bit like being a prostitute. It wasn't a great way to live, but I couldn't help warming to Jas. Perhaps if she'd been more calculating, it would have been distasteful. But she was so open and honest – so guileless – that there was something endearing about her.

She must have seen that I was struggling to control my disapproval, because she fiddled with her necklace and said, 'I know maybe it sounds bad, but I just like nice stuff. I guess cos I never had any growing up. Is there anything so wrong with that?'

Luckily there wasn't any time for me to come up with a reply. Right then, a tall, thin, humourless woman walked in, and a silence fell across the room. She looked older than us, maybe in her early thirties, with unnaturally black hair fashioned into a harsh bob, and bright red lips set against alabaster-pale skin. She wore a black trouser suit, like the doorwoman, and I could tell she was management of some kind.

'Come on, girls. Time to get to work.'

If she was aware that I was new, she didn't show it – in fact, she barely glanced in my direction.

'That's Mel, the assistant manager,' Jas whispered as we trailed out the door. 'Giles is a good guy, but she's a—' She pulled a face to show exactly what she thought of Mel.

But there was no time to talk any further. I followed Jas out for my first night working at Destination.

Chapter 5

The overhead lights were dimmed, giving the club's interior a chic subterranean feel, and ambient music pumped through the expensive sound system. A long silver bar ran one side of the room, backlit with neon blue. Low tables and modular seating surrounded a spacious dance floor, and the walls radiated a moody ruby glow.

It was a Wednesday night, and at first it was fairly quiet. But by midnight, the club was packed with wealthy-looking men and beautiful women. In fact, the crowd looked like they had been booked through Central Casting. Everyone seemed to be drinking champagne, served by the beautiful, hot-pants-clad hostesses, one assigned to each table. This wasn't the kind of place where people queued at the bar.

Jas and I were collecting empty glasses and bringing them to the bar. Jas was a fount of information, and seemed to know everyone. As we worked, she pointed out who was seated at the different tables – from Russian oligarchs to European nobility to City financiers.

'That's the most coveted table,' she said, pointing to the centre of the VIP section. The table was situated directly below the DJ booth, in prime location. 'It costs about ten grand to hire for the night.'

I let out a low whistle, and studied the people occupying it – two attractive Middle Eastern men who I guessed to be in their early twenties. 'Who are they?'

'Saudi princes, I heard.'

They looked on with cool detachment as three gorgeous women started to gyrate in front of them. 'And the girls?'

'Gold-diggers. There are always a few of them here, looking for a meal ticket. Management let a certain amount of them in because they're attractive, and rich men want to be surrounded by beautiful women.'

It seemed to be a theme of the place – you either got in because you were rich or because you were good-looking, and in a lot of cases it seemed people were both. It was elitism at its worst.

Jas nodded in the direction of two huge men standing discreetly to one side, and eyeing the table with professional alertness. 'They're the bodyguards, I reckon.'

It was like another world.

At one in the morning, there was a stir. I was up at the bar with Jas, ostensibly dropping glasses off while really listening to her gossip. But I looked up and did a double-take as I saw who was breezing through the door – it was the guy I'd seen the day before in Canary Wharf as I was leaving, the dark, chiselled Calvin Klein model lookalike with the ice-blue wolf eyes, who'd been waiting to see Duncan Noble.

Just like then, he stood out – mostly because of his I-don't-give-a-damn attitude. Most of the guys in the room were wearing suits, but he was flamboyantly dressed like before, in dark trousers and a white fop shirt – which reminded me of a seventeenth-century French courtier's – topped off with a black-leather coat. He'd clearly worn what he felt like, in the way that people do when they have nothing to prove.

I found myself watching as he crossed the room. He seemed to know everyone in the place. He stopped to talk to people at a few tables, before sliding into one of the booths in the VIP section. It was clearly one of the best seats in the house, and I guessed it had been reserved for him.

'And who's that?' I nodded in his direction, and Jas followed my gaze.

'That's Alexander Noble. His family own this place.'

The revelation floored me for a moment. And then suddenly it fell into place – the way he'd spoken about Duncan Noble, calling him 'the old man'. It hadn't even occurred to me at the time that he might have been referring to his father.

But then, having met preppy Giles, I'd never have guessed that Alexander was his brother.

'So that's Giles's brother?' I said, just to confirm I'd understood correctly.

'Yep. Alex is a couple of years younger – twenty-two, I think. He's also nothing like Giles. Alex is a total player. He's here most nights, surrounded by adoring girls. Gets one of the best tables in the place and blows a fortune on champagne.'

I looked back at Alexander Noble. He certainly didn't look like his older brother, either – if Giles had stepped out of a Ralph Lauren catalogue, then Alex was more Guess or Diesel. Right now, he was sprawled across the banquette, looking bored. There were three people in the booth – a tawny-haired man with a baby face and ruddy cheeks, and two expensive-looking blondes.

'Who's that with him?' I asked, hating myself for being interested.

'London's bluebloods,' Jas said, tossing her hair in a theatrical gesture. I raised an eyebrow, looking for a fuller explanation. 'You know the type. They've all grown up in Kensington or Chelsea, with wealthy parents, and attended the same schools and ski resorts, and now they hang out in the same clubs.'

'But it's a weekday. Don't they have jobs?'

She laughed. 'Yeah, well, that doesn't seem to stop them.'

I looked at her, waiting for a fuller answer.

She sighed. 'The girls tend to work in PR or art galleries or fashion. They're employed for their contacts, so no one cares if they turn up bleary-eyed. The guys who work in finance just do a line as a pick-me-up. And then there's the trust fund kids, like Alex Noble. The likes of him don't need to work.'

Her answer had just intrigued me more. But before I could pursue the conversation any further, raven-haired Mel materialised in front of us.

'Is there a problem here, girls?' Neither of us said anything. 'I thought not. So why don't you do a little less talking and a bit more work. After all, those glasses aren't going to collect themselves.'

The rest of the evening passed quickly enough. Just before closing time, I was walking by the bar, when a loud drunken banker stumbled off a bar stool and managed to spill beer all down my tunic.

Jas wrinkled her nose as she examined the damage. 'That stinks. You'd better go and change. You'll find a spare top in your locker.'

I hurried to the staff changing room. I hadn't expected anyone to be there, so I was already pulling my tunic up as I walked in, looking to save time.

'Don't mind me,' an amused male voice said.

I hastily pulled my top back down, and drew up short as I saw Alexander Noble before me. He was sitting astride the bench that dissected the room, looking like he'd stepped out of a photo shoot with his perfectly symmetrical bone structure and mussed-up black hair.

I wondered for a second what he was doing there. Then, as if to answer my question, he bent over, his silky dark hair falling across his face, and snorted a line of coke.

This wasn't an area of expertise of mine, but I'd seen enough TV programmes to have a rough idea of what was going on. He flipped his head back, and I watched as the high hit him. Then he wiped his nostrils and looked over at me, his ice-blue eyes extra bright.

Part of me was tempted to tell him he shouldn't be there – it was meant to be staff only – but then I reminded myself that he was the owner's son. I guessed he could be wherever he wanted.

He was regarding me expectantly, and I realised I was still just standing there staring at him.

'Sorry,' I muttered. 'I just needed to change my top.'

'Well, go right ahead. No one's stopping you.'

He seemed to be showing no signs of leaving, so I had no choice but to go to my locker. I kept the door open to shield my body from him as I changed.

As I closed it, I saw that he was frowning up at me, those wolf eyes studying me intently. When I went to walk by him, he rose, moving in front of me, his huge frame blocking my way.

'Now where do I know you from?' His voice was like honey – posh, yes, but also low and husky, in a way that jarred with his rugged appearance. I was about to tell him where he'd seen me, but a second later his expression cleared. 'That's it. I saw you yesterday. Over at the Wharf. You're the chauffeur's daughter, right?'

There was something mocking about the way he said it that immediately put me on my guard. 'That's right. I'm Nina. Nina Baxter.'

'Miss Baxter.' He gave a little bow of his head, his long dark hair falling across his sharp cheekbones. 'Lovely to meet you. My father told me all about you.' He held out his hand. 'I'm Alex, by the way. Alex Noble.'

I hesitated for a second, and then took the hand that he'd offered. His cool fingers closed around my slightly clammy ones. Everything about him seemed so calm and in control, whereas I felt like I'd been wrong-footed from the start of this exchange, and that I was out of my depth.

'Duncan Noble's son,' he added, probably mistaking my silence for confusion. 'In case you were wondering.'

'I know who you are.' As soon as the words were out of my mouth I felt myself flush, realising that it sounded like I'd been specifically asking after him.

Any hope I had that he might not have picked up on it

was quashed as he raised an eyebrow. 'Really?' he drawled. 'Been doing our homework, have we?'

'One of the other staff was telling me who all the customers were . . . that's all.'

'Hmm,' he said, in a way that made it clear he didn't believe me. 'Whatever you say.'

His eyes drifted over me again, appraising me in a blatantly sexual way. I was aware that he was too close, too much in my personal space. I swallowed hard, conscious that I should be putting an end to whatever this was, but not able to do it quite yet. But then he seemed to be moving closer, his hand reaching out behind me. It took me a split second to realise that he was trying to grab my bottom.

That was too much. Instinctively I took a step back, trying to put some distance between us.

'What the hell are you doing?'

I'd assumed my outraged tone would shame him, but he looked unperturbed . He cocked his head to one side, studying me through heavily lidded eyes. 'What exactly do you think I was doing?'

I crossed my arms over my chest. 'It seems pretty obvious.'

'Really?' An amused smile played on his lips. 'Because I get the feeling you thought I was trying to touch you up. When actually all I was going to do was this—'

Before I could stop him, he reached out again, exactly as he had done before. I felt his hand graze the back of my trousers, and then draw away. I had no idea what he'd done, until he held up a round orange sticker that read: *Ten per cent discount on bulk orders.*

I looked up and saw he was waiting for the moment when I worked out he'd actually been trying to do me a favour – not grope me, as I'd assumed.

I felt my cheeks heating up again. For once in my life, I was speechless.

'Oh, and trust me,' he said, making no effort to disguise the fact that he was enjoying my embarrassment. 'I don't need to go around molesting unsuspecting women. I have enough begging to be taken to my bed.'

Before I could formulate an apology, he screwed up the sticker and tossed it into a nearby bin. If I'd tried that manoeuvre, it no doubt would have bounced off the basket and landed on the floor, but for him, it went in perfectly.

He gave another little bow of his head. 'Lovely to meet you, Miss Nina Baxter.'

Then he turned and sauntered off.

It was only after he'd gone that I realised exactly what I'd done – not only had I humiliated myself, but I'd just insulted the owner's son. He'd seemed to take it well enough, but what if he chose to complain? And suddenly alongside my acute embarrassment at having misread the situation, I felt an overwhelming terror that I was about to lose my job.

Chapter 6

I found it hard to sleep that night. Every time I closed my eyes, my run-in with Alexander Noble went through my head.

But the following morning I resolved to put it from my mind. I had more pressing problems to deal with – like where I was going to live. It wasn't fair to keep imposing on Doreen, but my other options were limited. As a single adult in London, I wasn't exactly top of the priority list for housing.

Luckily our social worker Maggie had put in a word with her colleague in the housing department. He'd managed to find me a place in a bed and breakfast over in Wapping – where the council housed people while they looked into whether they deserved more permanent accommodation.

The manager of the B&B was a small, weasel-like man, with shifty eyes and a BO problem. He showed me a tiny room, which had just enough space for a single bed and an ancient wooden wardrobe. Masking tape covered the gap between the skirting board and the carpet, apparently to keep the cockroaches out.

I knew I should be grateful, but as I looked around at the peeling paint it was hard to see how living there was something to be pleased about. I could hear a baby crying through the paper-thin walls, while its mother tried to hush it. That wasn't going to make for a great night's sleep. But it was this or the streets.

On the way out, he showed me the dingy bathroom I'd be sharing with eight other people. There were no kitchen facilities. Fifty people resided in the building, he informed me – there were five floors with ten rooms on each. Given the number of children I saw, I had a feeling the number of people was actually a lot higher.

As we walked back down, I tried to ignore the smell of piss in the stairwell.

'Breakfast is from seven until 8.30,' he said. 'You need to be out by nine, and then you can come back in at four.' I thought of the late nights I was going to be doing at Destination. I'd have to get up and out, and then nap later.

He looked at me expectantly. 'First week's money up front,' he prompted, when I hadn't made a move.

I quickly handed over the cash. After paying for my mum's rehab, I had just enough savings left over to see me through to my first paycheque from Destination.

'Oh,' he said, once he'd counted it. 'I'm warning you now, don't leave anything valuable in your room. Not if you want to hold on to it.'

Hearing that, I couldn't wait to move in.

I left Wapping and headed over to the hospital. My mother was due to be discharged that day, and I'd arranged for her to be admitted into rehab. I took her straight there. It was a half-hour Tube ride away, in a leafy suburb in North London. She spent the whole journey talking about how it had been her wake-up call, and she was going to change her ways.

I listened with half an ear, and nodded along as I was expected to. But frankly I'd heard it all before, and had very little faith that anything would change. She'd let me down too many times in the past.

However, even at my most cynical, I couldn't help being impressed as we arrived. The entrance was tucked discreetly away on a wide tree-lined road. The long gravel driveway was heavily guarded with security cameras. At the end, there was a stunning honey-coloured mansion. It was like one of those rehab centres that celebrities went to.

We were given a quick tour of the facilities, which came complete with indoor pool and well-equipped gymnasium. The restaurant looked like it had received Michelin stars. I settled my mother into her room – beautifully decked out, if austere. It was then, just as I was preparing to leave, that she dropped the bombshell.

'Nina?' I was putting on my jacket, but the nervous tone in her voice made me turn. My heart sank when I saw the way she was perched on the bed, nibbling at her lower lip. I knew the look well – it meant she'd done something I wasn't going to be happy about.

'What is it now?'

She avoided my eyes. 'There's just one thing I need you to do for me . . .' I folded my arms and waited. 'I was running short a few weeks ago, so I borrowed a bit of money—'

'How much?' I knew my mother well enough to guess that it was more than 'a bit'. In addition to drinking, she was a dab hand at spending beyond her means.

'Nine grand,' she said sheepishly. 'Eleven with the interest.'

'Jesus, Mum.'

'Some of it was for Dave – some business venture or other. He promised to pay me back, but . . .'

But my mum's boyfriends were notoriously unreliable, and Dave had disappeared from the picture several weeks ago, triggering this current drinking binge. That meant the full debt was going to fall on us – or, more specifically, me.

'And who's the lender?'

'Sergei.'

I closed my eyes. This just got better and better. I knew exactly who she meant – Sergei Grekov, a Russian immigrant and leader of a band of thugs, who counted money-lending at extortionate interest rates as one of his many less than legal activities.

We'd been forced to borrow from him before on occasion – Mum wasn't the best at keeping a handle on finances. But it had always been small sums on a short-term basis – just to cover us for bills until I got my wages. This was more serious.

'And when are you due to pay?'

'This week.' Hearing that, I swore loudly again. 'I thought maybe if you could talk to him,' she went on hurriedly. 'Explain the situation . . .'

Yeah, because he was such a reasonable person.

'Don't worry,' I said tightly. 'I'll deal with it.' Like I had to deal with everything else.

On the way out, I was handed a leaflet reminding me that she wouldn't be allowed visitors for at least thirty days. It was the best news I'd had for some time. It would be a relief not to have to worry about her for a while.

The information about the debt weighed heavily on me as I got ready for work that evening. My plan was to contact Sergei and ask for additional time to pay off the money. But it had made me realise I needed this job at Destination now more than ever, and I was afraid I was going to lose it by having wrongly accused the owner's son of trying to maul me.

Fortunately the evening passed uneventfully. Alex and his entourage didn't make an appearance, and nothing was said about what had happened the previous night. My shift on Friday also went by without incident, and I began to relax. But then on Saturday, I was halfway through my shift when Mel came up to me and said that I was needed in Giles's office. My mind immediately went to the incident with Alexander Noble. 'How come?' I said uneasily.

She shrugged. 'Why don't you go and find out?'

There was no point putting off the inevitable, so I headed straight to Giles's office. I'd just have to hope that if I offered to apologise to Alex then Giles wouldn't sack me. Because without this job, I had no idea what I was going to do.

I knocked tentatively at the door. There was no answer, so I carefully pushed it open. No one was inside.

I was about to leave and come back later, when something caught my eye. On the desk there was a steel petty cash box – like the ones we used at the petrol station. From where I was standing, I could see that the key was inside the lock.

I don't know what made me do it, but I quickly checked the corridor. Once I was sure the coast was clear, I stepped into the room, and closed the door. Then I went over to the petty cash box, turned the key and lifted the lid.

Seeing the bundles of notes inside, I let out a gasp of surprise. At the petrol station, we kept about one hundred pounds in petty cash. But here there must have been thousands of pounds.

A wild thought occurred to me, one that must have been at the back of my mind when I first decided to walk into the room and look at the contents of the box. No one had seen me slip into the office. I could take the money now, leave quietly, and no one would be any the wiser.

I wasn't the type to steal. I'd always been honest, and fastidious about money – at the petrol station, I'd been the only cashier whose till always balanced, right down to the penny.

But back then my situation hadn't been so desperate. This would allow me to pay Sergei, or at least buy myself some time until I found another way to sort the situation out.

'Go ahead,' a husky, cultured voice said from behind me. 'Help yourself. I won't tell.'

I whirled round to see Alexander Noble leaning against the doorframe, watching me with a faintly amused look on his chiselled face. I could feel my cheeks flush red. He'd obviously been there for a while, and had guessed exactly what was going through my mind.

'I wasn't going to—' I started, and then stopped. Lying just made it worse. 'I was just looking,' I finished lamely.

'Of course you were.' He came into the room and sprawled in the leather chair across from Giles's desk. He swivelled round to face me. 'Day One – you accuse me of sexually assaulting you.' He counted on his long fingers. 'Day Two – you're caught stealing. Not one of my brother's better hires.'

I didn't know quite what to say to that. As much as I hated to admit it, he had a point.

'Is everything all right in here?' Giles said before I could respond. I looked up, and saw him standing in the doorway, frowning in at us. My stomach flipped over; I was afraid that he'd overheard our exchange. But then I realised his eyes were firmly on Alex. And he didn't look happy to see him. 'You harassing my staff again?'

Alex looked unfazed as he answered, 'Actually, I just dropped in to reclaim my coat.' He nodded over to the rack, where his black leather coat was hanging. 'And I found Nina —' I felt my heart turn over as he paused meaningfully. 'I found Nina here *waiting* for you,' he finished, his blue eyes dancing with wicked amusement that only I understood.

'Is that right?' Giles looked over at me for confirmation.

'Why are you asking her?' Alex said, a mocking tone in his voice. 'Are you saying you don't trust me?' He clutched a hand to his chest. 'You wound me, brother.'

Giles didn't bother to respond. I looked between the two men, unsure what all the tension was about. Even though they were brothers, the two of them couldn't have been more different – there was clean-cut Giles, the epitome of the hard-working businessman in a smart grey-wool suit, and bad boy Alex, who looked more like an indie rocker today in black jeans and a black T-shirt.

'Nina?' Giles looked at me for confirmation.

'Everything's fine,' I said hastily, worried that Alex might get annoyed and start revealing what had actually happened.

'See?' he said. 'As I told you, everything's fine here.' He stood, and collected his coat. 'So, as much fun as this has been, I'll be on my way now, and leave you two to it.'

He gave a theatrical bow and exited.

Once Alex was gone, I felt relief flood through me. For whatever reason, he'd obviously decided not to rat me out.

Giles turned to me.

'Sorry about that, Nina. Now what was on your mind?'

I blinked, feeling confused. 'I thought you wanted to see me.' He frowned, clearly as lost as I was. 'I got a message that I was needed in your office—'

Giles's expression cleared. 'And let me guess – you got here and Alex just happened to turn up?'

'That's right.' I spoke slowly, as I began to understand what he was getting at. 'You're saying he was the one who asked Mel to tell me to come to your office? But why would he do that?'

Giles gave me a rueful smile. 'I gave up trying to understand my brother a long time ago.' He walked over and dropped into his chair. I would have made my exit, but I had a feeling he wasn't done talking yet. I could see him considering his words carefully before he spoke. 'Look,' he said finally. 'Alex is my brother, and deep down I believe he's a good guy. But he's got a reputation. He likes to party hard—'

'I've already heard about the drinking and women.'

He gave a grim smile. 'That's just the tip of the iceberg, believe me.' I wanted to ask more, but he went on before I could. 'Look, Alex can be very charming when he wants to be. I just don't want you getting dragged into anything by him. He may be my brother, but take it from me, he's not the kind of person you want to get involved with.'

The thought that I'd be influenced by some superficial charm amused me.

'Don't worry,' I said. 'I understand what you're saying.'

'Good.' He gave a brisk nod, but I could see he was still a little concerned. 'My father asked me to look out for you, Nina, and that's what I'm trying to do. He and Alex – well, let's just say they don't have the easiest relationship.' I thought back to that meeting in Canary Wharf, when Duncan was clearly exasperated by his son turning up late. 'To say Dad wouldn't be happy to hear you were hanging out with Alex is something of an understatement. So take my advice, and steer clear of my brother. It's in your best interests.'

I got the message. Duncan Noble had given me this job, and he could just as easily take it away from me if I went against his wishes. That meant staying away from his youngest son. And from what I'd seen so far, that was fine by me.

I didn't have time to dwell on our conversation. It was a busy night in the club, and I spent the whole of my shift rushing around. By a quarter to three I was exhausted. The DJ was ramping up the music for the end-of-night climax, and most people were on the dance floor. I was at the bar, dropping off the empties, when Jas came up beside me.

'I just want this night over with,' she said. 'My feet are killing me.'

I knew what she meant. Even in the flat black pumps that were standard issue, the standing up became tedious after a while. But while the balls of my feet were aching, there were other parts of me that hurt worse. 'It's my back.' I rubbed my lower spine. 'All that bending over those low tables to collect glasses . . . It's torture.'

'Still.' Jas winked at me. 'Mustn't complain.'

I grinned. 'That's right – mustn't complain.' It was one of Mel's catchphrases before sending us out every evening – a warning not to let the customers hear us complaining.

'I don't know about that,' a male voice drawled from behind. 'A complaint to management sounds like an excellent idea. All this pain you're in – you should ask for a well-deserved pay rise.'

I turned to see Alex, a smile hovering on his lips. His ice-blue eyes were fixed on me.

'There was something I wanted to ask you earlier, before my brother so rudely interrupted us.'

'Oh?' I tried to sound uninterested.

'I've got a few people coming back to my place after this closes tonight, and I hoped you might like to join us.' His gaze flicked over to Jas. 'You too, of course.'

So that was why he'd asked me to his brother's office earlier. My first instinct was to refuse. I didn't quite understand why Alex Noble was trying to get to know me, but whatever the reason, I needed to stay away from him. I had enough problems without getting involved with some charming party boy.

But before I could decline Jas said, 'Sounds great! Count us in!'

'Good.' Alex answered her, but his gaze was on me. He rattled off the address, telling us that it was right opposite Knightsbridge Tube station. 'I'll see you both soon then.'

I watched him stroll back to his friends, and they all rose to leave. Another prickle of unease passed over me. Instinct told me that I should stay away tonight. But looking over at Jas's excited face, I wasn't sure how much choice I'd have in the matter.

Chapter 7

Our shift had ended, and Jas and I were in the staff changing room, arguing about whether to take Alex up on his invitation. My instincts were still screaming at me that it was a bad idea.

'It's so late now,' I said. I was sitting on a bench, watching Jas rifle through her locker. 'I just want to fall into bed.'

Jas turned to face me, hands on her slim hips. 'You can sleep all day tomorrow.'

'Honestly, Jas, I really don't want to go. It's been a long week for me . . .'

'Don't say that!' She rushed over to crouch in front of me, gripping both my arms as she looked up at me with huge, pleading eyes. It was theatrical and melodramatic, and designed to win me over. 'Please, please do this for me. I've been dying to go to one of these parties for ages. Besides,' she added, with a wicked glint in her eye. 'If you don't come, then I'll have to go alone, and then I'm much more likely to get into trouble . . .'

She'd just said the one thing guaranteed to get me along. There was no way I was going to let her go into that lion's den alone. I sighed, feeling myself giving in.

'Fine. I'll go. But only for an hour or so—'

Before I could finish that last part, she let out a little squeal of pleasure, and threw her arms around me.

'Thank you, thank you, thank you. You won't regret it. I swear.' She turned away and hurried to her locker, where she seemed to have a whole wardrobe of clothes. 'By the way,' she said, as she rifled through them. 'What did you do to get invited to one of Alex Noble's parties?'

'Oh . . .' I tried to sound casual. 'Nothing, really. I just bumped into him the other day and we started talking. It's no big deal.'

'Well, I hope it isn't.' She sneaked a look back at me. 'Because he's a total player. Too much even for the likes of me to handle – let alone you.'

I let the warning slide – it wasn't as though I needed it.

After that, it didn't take her long to get ready. She pulled on a tiny burgundy dress, which showed off her hourglass figure, and slipped into heels so high that I had no idea how she was ever going to walk in them. I watched in fascination as she applied lashings of mascara and dark lipstick, and shook her raven hair loose, so it settled in soft waves around her shoulders.

It was only then that she seemed to realise that I was still sitting there in my jeans and T-shirt, with no make-up.

'You're not going like that, are you?' She wrinkled her nose, showing me exactly what she thought of my appearance.

I looked down at myself and shrugged. 'Yep. Why?'

'It's just . . . well, you look a bit masculine, that's all. I mean, don't get me wrong,' she said hurriedly. 'You're gorgeous. You've got really strong features – big eyes and lips – which helps you pull off that pixie cut . . .'

Hearing that, I couldn't help laughing. That term – 'pixie cut' – seemed to imply I'd deliberately opted for a style, when in fact it was just easier to wear it short. My mother had cried the first time I'd had my long, heavy dark hair cut off, and routinely begged me to grow it out. But that just made me more determined to keep it this way.

Jas stepped closer, studying me. 'I've got a dress that you could borrow. And maybe I could just put a bit of make-up on you . . .'

But I was already shaking my head. 'No way. I'm going just the way I am.' She opened her mouth to object, but I held up my hand. 'And if I hear any arguments from you, I won't go at all.'

She mimed zipping her mouth closed.

'That's more like it,' I said. 'Now let's get this over with.'

Outside the club, the bouncers called a cab to take us over to Knightsbridge. It was policy at Destination that all staff members were provided with a taxi home after midnight. Jas chattered non-stop throughout the journey, mostly about the guys who were going to be there and how she hoped one of them would notice her. In the dress she was wearing, I didn't see it being a problem.

The cab dropped us by Knightsbridge Tube station. Right opposite was the super-luxury apartment block where Alex lived. I'd read about the state-of-the-art building, which came complete with bulletproof glass, and was home to the likes of Russian oligarchs and newly minted Chinese entrepreneurs. I'd never expected to be invited to a party there, though.

Inside the plush reception area, sharp-suited security guards checked our bags before directing us towards the lift. They didn't seem perturbed that we were turning up at such a late hour, and I got the feeling they were used to Alex receiving visitors at all times of the day and night.

Naturally Alex owned one of the penthouses. The dedicated lift opened directly into his apartment, something I'd only ever seen on TV before. We stepped into a striking hallway, with gleaming white walls and polished-concrete floor. It was all modern, sharp lines, like an exclusive art gallery.

'Wow!' Jas breathed. 'This place is unbelievable.'

I didn't reply. I was determined to appear indifferent to everything tonight, so I might as well start practising now.

Ahead of us, a door swung open. A snooty blonde emerged from what looked like a guest powder room. Unlike Jas, she wasn't beautiful, but she was attractive in that expensive, well-groomed way – hair extensions; spray-tanned limbs; and a toned body no doubt courtesy of a personal trainer. She wore a tiny sequinned backless dress that looked like it cost a small fortune, and even though I hated to admit it, she carried it off. It was something to do with the arrogant tilt of her chin.

I'd seen her around at the club with Alex. She must have recognised us too, because she stopped in front of us and wrinkled her nose.

'Who the hell invited the help?'

'Alex,' I said, enjoying the O of surprise her mouth formed. 'He asked us personally. Said it wouldn't be the same without us here, didn't he, Jas?' I knew it was hypocritical to suddenly be bragging about Alex inviting us, after I'd been wishing he hadn't. But I didn't like the way the blonde was looking at us as though we were scum.

I pushed past her before she could say another word, and grabbed Jas's hand, pulling her after me.

'Who was that?' I asked.

'Victoria Cavendish – or Tori, as she's known. Her dad's in property. He owns half of London. She's a big spender at the club, and an even bigger bitch.'

Somehow it wasn't hard to believe that last part.

It was only as I walked purposefully along the hallway that I realised I had no idea where I was going. But I used my common sense and followed the noise.

At the end of the corridor, we entered a vast, open-plan living area. Like the hallway, the walls and floor were gleaming white, which along with the double-height ceilings, created a feeling of space and light. A statement staircase led up to a mezzanine, where I presumed the bedrooms were, and a huge set of patio doors stretched the length of the room, providing magnificent views across London. It was exactly the kind of place I imagined a wealthy playboy to live.

The décor was equally impressive. Low-slung cream-suede couches surrounded the biggest plasma screen TV I'd ever seen, and a pool table took up one corner. At the far end of the room, there was a state-of-the-art kitchen, and that's where everyone was – about twenty people crowded round one side of the kitchen island, while Alex played bartender on the other. He was standing on a chair, and had a line of shot glasses in front of him.

'Come on, Noble!' someone called.

'Just do it already!'

To the sound of cheers, he picked up a bottle of Sambuca, and poured it back and forth across the shot glasses, filling them to the brim. The catcalls increased as he grabbed a lighter and ran it across the top of the clear liquid, creating a line of blue flames, like candles on a birthday cake.

He held up his hands, letting everyone admire his handiwork. Then a second later, he grabbed a beer mat, slammed it on top of the first glass to extinguish the flame, and downed the shot.

The group let out a roar of approval, and then they all followed suit. There was a glass for me, but I didn't walk over to join in. I'd never been one for drinking. Seeing my mother's battle with alcohol had made me wary. I never touched spirits, and I was probably one of the few nineteen-year-olds who'd never been drunk.

I'd assumed Alex was too caught up in his guests to notice me. But now he looked over in my direction. He held out one of the shot glasses, but I shook my head, and looked away. I wasn't sure why he was paying me so much attention, but I certainly didn't want to encourage it.

'Oh my God!' Jas squealed. 'This party is going to be amazing.' She clutched at my arm. 'Thank you so much for this.'

Seeing how happy Jas was, I found it hard to regret coming.

'Hello, ladies.' The male voice was slightly nervous. We looked round and saw a tawny-haired, ruddy-cheeked young man, who'd been with Alex my first night at the club. In chinos, a pink shirt and blue blazer, he looked almost a parody of a country gent. 'You two work at Destination, right?' He stuck out his hand in a slightly formal manner. 'I'm Hugh.'

He shook hands with both of us, but his interest was most definitely in Jas – and I didn't blame him. With her jet-black curls and smooth coffee skin, she was by far the most beautiful girl in the room.

'You're Hugh Forbes, right?' Jas said. 'Isn't your dad an MP or something?'

Hugh's ruddy cheeks turned an even brighter shade of red. 'He's a minister.'

I searched my mind and suddenly worked out who his dad was – a pompous right-wing ass. It was amusing to think of his son having a crush on a former stripper. I wondered what Daddy would have made of that.

But whatever Daddy would have thought, Hugh was clearly smitten. His eyes were fixed on Jas as he said, 'I wondered if perhaps I could, uh, get you a drink?' He sounded a little unsure of himself as he spoke, and I had a feeling he was worried about being rejected.

Luckily Jas looked delighted.

'That sounds lovely,' she said, affecting a fake accent. Then she shot me a worried look. 'You don't mind, do you?'

'Not at all. Go.' I made a little shooing sign with my hand. 'Have fun.'

I watched them walk off, Jas chatting away to an enamoured Hugh. I was pleased to see things working out for her – at least then it wasn't an entirely wasted night.

There was an ice bucket nearby, with a few bottles of beer upended in it, so I grabbed one, as much for something to do as anything else. Everyone was still crowded around the bar, laughing and talking. But I had no interest in joining in. These weren't my kind of people, and I was sure I'd have nothing to say to them.

I noticed then that the folding glass doors led to a terrace. I headed outside, wanting to be on my own. It was ice-cold and pitch black, a starless night. I pulled my coat around me, blowing on my hands. My breath looked like white smoke in the freezing early morning air.

I surveyed the terrace. It was huge, at least forty feet long and fifteen feet wide. It had clearly been designed in keeping with the apartment, and there was a modern, almost Mediterranean feel to it. Blue lights beamed up from the huge white tiles.

I walked over to the Ibiza-style rattan furniture, and curled up on one of the sofas, sinking into the soft cream cushions. It was cold, but somehow peaceful out here, with the sounds of the party behind me.

'Mind if I join you?'

I looked up and wasn't at all surprised to see Alex there. He was carrying an ice bucket with a bottle of champagne and two flutes. He set it all down on the low table and took the chair opposite me. He popped the cork of the champagne bottle and looked at me expectantly before he poured. I held up my bottle of beer and shook my head.

'I'm fine with this.'

He raised an eyebrow. 'I've never known a girl turn down champagne for beer.' He thought about it for a moment. 'You didn't down the shot either.'

'I don't drink much.' I'd be lying if I said I wasn't tempted – after all, I'd never had champagne before. But children of alcoholics went one of two ways – either totally irresponsible, or too responsible. Given the choice, I'd rather opt for the latter.

I'd worried that he might try to pressure me further, but he didn't. Instead, he took a swig from the champagne bottle – clearly the glasses had just been for my benefit – and settled back in the chair, regarding me with interest.

'So what brought you to Destination?'

I took a sip of beer, playing for time before answering. Obviously his father hadn't told him the whole story, and I wasn't sure how much of it I wanted to reveal. 'What do you mean by that?'

His mouth turned up at the corners, as if to say *you can't fool me*. 'From what I understand, my father hadn't heard from you in years, and then you suddenly turn up out of the blue. And what – you expect me to believe you just decided one day that it would be nice to get in touch? Please. Give me more credit than that.'

He was right – and also far more observant than I'd imagined.

'I lost my job. I needed another quickly, and so I got in touch with your dad. He'd said once that he'd help me if I ever needed him to, and I decided to take him up on his offer.' I shrugged. 'So . . . now you know. That's my story.'

'Not all of it.' His eyes were shrewd. 'I'm guessing there's more to it than that.'

I didn't say anything, just sipped my beer.

After a moment, Alex gave a soft laugh. 'Fair enough. Keep your secrets.' He settled back in his chair. 'But just tell me one thing – what did my big brother say about me today? Did he tell you to stay away from me?'

The question took me by surprise. I thought of trying to be evasive, but I'd already used up all of my moves. 'What if he did?' I said.

He grinned. 'Then I'd tell you to make up your own mind.'

Fortunately, before the conversation could go any further, Tori, the bitchy blonde I'd come across earlier, stepped outside. I never thought I'd be so relieved to see her again.

'What on earth are you doing out here, darling?' She walked over, pouting at Alex while ignoring me. 'It's absolutely freezing! Come back inside and warm me up.'

It was little wonder she felt cold. In that silver sequinned backless dress and matching heels, she wasn't exactly dressed for outside. Her long blonde hair swished around her delicate shoulders as she grabbed Alex's hand and tried to drag him up.

'I'm fine out here for the moment.' He pulled his hand gently away. 'But you should go back inside. I'd hate you to catch your death of cold.'

It was said so charmingly that she had no choice but to do as he suggested. But she didn't look too happy about it.

'Fine,' she snapped. 'But just to let you know, I'll probably head off soon.'

It was obviously a threat to see if she could get him to follow her in, but Alex appeared unmoved. When he didn't react the way she'd hoped, I watched her flounce back inside.

'I don't think your girlfriend's too keen on you staying out here with me,' I said.

'She's not my girlfriend. We're just friends.'

'Friends who sleep together?' The words were out of my mouth before I could stop them. The last thing I wanted was for him to think I cared about his love life.

'Something like that.' He waited a beat. 'You don't approve?'

I tried to look nonchalant. 'It's really none of my business.' I should have left it there, but my curiosity got the better of me. 'I just don't understand why you'd rather sit out here with me, when you could be inside with her.'

'I would've thought it was obvious.' He leaned forward and stared at me intently. 'I've never met anyone quite like you before. I find you intriguing.'

I swallowed, hard. It was difficult to know what to say to that. Alex's eyes were so fixed on mine that it was unnerving. I sat back, trying to create a distance between us, and forced a smile in an attempt to lighten the mood.

'And here was I thinking you were just slumming.'

He smiled at that, but his eyes were shrewd as he said, 'Oh, I think you know there's far more to it than that. As much as I like Destination, I rarely go there twice in a row. I was only there tonight because I'd met someone who interested me.'

I felt a shiver run through my body. I was beginning to feel out of my depth. I didn't have much experience with the opposite sex – I'd never had the time or the inclination for a boyfriend – and someone like Alexander Noble didn't feel like a good place to start. My life was all about responsibility and staying in control. I didn't want to be with someone who spent their time drinking, taking drugs and sleeping around.

'Look.' I gave a deliberately world-weary sigh. 'I don't know what your game is, but let me set you straight right now: I have no interest in being another notch on your already well-scored bedpost. So whatever you think you're doing here, there's no point. I'm not interested.' Before he could say anything, I swigged down the last of my beer, and stood up. 'Anyway, I should see where Jas has got to.'

I'd worried that he might try to stop me, but instead he gave a brief nod.

'Of course.' He grinned. 'Although I'm not sure she'll appreciate you interrupting her and Hugh.'

I tried not to show my surprise that he'd noticed them together. Was there nothing he missed?

I jammed my hands into my jeans pockets and headed back inside. It took all my effort not to look round and see if Alex was watching me.

I found Jas on one of the sofas, straddling Hugh. His hands had pushed up her dress and were splayed across her exposed thighs. A group of guys were standing in the corner, watching them and laughing, while a separate group of girls were looking down their noses at Jas. I felt bad for my new friend, being made a spectacle like that.

'Jas!' I called out loudly as I walked over. 'Have you got a second?'

Luckily my voice broke her out of what she was doing. She pulled away from a protesting Hugh, her cheeks flushed.

I took the opportunity to grab her by the arm and drag her out into the hallway.

'What were you and Alex doing out there?' she giggled before I could speak. Her eyes looked glassy, and I could tell she was already tipsy.

'Just talking.'

'Yeah, right.' I could see the scepticism on her face. 'A likely story.'

Tori was standing just inside the doorway, eavesdropping, a frown on her pretty face. I felt bad then. I might not have liked the girl, but I had no desire to hurt her either.

'Honestly, it was nothing. He was just being polite.' I hoped that was enough to reassure Tori that I was no threat to her. 'Anyway,' I said quickly, changing the subject. 'I'm going now. Are you coming with me? I can make up a bed for you in my room.'

We'd talked about her staying the night with me on the way over, but now she giggled again, and shook her head. When she spoke, it was in a stage whisper. 'Hugh's asked me over to his flat. I think he might have a bed for me there.'

She laughed at her own joke, but I couldn't see the funny side.

'Oh, Jas.' I pulled a face, like the one she'd pulled at my outfit. 'Do you really think you should? This is the first time you've even talked to him!'

She gave me a playful slap. 'Don't be so judgemental.' Her eyes flicked to the open doorway. 'He's gorgeous and he likes me. It's just a bit of fun.'

I regarded her for a moment. She was old enough to do whatever she liked. I had no reason to lecture her, and I wasn't sure why I felt so protective when I'd only just met her. Maybe I was too used to looking after my mother and sister, but I couldn't stop myself interfering. It felt like she was out of her league here.

'If Hugh likes you, he'll take your number and call you to invite you out.' I gave the advice that millions of mothers would give to their daughters. And I had a feeling it was just as likely to fall on deaf ears. 'Let him work for it.'

She frowned. 'But that's the point. I don't want him to.'

Before I could argue with her, Hugh joined us in the hallway. Every time I looked at him, all I could think of was fox-hunting and country shoots.

'You ready to go, Jas? I've got a car coming.'

She linked her arm through his, and beamed up at him. 'Sure thing!' She turned to me. 'I'll call you tomorrow.'

She was gone before I could say anything more. I went back in to the room and looked around, just in time to see Alex disappearing upstairs with some leggy redhead I didn't recognise. Well, that hadn't taken long.

There was no reason for me to stay. So I headed out into the night alone.

Chapter 8

The blare of a car horn woke me the next morning. I groaned as I checked my watch. I'd only got to bed a few hours ago, and I could've done with more sleep. I shifted uncomfortably, feeling every one of the springs in the old, thin mattress. It was only three days since I'd moved into the B&B, and already it felt like far too long.

As usual, there was a queue for the bathroom. I spent as little time as possible in there when my turn came. Something must have overflowed, and the mess hadn't been mopped up properly, so the tiled floor was covered in a layer of dirty water. The woman before me hadn't bothered to flush the toilet. I had a quick, cold shower, which didn't make me feel much cleaner, and then went back to my room to dress.

I went to the canteen for breakfast. I grabbed coffee and some toast, and sat at the end of the long plastic table, trying not to make eye contact with anyone. There seemed to be kids everywhere, which just depressed me. It also made me more determined than ever to get as much money together as possible so I could find us somewhere to live as a family. Whatever happened, I didn't want April to end up in a place like this.

Back in my room, I called my sister. We'd worked out a system – I'd leave a message and then she would call me back when she got a chance.

I was lying stretched out on my bed, reading, when April phoned ten minutes later. It was hard to hear her, and I had to keep asking her to speak up. Something didn't feel quite right, and when I heard the sound of running water I decided to ask.

'Where are you?'

She hesitated for a second before answering, and I could tell she was debating whether to lie or not.

'April . . .'

'I'm in the bathroom,' she whispered.

'Why on earth are you calling from there?'

'Cos there's this girl, Racquel, who keeps stealing my things. You know, the one who took my lunch money the other day? If she knows I've a phone, it'll be gone straight away.'

I winced at the distress in her voice. 'Do you want me to have a word with her?' After what Maggie had said, I'd ruled out making a formal complaint, so it was the only action I could think of. I had no problem standing up to bullies, but my sister was a lot softer than me.

There was a pause at the end of the line, as April considered this. 'No,' she said eventually. 'If you get involved, it'll just antagonise her.'

That was the last thing I wanted. 'All right. It's your decision. But if things get worse, let me know and I'll do something about it straight away.'

In the meantime, I told her to keep doing what she was doing – hide the phone, and we'd talk every day at this time – that way, she could arrange to be somewhere secluded to speak to me. At least I'd be seeing her soon. As part of the Care Order, Maggie had arranged for me to see my sister every Tuesday evening for two hours.

As we said goodbye, April asked me the question I'd been dreading. 'When do you think I'll be able to come and live with you?'

'Soon, I hope. I'm doing everything I can.'

I couldn't say more than that, and fortunately she didn't press me on the subject.

After that, it was time for me to leave the B&B. I needed somewhere warm to sit – preferably where I wouldn't have to pay for coffee – so I headed over to Rotherhithe library, which was thankfully open on Sunday. I'd just selected a newspaper from the rack, when my mobile phone beeped. I mouthed an apology to the glaring librarian, but as I took my phone out to put it on silent, I saw that I had a message from Jas. It read:

Doing the walk of shame! Will give u FULL deets when I c you.

She'd added a smiley face with a wink. Usually I hated it when people did that, but with Jas it made me smile. I was pleased that despite my naysaying she'd obviously had a good time. It was clear I'd be hearing all about it later.

The events of the previous evening were still running through my head – mostly that conversation outside with Alex Noble. I wasn't sure why he'd singled me out. All I knew was that I needed to stay away from him. I had enough problems in my life without developing a crush on some womanising bad boy with too much time and money on his hands.

Having a boyfriend had never held that much interest for me. My mum had spent the past six years fawning over a never-ending parade of losers, desperately trying to alleviate her loneliness. I had no desire to let my happiness revolve around a man.

But obviously Jas didn't feel the same way. When I walked into the staff changing room at Destination the following Wednesday evening, she came bounding up to me, dying to divulge everything about her night with Hugh.

'His flat was a-may-zing.' She dragged me over to one of the benches, clearly settling in for a good gossip. 'Honestly, babes, you should've seen the place. His bed's bigger than my bloomin' bedsit!'

'Shush.' I gave a quick glance round to check that no one was eavesdropping. I didn't want Jas to get into trouble for fraternising with a customer. But she didn't seem to care.

'What're they going to do, sack me? I can't see Hugh standing for that!'

I didn't like to point out that it was possibly a bit too soon to start relying on him. Even if I had, I'm not sure she'd have listened.

Luckily before she could go into further details about what had happened at his flat, Mel came in.

'Come on, girls. Let's get moving.' She clapped her hands. 'It's going to be a busy one, I can feel it.'

To my surprise, Jas was already up, pulling me to my feet and across the room.

'Why're you so eager to get out there?'

She turned and fluttered her eyelashes at me. 'Because Hugh'll be there.'

'You're such a tart.' I punched her affectionately.

'And proud of it!'

Mel was right. By midnight, the place was heaving. We were all pretty much rushed off our feet collecting dirty glasses and bringing the clean ones back from the kitchen, so there was no time to chat. But every now and then I'd pass Jas, and she'd whisper to me, 'Have you seen him?' and I would shake my head.

It was almost one in the morning, and I was rushing over to clear and clean a table that had just been vacated, when Jas grabbed me.

'He's here!' Her eyes were bright with excitement. I followed her gaze, and saw Hugh seated at one of the best tables along with two very serious, swarthy-looking guys in expensive suits. Two leggy blondes approached and slid into the booth with them, and I could feel Jas stiffening next to me.

'What the hell do they think they're playing at?' Before I could say anything, she took down her ponytail, shook out her hair and struck a pose in front of me. 'How do I look?'

'Great, but—' I'd been about to ask if she thought it was a good idea to go over and see him, but she was gone before I could finish the sentence.

I watched as she approached the table. She looked happy and confident as she went up to Hugh. She must have said his name to get his attention, but as he turned towards her he looked blank, as though he'd never seen her before.

Jas froze, clearly confused by what was going on.

One of the blondes said something – she must have been telling Jas to clear the table, because I watched irritation cross my friend's face. She hesitated for just a second, and I could sense she wanted to tell the girl where to go. But instead she seemed to take a breath, and picked up the dirty glasses. She shot Hugh a contemptuous look, and then walked back over to me. Hugh didn't so much as glance in her direction.

'Bastard pretended not to know me,' Jas said as she reached me. She wiped her hand across her eyes, smearing her mascara a little. I could tell she was trying to look angry, but it was obvious she was more hurt than anything else. 'Guess I'm not good enough for his rich friends.'

In that moment, I wanted to go up and punch him.

'Forget him. He's not worth it.' I wasn't really the hugging type of person, and even if I had been it wasn't appropriate right there in the middle of the club, so I settled for reaching out to wipe the black smudges of make-up from around her eyes. 'In fact, weren't you just about to tell me how lame he was in bed?'

She managed a weak smile. 'Yeah, I guess I was.' Then her face dropped, and she sighed. 'You were right, weren't you? I shouldn't have slept with him.'

'Well, what did you expect?' We whirled round to see Tori Cavendish, the expensive blonde who'd been rude to us at Alex's party. She'd clearly overheard every word we'd said, and had a catlike smile on her pretty face. 'The likes of Hugh Forbes don't date ex-strippers.' She shot Jas a look of disdain. 'To him, you're a one-night stand, nothing more.'

With that parting shot, she flipped her long blonde hair and glided off.

My hands clenched into fists at Tori's unnecessary cruelty. I felt especially bad, because I suspected that she'd only been mean to Jas to get back at me for monopolising Alex's attention at his party. I was about to go after her, and demand that she apologise to my friend, but Jas put a restraining hand on my arm.

'Leave it.'

I followed her gaze, and saw Mel watching us through narrowed eyes. I imagined she wouldn't take too kindly to me insulting one of the customers, so I forced myself to take a deep, calming breath.

We both hurried away, and for the rest of the evening we had no opportunity to talk. I spotted Jas a couple of times, looking sad and a bit spaced out, and I couldn't help feeling furious at Hugh for hurting her like that. But in some ways, maybe it was a good thing. At least it would cure her of hanging out with rich guys who treated her as though she was dirt.

The club officially closed at three, but it was half past by the time all the members had left and the cleaners had arrived. I caught up with Jas in the changing room, and once we'd put on our street clothes, we walked out together. As we passed the staff break room, I saw that Alex was in there, with half a dozen of his friends – London's bluebloods, as Jas had called them. They were gathered round a table, playing poker.

We paused in the doorway.

'Why're they back here?' I asked Jas.

'Owner's son can do what he likes – including have his own after-hours parties.'

They were so engrossed in their game that they didn't notice us at first. Tori had somehow persuaded them to let her join in, but she clearly had no idea what she was doing. She kept asking Alex for help, and was giggling, not even bothering to try to take it seriously. The game ended, and she revealed a weak hand, losing all her chips in the process.

'Oh no!' she pouted prettily. 'Can't I have another go?'

'No way, Tori.' It was Jamie Lancaster, the portly son of a duke, who was known among the waitresses for being a bit hands-y. 'As I said before, girls can't play poker.'

I thought I'd just mentally rolled my eyes at that, but I must have made a scoffing sound in the back of my throat, because everyone turned to look at me.

'I think someone begs to differ on that point.' It was Alex who spoke. He had such a distinct turn of phrase. He'd use these words – odd, almost old-fashioned expressions – as though he was permanently mocking those around him.

He pulled out the free chair next to him, inviting me to sit down. 'Well?' His wolf eyes held a challenge. 'Are you going to show us how it's done?'

I hesitated. I didn't want to back down on a challenge, but I'd also planned to stay away from Alex Noble unless absolutely necessary. Then I caught the look of unease on Tori's face. She was worried that I would show her up. And the prospect of doing that was too good to pass up. It would be my way of paying her back for upsetting Jas.

'What's the buy-in?' I said finally.

'What can you afford?'

Officially, nothing at all. But my pride wouldn't let me back down. I thought of the tip money in my pocket. It was fifty pounds, and I really couldn't afford to squander it on some silly game. But part of me was confident that I wouldn't. My dad had taught me how to play when I was very young, and I'd honed my skills over the years. It was the one benefit of my mum spending so much time in pubs. There had been little else to do other than play, and I'd picked up tips from the best.

I just hoped my skills would hold out now. Otherwise I was going to look really stupid.

Offering up a silent plea not to make a fool of myself, I said, 'Fifty pounds is my limit.'

'Then that's what we'll play for.'

Jamie glared at me in disbelief. 'Seriously? This isn't a game of snap, little girl.'

A retort sprang to my lips, but Alex beat me to it. 'If she wants to play, then she can,' he said.

Jamie looked like he wanted to argue back, but didn't dare. 'Fair enough,' he gave in, moving his eyes to me. 'Just don't expect me to go easy on you just because you're clueless.'

'Treat me like everyone else,' I told him.

He rolled his eyes.

I was about to head over to take my place, but Jas put her hand on my arm. 'Nina, are you sure this is such a great idea?' she said in a low voice.

'Why wouldn't it be?'

'Because I've seen these guys play before. They're really good.'

'Oh.' I feigned a frown, as though that hadn't occurred to me. 'Well . . . I'll just give it a go for a couple of hands. How hard can it be?'

Standing nearby, Tori snorted a laugh. I ignored her, and walked over to the table. But instead of taking the seat next to Alex, I chose the one opposite him instead. If I was going to win, I needed to eliminate any distractions.

As everyone settled down to play, Giles appeared in the doorway. He must have been about the same age as most of the people in the room, but in his Italian wool suit and with his clean-cut looks, he appeared a lot older. He nodded a brief greeting to a couple of Alex's entourage, who I guess he knew as clients, but his attention was on his brother. And he didn't look happy.

'Alex?' he said. 'What's going on here?'

'What does it look like? We're playing poker.' He held up his hand in a parody of the Scout's honour sign. 'Very low stakes. I swear.' He gestured at the seat. 'You're welcome to join us, if you like.'

'I'm fine right here, thanks.' Giles folded his arms, making it clear he had no intention of leaving. I wasn't entirely sure what the tension was about, but he obviously planned to keep an eye on what was going on.

Jamie was acting as dealer. I handed him my fifty pounds, and he doled out my chips. I looked at my first hand. It was actually pretty decent. Getting a winning hand was all down to card ranking, and I knew I should be aiming to get cards of the same number, suit or in a consecutive series. If I'd been playing properly with the cards I had, I'd have aimed to build up my hand in the same suit. But for the time being, I wasn't looking to win.

I made a hash of the first hand, losing most of my chips. I didn't play anywhere near as badly as Tori had, but my mistakes were still pretty basic. There were some derisory snorts from Jamie, and I pretended to look ashamed.

'Hey, you.' It was Tori who spoke, and I could tell she was talking to me. I thought about ignoring her, but I had a feeling she'd just keep going until she got my attention. So I looked up and saw her smiling smugly at me. 'Looks like it's not as easy as you thought.'

It took all my willpower, but I swallowed hard and dropped my eyes, faking embarrassment.

I continued to lose for the next couple of hands.

At one point Jas came up to me. She looked worried.

'Come on, Nina. Don't you think it's time to bow out? You know you can't afford to lose this money. There's nothing to be ashamed of. These guys are good and you're just a beginner.'

I sighed. 'Maybe you're right . . .' I pretended to think it over. 'I'll just play this one last hand, and then I'm done.'

My friend gave me a resigned look – as if to say that she'd tried her best with me, so what more could she do.

It took just two hands for me to win back my chips, and decimate most of the other players. There was nothing like luring people into a false sense of security.

Jamie, who now had no chips left, swore loudly, and threw his cards onto the table. 'Beginner's luck,' he muttered.

'Really?' Alex arched an eyebrow. 'Because I was going to say sore loser. What was it you said before about girls not being able to play poker? It seems that was just Tori.'

There was a tittering from around the table, and Jamie's glare deepened. Tori looked like she'd swallowed glass, and I bit back a smile. I shot Alex a grateful look. Our gaze held for a second, and then I forced myself to look away. This was no time to lose focus.

Alex was one of the better players. I'd used my time when I was deliberately losing to study my opponents, looking for tells. Out of everyone, Alex was the most guarded – his naturally cool demeanour meant he gave little away. But no one could keep their body totally still – and over the course of the game I'd noticed that when he was bluffing his breathing would slow just a fraction, as though he was deliberately trying to keep himself calm and give nothing away. I was sure that information would come in useful.

Three hands later, we were the only two left at the table. Everyone else had folded.

'Well?' Alex said, his wolf eyes on me, an unmistakable challenge there. 'Your move.'

I studied him for a long moment. He'd been upping the stakes throughout this game, as though he had a strong hand. But I suspected he was bluffing. I'd noticed his breathing slow when he was first dealt his cards.

I'd already increased my stakes twice, borrowing money from Jas. I wouldn't have done it if the players had been staff, but I had no problem taking Alex's money.

Without a word, I tossed the last of my chips in. Then I placed my cards face up on the table. I had a full house – three Jacks and two sevens.

'Good,' I heard Jas murmur, obviously assuming my cards were unbeatable.

I looked to Alex. He gazed coolly back at me for a moment. I saw the faintest smile cross his lips, and a feeling of unease crept over me. I knew in that moment that I'd been played.

In his usual cool, detached way, he spread his cards across the table. There was a moment of stunned silence as everyone took in what his hand showed – the ten, Jack, Queen, King and Ace of hearts. A royal flush.

'Oh my God!' It was Jas who spoke, the shock evident in her voice. She looked from the cards up at me, mouthing, 'I'm sorry.'

'Oh, shame.' Tori sounded positively gleeful to have witnessed my misfortune.

I was aware of everyone's eyes on me, gauging my reaction to being beaten. It took all my willpower, but I managed to just shrug.

'That's the way it goes.' I tried to look nonchalant, not wanting anyone to realise how upset I was. It wasn't really about the money – although I could have done without losing that – but I hated being played. It was my own fault though – my arrogance had cost me dearly.

I forced myself to face Alex. 'Good game.' I offered my hand to him across the table.

'You too.'

I felt Alex's cool fingers close around mine, and a jolt of electricity shot through me, taking me by surprise. I pulled my hand away quickly and stood up. Jas rushed over to console me.

'I can't believe you lost!' Jas's eyes were sympathetic. 'I really thought you had him!' She shot a dirty look in Alex's direction. 'I can't believe he played you like that. It's not as if he doesn't have enough money as it is. You'd think he'd have some shame about taking it from you.'

'Well, he won it fair and square,' I forced myself to say. But there was a hollow pit forming in my stomach as I thought of the money I couldn't afford to lose. I'd been so stupid.

Right then, Alex came over. Jas instinctively drew in front of me – as though she was trying to protect me.

'Give us a second, will you?' Alex's words were clearly addressed to Jas, but his blue eyes were on me.

Jas looked at me to check that was what I wanted, and I just shrugged.

'I don't want the money back,' I said as soon as she'd gone, imagining that was why he wanted to speak to me.

He grinned. 'That's good to know. Because I wasn't intending to give it to you.'

That stumped me. 'Then what do you want?'

'I want to know where you learnt to play like that.'

I shrugged, unsure why he cared. 'In pubs growing up. One of my mum's boyfriends thought it was hilarious to see a thirteen-year-old girl take money from grown men.'

I could see him frown a little at that.

'And I'm guessing you can deal?'

The question threw me. I had no idea what he was getting at.

'Well?' he said. 'Can you?'

'A damn sight better than Jamie did just now.'

'Good.' I had no idea what this was all about, but to my surprise he drew a business card from his wallet and handed it to me. 'You should come to this location on Sunday evening. Sometime after eleven should be good.'

I studied the card. It was plain white and glossy, with an address printed in black on one side. It took a moment to digest what he was asking of me.

I looked from the card to him. 'What is this?'

'I can't tell you that. But if you come on Sunday, everything will be explained.'

'Are you serious?' I gave a laugh of disbelief. 'You want me to go alone at night to a strange address on your say-so?'

'That's right.'

'And why on earth would I do that?'

'Because from the way you were eyeing that petty cash box the other night, I got the feeling you need money, right? And I suspect you need it badly.'

I didn't say anything, which was obviously answer enough, because he gave a small nod.

'Well, put it this way – Sunday night is the solution to all your money troubles. So trust me when I say you *are* going to want to come along.'

He turned away, signalling the end of our conversation. But then he looked back over his shoulder, as though something had occurred to him.

'Oh, and this needs to be our little secret. So don't go spilling your guts to anyone.' His eyes flicked over to Giles. He'd been cornered by one of the gold-diggers Jas had pointed out the other night, but his attention was clearly on us. 'Especially not my brother. I'm trusting you to keep it to yourself.'

After he'd gone, Giles managed to extricate himself from the gold-digger, and came over to me. I quickly tucked the card into my pocket before he could see it.

'So what did Alex want?' Giles looked concerned.

I hesitated before answering. Part of me longed to tell him. He seemed to have my best interests at heart, and it didn't feel right to keep information from him. But then I thought about what Alex had said – that this could solve my money problems.

'Nina?' Giles prompted. 'What was that all about?'

I looked over at him and shrugged. 'I have absolutely no idea.' In that moment, it was the most honest answer I could give.

Chapter 9

Sunday evening, just before midnight, I stood across the street from the Manor Hotel, wondering what to do. The Manor Hotel was one of London's premier five-star hotels, and part of Noble Enterprises. Conveniently located on one of the elegant squares off Old Bond Street, it had an old-fashioned grandeur to it. Outside, two liveried porters greeted guests as they came and went – hailing black cabs, and opening chauffeur-driven-car doors.

I'd been debating all day about whether to go there. I'd tried to come up with ideas as to why Alex Noble would want me to, but I'd drawn a blank. All I knew was that I didn't trust him, and that was reason enough not to be there. But his invitation had intrigued me, as he'd known it would. And when he'd said that it would give me the opportunity to earn money, I could hardly walk away.

But now, standing there and watching all the wealthy people coming in and out of the plush hotel, I was beginning to wonder if I was making a huge mistake. What business could I possibly have somewhere like this? But I'd come this far – I couldn't turn back now.

I took a deep breath, steeling myself for what was about to happen, and crossed the street to the hotel entrance. One of the porters held the door open for me, and I slipped inside, feeling like a fraud. In my jeans and biker boots, I stood out a mile.

The hotel was known for its opulence. The lobby was all dark mahogany wood and plush sofas. I crossed the marble floor to the reception desk, and asked to be directed to the Empire Suite. I could feel the smartly dressed receptionist looking me up and down. I could sense her suspicion as she politely asked for my name and called up to the suite to check that I was expected. Her demeanour changed once she'd received confirmation that I was meant to be there. She was all smiles when she came off the phone, and directed me to the lifts that would take me up to the top floor.

'Mr Noble said to go right up,' she said.

Despite the old-style elegance, the newly refurbished hotel was all mod cons. There was a separate lift for the suites, and it whizzed straight up to the top floor. I stepped out and walked along the corridor to the Empire Suite.

A huge man in a dark suit stood outside. It took me a minute to work out that he was a security guard.

I felt a prickle of trepidation. What the hell was this? I'd grown up on one of the roughest estates in London, but somehow being among the rich and entitled felt more dangerous than anything I'd ever experienced there. But it was too late to turn back now. I gave him my name, he checked it through an earpiece, and then he opened the double doors and I stepped inside.

I wasn't much of a connoisseur of hotel rooms, but I'd sensed that the Empire Suite was going to be plush. It didn't disappoint – it must have been bigger than most flats in London. I stepped into a huge marbled entrance hall, where a pretty brunette took my coat and directed me through to another room. I could hear voices coming from further inside, so I followed them. I rounded the corner into a huge living area. There wasn't a bed in sight, so I presumed the bedroom was elsewhere.

In the middle of the room there was a table with half a dozen guys and two women seated round it. They were all holding playing cards, and had bundles of money next to them. A huge stack of notes lay at the centre of the table. Standing to the side, a safe distance away so they couldn't see anyone's hand, were about a dozen spectators. Alex was among them.

It took me a second to get what was going on.

This was a poker game. A very high-stakes poker game by the look of it.

No one seemed particularly interested in my presence, so I hung back, leaning against the long bar that stood at one end of the room, content to watch from a distance. Everyone was engrossed in the game. It was clearly at a crucial point.

There were two players left in that hand. They both must have been confident in their cards, because they each kept raising the ante. Finally, one of the men called. He had a good hand, but his opponent's was stronger. He crashed out, lost all his chips.

To my surprise, he didn't look particularly fazed by losing such a huge amount of money. Instead he calmly turned to the dealer. 'I'll buy back in.'

I watched as he took a huge pile of cash from a holdall and placed it on the table. From where I was standing, I could see the dealer hand over fifty thousand pounds of chips.

As the next hand started, Alex finally looked up, his blue eyes searching for me. When he saw where I was standing, he came to join me, taking up the spot by my side so he still had a view of the table.

For the first time since I'd met him he was wearing a suit, but it wasn't the business kind – it was black, with a matching black open-necked shirt underneath. It made him look sleek, authoritative and slightly dangerous all at once.

'So what do you think?' he said.

'What?' He clearly wanted me to be impressed, and I was determined not to be. 'About a bunch of rich wankers losing obscene amounts of money to each other?'

He pulled a face. 'You make it sound so tawdry.'

'Honestly?' I gave a sweet smile. 'I'm just surprised you're not playing.'

'Ouch.' He affected a hurt look. 'I think I've just been insulted.'

'I'm sure it's not the first time.' He laughed. I waited for him to elaborate on why he wasn't playing, but he didn't. His eyes were fixed firmly on the game. 'So why aren't you?' I said eventually.

'What? Playing? Because I'm organising.' I raised a questioning eyebrow. 'I host these things.'

Ah, so that explained the suit.

I glanced around the room. 'And why the cloak and dagger routine?'

'Because it's not strictly on the up-and-up.'

'It's illegal? Why?' To my mind, who cared if a bunch of obnoxious wealthy people wanted to gamble money they could afford.

'Because I take the rake.' I must have looked as confused as I felt, because he grinned. 'So you're not quite as streetwise as you'd like everyone to think.'

'Or maybe I've just got better things to do with my money than fritter it away on some stupid game.'

'Right.' He nodded with exaggerated patience. 'That must be it.'

I waited for him to explain, but he didn't. I debated whether to let it go, rather than admit to being interested, but curiosity got the better of me. 'So?' I said. 'What's the rake?'

'It's the commission I take for hosting the game. About two and a half per cent of the pot.'

I looked at the piles of money on the table, and let out a low whistle. 'I'm guessing that adds up.' I frowned then. 'But what's the point? Is your allowance from Daddy not big enough?'

I saw his jaw tighten a fraction. I'd clearly hit on a nerve. His eyes flitted over to me. 'I haven't taken a penny from my father since I was eighteen. This is how I earn my living.' He nodded at the poker table. 'For now.'

I wasn't sure if I was meant to be impressed, but I was determined not to be.

'And he knows you hold these games here?'

'Not exactly.' The ghost of a smile crossed his face. 'That's part of the fun.'

There was a trace of bitterness in his voice, and it sounded like there was more to that story.

Before I could pursue the topic any further, Tori came up to us. She didn't look happy to see me.

'What's she doing here?' Her arms snaked proprietorially around Alex.

'That's what I've been wondering,' I said, trying not to bristle at the way she talked about me as though I wasn't there. I still couldn't quite make out their relationship. I'd seen Alex with a bunch of girls, so they certainly weren't boyfriend and girlfriend. Yet it was clear Tori felt she had some right to him.

But more importantly, I couldn't figure out what Alex's angle was. He surely didn't want me to join the poker game – it wasn't like I had anywhere near the money for that. And even though I was good, I wasn't in the league of the people playing.

'It's very simple.' To his credit, he ignored Tori and directed his answer at me. 'I'm in need of a dealer. Someone who knows the game but who's also discreet and trustworthy.'

I must have been staring blankly at him, because to my shame I still wasn't getting what he was saying.

'I invited you because I want you to come and work for me,' he explained with slow deliberation. 'I want you to be a dealer at my poker nights.'

'I don't understand,' I said. 'You've already got a dealer, haven't you? Why do you need me?'

It was four hours later, the early hours of the morning, and the poker game was over. After dropping his bombshell, Alex had said he needed to get back to the game and asked me to wait around so we could talk once it was finished.

I'd been in too much shock to object. He'd gone back to overseeing the game, and I'd been drawn into watching it, too. There was something fascinating about seeing those huge sums of money being won and lost.

Alex and I sat opposite each other on the plush sofas in front of the roaring fire. Tori was still there – although thankfully far enough away not to be able to hear our conversation, draped over a beautifully upholstered ottoman as she tapped away on her iPhone.

'Unfortunately I need a new dealer.' Alex regarded me with cool eyes. 'Lai-King – the girl dealing tonight – is going back to Macau. I want you to take her place.'

I chewed at the inside of my lip. I hated to admit it, but I was intrigued.

'So what would that entail?'

'I hold one of these nights every week or so. Sometimes more regularly, if there's demand. It pays well – a thousand pounds a night, plus tips.' He grinned. 'And, trust me, these guys are generous tippers.'

I chewed at my lip. He made it sound so tempting – which I presumed was deliberate. He knew I was desperate for money. I had to tear my thoughts away from the cash, and focus instead on more pragmatic details.

'But you said it's illegal. What if we get caught?'

He sat back and laced his hands behind his head, his long legs stretching out in front of him. 'That's not going to happen.'

'Really? And how can you be so sure?'

'Because I'm very, very careful. The players are all personal contacts. The venue is always somewhere high end' – he cast his eyes around the hotel room, as if to prove his point – 'and the exact address is only revealed at the last minute. Trust me, I have all bases covered.' He paused, waited a beat, and then said, 'So? Anything else you want to know?'

I didn't answer straight away. The truth was, I did have one more question – one that had been nagging at the back of my mind since I arrived. But I wasn't entirely sure I wanted to hear the answer.

'Why me?' I said finally.

He frowned a little. 'What do you mean by that?'

'I mean why are you offering this role to *me*, specifically? I get that I play cards well, and I suppose you think it will titillate your players to have a female dealer.' I remembered reading in an article somewhere that casinos were looking to employ more women. 'But it's more than that, isn't it? I'm sure you could find plenty of other girls willing and able to do this job. So why are you asking me?'

Alex leaned back on the sofa, his ice-blue eyes strangely mesmerising. 'Because it means I get to spend more time with you, of course.'

He spoke in that slightly mocking tone, which made it hard for me to work out how serious he was. But something about the way he was looking at me made me feel like he really meant it.

I was suddenly aware of just how dry my mouth was. I picked up the glass of water in front of me and took a long swig. My mind was racing. Alex's offer was tempting – more tempting than I cared to admit. But I was worried about where it would lead. The business side of things I could handle – it was just the personal stuff that scared me. I had enough problems sorting out my mother. I didn't need to get involved with someone equally damaged.

'I'm sorry, but I can't do it,' I said. 'I know you said we won't get caught, but I just can't risk it. The last thing I need is a criminal record.'

I thought I saw a look of disappointment flicker across his face, and I was worried that he was going to try to convince me further. But instead all he said was, 'That's a shame.' His eyes flicked to the windows. Even through the blackout blinds, I could see the cold, harsh glare of the early morning sun. 'It's light outside. You'll be safe getting home.' He reached into his pocket, pulled out his wallet and tossed a handful of notes onto the table. 'This should cover your cab fare and your time tonight.'

That was the last thing I'd been expecting. 'There's no need for that—'

'Please. Take it. I insist.'

With that, he stood and went to join Tori. Once they were gone, I collected up the money and headed out into the ice-cold air. For some reason I couldn't understand, I felt strangely empty. But I didn't have time to dwell on that. I had far more important things to worry about – because at eight o'clock that morning I was due to meet with Sergei.

After my mother had told me about the loan she'd taken from Sergei, I'd called to inform him that I'd be the one paying him back. He'd arranged to meet me to discuss payment terms.

So two hours after leaving the Manor Hotel I found myself standing outside Le Grand Café, the bizarrely named greasy spoon situated by a busy crossroads on the Tower Bridge Road. It was one of several dingy working men's caffs in the area that served as Sergei's unofficial office. He always insisted on meeting in public – which was fine by me. I had no desire to be anywhere alone with him.

I spotted him as soon as I walked in. He was already seated at his usual table in the corner, conveniently away from anyone else. From a distance, he didn't look like an especially dangerous individual – he was in his early sixties, and not physically impressive. He was only a little taller than me, and slightly built; he wore a bad wig to cover his receding hairline. In his dark suit and white shirt, he could almost have passed for a legitimate businessman. But when you got closer, you could see that this was just a front for a hardened criminal – his face was like leather, criss-crossed with scars, and there was a coldness and cruelty in his eyes.

Three of his enforcers sat at a nearby table. They were silent and watchful, showing off meaty arms that were thicker than my thighs. If their purpose was to intimidate, then they could consider it fulfilled.

Sergei was halfway through a full fry-up as I slipped into the plastic seat opposite him.

I waited for him to speak as he finished chewing down some black pudding.

'You want something?' He didn't look up at me as he asked this, just continued eating.

'I'm fine.' Even though I was hungry, I knew there was no point ordering anything. Meetings with Sergei tended to rob me of my appetite. 'I just wanted to talk terms for paying back my mum's debt.'

Finally he finished chewing. He threw his knife and fork onto his plate, slurped down some tea, and then turned his attention to me.

'Your mother's debt,' he mused. 'That's right. Now, what is it she owes me? Eleven grand, isn't it? And from what I remember, it was due to be repaid last week?'

I gave a brief nod to confirm, trying to ignore the way my stomach was twisting into knots.

His eyes narrowed as he studied me. 'And I'm guessing by the look of you that you don't have it.'

'Not right now. But if you give me some time . . .' Unfortunately he was already shaking his head.

I had no idea what I was going to do. I had no savings left after paying the rehab facility. I'd thought I might be able to reason with Sergei. But that didn't seem to be the case.

'Nina, Nina.' He said my name like a rebuke. 'I can't have you and your mother disrespecting me like this. You know that.'

In that moment I remembered a story I'd heard about one of the young women who'd lived on our estate – a stripper, who went by the stage name Star. She was a beautiful girl – turned heads when she walked down the street – who'd borrowed money from Sergei to get breast implants, hoping it would boost her career. For a time, it had done just that – she'd begun to get work as a glamour model; talked about being the next Jordan. But she'd spent what she'd earned, and fell behind on her repayments to Sergei. One night she was attacked in a stairwell in Hayfield Court – her face carved up with a Stanley knife.

After that, her career was over, and small children squealed in fright when she walked by. A year to the day after the attack, she was found dead of an overdose.

Now, while I wasn't one to fuss over my appearance, I certainly didn't fancy having my face shredded.

'I'll get the money. I promise. I just need some time. Maybe if I could pay it in instalments—'

'Instalments?' Sergei said this as though it was the most outrageous suggestion he'd ever heard. He stroked his chin, feigning deep thought. 'I suppose that would be all right. What did you have in mind?'

I did a quick mental calculation. With tips, I was making about five hundred pounds a week at Destination. Along with my own living expenses, and trying to slip April some money, I also needed to save up for a deposit on a flat.

'Three hundred a week?'

He thought for a moment. 'Make it one and a half, and we have deal.'

It took me a moment to understand what he was saying – that he wanted one thousand five hundred pounds from me each week.

'No!' The word was out of my mouth before I could stop it. 'There's no way I can get all that.'

'That's what I want. One and a half grand a week, for the next eight weeks. No arguments.'

I did a quick mental calculation.

'But that's twelve grand. You said we owed eleven—'

'The extra thousand is for the inconvenience of making me wait.'

I felt panic rising up in me. 'I've no idea how to get that for you—'

'This is not my problem.' He picked up his fork, his attention back on his plate. 'You have the first lot ready this time next week. I send someone round to collect it from you.'

He didn't need to utter the 'or else'.

He began to shovel food into his mouth, signalling the end of our conversation.

I got unsteadily to my feet. I was halfway to the door when Sergei called my name. I turned back, hoping that he might relent and let me pay back a smaller amount. But instead he said, 'And don't even think about running. I know where your sister goes to school. And if I can't find you, I'll go after her.'

A chill passed through me. He'd just said the one thing guaranteed to get him his money. If he was planning to go after April, I'd do anything he asked. And he knew it.

I spent the rest of the day trying to think of a way to repay Sergei. Part of me had wondered about going to Duncan Noble, and asking him for a loan. But I was worried that he would ask why I needed the money – and if I told him, who knew what he might do with that information. Most people would advise going to the police, but in my experience that would just make the situation worse. I had no proof that Sergei had threatened me, so they wouldn't be able to hold him – which meant he'd be free to exact his vengeance on me, or worse still, my sister. And I couldn't take the risk.

Not when there was another solution open to me – however unpalatable that might be.

So early that evening I did what I'd sworn not to – I called Alex, and told him that I would take part in his poker games, after all.

Chapter 10

The week passed uneventfully. I met my sister at a coffee shop on Tuesday evening, as per the visitation rights dictated by the Care Order. April seemed well enough – Racquel appeared to have lost interest in bullying her – although she was still impatient to get back home. I'd told her that we wouldn't be able to even consider applying to the courts until Mum got out of rehab, but I think she still kept hoping for some kind of loophole to turn up.

The counsellor from the rehab centre called me with an update on my mum's progress. She told me that it had been a tough week for my mum, but that she was doing her best to stay strong. I didn't make much comment. I had no intention of getting my hopes up where my mother was concerned. Especially since she'd landed this Sergei mess on me. Right now, getting him his money was my top priority.

That was on my mind the following Sunday evening when, just before ten, I arrived at the Manor Hotel for my first night as a dealer at Alex's poker games. I had to keep reminding myself of why I was there, otherwise I was liable to bolt.

In the meantime, I'd gone on the Internet to try to find out a bit more about Alex. Mostly there were pictures of him falling out of nightclubs or partying in various glamorous locations around the world, always accompanied by some gorgeous girl. But there was one article that was more revealing. It was one of those gossipy tabloid pieces, written after Duncan Noble made some acquisition, but focusing more on him and his sons rather than the business. It was made up of hearsay and assumption, and extensively quoted 'a source close to the family', but the spirit of the piece made sense. It talked of a rift between Duncan and his youngest son Alex, which went back years.

Apparently Alex and Giles were half-brothers. Giles's mother had been Duncan's first wife, Anne, who by all accounts was a warm, sweet woman, who'd sadly died of ovarian cancer shortly after her son was born. Duncan had been devastated by the loss, and had still been grieving when he'd met a beautiful aspiring actress, called Eva. She'd been the life and soul of the party, a social butterfly. They'd had a whirlwind romance, and married within months, and Alex had been born a little while later.

But by then Eva had already tired of domestic life. She'd taken no interest in her stepson, or her own child. Less than a year after Alex was born, she'd left Duncan for an impoverished artist. They'd been found dead of an overdose in his studio in Paris a few months later.

So Giles's mother was a saint, and Alex's a sinner. It explained a lot.

The article had gone on to say that Alex had grown into a playboy, who partied his way round the world, and had turned his back on the family business. And that this had led to a rift with his father, who favoured his more sensible older son Giles. From what I'd seen, this appeared to be pretty accurate.

Even though the article hadn't told me much more than I'd already guessed, it was good to get some context – because whether I liked it or not, for the moment the Noble family seemed to be a fixture in my life.

As I went up in the lift, I caught sight of my reflection. I looked smarter than usual, and I just hoped my outfit was good enough. Having attended one of the poker games, I'd realised that my usual jeans and T-shirt weren't going to cut it. I wasn't one for skirts and dresses, so I'd tried to find something chic and sophisticated, but also comfortable. I'd spent the previous day trawling thrift shops, and finally came up with a tuxedo-style black suit, which I paired with a white dress shirt. I slicked my short dark hair back from my face. I didn't usually wear make-up, but just to soften the look a little I put on some mascara and black-cherry lip-gloss. The whole effect was almost 1920s androgynous. It was an older and more professional look – which was what I was going for.

But even though I looked the part, I still felt nervous as I stepped out of the lift and walked along the corridor. When I'd called Alex to say I wanted to take him up on his offer, I'd expected there to be a practice run. But he'd told me that I'd be auditioning on the job – a baptism of fire, where I'd either sink or swim. The thought made my stomach churn, and as I stood outside the suite, I had to wipe my damp hands on my trousers before I knocked.

Alex opened the door to me. None of the players had arrived yet. He'd told me to come early, so I could get acclimatised before the game began.

He looked me over, and nodded approvingly.

'Good choice,' he drawled. When I'd asked him what to wear, he'd said he'd leave it up to me, and even offered me cash to buy an outfit. I think he was shocked that I'd managed to come up with something decent on my own. His eyes moved down to where the top button of the shirt struggled to close across my cleavage. 'I just hope you don't distract the players.'

'I'm sure it won't be a problem.'

He moved over to the bar. 'Drink?'

'Just water.'

'That's right,' he said, pouring me a glass, and adding ice and a slice. 'Keep a clear head and you'll be fine.'

He handed me the glass and I was embarrassed to see that my hand was shaking. Part of me wanted to ask him questions about the evening – to get reassurance that everything was going to be all right. But before I could find the words, there was a knock at the door. The first player had arrived.

Over the next twenty minutes, all the guests congregated in the room. Alex gave me a rundown of who they all were as they came in: they included two businessmen, a well-known actor and a government minister. I'd seen Alex talking to a few of them at Destination. I guessed that was where he'd met them. It made more sense now: that was why he spent so much time there – it was his recruiting ground.

I stood to one side, watching as Alex interacted with them. He was the perfect host – confident and comfortable among all these heavy hitters.

By 10.30 everyone had arrived, and the game was due to begin.

As the players took their places at the table, I sat down with them. I looked around at all these important people, and my mind went blank. As the dealer, I was meant to take control, but I'd never felt more out of my depth.

I felt like a fraud, and part of me wanted to run away. Why had I ever agreed to do this in the first place?

Because you need the money, a little voice reminded me. *Otherwise Sergei will hurt you and go after April.*

With that thought, I picked up the deck of cards, shuffled it, and started to deal.

Halfway through that first round, though, I managed to accidentally flip a card over, so a few of the players saw a flash of the Jack of hearts. It wasn't the end of the world – it happened a lot – and I did what etiquette dictated, and took the card out and placed it face up in front of the player it should have been dealt to. Then, once all the cards were dealt, I would use it as the first burn card.

I continued dealing as though nothing had happened. But the incident must have made me jittery, because I managed to flash another card – the five of spades.

This time, I had to stop. There could only be one flashed card per deal. Now that more than one card had been exposed, the deal was considered a misdeal.

'S-sorry,' I stuttered, as I collected up the cards. I hated the nervousness in my voice, knowing that it made me seem weak. I wondered what on earth I should do – whether it would be best just to walk out now. I couldn't see a way to come back from this.

But just as I was considering whether there was any chance of the floor opening up to swallow me, Alex came over and bent down to whisper in my ear. I was expecting him to tell me to leave, but instead he said, 'Just take a deep breath and calm down. You can do this. There's no reason to be nervous.'

He squeezed my shoulder before moving off.

I wasn't sure what it was – maybe the unexpected kindness – but Alex's words had a surprisingly calming effect. I closed my eyes for a second, and did as he'd suggested – breathed in deeply, then slowly exhaled.

My eyes flipped open and I picked up the deck of cards.

'Right,' I said, with a confidence that surprised even me. 'Let's try this again.'

After that, the rest of the game went off without a hitch. When we finished five hours later, the players all thanked me as they left.

'Here you go.' The winner pressed some cash into my hands. After he'd gone, I counted it – a three hundred-pound tip. I couldn't believe it. Given the stakes they'd been playing for tonight, it meant nothing to him – but it was everything to me. Along with what Alex was paying me, and my wages from Destination, I'd be able to comfortably pay Sergei the first instalment this week.

After Alex had seen the players out, he came up to me. 'Thanks for tonight. You did a good job.'

'Oh, I don't know about that.' I felt flushed with exhilaration, my heart pounding fast. 'I messed up at the beginning. When I fumbled the cards at first I was just about ready to run out, but then you came over and—'

'You did good,' he said, cutting off my tirade. 'I was impressed.'

For a moment we stood like that, our eyes locked. I felt suddenly aware of how close he was to me – and confused by how this made me feel. He was everything I was meant to be staying away from, and yet here I was taking comfort from him. My heartbeat speeded up a little, and I wet my dry lips.

I was wondering what to say next when a slim brunette, who'd been watching the game, approached and draped herself over Alex, ruining the moment. 'Come on, sweetie,' she pouted up at him, as though I wasn't there. 'Aren't you ready to go yet? You know I need my beauty sleep.'

'Just give me a second to finish off with Nina and we'll get out of here.'

She gave a quick, disparaging flick of her eyes in my direction, and then she turned and stalked off, flopping down onto one of the nearby sofas. I watched her pull out a baby-pink phone and start to text someone.

'Here.' I turned at Alex's voice, just in time to see him reach into the leather sports bag he had with him and pull out a wad of notes. The moment we had shared – whatever it meant – was now gone, and he was back to business.

He waited as I quickly counted the notes. One thousand pounds – exactly as he'd promised.

I looked up. Alex was still standing there.

'Do you think you'll need my help again?' He looked amused at my eagerness. I'd gone from swearing I'd never do something like this to wanting to do as much of it as I could. But that was because it would be the quickest way to clear my family's debt, as well as earn enough money to rent somewhere decent for us all to live.

'What happened to never doing anything illegal?' His tone was faintly mocking, but I refused to be shamed into backing down.

'I told you – I need the money.'

'Yes. You said that.' He studied me closely. 'I'm just wondering what for.'

I looked around the room. I was tempted to tell him, but it just didn't feel like the right place. Not with that girl waiting for him. 'Does it matter?' I said lightly. 'Just – do you need me again?'

'How does next Sunday suit you?'

Relief coursed through me. If he kept using me for the games each week, I'd be able to maintain the payments to Sergei. 'That would be great.'

'Alex?' the leggy brunette called impatiently from the other side of the room. 'You ready to go?'

He frowned, clearly irritated. 'Give me a minute.'

'Don't hang around on my account,' I said lightly. 'Although whatever will Tori say about your new friend?'

'She won't say anything. Tori knows the score. She knows I'm not a one-woman man.' He took a step towards me. 'In fact, say the word and I'm happy to ditch her.' He inclined his head towards the brunette.

'I told you before, I'm not sleeping with you.'

'I know. I'm just saying – I'm happy to ditch her if you want me to drive you home.'

For once, he looked serious, and I wasn't sure how to react. I attempted to look disdainful. 'As flattering as your offer is, I'm not planning to get into a car with someone who's been drinking or doing drugs.'

'Who says I have?'

'Well . . . I've seen you.'

He frowned, looking genuinely confused. 'What? Tonight?'

Now he said it, I realised I hadn't. 'I suppose I just assumed . . .'

'So just because I've been known to have a drink or indulge in some recreational pharmaceuticals, you assume I'm out driving around drunk or coked out of my brain? That's quite a leap.'

I realised he was right. I swallowed hard, and tried to bring things back to the original question. 'Still . . . I'd rather get a cab.'

'Fair enough. Suit yourself. But just for the record, I haven't had so much as a sip of low-alcohol beer tonight. Just because I don't play by the rules like Giles doesn't mean I'm an idiot.'

He turned away without another word, and I watched him walk over to the brunette, who I was sure I recognised from the front cover of one of that month's magazines. I couldn't hear their exchange, but he offered her his hand, and pulled her to her feet. They laced arms and walked towards the exit.

As the door slammed closed, the noise echoed around the empty room. I realised then that I was the last one there, alone in the vast room. I suddenly felt a huge sense of anti-climax. I'd enjoyed the night more than I wanted to let on, even to myself. Even though I hated to admit it, it felt good for once to do something wild and dangerous.

I pushed the thought away, and tucked my money into the inside pocket of my jacket and headed out into the cold, bright day. Sergei's enforcers were due round to collect the first instalment of his money, and I had no desire to make them wait.

Chapter 11

'Nice work the other night,' Alex said. It was the following Friday evening, and he'd cornered me just as I was dropping some glasses at the bar. I hadn't seen him at the club so far that week, but he'd turned up tonight about an hour earlier. 'Are you still up for Sunday?'

I felt adrenalin course through me – fear mixed with excitement at the prospect. 'Sure.' I tried to sound casual, but secretly I was pleased to hear that the game was still on. I'd paid Sergei the first instalment, but another was due on Monday.

Something must have caught Alex's eye, because his gaze shifted upwards. He looked amused as he said, 'I think we have an audience.'

I looked over and saw Jas watching us. I could see the quizzical look on her face, and knew she was wondering why I was talking to Alex again. Great. The last thing I needed was her jumping to conclusions and assuming I'd become one of the gold-diggers who fawned all over the wealthy clientele.

'I'd better go.'

'Why the rush?' Alex was standing in front of me, and I had my back pressed against the wall, so the only way I could get out was for him to move aside to let me. But instead of backing away, Alex took a step closer, his eyes glinting with mischief. Before I could stop him, he reached out and took a strand of hair that had fallen across my face and smoothed it behind my ear, his hand trailing down my cheek and coming to rest on my shoulder in a deliberately intimate gesture. 'Worried your friend will disapprove of you fraternising with me?'

His hand was still on my shoulder, and he began to gently massage my collarbone. I knew he was trying to cause trouble – and trying to get a rise out of me – so I made sure to return his gaze levelly, refusing to give him the satisfaction of seeing a reaction. 'I'm just surprised you're trying to draw attention to the fact we're hanging out together. I thought we'd agreed no one was meant to know about this?'

'Hmm.' He cocked his head to one side, studying me, and for a moment I wondered if he was going to make a scene. But then he held up his hands in mock surrender. 'You're right. As always.' He looked over again at Jas. 'I'll leave you to explain our little tête-à-tête, and text you the details about Sunday later.'

I walked over to where Jas was standing.

'You two seemed very cosy,' she said. 'What was that all about?'

'Nothing.' My eyes flicked over to where Alex was walking across the floor to his usual group. Two girls – blondes, of course – made room for him on the sofa. As he dropped down between them, I watched his arms snake round their shoulders. It gave me an idea. 'He was just trying it on with me.'

Jas groaned. 'You and every other girl in the room. I hope you told him where to go.'

I forced a smile. 'That's exactly what I did.'

'It's like that scumbag Hugh,' she muttered darkly. 'He's here tonight, giving me puppy-dog eyes. Like I'm just supposed to forget him blanking me last week.'

I followed her gaze, and saw that Hugh was sitting across the room, staring back at her. He gave her a hopeful little smile and a wave, but she just huffed and turned away. I couldn't help feeling proud of her for not caving in.

Then, just before three, I stood by the bar, taking a quick break. It was coming up to closing, which was always a slower time for us. Pretty much everyone was on the dance floor, so there was no point trying to collect glasses until the clubbers had begun to filter out.

I glanced around the room, and caught sight of Jas standing over to one side in the corridor leading to the powder room. Hugh was there, too. She stood with her back against the wall, arms folded, while he was in front of her holding her hand and, from the anguished look on his face, clearly apologising. She looked stony-faced, like she was refusing to accept what he said, and I felt proud of her.

Then, a moment later, Hugh dipped down onto his knees, clasping his hand over his heart in a theatrical gesture as he spoke. I watched as Jas's mouth twitched. She was clearly trying not to give in to him, but a second later she lost her battle and started to laugh. I rolled my eyes as she gestured for him to get up off the floor.

Jas obviously felt my gaze, because she glanced over in my direction. The disapproval on my face must have been clear, because she said something quickly to Hugh and then hurried over to me.

I probably shouldn't have said a word, but after so many years of seeing my mum make a fool of herself over a worthless man, I couldn't hold back.

'What the hell, Jas?'

'Oh, don't be cross. It wasn't how it looked.'

'Oh?' I crossed my arms, waiting for the explanation.

'Honest. Hugh explained everything. He was with these clients he was trying to impress, and they can kind of be chauvinist pigs. He didn't want to introduce me cos they wouldn't understand me working here, and he thought they'd take liberties.' She chewed at her lip, her voice growing smaller under my gaze. 'He was just protecting me, really.'

'I see.' I didn't bother to keep the scepticism out of my voice.

'Oh, babes, I know you don't buy it. But he's a good one, I know it. He said he's sorry, and I believe him.'

'And what – you're just happy to give him a second chance? How can you trust him after what he did? What if he hurts you again?'

She thought about it for a moment, and then shrugged. 'Then I guess I'll cry about it and move on. But I'd rather risk getting hurt than pass up the chance to be with someone I really like because I'm scared.'

Her reasoning drew me up short. I'd assumed she was just being naïve, but it seemed like she'd given it a lot of thought. Still, it didn't mean she was doing the right thing.

'It's up to you, Jas. But just be careful of him, that's all.'

'Don't worry, babes.' She patted my cheek. 'I can look after myself.'

I watched as she ran over to him, her face lighting up as they spoke. But however happy she looked, I couldn't help feeling that she was making a huge mistake.

* * *

Over the next couple of weeks, my life settled into a routine. I saw April on Tuesday evenings; got an update from my mother's rehab counsellor on a Friday; and worked at Destination Wednesday through to Saturday. And then on Sundays, I acted as dealer at Alex's poker nights.

The second game ran much the same as the first one. There was another the following week, and that went smoothly, too. I got paid a thousand pounds for each, plus healthy tips. After the third game, I'd already paid off four and a half thousand of the twelve thousand I owed Sergei. The money was so good that it began to make me forget all about the risk.

But the night of the fourth game, just before we started, the door of the Empire Suite opened, and Giles appeared. At first I thought he'd been invited – but then I saw how unhappy he looked.

Alex was in one corner, briefing the bouncers. When he spotted Giles, he stopped and held out his arms in a theatrical welcome. 'Brother! I don't remember inviting you.'

But Giles didn't seem in the mood to be charmed. 'Jesus, Alex. I can't believe you're up to your old tricks.' He gave a pointed glance around the room. 'Using our hotel suites for your illegal poker games?' He ran a hand through his short sandy hair. 'You know if you're caught you'll go to jail and the hotel could get closed down. Or is that what you're hoping for?' I stood up from the couch where I'd been sitting, feeling like I needed to make my presence felt. Giles's eyes widened when he saw me. 'And you've dragged Nina into this, too?' He shook his head, as though my involvement upset him most. 'What the hell's wrong with you?'

'Nina's perfectly fine.' Alex looked unperturbed. 'You worry too much. We're not going to get caught. As long as you're not going to blab, that is.'

The last part was said almost as a question, and Giles shook his head. 'You know I'm not about to do that.'

'Good.' Alex waited a beat. 'And just how did you find out about this, anyway?'

'It wasn't that hard to figure out. I remember all your tricks from last time. I saw you recruiting players at Destination, and then I checked the hotels to see which suite you were using.'

'Well, aren't you the smart one? Now I remember why you're our father's favourite.'

Alex made to walk away, but Giles caught his arm. 'You can't keep holding games here, Alex. This is the last one, or I will tell Dad.' Giles's eyes flashed over to me. 'And if you do anything to get Nina into trouble, so help me . . .'

They stared at each other for a long moment, and then Alex wrenched his arm away and walked off to speak to his guests, leaving me alone with Giles.

He turned to me. I could see his disappointment. 'Oh, Nina – how the hell did he rope you into this?'

I couldn't help feeling ashamed. Giles had been good to me these past few weeks – always stopping in the corridor to ask how I was getting on, and seeming genuinely interested in the response. Now I felt like I'd let him down – he'd asked me to stay away from Alex, and I'd managed to get myself caught up in one of his schemes.

'I needed the money,' I said in a small voice.

'Then why didn't you come to me? I'd have given it to you – no questions asked.'

Maybe he would have – but I'd still have felt obliged to pay him back at some point. And earning the money doing these games was so easy – a quick way of paying off the loan.

When I didn't say anything, he sighed. 'Look, I don't know how Alex managed to drag you into this, but I just want you to think twice before you continue working for him. He's my brother, and I care about him, but he's self-destructive. Don't let him drag you down, too.'

'It's just a few games—'. But even to my own ears that justification sounded weak.

'No, it's not. What you have to understand is that Alex wants to be caught. That's his way of hurting our father.' I went cold at the thought. 'I'm not going to tell Dad about your involvement, but understand this – if he finds out, then you'll be gone. And that's not the worst of it. If the police raid one of these things, you'll end up in prison. I'd hate that to happen to you.'

First Jas, and now Giles. The warnings from these people – people I trusted – about Alex made me think twice about what I was doing. Somehow I'd begun to warm to him. But now I realised how important it was to remember the kind of person he was. He was jaded and dangerous, someone who lived on the edge. My association with him was through necessity – and I would do well to remember that.

Movement across the room made us both look up. The players were taking their places at the table. The game was about to begin.

'I'd better get out of here,' Giles said. 'And if you've got any sense you'll do the same. Just give what I said some thought, will you?'

He squeezed the top of my arm reassuringly, and then left. I had no doubt that he was right – I should have been leaving. But my situation gave me no option but to stay.

Later that night, after the game, I stood waiting for Alex to pay me. I still felt shamed by Giles's words. Alex must have noticed the dip in my mood, because just as he was about to hand the money over, he cocked his head to one side, studying me closely. 'What's up with you?'

'Nothing,' I said.

'Oh, come on. This isn't about what Giles said earlier, is it?' My silence said everything. 'Well, take my advice and don't pay any attention to him. You're doing this for the money, no other reason. You have nothing to feel guilty about. My brother's just a goody two-shoes. He always has been. It can be quite irritating.'

The dismissive way he said that annoyed me. Giles had only been looking out for me – which was more than Alex was. 'Your brother's a good guy,' I said quietly. 'He takes his responsibilities seriously. And he's been very kind to me.'

Alex stared at me. 'Well, well.' His mouth twisted into a smirk. 'It seems like you and my brother have quite the admiration club going. I've never seen him quite so defensive over a girl before either.'

'I'm just saying, he seems like a good guy.'

'Unlike me, I suppose.' He held out the money I'd earned for the night. 'Shame that I seem to be a necessary evil at the moment. But then we're often forced to take strange bedfellows.'

I snatched the notes from him, and turned away before he could say anything more. But as I left the hotel suite, I realised Giles's warning had shaken me more than I would have liked.

I needed to end my association with Alex sooner rather than later. He was the kind of person who could easily lead me astray. I'd always been so good at sticking to my principles, and prided myself on having such a clear sense of myself – I wasn't about to let some guy corrupt me.

* * *

133

Half an hour later, I was standing outside the door of my room at the B&B, my hand in my bag searching around for my keys.

'Hey,' a heavily accented male voice said.

I started at the sound, and whirled round, my heart thumping loudly.

Two thickset men stood shoulder-to-shoulder in the hallway. It was Viktor and Vladimir Osipova, identical twins who were renowned on our estate for being two of Sergei's most vicious enforcers. They weren't especially tall – maybe just five ten – but they were built like brick walls. Just in case their physiques alone weren't intimidating enough, they both had shaved heads, angry scars on their faces, and their arms and necks were covered in tattoos.

I felt my stomach twist into knots – which always happened when I saw these two. For the past three weeks they had turned up first thing on a Monday morning like this, just in time for me to hand over the one and a half grand instalment of what I owed to Sergei. Once I'd given them today's, I'd have repaid six thousand pounds of the debt. That meant only another six thousand to go. Four more poker games and I'd be done.

'You have money for us?' It was Viktor who spoke. I could tell it was him from the long scar that zigzagged across his right eye.

I unzipped my backpack and took the envelope of cash out and passed it to Viktor.

He opened it and quickly flicked through the contents before stuffing it into the inner pocket of his jacket.

'Right.' I shifted from one foot to the other, keen for them to leave now. 'If that's all sorted, then I should get going—'

Viktor held up his hand, and I could feel the knots in my stomach tightening.

'Not so fast, my lovely.' I froze, knowing this wasn't going to be good. 'Sergei is pleased you get him money on time.'

'That's good,' I said warily, already sensing where this was leading.

'But it has him wondering – maybe you get him rest quicker. Say, three thousand by next Monday.'

'What?' I couldn't keep the horror out of my voice.

'You heard.'

'But that wasn't what we agreed.'

Obviously Viktor wasn't too bothered about his boss being thought of as a man of his word, because he simply shrugged.

'He change mind.' He picked at the dirt under his nails. 'He want cash sooner.'

I had no idea what I was going to do. Unless Alex magically had an extra poker night for me, I had no chance of getting that money together.

'I can't . . .' I did a quick mental calculation. I'd managed to save a bit from my tips and wages at the club. 'I could maybe scrape together an extra few hundred pounds—'

'This is not our problem.' Viktor's voice was firm. 'You have three thousand by time we come next week.'

He didn't need to utter the 'or else'.

Before I could say anything more, Viktor nodded at his brother and they turned away – signalling that this wasn't open to further discussion. And leaving me wondering – what the hell was I going to do now?

I was on the lookout for Alex at Destination on Wednesday. I'd thought about calling him up, but it felt like something that should be discussed face to face. I managed to pull him to one side, and said, 'Do you have any other nights you need me for? Like, maybe Friday or Saturday this week?' He'd asked me before about working those nights, but I'd told him I couldn't, because of my job at Destination. But now I wasn't so fussy. I looked around, making sure no one could hear. 'I can always call in sick here if I have to . . .'

He cocked his head to one side, and studied me. 'You really are desperate for money, aren't you? Now the big question is why. I might ask if you've got some secret coke habit you're funding, but you're far too straight-laced for that. So do you care to enlighten me?'

I thought about it for a moment. Part of me wanted to tell him, to share the burden of my situation. But I was worried about what he might do if he knew the truth. I couldn't imagine Alex insisting I go to the police, but I couldn't take the risk.

He must have sensed my hesitation, because finally he shrugged. 'I see. So you still don't want to share.' I saw the wicked glint in his eye. 'Of course, I could make the work contingent on you telling me . . . But I won't,' he added hastily, no doubt having seen the look of horror on my face. 'Anyway, Sunday's all I've got. With Giles turning up, I've had to rethink venues, so the other games got cancelled.'

My heart plummeted.

He must have seen the worry on my face, because he frowned. 'Look, if you're that desperate for cash, I can give you an advance.'

I looked up at him, and thought I saw genuine concern in his usually mocking eyes. It was tempting – the money meant so little to him, while it was the world to me. But I'd try to reason with Sergei first. Getting the money from Alex could always be a last resort – if I thought that there was any imminent danger to my sister.

'Thanks, but I'll be fine.'

It seemed like he wanted to press it further, but then decided against it. 'If you say so.'

I made to go, but before I could walk away, he caught hold of my arm. I turned round, and was surprised to see him serious for once.

'Look, I meant what I said. If you need money now, the offer still stands.'

I was so used to him looking either bored or mocking that seeing him so obviously concerned was hard to take.

'I'll bear that in mind.'

That night, I called Sergei to let him know that I wouldn't be able to make the additional payment on Monday. He seemed agreeable enough on the phone. But I couldn't help feeling unnerved. I suspected that now he'd got it into his head I could pay more he wouldn't let up.

My only consolation was that April was away on a geography school trip over the weekend. I'd be able to see how the land lay with Sergei on Monday, and make a decision about what to do from there.

Chapter 12

After Giles's threat, Alex was forced to move the venue for the next poker game. So instead of the hotel it was a private apartment in the heart of Chelsea. When I asked Alex who it belonged to, his reply was vague – a friend, who was out of the country and had let him use it for the night.

The mansion block was quiet and discreet, and the apartment itself was as chic and impersonal as the hotel. The game passed uneventfully, and I made another one and a half thousand pounds – a lot of money, but still not enough to meet Sergei's new demand.

When I left the apartment at four in the morning it was raining heavily, the water bouncing off the pavement. Unlike at the hotel, there was no doorman, so I huddled in the doorway, keeping an eye out for a cab.

I'd been waiting for about ten minutes, when a sleek silver Porsche pulled up in front of me. I looked up, expecting to be asked for directions, but instead I saw Alex leaning over from the driver's seat.

'What the hell are you doing out here?' he called as the electronic window wound down.

'What does it look like? Waiting for the chauffeur to bring round my car.'

His mouth twisted in amusement at the sarcasm in my voice.

'Come on. I'll drive you home.'

I hesitated for a split second. He saw my doubt, and swore under his breath.

'Oh, for God's sake.' I could see his hands tightening on the steering wheel. 'It's just a lift. You'd seriously rather get soaked out there than get in a car with me?'

I suddenly realised how ridiculous I was being. After the game, I'd changed back into my street clothes, but even they weren't standing up well in the weather – my trainers and the bottoms of my jeans were already soaked, and the wind kept whipping sheets of spray towards me. And I was turning down a lift from Alex because . . . well, why exactly?

Before I had a chance to change my mind, I sprinted across the pavement to the car. I threw open the door and jumped inside, shaking my hair out like a wet dog. I rubbed a hand across my face to clear the water from my eyes, and realised that I'd dripped all over the smooth buttery leather of the bucket seats. But that wasn't my only concern.

As I looked down, I saw my T-shirt was soaked through, so you could see the outline of my bra, as well as my cold, erect nipples pressing through the thin material. It was then that I felt Alex's eyes on me. I turned to see a little half-smile playing on his lips.

'What?' I folded my arms across my chest, trying to preserve some modesty.

He affected an innocent look. 'I'm just waiting for you to tell me where I'm taking you to. Or would you rather stay here all night?'

I felt myself flush as I realised my mistake. 'Oh . . . right.'

I told him the address, and once I'd fastened my seat belt Alex sped off. I settled back in my seat, content to watch the city slip by. I loved London in the early hours of the morning. The streets were empty, and the bright lights of the streetlamps shimmered in the puddles like rippling rainbows.

It had been a long night, and neither of us bothered making conversation. It was only as we neared my road that I began to wonder if I'd made a mistake. I thought of the rundown building, and realised that I didn't especially want Alex to see my current abode. But I knew there was no way I was going to be able to get him to drop me elsewhere, so I'd just have to put up with it.

As the streets grew rougher, I could see Alex looking out of the window, assessing his surroundings. He didn't make any comment, and his customary impassive face revealed little, but I knew he was aware of just how squalid the area was.

Finally he pulled up in front of the entrance to my building.

'You live here?'

I could hear the shock in his voice, and for a moment I saw the block through his eyes. It was a shame that the resident meth-heads were hanging out on the steps. They didn't really do much to raise the tone of the neighbourhood.

'Not all of us get to buy luxury apartments with our trust funds,' I said, trying to lighten the moment. But Alex didn't look amused. Instead, his eyes were firmly fixed on the dilapidated red-brick building.

'I get that, but still . . .'

I unfastened my seat belt, and went to open the door. To my surprise, he did the same.

'What are you doing?' I asked.

'Coming in with you.'

'Oh, please,' I scoffed. 'I'm not exactly the kind of girl who needs to be walked to her door. And you're certainly not the kind of guy who does the walking.'

'Then consider this virgin territory for us both,' he fired back.

Before I could stop him, he was out of the car. I could have argued back, but it seemed easiest just to let him accompany me upstairs.

My room was at the top of the building, which meant an excruciating trek up five flights of stairs. We didn't speak as we began the climb. I expected him to give up halfway, but he kept following me up, uncomplaining. He really was serious about making sure I got to my room safely.

Finally we reached my corridor.

'Well, you can go now,' I said as we walked past my neighbours' doors. 'This is me—'

The words were hardly out of my mouth when I stopped abruptly. My door was ajar, and it didn't take a genius to see from the paint scratches by the handle that the flimsy lock had been jemmied with some kind of tool.

I looked up at Alex, and saw him frowning. It was too much to hope that he wouldn't have noticed.

'I'm guessing you didn't leave it like this?' he said.

Before I could reply, he moved in front of me and pushed the door open. The light switch was right inside the door, and he found it straight away.

I gasped as I saw the state of the place. It had been perfectly neat and tidy when I had left, but now it was torn apart. All the furniture was upturned and my clothes lay strewn across the floor. Someone had taken a knife to the mattress and pillows, so there were white feathers scattered over the room. It might have looked pretty if it wasn't so obviously threatening. But what stood out the most was the blood-red writing sprayed across the walls, which read: *Pay Up.*

I stared at the words, unable to tear my eyes away. Cold fear spread through the pit of my stomach. What if I'd been there? What would the men who did this have done to me? And as I wasn't there, would they have moved on to April?

That thought hit me like a punch. For a moment, I couldn't catch my breath. And then I remembered – she was away on a school trip until Tuesday. I just needed to have this all sorted out by then – which I would. I should have taken Sergei's demand more seriously. I wouldn't underestimate him again.

'Nina?' I jumped as Alex said my name. I'd forgotten he was there. All I could think about was the threat of physical violence, visible throughout my room. I looked over at him now, wondering what he was making of it all. He lifted an eyebrow. 'Are you all right?'

'Not really.'

He started to move around, righting furniture as he went and searching through my belongings. I had no idea what he was up to until he pulled out a backpack and tossed it over to me.

'Here,' he said, as I caught it. 'Grab what you can and let's go.'

I looked down at the bag, confused. 'What do you mean?'

'I mean you can come and stay with me.'

'Why would I want to do that?'

'Why wouldn't you?' He gave a pointed glance around the room. 'You can't exactly stay here, can you? It's not safe.'

'I'll be fine. This is nothing.' Even as I said the words, I knew I didn't believe them. 'It's just a—'

'Threat? Yes, I can see that.' He shook his head in exasperation. 'Seriously? You'd prefer to stay here than come back to my flat for the night? What the hell do you think I'm going to do to you?'

'Nothing!' I felt myself redden at the implication. 'I just wouldn't feel very comfortable, that's all.'

He took a step forward, his blue eyes deadly serious. 'Then let me put it another way – I'm not leaving you here alone for whatever madman you pissed off to decide to come back for you. So start packing or come as you are.'

I hesitated for just a second. His tone didn't invite any argument, but that wasn't my only reason for giving in. Part of me didn't want to stay here alone. Sergei had been kind enough to leave a Stanley knife on top of my demolished bed. That's what he'd used to carve up my mattress, and I couldn't help wondering what it could do to my face.

Alex must have taken my silence for reluctance because he said, 'If it makes you feel more comfortable, think of it as me protecting my investment.'

He held out the bag to me, and this time I took it.

* * *

Half an hour later, Alex drove his Porsche into the under-ground car park beneath his luxury apartment block in Knightsbridge. He nodded at the security guard as we passed his booth and pulled up in his designated space.

Because it was early in the morning, no one was around. He got out of the car without a word, grabbed my bag from the boot, and started to stroll towards the lifts at the other end of the basement.

Alex had a key-card to operate the lift. When the doors pulled open, he gestured with his hand. 'After you.'

We went through to the open-plan living space. It was just as impressive as I remembered – and easier to appreciate without the crowd that had been at the party. Floor-to-ceiling windows dominated the room, with a view across London. I walked over, inextricably drawn to them, and pressed my hand against the glass, liking the cold feel against my skin. Lights sparkled below, like pinpricks in a blanket of darkness.

'This place is unbelievable,' I breathed.

I turned to face Alex. He was standing in the huge, state-of-the-art kitchen, the kind where the cupboards and drawers have no handles, and the electrics are touch-button. There was a central island with bar stools on one side.

I watched as Alex pulled out a bottle of whisky and fixed himself a drink. He looked around in a detached way.

'It's a good investment.' He held up the bottle. 'Drink?'

I shook my head. 'I'm fine.'

'So clean-living,' he said mockingly. He drank the contents of the tumbler down, and poured more – I presumed just to prove he wasn't going to be shamed into not drinking by my abstinence.

Whisky in hand, he walked over to the seating area, and collapsed onto a plush cream couch, gesturing to me to do the same. He took a drink, and fixed me with a stare. 'So are you finally going to tell me what this is all about? Why you need the money from these poker nights?'

I looked at him for a long moment. Because of what he'd seen and how he'd taken me in, it felt like I owed him the truth.

He listened impassively as I told him about my mother and April, and why I'd come to work for his father, only interjecting to ask the odd question or clarify a detail here and there.

Once I'd finished explaining about Sergei, he said, 'So how much do you need?'

'Six thousand to clear the debt.'

He didn't say anything. Instead he got up, went to the wall and removed a picture to reveal a safe. I watched as he opened it. From where I stood, I could see the stacks of cash inside. He pulled out several bundles, carried them over to the table and placed them in front of me.

'Here. It's all there.'

At first I didn't understand what he was saying. And then I realised: he wanted to settle my debt. I recoiled at the thought. 'I can't take that from you.'

'Why not?'

'This is my debt. My problem. I'll find a way to pay it.'

He looked like he was going to argue with me, but then stopped himself. He could obviously see that I was deadly serious. 'Fair enough. Well, if you really don't want to take the money, then think of it as an advance on your wages.'

I looked down at the cash and then back up at him, torn over what I should do for the best.

He could obviously see my indecision, because he said, 'If you don't want to do this for yourself, then think of your sister. You're not going to be much good to her if you wind up in hospital – which I suspect is exactly what's going to happen if you don't pay that Sergei guy. And what's to stop him skipping you and heading straight to her once she's home?'

It was hard to argue with the logic of what he was saying. 'All right,' I said. 'If you don't mind giving me the money as an advance, then I'd love to take you up on your offer.'

'Good.' He nodded his approval. 'So why don't you call this Sergei guy now? Tell him you have the money, and you'll meet him whenever he wants.'

Alex went upstairs while I made the call. Sergei didn't sound remotely surprised to hear from me. Sending round his thugs obviously had a way of making people pay up. He arranged to meet me in a couple of hours' time, in the same place as before, Le Grand Café.

When Alex came back in, I told him the details.

'And when are you meeting?' he wanted to know.

'Eight thirty.'

'Good. Then we'll leave here just before eight.'

He said it so decisively, as though it was the most natural thing in the world for him to accompany me.

'You don't have to come.' He'd been good to me so far, but I had no wish to drag him into this any further. 'I know it looked bad tonight, but if Sergei knows I have his money, he won't hurt me or anything.'

'I'm still going with you.'

I was going to argue back, but seeing the determined jut of his chin I decided it would be easiest to give in – mostly because I was pretty certain it was all talk, and he wouldn't bother coming in the end. No doubt eight o'clock would roll around, and he'd still be in bed, and I'd end up going alone.

'If that's what you want.'

There was a silence, and then he said, 'Just one last question – why didn't you let me lend you the money when I offered?'

He seemed genuinely curious. I thought about it for a moment, and then shrugged. 'I don't like relying on other people for help.'

He stared at me for a long moment. 'You know, Nina, I don't think I've ever met anyone quite like you before.' He looked at me with what seemed to be admiration. 'Most girls I know, all they care about is what they look like or who they're going out with. And here you are, sacrificing everything for your family.'

I looked away, feeling embarrassed at the unexpected praise. 'I just do what I have to do.'

He didn't say anything to that. The silence dragged on, so I flipped my eyes up and found him still staring at me. There was something in his gaze that I hadn't seen before, and I could feel my heart speeding up. My lips suddenly felt dry, and I wet them a little.

'I should get some sleep,' I said, suddenly anxious to be away from him.

I was worried he might argue back, but instead he gave a swift nod. 'Of course.'

He swallowed down the last of his drink, then led me upstairs to where the bedrooms were situated. The room he showed me to was huge and expensively decorated – with a walk-in closet and an en suite bathroom that came equipped with huge, fluffy towels and Bvlgari toiletries. It was a bit like being in a five-star hotel – or so I imagined.

Alex placed my scruffy bag on the huge king-sized bed, and came to stand in front of me. I was suddenly all too aware of the fact that we were alone in a bedroom.

'Is there anything else you need?'

I shook my head. 'No. This is perfect.' The words seemed inadequate to describe what he'd done for me.

'I know it won't be easy, but try to get some sleep.'

'I will.' He was at the door, when I said, 'And, Alex?'

He turned back. 'Yes?'

'I just wanted to say thank you – for everything. I don't know what I'd have done without your help.'

'I'm sure you'd have sorted something out.'

With that, he left the room. I hurried over to close the door and, pressing my back up against it, I sank to the floor. The last thing I needed was to complicate my life by being attracted to Alex. A fun statistic about children of alcoholics – they were four times more likely to become alcoholics themselves, or end up married to one. I planned to be the exception to the rule. Alex might not be an alcoholic, but he was wild and unpredictable – everything I wanted to avoid. I hated looking after my mother, and I wasn't about to trade one co-dependent relationship for another.

So why did it feel like, as hard as I tried to push him away, he was still getting under my skin?

With that disconcerting thought, I went to bed.

Chapter 13

I hadn't expected to be able to sleep. So when my alarm went off at 7.30, I was surprised to find I'd dozed off. I suppose the events of the previous night had drained my energy.

I quickly got ready, wanting to leave lots of time to get to my appointment with Sergei. But when I got downstairs, to my surprise, Alex was already up and dressed, sitting at the kitchen island drinking coffee.

He swivelled round as I entered. 'Morning. How did you sleep?'

'Fine,' I answered automatically. I shook my head, trying to clear my confusion. 'You're really coming with me ?' I couldn't keep the surprise out of my voice.

He frowned, setting down his mug. 'Didn't I say that I would?'

'I know you did. But—' I stopped, unsure how to explain my thought process.

'But what?'

I walked over to where he sat, and slipped onto one of the stools. 'I told you before that my mother's an alcoholic?' I accepted the mug of coffee he'd poured me, and took a sip before continuing. 'Well, the thing about alcoholics is that they tend to be pretty self-absorbed.' I looked down into my mug as I spoke, unable to meet his eye. 'She'd forget birthdays; wouldn't turn up for parents' evening at school . . . That kind of thing. And because of that . . . well, let's just say I stopped expecting people to keep their promises a long time ago. So even though you said you'd come today, I didn't believe that you really would.'

There was a silence after my confession. 'Well,' Alex said presently. 'I'm not your mother. And whatever you think of me, I don't make promises I'm not prepared to keep.'

I raised my eyes to meet his. 'I can see that,' I said softly. The events of the past night had made me wonder if perhaps I had misjudged Alex. Beneath his rakish exterior maybe he was a good guy after all.

Our gaze held for a moment. Then he glanced at his watch.

'It's nearly eight.' He swallowed down the last of his coffee. 'We should get going.'

The traffic was building up at that time in the morning, but we still made it across to East London before 8.30.

My heartbeat seemed to double between getting out of

the car and reaching Le Grand Café. I hesitated for just a moment as we got to the entrance. Alex put his hand on my shoulder. I looked up at him and he gave me a reassuring smile. Trying to look calmer than I felt, I pushed open the door.

The place was fairly empty at that hour of the morning. Sergei was there in his usual spot, with the Osipova brothers hovering nearby for backup. A couple of other tables were occupied, by the usual builders and lorry drivers, but no one gave us so much as a glance as we walked in.

I headed straight over to where Sergei sat. Alex followed behind me. We'd agreed in advance that I'd do the talking, and that Alex wouldn't get involved unless absolutely necessary. I just wanted to get it over with as soon as possible.

I kept conversation to a minimum, and simply handed over the envelope of cash to Sergei. He took his time counting it, but finally he put it away in the locked briefcase he carried with him. Then he turned his cold black eyes on me.

'I knew you'd find a way to get me the money, Nina. All you needed was a little persuasion.'

I clenched and unclenched my fists, my body stiff with tension. 'That's it now, then? The debt's paid?'

'Of course, Nina. Of course.' He smiled a snake-like smile. 'And may I just say, I look forward to doing business with you again.'

Alex stepped up, planting both hands on the table as he loomed over Sergei. 'Let's be clear, there is no again,' he said quietly. 'This ends now. You have your money. The debt is paid. You don't go near Nina or her family again. Understand?'

'Hey!' Viktor was already on his feet, closely followed by his brother. 'Who do you think you are talking to?'

'Alex,' I said warningly, as the twins advanced towards him.

But he was already straightening up and turning to face his attackers, with a speed that left me breathless. I stood frozen with shock as he punched Viktor on the nose, his knuckles crunching against bone, and landed a blow to Vladimir's stomach. The two brothers stumbled backwards, Viktor clutching at his nose, Vladimir bent over, clearly winded.

They weren't down for long, though. This wasn't the first time they'd been hit – it was their job after all. I looked from them to Alex. He'd assumed a boxer's stance, and his wolf eyes were blazing. He was clearly ready for a fight, and very proficient at it. He had a lightness to his moves that looked honed over years of training. But even though I didn't doubt his skill, I still didn't like his chances against the twins – there were two of them, after all.

The few other people in the café were also obviously sensing that the situation was about to escalate, and didn't want to get involved. The waitresses were suddenly nowhere to be seen, and the customers were hastily throwing cash onto the tables, and leaving half-finished food as they made for the door.

As the brothers advanced towards Alex, my mind was racing as I wondered what to do. And then—

'Stop!' Sergei's voice rang out. The twins came to an immediate halt, like Duracell bunnies that'd had their batteries removed. 'No more fighting,' he instructed his thugs. He turned to nod at Alex. 'He's right. I have my money. There is nothing to be gained from making a scene, apart from dragging the police in, and I do not want that.' Relief coursed through me. Although I'd been impressed by Alex's moves, I hadn't really wanted him to put them to the test. Then Sergei turned to me. 'Just tell your mother not to come looking for any more loans from me. I don't need this grief.'

There was nothing more to say to that. I just wanted to get out of there, and forget what had happened. Alex rested a hand on my shoulder, and the two of us left the café.

Once we were outside and safely in his car, I felt all the tension leave my body. I turned to Alex.

'So where did you learn to do that?'

He grinned. 'Would you believe boarding school? The gentleman's sport of boxing has had quite the renaissance over the past decade.'

'Seriously? You had lessons in how to beat each other up?' I shook my head in disbelief. 'At my school, the teachers spent most of their time trying to make sure we didn't kill each other.'

It was rush hour by now, and it took a while to get back to Alex's apartment. As we stepped out of the lift into the hallway, I said, 'Thanks again for everything. Obviously I'll get out of your way now—'

He frowned. 'Why would you do that? I told you last night you could stay.'

'I know, but now everything with Sergei is sorted out, I can go back to the B&B.'

'Oh, please.' He shook his head dismissively. 'Why on earth would you want to live in that fleapit when you can stay here?'

It was a fair point. There weren't many people who'd choose to live in a cockroach-infested room rather than a luxury apartment. But still . . .

'Just tell me one thing,' I said finally. 'This isn't some ploy of yours to get me to sleep with you, is it?'

'No. It's not.' He grinned. 'Although it's always nice to be reminded of what a low opinion you have of me.' He sighed. 'Look, if you want to justify it to yourself, think of it like this. I paid off your debt. In exchange, you promised to continue working for me. To do that, you need to stay safe, and I'm not sure that's going to happen if you carry on living in that hovel.'

For some reason, his words deflated me. He only thought of me as a commodity – something he had invested in. I wasn't sure why I was so surprised. Had I really been expecting him to say he cared about me?

'Fair enough,' I said quietly. 'I'll stay until my debt's cleared. If that's what you want.'

'It is.'

Right then, my phone bleeped in my pocket. I pulled it out and saw a text from Jas. We were meant to be meeting for lunch at her flat, and she was letting me know that she'd be a bit late, because she'd spent the night at Hugh's.

'Unbelievable,' I muttered.

'What's that?'

'Jas.' I sent her a quick text saying that was fine, and then tucked my phone back into my pocket. 'She's with Hugh.'

Alex must have sensed my tone, because he looked over at me, his eyebrow raised. 'And that's a bad thing?'

'Well, it ain't good.'

'Why do you say that?'

I looked at him. 'You're seriously asking me that? The guy's just using her.'

'For what?'

'You know what for.' When he continued to pretend to be confused, I gave a big sigh. 'Fine. I'll say it then. He's using her for sex.'

Alex frowned. 'I sincerely doubt that. Hugh's a good guy.

I've known him since prep school. He doesn't have a bad bone in his body.'

'Yeah, well. You would say that.'

'What do you mean by that?'

'Well, he's your friend, isn't he? You probably think it's fine for him to shag the trashy waitress and then ignore her until he wants to have sex again.'

Alex burst out laughing. 'You really do have a suspicious mind, don't you? Honestly, nothing could be further from the truth. Hugh's crazy about Jas.'

'Well, I guess we'll see who's right eventually,' I said a touch primly. 'Anyway, talking of Jas – I'm really going to have to tell her that I'm staying here. I can't risk her finding out for herself. And she's going to ask questions about why we were hanging out together . . .'

He paused for a moment. 'I suppose you're going to have to tell her the truth, then.' His eyes glinted as he added, 'That should be a novel change for you.'

That afternoon, Jas and I sat drinking tea in her tiny living room. She listened wide-eyed as I told her everything – from my mother's drinking to the poker nights and Sergei.

'So now you're staying at Alex's?' she asked, once the whole story was out. 'I knew there was something going on between you!'

'Trust me. There isn't.'

'Yeah, a likely story.' She threw a cushion at me. 'And you had the cheek to give me a hard time about Hugh.'

'How's that going, by the way?' I asked, looking to change the subject.

'Oh, don't say it like that. I know you don't approve. But he's been really good to me.' Her eyes went dreamy as she spoke of how he'd cooked her dinner and brought her breakfast in bed.

It all sounded lovely, except for one thing: they didn't seem to be spending time with anyone other than each other. 'What about his friends and family?' I said casually. 'Have you met any of them yet?'

She frowned. 'Well, no.' I could see her chewing at her inner lip. 'But we haven't been together for that long. I'm sure that'll happen.'

I just nodded, and hoped for her sake that she was right about him.

When I got back to the flat that night, Alex was waiting for me. He was smiling.

'You're looking very pleased with yourself.'

'I am.' His smile widened. 'I've got something for you.'

'Oh?'

He reached into his jeans pocket, pulled out a piece of paper and handed it to me. It was a concert ticket for Tumbleweed, my favourite band.

I looked up at him, a question in my eyes.

'Jas mentioned you liked them, so I got us all tickets. You, me, Jas and Hugh. I thought it'd be a good way for you to get to know him a little better – make sure that his intentions towards your friend are honourable.'

I looked at the date, and bit my lip. It was for a Tuesday evening over in the Caledonian Road, North London. And Tuesday was the night I met up with April.

'What's wrong?' Alex had clearly seen my reaction.

'I can't go.' I knew I needed to give more explanation. 'It's the night I meet my sister. I can't let her down.'

His brow furrowed. 'Can't you change it to another night?'

I gave a short, harsh laugh. 'Spoken like someone who's never had to deal with Social Services.' He looked at me quizzically. 'Trust me – the system isn't set up to be that flexible.'

'And you can't skip it for once? Your sister would understand.'

'I can't do that to her.' I handed the ticket back. 'I'm sorry if you wasted your money. But I'm sure you'll find someone else who'll be dying to go with you.' I waited a beat, and then couldn't help adding, 'Tori, maybe. I can see it being right up her street.'

He smiled at that.

He pocketed the ticket, but I could tell the conversation

wasn't over yet. He sat back and regarded me with an intense stare.

'What?' I said finally.

'Why are you always so restrained? This isn't me hassling you about the ticket,' he added hastily. 'It's just that you're always like this. You work and you take care of your family. But you never seem to have any—' He hesitated. 'Well, you don't seem to have any *fun*.'

'I told you before. My mother's an alcoholic.'

'I know that. And I get the not-drinking part. But there's more to it than that. You're always so—' He trailed off, as though searching for the right word.

'So what?' I sounded as defensive as I felt. Somehow I had a feeling whatever he was about to say wasn't going to be complimentary.

'I was going to say so responsible.'

'Someone had to be.' I tried to sound nonchalant, but deep down I wasn't. There were times over the years when I'd wished I could have had more of a childhood. But I'd also learnt that there was no point feeling sorry for myself. Someone had to try to hold our family together – to pick up the pieces after my mother and look after April. And there was no one else but me.

I preferred not to think about it, but Alex didn't seem willing to let it go.

'It's not very fair on you, though, is it?' he said. 'You're only nineteen. You shouldn't have all this responsibility.'

'Well, what do you suggest I do? Leave my sister in foster care and swan off enjoying myself?'

'No.' He sounded like he was trying to be reasonable. 'I think it's great what you're doing for your family. I'm just saying you should give yourself a break now and again. The world won't fall apart because you have one night off.'

'Yeah, well, that's easy for you to say. You've never had to worry about anything apart from enjoying yourself. Don't judge me when you have no idea what my life is like.'

'Fair enough, I won't.' He waited a beat. 'As long as you do me the same courtesy.'

It took me a moment to figure out what he meant. It was a good point, and I felt my cheeks heat up as I realised what I'd done. I hated that he was always so quick and smart with his words. He always seemed to get the better of me.

'I should go and try to get some sleep.' It wasn't the wittiest reply, but it was all I had.

'Just think about coming to see the band next week. It'd do you good.'

There was no point discussing it further. He didn't seem to realise how much I'd have loved to go – but I just couldn't. I got up and headed to my room.

Chapter 14

The next few days I settled into my new surroundings. Alex was rarely there, so I didn't see him apart from very briefly as he was coming in or going out.

I met April on the Tuesday night, once she was back from her trip, and told her about my new living arrangements – saying that I was staying with a friend I'd met through my new job. Usually she'd have wanted to hear all the details, but she was more preoccupied with her own circumstances. She assured me that Racquel was no longer bullying her, but said that even so she'd rather be back home with me and Mum. I couldn't say I blamed her.

It was as though some higher power knew I was already fed up enough with my family situation. When I got up the next morning, I had a message to call the rehab centre. It was over a month since my mother had been admitted, and when I phoned back, her counsellor told me that she had been doing so well that they thought it was time for me to join her in one of her therapy sessions. She apparently wanted to apologise for all the times she'd let me down over the years. If it was convenient, I could come in one afternoon.

'Do I have to?' I said.

For some reason, they didn't seem to think I was serious.

The following Tuesday afternoon, I made my way out to the centre.

The meeting had been set up in a formal room, and it was clearly a big deal. Tea was served in fine china, and I could see again why this place was setting me back so much.

After ten minutes my mother came in, and delivered her prepared speech to me. Her counsellor sat nearby, and they'd clearly been working together on what she should say. The counsellor nodded encouragingly as my mother spoke, sometimes mouthing the words along with her.

It was hard to listen to my mother apologising. I tried to appear engaged, but I'd heard it all before. She was looking for forgiveness, and I just didn't have it in me. But I said what she wanted to hear – that I accepted her apology, and believed she really was going to stay sober this time – mostly so I could get out of there.

The counsellor asked to speak privately with me afterwards. I didn't exactly feel like I had a choice in the matter.

She took me into her room, smiling like we were sharing a secret.

'That wasn't easy to hear, was it?' She gestured to me to sit down.

I just looked at her.

'You know she means what she says, don't you?'

'She always does.'

After half an hour of listening to the counsellor making excuses for my mum, and explaining how hard she was trying, I was finally free to leave.

I was feeling thoroughly fed up by the time I got back to the flat. I didn't have the energy to make it to my room, so I flopped onto one of the sofas and closed my eyes. I was due to meet April at seven, but for the first time I had no desire to go. She'd ask me about our mother, and I didn't have it in me to pretend I gave a damn about the woman.

I'd been there for about ten minutes when I heard someone running down the stairs. I opened my eyes, and saw Alex. His hair was damp and he had his jacket on, and he was clearly on his way out somewhere. Then I remembered he was going to the concert with Jas and Hugh.

He probably wouldn't have even noticed me there, but as he got to the last step he happened to glance in my direction. 'I didn't know you were back,' he said. I just shrugged. I must have been wearing my mood on my face, because he frowned. 'So what's up with you?'

I shook my head, not wanting to go into it. 'I've just had a really bad day.'

'And what's in store for the evening? Something fun, I trust?' He made no effort to keep the sarcasm out of his voice.

I just shook my head again. I was worried if I tried to speak, I might start crying.

'Then instead of moping around here, why don't you come out with us instead?'

'I can't.'

'Of course you can.' He took a step towards me, his eyes glittering with challenge. 'I've still got that spare ticket for tonight. For once in your life, live a little. Don't you want to know what it's like to have fun?'

I sat up a little, smarting at his implication. 'I know how to have fun.'

'Really?' He stood back and folded his arms. 'Then show me.'

I knew he was goading me into agreeing to his suggestion, and I wanted to think I was smart enough not to fall for it. He was calling me chicken to get me to do something I shouldn't – it was so transparent. But in that moment I realised I didn't care. Because it suddenly dawned on me just how much I wanted to take him up on his invitation. It was wrong of me, but I just needed one night to be around people my own age; for one night I wanted to let my hair down and forget all my responsibilities.

'You know what?' I said. 'I will come with you.'

I felt a pang of concern as I noted the self-satisfied smile that crossed his face, but I pushed it to one side. 'Good,' he said, and then gave a quick glance at his watch. 'But we need to leave soon.'

I smiled. 'Give me five minutes and I'll be ready to go.'

I hurried to my room, aware that I didn't have long. That was fine by me – I wasn't planning to make a great deal of effort. I pulled off my jumper, but decided there was no point changing out of my old jeans, white tank top and Converse trainers – if we were going to see a band, then I knew the floor would be swimming in beer. I pulled a hand through my short dark hair, and applied mascara and some black-cherry lipstick, just so it looked like I'd made some kind of effort. I finished the look with my favourite item – a fitted vintage brown-leather jacket, which had cost me a tenner from Portobello Road market.

I regarded myself in the mirror. I might not have looked glamorous and chic like the girls Alex usually hung out with, but I was definitely pulling off rock chick. For a moment I wondered why it was important to me that he liked the way I looked, but I pushed the thought away, not wanting to dwell on it too much.

I tried to call April, but couldn't get through, so I left her a message apologising for not being able to make it, and saying that I'd pop round to her school at lunchtime tomorrow instead. I felt bad as I did it, and after I put the phone down I almost changed my mind about going out. But then I thought: What difference will one night make? I can always make it up to her – perhaps even see if I can take her out during the day on Saturday.

As I headed back downstairs, I pushed my guilt to one side. If I was going to take this night for myself, I might as well enjoy it.

Alex was waiting for me at the lift. His eyes swept over me, and he smiled approvingly.

'Ready?' he said, and I nodded. 'Good. Then let's go.'

The Caledonian Road wasn't exactly the swankiest area of London, and I'd worried about being dropped off in some chauffeur-driven car. Or worse still, that Alex would bring his Porsche, which would undoubtedly get nicked within five minutes of us arriving. But he seemed to have considered that. Instead, we took a cab, picking up Jas and Hugh from his apartment along the way.

'You came after all!' Jas beamed as she clambered into the taxi, squeezing my arm as she settled down on the leather seat next to me. 'That's brilliant! Tonight's going to be amazing.'

I watched Hugh get in next, carrying Jas's sparkly handbag for her. Seeing that was almost enough to get me to believe that Jas and Alex were right, and he was a nice guy. But I was still reserving judgement.

It was a squeeze in the taxi, and Jas hugged up to me, inadvertently pressing me against Alex. I couldn't deny how aware of him I was. As Jas chattered on, I contented myself with staring out the window, watching the bright lights of the West End fade as we got further out into the dinginess of King's Cross, until the cab pulled up in the Caledonian Road.

The venue was a former church, where club nights were held and up-and-coming bands played. When we arrived it was already swamped, and we joined the crowd that was pouring through the arched doorway. The place was rough and down-at-heel, shabby compared to the urban sophistication of Destination. But to my surprise, Alex looked just as at home as he did in a private members' club. He had that laid-back cool that made him instantly fit in wherever he went.

Inside it looked a bit like a beaten-up theatre, with a stage at the front, a bar at the back, and a dance floor/mosh pit in between. The walls were all painted black, adding to the dingy feel.

The warm-up band had already started playing. Alex turned to us to take our drinks order. The others all asked for shots of tequila. He looked at me quizzically. I thought for just a second.

'Same for me.' Tonight I was going to forget everything and let my hair down.

Jas cheered. Alex regarded me with undisguised curiosity. I knew he was wondering what exactly I was playing at.

Soon he was back from the bar, juggling the four shot glasses. We all clinked glasses and downed the bitter liquid.

'Same again!' Jas said. I didn't object.

Alex didn't say anything for the first three rounds of shots, but by the fourth he looked concerned.

'Are you sure about this?' He dipped his head towards me, so only I could hear. 'It's not a good idea if you're not used to drinking.'

The sensible part of me knew that he was right. But the alcohol had already gone to my head, and I was at that stage where I felt invincible. 'Don't you worry about me.' I tapped my finger against his chest, in what I knew was a flirtatious manner. 'I can take care of myself. Promise.'

He came back with the shots like before, but this time he also brought bottles of water. After we'd downed the tequila, he handed me one of the waters.

'I like seeing you like this, letting go a little. But let's not go crazy. I don't want to be holding your head over the toilet bowl before the night's over.'

I rolled my eyes at him, but dutifully drank the water down.

Then, before there was time for any more tequila, the lights dimmed and, to a chorus of cheers, whoops and wolf-whistles, Tumbleweed took to the stage.

The place was jammed from wall to wall, and as the band struck up everyone surged towards the stage. Someone bumped into me, and I staggered to one side, but Alex grabbed me from behind. His arms went protectively around my waist. I felt the tips of his fingers pressing into the curve of my hip bones.

'Are you all right?' His lips were so close to my ear I could feel his breath on my skin. I shivered against him, and his arms tightened around me.

'I'm fine.'

He made no effort to let me go, and I didn't object. Everyone around us seemed to be dancing, so when Alex began to move behind me, I couldn't help responding. His hands splayed across my stomach, drawing me closer so I could feel his body pressing against mine. I'd seen him do this with a dozen girls at Destination, but I closed my eyes and shut out the image, just wanting to be in the moment.

As the set wore on, the beat of the music shook the room. Strobe lights flashed, and the smoke machine pumped out clouds of white mist. The crowd swelled again, swallowing Jas and Hugh, and crushing Alex and I together, my buttocks grinding against his hips. My t-shirt rose up, and his fingers grazed my bare midriff, making me gasp.

Alex must have felt my reaction, because he bent his head, so his mouth was next to my ear, and said: 'Do you want to go outside and cool down?'

I knew what he was really asking, and for a moment I hesitated. There was enough of the sensible part of me left to know exactly what I was getting myself into. I nodded, not trusting myself to speak.

He grabbed my hand and led me out to the little alleyway behind the building, where clubbers came to take a break from the heat and noise. The cold air hit me as we emerged into the night, and it was a relief against my burning skin.

At the back of my mind, I knew this was a bad idea, something I was bound to regret. But I didn't want to think about the consequences. For once, I wanted to act without thinking – to just go for what I wanted, even if it wasn't good for me.

There was just a handful of people outside – a few smokers and a bouncer. But Alex took me round the corner, away from their prying eyes. Then he stopped, and looked down at me, his eyes searching mine. My heart was beating so hard in my chest I was sure he could hear it. I knew that if I was going to object this was the moment. That's what he was waiting for. But instead I returned his gaze, strong and steady.

He needed no further encouragement. With that, he grabbed me by the shoulders, backed me up against the wall and kissed me.

I felt the urgency of his mouth on mine, the hard weight of his body pushing against me. His hands moved from my shoulders to my face, pulling me closer as his kiss deepened.

The music and noise from inside felt so far away as Alex's lips dropped to my neck and he ran the tip of his tongue along my collarbone.

I couldn't stop myself from letting out a moan, deep in the back of my throat.

The sudden sound of laughter and chatter startled me as a group of clubbers rounded the corner to where we were. Alex continued to kiss me, before breaking away with a groan. He drew his head back so he was staring down at me, and I could see the pure, unguarded lust in his eyes.

I could hear the others giggling as they realised exactly what they'd interrupted.

'Get a room!' one of them called.

Neither of us even bothered to glance in their direction. It was as though they weren't there. I could see Alex struggling to get himself under control. He took two deep breaths, his chest rising and falling, before he finally spoke.

'Do you want to get out of here?' His voice was thick and gravelly.

I nodded. I didn't even have to think about it.

'Wait here. I'll grab our jackets and tell Hugh and Jas we're heading off.'

His hand swept over my cheek before he went back inside.

I rested my head against the cold brick wall and closed my eyes. I had no idea what I was doing. All I knew was that for once I wanted to do something irresponsible, just for myself.

It was then that I felt my phone vibrate. I pulled it from my jeans pocket, flipped it open, and saw that I had ten missed calls. It took me a second to recognise the number – it was Denise, my sister's foster mother – and I felt a cold sense of foreboding.

I listened to the message with a sense of dawning horror.

'I'm calling to let you know that your sister had to be rushed to hospital earlier this evening. April . . . er . . . fell down the stairs . . . She's broken her arm. But please don't be alarmed. She's back home now, and everything's all right.'

I felt sick as I listened to a message from April, too – she was in tears and begging me to come to see her.

I felt like I was going to be sick. I'd cancelled on April tonight, and she'd ended up hurt. If I'd kept our appointment, this would never have happened. She would have been with me instead. And then, to make matters worse, when she'd called me I hadn't been there for her. My sister had been frightened and in pain, and here I was, drinking and making out with some charming womaniser who would be no good for me.

It dawned on me then who I'd behaved like tonight – my mother. Bile rose in my throat at the realisation.

I looked at my watch, and realised I was shaking. It was after midnight, but I wanted to see April.

I hurried away from the alleyway, reaching the door just as Alex was on his way back out. He had our jackets under his arm.

He stopped when he saw me. It was like he could tell from the look on my face that something had changed. His brow furrowed.

'What's going on?'

'It's my sister. She's been hurt—' I shook my head. I couldn't deal with explanations. 'I need to see her. Right now.' I pushed past Alex.

'Wait a minute. I'll come with you,' he called after me.

That drew me to a halt. I rounded on him. 'No!' I was suddenly completely sober. 'I don't want you anywhere near me. You've already done enough for one night.'

His eyes narrowed. 'What's that supposed to mean?'

'It means I should never have listened to you and come here tonight.' Deep down, I knew I was being unreasonable, blaming it all on Alex, but I was feeling angry and scared and guilty, and I needed to take it out on someone. 'I should have gone to see April like I'd planned. Maybe then this wouldn't have happened.'

'Seriously?' He shook his head in disbelief. 'You're blaming me for this?'

'No,' I said, my voice surprisingly even. 'I'm blaming myself. I knew from the beginning that it was a bad idea. I've spent the last six years living with someone irresponsible. And the last thing I need is to get involved with anyone else like that. You're selfish and reckless, and that's great for you. But I can't be that way. So please – I'm asking you to stay away from me. Because I have enough problems in my life without you in it, too.'

With that, I turned and ran towards the nearest taxi, trying not to think of the look of fury on Alex's face.

Chapter 15

I couldn't get hold of anyone on the phone, so I decided to go straight round to the foster home. By the time I got there, the house was in darkness. I rang the doorbell once, and when there wasn't a response I kept ringing until finally a light went on in what I presumed was an upstairs bedroom.

I waited impatiently for the sound of footsteps on the stairs. When Denise opened the door she didn't look happy to see me, and when I asked to see my sister she told me in no uncertain terms that it wasn't possible, because April was asleep – along with the rest of the household.

'Best if you come back in the morning,' Denise said. She had on a huge pink dressing gown, and it was clear I'd got her out of bed. But I didn't care. 'I'm not disturbing her now,' she added.

She stepped outside and pulled the door to, making it clear I wasn't getting in.

'You can't stop me seeing her. I'm her sister, and she needs me. She sounded so upset earlier, and I want to make sure she's all right—'

Denise folded her arms across her ample chest. 'I've told you, it's not a good idea. She's asleep, and anyway I think it would just upset her more to see you like that.'

She gave me a very pointed once-over, and I felt my cheeks redden. I knew exactly what she was referring to. I could tell she smelt the alcohol on my breath, and wasn't impressed. I wanted to explain that this wasn't me – it was a stupid one-off. But no doubt she wouldn't believe me. Like mother, like daughter.

I banged my hand against the doorframe, and swore under my breath. 'How could you let this happen to her?'

Denise stared impassively at me, unmoved by my display of temper. 'I can't have eyes everywhere. I do my best, and can't do no more.'

I knew she was right. I was only taking my anger at myself out on her. She was around forty-five, and had been foster-ing for ten years after finding she couldn't have her own kids. She had that no-nonsense, I've-seen-it-all-before way about her. I knew she ran a good house, but even she couldn't be everywhere at once.

'I'm sorry—' I began, but she waved my apology away.

'Go home now,' she said more kindly. 'I'll have her ready early tomorrow morning and you can see her before school.'

It was hard to argue with her logic. I didn't want to go back to Alex's apartment. Even though it might sound silly, I wanted to stay physically close to my sister. So I headed to an all-night kebab shop on the Jamaica Road, to wait for the morning to come round.

At seven, I went back to the house to catch up with April before school, like Denise had suggested. I was shocked when I saw her. She had a cast on her wrist, and a long scratch across her cheek – from a fingernail, I guessed – and looked even paler than usual in her burgundy uniform.

We went to a coffee shop that was on her route to school, and I made her tell me the whole story. It turned out she'd been lying to me, and Racquel had continued to bully her. It had come to a head when the other girl had heard April calling me. She'd tried to snatch the phone from my sister's hands, and in the struggle April had ended up falling down the stairs.

The good thing to have come out of it was that one of the other kids had witnessed the altercation, and reported it to Denise. It wasn't the first time Racquel had been caught acting violently, and it turned out she'd been on her last warning. So as of that morning, Racquel had been removed and taken to a care home.

But even though I probably should have been relieved, it upset me to know that April had hidden something so major from me.

'You should have told me what was going on! I would have done something about it. Why did you say everything was fine?'

'Because I didn't want you to worry. You spend so much time looking after me and Mum. I didn't think you needed any more on your plate.'

I felt my eyes water. None of this was fair. She shouldn't be dealing with this stuff at her age.

'Don't ever think that. I want to know what's going on with you. All right?'

She stared forlornly into her hot chocolate, before shrugging her shoulders. 'I suppose.' After a moment, she looked up at me. 'Where were you last night, anyway? How come you couldn't meet me?' It was the question I'd been dreading. She didn't look annoyed or accusatory – just curious.

I couldn't bring myself to tell her the truth.

'I just had some things to do.' I took a sip of coffee, and looked away. I knew I was being evasive, but how could I tell her I'd been out drinking and flirting with some guy I'd known for all of five minutes?

April had to go to school then. I walked her to the gate and gave her a big hug, and promised that I would see her at the weekend. But she didn't seem as excited as usual about the prospect of meeting up. It was only after she left that I noticed for the first time she hadn't asked me when we'd be back together as a family. My sister had obviously given up on me, and I couldn't blame her.

I headed back to Alex's apartment, aware that I owed him an apology for what I'd said the night before. I'd been feeling guilty and I'd taken it out on him, and in the cold light of day, I could see I'd been unfair.

The place was silent when I got in, but his jacket and shoes lay on the hallway floor, so I knew he was back, and probably still asleep. I went into the kitchen to make myself some tea. As I waited for the kettle to boil, I sat up at the central island, running my hand over the granite worktop. But as I did so, I heard Alex clearing his throat behind me.

I started at the sound, and whirled round, preparing my apology. But the words froze on my lips as I saw he was wearing nothing but a pair of jeans that hung low on his hips. He was naked from the waist up, and his ripped chest would have put a Calvin Klein model to shame.

He leaned one muscular shoulder against the doorframe, and regarded me with hooded eyes.

'So you're back.'

All I could do was nod. I didn't know where my head was at. Having assumed he was asleep, and that I'd have some time to prepare my apology, I was thrown by seeing him like this.

'And your sister? Is she all right?' His voice was cool, giving no clue to what he was thinking. The expression on his face also gave nothing away.

'Yes,' I said, finally finding my voice. 'She's fine now, thanks.'

'I'm glad to hear it.' His expression hardened. 'After all, I'd hate to think my reckless behaviour had caused her any undue harm.'

I studied the floor. I'd hoped he might make this easy on me, but it seemed he was holding a grudge about last night. In some ways, I didn't blame him. It looked like I was going to need to do some serious grovelling.

'Look, Alex.' I took a breath, trying to compose myself. 'About what I said last night—'

Before I could finish my sentence, I heard light rapid footsteps on the stairs from the mezzanine.

'Alex?' a posh female voice cooed. 'What on earth are you playing at? I was getting lonely up there—'

An expensive-looking blonde appeared. She was wearing a man's white shirt, unbuttoned, over a pair of black panties, and nothing else. Her long, tanned legs seemed to stretch forever, down to perfectly manicured toes. I suddenly realised why Alex was barefoot and shirtless. I must have interrupted them in his bedroom, and he'd only had time to pull on his jeans. I felt my cheeks redden at the knowledge of what they'd been doing.

When the blonde saw me, the smile died on her lips.

'Who's this?' Her sharp eyes were on me, but the question was clearly directed at Alex. It was annoying, the way she looked at me like I was some kind of insect she'd found in her salad.

'It's my charity case,' Alex drawled. 'You know me – always doing my bit to help life's unfortunates.'

So I'd been right – Alex was holding a grudge.

The blonde's eyes narrowed; she was clearly confused. 'And will she be joining us?'

Alex gave a faint sigh of exasperation. 'Of course not, Lavinia. I'm just trying to finish my conversation with the young lady, and then I'll be all yours.'

Lavinia didn't look happy, but she must have realised there wasn't much she could do, because she gave a little shrug. 'Fine. Do whatever you need to. But don't be too long.'

She gave me one last, contemptuous look, and disappeared upstairs.

'She seems charming,' I said without thinking.

'You're right. Charm isn't one of Lavinia's strong points.' He raised his eyebrows suggestively. 'But trust me, she has others.'

The blatant innuendo, coming from someone I'd been making out with the night before, floored me. I knew that if we hadn't been interrupted I would have ended up in bed with him. Had it meant so little to him that he'd moved on to someone else already?

But before I had time to dwell on the thought, Alex walked over to the fridge and pulled out what looked like an expensive bottle of champagne.

'Bit early for it, isn't it?' The words were out of my mouth before I could stop them.

He turned, his eyes narrowing as he studied me. 'If I didn't know better, darling, I'd think you were jealous.'

'Jealous?' I sputtered, hardly able to get the word out and my thoughts together.

But he didn't seem interested in my outraged denial. Instead, he took out two champagne flutes from the cupboard, used some gadget to chill them, and then strolled towards the stairs.

I stood up, not sure what to do with myself. On the bottom step, he paused and looked back at me, a small smile playing at the corners of his mouth.

'You know, Nina, you had your chance with me last night. But I'm always willing to give you another go – although next time, you might have to beg.'

I was so incensed that I couldn't even speak. Then he was gone, his mocking laughter floating down the stairs behind him.

Chapter 16

I managed to avoid Alex the rest of the day by steering clear of the apartment. But I went into work that night with a feeling of nervous dread hanging over me. If he decided to turn up at Destination, then I'd be forced to spend the evening watching girls like Tori and Lavinia fawn all over him, and I wasn't sure how much of that I could stomach.

However, I needn't have worried. There'd been a leak in the ladies' toilets, and it looked like the place wouldn't be opening. We were told to hang around for a bit to see if the problem could be fixed, but after an hour, Mel announced that nothing would be resolved that evening, so we could all go home.

I was on my way out, when Giles caught up with me. He looked more dishevelled than usual, with his shirtsleeves rolled up and his dark-blond hair mussed up, and I guessed he'd had a difficult night.

'Nina? Do you have a second?' Immediately I wondered what I'd done. He must have seen the anxiety on my face, because he flashed his usual charming smile, his cheeks dimpling a little. 'It's nothing to worry about. I promise.'

'Sure.' I said goodnight to Jas, and followed him through to his office. Giles gestured for me to sit on the small couch, while he perched on his desk. Despite what he'd said, I couldn't help feeling nervous.

'Sorry to frighten you back there. I just wanted to catch up. Find out how everything's going with you.'

He lowered his voice meaningfully, and I smiled, touched by his concern. 'You mean with the illegal gambling?'

'Well, yes. There's that,' he said slowly. 'But I also heard a rumour that you'd moved in with my brother.'

I was aware then of just how keenly he was watching me. I felt my cheeks flush, giving him the answer he wanted.

'So it's true,' he said. He looked strangely disappointed. 'Is there something going on between you two?'

'No!' The memory of what occurred at the Tumbleweed concert flashed through my mind, but I pushed it away. There would be no repeat of that, not after everything else that had happened. 'I just had some trouble, and he offered me a place to stay for a couple of weeks. That's all.'

Giles studied me for a long moment, as though weighing up whether I was telling the truth. Finally, he gave a brisk nod. 'I'm glad to hear it.' He gave a wry smile. 'Alex can be very charming when he wants to be, so forgive me if I jumped to the wrong conclusion. And I didn't mean to pry. I'm just worried about you, that's all.'

'I know. Your dad asked you to look out for me, and you're just doing what he wanted.'

'That's not the only reason I'm asking, Nina.'

The way he gazed at me was unnerving. I dropped my eyes. 'Yeah, well.' I cleared my throat. 'Just so you know, I'm nearly done with the poker. I promise. And then I'll be moving out of Alex's apartment, too.'

'That's good to hear.'

I risked sneaking a look back at him. He'd resumed his usual businesslike expression. I felt confused. Maybe I'd just imagined the tension before.

'There's just one more thing,' he said.

'Oh?'

'My father would like to have dinner with you.' It was pretty much the last thing I'd been expecting him to say. 'He said your first meeting was very brief, and he'd like a chance to get to know you in a more informal setting.'

I couldn't think of anything worse, to be honest, but given my job at Destination was contingent on his good-will, it wasn't like I had much choice.

'It'll just be the three of us,' Giles went on, as if sensing my hesitation. 'He just wants to get to know you a little more.'

There really was no way out of this. 'Sure. I'll have dinner with him, if he wants.'

Giles looked relieved. 'He suggested next Sunday evening, at his house.'

Sunday was usually poker night, but for the moment Alex seemed to have given up on organising any events. 'Sounds fine.'

Giles was on his feet now, bent over his desk with his back to me, searching for something.

'Good,' he said briskly. 'I'm glad to hear it.' He straightened up, and turned to me, holding his car keys in his hand. 'I'm done here for the night, so why don't I give you a lift home?' I was about to object, and say I was happy getting the Tube, but then he said, 'Honestly, it's not a problem. It's on my way.'

Giles drove a Jaguar XJ, in dark grey. It was a sophisticated car, which suited him perfectly.

We chatted easily in the car, mostly about Destination.

When we reached Alex's apartment block, Giles pulled up in the valet parking area, right by reception.

'So Alex won't be at this dinner?' I said as I unbuckled my seat belt.

'No. He avoids family gatherings whenever he can.' Giles frowned. 'In fact, I probably don't need to tell you this, but it'd be best if you didn't say anything to my dad about the poker nights and staying with Alex. It would just cause problems.'

'Sure. I understand.' I grabbed my bag. 'And thanks for the lift.'

'It's no problem,' he said.

To my surprise, Giles leaned over and kissed me on the cheek. As he did so, I felt someone's eyes on me. I looked up and saw Alex in his Porsche, pulling slowly into the underground car park.

At first I couldn't understand the reason for his interest. But then I realised what it must have looked like. The kiss between me and Giles had been purely platonic, but all Alex could see was the back of his brother's head.

Giles seemed to sense my mood change. 'What's wrong?' He looked around, but Alex had already driven inside.

'It's Alex.' I gnawed at the inside of my mouth. 'He saw us as he was driving in, and I think he might've got the wrong idea.'

'Really?' Giles gave a short laugh. 'Well, that should be interesting.'

I didn't ask what he meant. Instead, I thanked him again, and headed inside.

I'd have loved to have avoided Alex, but the only way to my room was through the open-plan living space. I walked in to find him lounging across one of the sofas, a tumbler of what looked like whisky in his hand.

'So,' he drawled. 'Looks like you've moved on to my brother. That didn't take long.'

I rolled my eyes. 'Don't be ridiculous.'

I made my way to the stairs, intending to head up to my room, but his voice stopped me.

'What's so ridiculous?' The light-hearted tone was still there on the surface, but beneath it I could hear an edge. 'From what I saw just now, the two of you looked awfully cosy.'

I turned back slowly to face him. He was sitting up now, his ice-blue eyes regarding me intently. It would have been easy enough to set him straight, but I was still hurt over what had happened that morning.

'And?' I raised my chin in defiance. 'What if I am interested in Giles? I didn't see you asking my permission to have Lavinia stay over.'

His eyes dropped to the floor. 'Yeah, well . . .' He ran a hand over the bristles of his permanent five o'clock shadow. 'You'd made it clear you weren't interested in me. I just found someone who was.'

'Is that right?' I was stung by the idea that it had been so easy for him to go from me to someone else. 'Well then, maybe I just found someone who's more my level.'

Alex went very still. 'And what's that supposed to mean?'

'It means if I'm going to go out with someone, I want it to be a guy like Giles. Someone who's responsible and hard-working. Someone I can trust.'

He sucked in a breath.

'Anyway,' I went on, before he could say anything else, 'I don't know why you're making such a big deal of this. Surely you've got girls like Lavinia queuing up to sleep with you. Why don't you go and harass one of them instead?'

His jaw tightened. 'You know what?' he said after a moment. 'I think that's exactly what I'll do.'

He downed his drink, grabbed his wallet and headed back out. Only when he was gone did I finally let out a deep breath.

My eyes blurred with tears, and I quickly wiped them away. I had no right to be upset. Alex was a free agent. He could do whatever he wanted – I'd even told him to.

But that didn't stop it hurting. With that thought, I took myself off to bed.

I woke to the muffled thump of music reverberating against my bedroom floor. Screams of laughter floated up from downstairs, a mix of male and female voices. It sounded like there was a party going on. I sat up a little, so I could see my alarm clock. The neon numbers showed that it was only half three in the morning.

Groaning, I hunkered down under the duvet, determined to go back to sleep. But a second later someone cranked up the music even louder, and a cheer of appreciation went up. That was the final straw. I shoved back the covers, jumped out of bed and headed to the mezzanine balcony to check out what exactly was going on.

From there I had a direct view into the living room below, and I could see there were about half a dozen people downstairs. Tori was sitting to one side, talking to some guy I didn't recognise, while Alex was on the couch, with one semi-naked girl sitting on his knee – who he was kissing deeply – while another nibbled at his neck. The three of them looked like they were practically having sex.

I couldn't take it any longer. I went back to my room, quickly got dressed, and threw my few belongings into a backpack. I was sure Jas would let me stay at her place for a few days. It would be cramped, but at that moment I wanted to be anywhere but Alex's.

I headed down the stairs, hoping to sneak out unnoticed. But I was almost at the doorway into the hall when I heard Alex's voice.

'Hey. Where do you think you're going?'

It was tempting to pretend I hadn't heard him, but we'd have to have this conversation at some point. So I slowly turned round to face him.

He hadn't bothered to stand up. Instead, he gazed lazily up at me from the couch, one hand casually stroking the nearest girl's hair, making it clear he had no intention of disengaging himself and talking to me alone. Whatever I had to say, I was going to have to do it there, in front of everyone.

'I think I should move out,' I said.

'Oh?' He looked bored. 'And why's that?'

I cast my eyes around the room. 'I think that's pretty obvious.' I lowered my voice a little. 'You're turning the place into a knocking shop.'

'And why does that bother you?' He waited for me to come up with an answer, and when I couldn't, he smiled. 'Unless, like I said, you're jealous?'

I rolled my eyes. 'Oh, please. Don't flatter yourself.'

'Well, if you're not jealous, then why should you care what I'm up to?'

'Because . . .' I lost my train of thought. The two girls were both nibbling at him now, which was distracting enough, and his calm tone was making me even more irritated. 'Because I don't want to be around this all the time.'

He regarded me for a long moment. 'Fair enough. Go if you want.' Relief flooded through me, until he said, 'But you need to pay me back first.'

'What?'

'It's very simple. Pay me back the money I gave you to clear your debt, and then you can leave.'

'You know I can't do that.' I couldn't believe he was going to hold me to this.

'Then I suppose you'll have to stay. That was our deal, wasn't it – you stay here until you've worked off your debt.'

I stared at him, unable to make sense of what I was hearing.

'Now, if you'll excuse me.' He turned his attention to the two girls who had been fawning and petting him through-out our conversation. 'Shall we take this upstairs, ladies?'

The girls scrambled off his lap, and he stood up, offering them each an arm. I could do nothing but watch as they headed upstairs.

I contemplated leaving anyway – after all, what exactly was he going to do to stop me? But then he might not have me working at the poker nights any longer, and I'd never be able to pay him back – which I had every intention of doing. And part of me couldn't help feeling that some of this was my fault – if I hadn't overreacted at the concert, we wouldn't be in this position.

So I put down my bag, and went over to the kitchen to make a cup of tea.

'Hey,' a voice said as I took out a box of tea bags from a cupboard. I looked over to see Tori slipping onto one of the stools that lined the breakfast bar. It was pretty much the last thing I needed – her rubbing my face in Alex's behaviour. But to my surprise, instead of making a bitchy comment, she said, 'So what the hell happened between you two?'

'Nothing worth talking about.' I was hardly about to open up to her – the girl who'd been a bitch from the beginning.

'Well, whatever it was, you must have touched a nerve with Alex. I haven't seen him like this for a while.'

'What do you mean? I thought this was exactly how he always behaved.'

Tori wrinkled her nose. 'The women and partying?' she mused. 'Sometimes it's worse. He tends to go off the rails when someone has a go at him. Like he thinks – well, if they have such a low opinion of me, then there's no point trying to prove them wrong.'

'But why?'

Tori sighed. 'I guess it goes back to when he was younger. You know his mother left his father?' I nodded. 'Well, Duncan . . . he was a proud man, who didn't deal well with being cuckolded. He never forgave Eva for walking out on him, and he took it out on Alex.

'Alex . . . he looks so much like his mother. And he has her personality, too – charming and witty, the life and soul of the party . . . Duncan's very different. He's much more serious – a real businessman, who puts duty first. And you know Giles – he's like that, too. So unfortunately Duncan found it hard to ever really connect with Alex, and he gave him a very hard time. At first, when Alex was little, Duncan avoided him because he reminded him of Eva. And then when he grew older, any time Alex got into scrapes, he would tell him that he was just like his mother. He was always comparing him to Giles, telling him he should be more like his older brother. But nothing Alex ever did was good enough.' Tori smiled ruefully. 'So I think in the end, Alex began to play up to it. He got into a lot of trouble at school; never bothered with university or a career. He just left all that to Giles. The more Duncan told him he was bad, the more he seemed determined to prove him right. I think now it's become a habit. If he's attacked, he acts out.'

I chewed at my lip. It was fascinating, hearing about Alex's upbringing. It explained his recent behaviour. It had all started with that night at the concert. Did that mean Alex was only being like that because I'd rejected him? And then told him I'd prefer someone responsible like Giles? Perhaps. But that was still no excuse. And no guarantee that even if we hadn't argued he would be acting any differently.

But something was bothering me. I studied Tori through narrowed eyes. Even at this time in the morning, having been up all night partying, she looked perfect, with her long blonde hair and fine features.

'Why are you telling me this?' I said.

'What do you mean?'

'Oh, come on. You've made no secret of the fact that you

don't like me. You've been a bitch from the beginning. Why do you suddenly care what I think of Alex?'

'Because I care about him, and I hate seeing him on this self-destructive streak,' she said levelly.

'And what's that got to do with me?'

Tori just looked at me. 'Oh, please. Don't play dumb. It doesn't suit you.'

She slipped off the stool, turned to go, and then stopped. 'And is it any wonder I was a bitch? It wasn't exactly fun being rejected for you.'

'But that's ridiculous! Nothing's happened between us.' Well, not until we went to the concert, but I had a feeling that wasn't what she was referring to. 'I never made any play for him.'

Tori gave a rueful laugh. 'But that's what made it even worse. It didn't matter that you weren't actively trying to seduce Alex – he still showed far more interest in you than he ever did in me. Maybe that wasn't your fault, but it didn't exactly make me want to be best friends with you.' I could see her green eyes water a little. 'Every time I look at you, I see the person that Alex chose over me. So if I was mean to you, can you blame me? Whether you knew it or not, he wanted you, not me.'

With those last words, Tori left. And I stood there in the kitchen, feeling bad for her. All this time, I'd thought of her as a rich bitch, and hadn't considered what was making her lash out that way. Had I been wrong about Alex, too?

I finished making my tea, and sat curled up on the couch drinking it, while thinking about everything I'd learned about Alex. I'd always thought of him as this entitled charmer, who had the world at his feet. Somehow, hearing about his tragic childhood made me soften a little towards him.

Then I looked around at the state of the room. There were empty champagne bottles; traces of coke on the black-glass coffee table; and a discarded halter top one of the girls had left . . .

Even if there was more to Alex, there was no denying he was still a deeply troubled person. And I already had enough problems dealing with my mum.

Chapter 17

The following Sunday night, I stared at my reflection in the mirror, wishing I had time to change. Unfortunately I was due round for dinner at Duncan Noble's house in Chelsea, so I was stuck.

However informal the dinner was meant to be, I'd guessed that jeans and a T-shirt were going to be a bit too casual. So given the limitations of my wardrobe, I'd been forced to ask Jas to lend me an outfit. Most of her clothes were too tight and short, but I'd finally settled on a black-satin baby-doll dress. She'd advised me to pair it with sheer stockings and heels, but instead I'd kept true to myself, and worn opaque tights and my biker boots, to give it a casual feel, more in keeping with my style. The thought made me laugh – like I had a style.

I'd put on some make-up, and blow-dried my hair so it fell softly around my face. I'd been pleased with myself for looking more feminine, but now I wondered if it was still too biker chick for the occasion.

I wasn't even sure whether it was the outfit or the prospect of the dinner itself that was making me feel uncomfortable. I'd been dreading this evening ever since I'd agreed to it. It wasn't like Duncan Noble had been particularly friendly to me when I'd gone to his office. But given that he'd been good enough to help me out, I didn't feel I was in a position to turn him down.

When I came out of my bedroom, I saw from the mezzanine landing that Alex was downstairs in the living room, stretched out on the sofa. To my surprise, he was alone. This past week, he'd seemed to be holding a permanent party at the apartment. He'd go out in the early evening, and come back late with a noisy group in tow, playing music at full blast. Each morning, I'd come downstairs to find the living area in disarray, and be forced to watch as Alex said goodbye to a different girl.

At first, I assumed he was sleeping – no doubt worn out from his late-night antics – but as I began to walk downstairs his eyes flew open.

'Hmm.' His gaze swept over me. 'Where are you off to in that get-up? No—' He propped himself up on his elbows. 'On second thoughts, don't tell me – let me guess. Some rich guy's offered to take you out in exchange for a little cash.'

I rolled my eyes in response, and just continued down the stairs. I was feeling nervous enough about this evening without being told I looked like a high-class hooker.

'But just between us,' he said as I reached the bottom. 'Whatever he's told you, he *is* expecting more than just dinner. A lot more.'

That finally got to me. I stopped and turned, a bright smile on my face. 'Actually, Alex, you're right. I am meeting a rich older man tonight.'

His eyes narrowed a little. 'Oh?'

'Yes. If memory serves me right, I think you call him Daddy.'

He swung his legs round, and sat up. 'Ah, so you've been invited to dinner at my father's house. Lucky you.' He waited a beat, and then said, 'And will my brother be there, too?'

I raised my chin a little, refusing to sugar-coat it for him. 'That's right. In fact, Giles is picking me up right now. So,' I said, ignoring the irritated look that crossed his face, 'enjoy your evening here alone – or with whatever poor girl has such low self-esteem that she feels flattered into sleeping with you.'

I was deliberately being cruel, hitting at what I knew were sore points – his relationships with his father and Giles – but I'd had just about enough of him in the last few days. With that parting shot, I turned and walked out.

As he'd promised, Giles was parked outside the apartment block, waiting for me. We'd agreed it was better for me to come down to meet him, rather than him risk having a run-in with Alex. Though I had a feeling I'd managed to stir things up there, anyway.

Giles was as charming as ever, holding open the car door for me, and complimenting me on my appearance. But to be honest I was too distracted to really care. I'd already been dreading the evening, and now the conversation with Alex had rattled me further.

Ten minutes later, we were driving through the streets of Chelsea, passing elegant white townhouses and manicured squares. As we pulled up outside Duncan Noble's house, I tried not to show how impressed I was. The five-storey building was set on the crescent of the road, making it one of the most expensive houses on the most expensive street in London. So this was what running a successful luxury leisure group got you.

It was just after seven when we arrived. Duncan was there to greet us. He looked less formal than when we'd first met, in chinos and a blue shirt. Now he and Giles were together, I could see the resemblance between them even more keenly.

'Nina, I'm glad you could make it.' He kissed me on both cheeks. 'Come through, will you?'

I followed him along the corridor to the drawing room. I perched on the sofa as a waitress dressed in a black pencil skirt and fitted white shirt brought round champagne and canapés. I stuck with water, deciding I'd need to keep my wits about me.

'Now,' Duncan said to me once she'd withdrawn from the room. 'I was aware that I was a little abrupt at our last meeting, so I was hoping we'd have a chance to get to know each other a bit better tonight.'

'Great,' I said, trying to look as though I couldn't think of anything I'd rather be doing.

'So on that note, why don't you tell me what you've been up to?'

Given that I'd hidden the details of my mum's alcoholism from him, it wasn't the easiest of conversations to have. But I spoke a lot about April, and somehow we managed to fill the time.

Three-quarters of an hour later, we finally went through to a formal dining room. A long table made of polished mahogany dominated. It could have easily seated twelve, so it felt a little empty with just three of us there. But I didn't have time to dwell on the awkwardness, because Duncan Noble was already firing more questions at me.

We had just finished our starter of scallops, and the last plates were being cleared, when the doorbell sounded. I saw Giles and his father exchange looks – this wasn't the type of area where visitors just dropped in. The maid had obviously answered the door, and we could hear muffled voices – her high-pitched female tone, followed by a deeper man's voice. Then there was the sound of heavy footsteps in the hallway, and a second later Alex swept into the room.

He'd made no effort to shave or tidy himself up, and was wearing what looked like his oldest pair of jeans and a T-shirt that was ripped at the neck. I could smell the alcohol off him from all the way across the room.

'Deepest apologies for my tardiness,' he said. 'Car wouldn't start.'

It was so obviously a lie, that it was hard not to laugh. I could feel a snigger rising until I caught sight of the look of fury on Duncan Noble's face. I managed to bite it back.

'I didn't realise you'd be joining us, Alexander,' Duncan Noble said. His tone was chillier than the Arctic.

'Family dinner?' Alex pulled up a chair and collapsed into it. 'Wouldn't miss it for the world. Such a shame I had to hear about it second-hand, though. I presume your PA forgot to call me.'

Duncan Noble winced at this. He was obviously aware that Alex was peeved about not being invited, and that his son had come here tonight intent on payback.

'No need to worry, though,' he went on, his gaze moving to me. I could see a wicked playfulness in his eyes. 'Nina was kind enough to fill me in on the details.'

Duncan's jaw tightened, and he looked between us. 'Oh? You two know each other?'

I went very still, unsure how to respond. I remembered how adamant Giles had been about not letting on to Duncan about my connection with Alex. But if he wanted to tell his father, there was nothing I could do about it.

'Well, of course I know Nina,' Alex said, a little smirk playing on his lips. 'She works at Destination. I was bound to run into her.'

There was a silence. I felt Alex, Giles and their father exchange looks, but I had no idea why. Fortunately at that moment, the waitress came in with the main course of guinea fowl. She said that the cook was making up a plate for Alex, and while I marvelled at being in a house that had what appeared to be a whole range of staff, Giles took the opportunity to move the conversation on to more neutral topics.

For the next hour, we stayed on current affairs. Alex was surprisingly well-versed in world events, and the debate was animated, though without the heat of the more personal subjects.

I'd almost managed to relax, but just as coffee was being served Duncan turned to Giles. 'I reviewed your plans for renovating Destination, and I have to say so far I'm impressed.'

'I'm glad.'

'I just have a question on cost. It seems a little higher than I'd anticipated, and we don't seem to be using our usual contractors.'

Giles nodded along as his father spoke, as though he'd been anticipating these questions.

'I basically went for quality over cost savings. I thought this new firm would create a better finish.'

Duncan nodded approvingly. 'Good thinking.'

'The golden boy strikes again,' Alex said softly, but still loud enough for his father to hear.

His head snapped round to glare at his son. 'Yes, Alexander, you're right – we've heard quite enough from Giles tonight. Why don't you fill us in on your latest achievements instead? I'm sure everyone at the table is dying to hear how you're spending your time.'

Alex rolled his eyes. 'Oh, Father, give it a rest, will you?'

'Still no thoughts on joining us in the world of work, then?'

Alex took a sip of wine before answering. 'Not really my scene.'

'No?' Duncan raised an eyebrow. 'So what is your "scene" these days? Falling out of clubs drunk with whatever girl happens to be flavour of the week? Does that constitute a "scene"?'

Alex put down his glass. He looked serious, and far more sober than I'd realised. 'Actually, I have been working on something. A pop-up restaurant with guest chefs. I'm just looking for investors at the moment.'

'Oh? And let me guess – you want me to fund you?'

Alex's jaw tightened. 'When have I ever asked you for a penny? I'm doing this on my own. Without any help from you.'

For a moment, Duncan looked surprised. Then he recovered. 'That's very admirable. I just hope you stick at something this time.'

I cringed. Somehow he'd managed to compliment Alex and put him down at the same time.

Alex reached for his wine glass again, and Duncan frowned. 'I hope you're not planning to drive after that.'

Alex drained his glass, and then set it on the table. 'Actually, no, I'm not planning to drive. I got a cab here, and I'm going to get a cab back. But it's always good to know what a low opinion you have of me.'

Instead of apologising, Duncan said, 'Well, can you blame me? I've given up counting the number of times you've been selfish and reckless over the years.'

Alex gave a harsh laugh. 'And you wonder why I don't come to family dinners more often?' He looked round at me and Giles, and shook his head. 'You know what? I don't need this. I'm out of here.'

With that, Alex pushed his chair back from the table, and left the room.

I didn't think twice. I stood up and hurried after him. But he was too fast for me. He was already at the front door while I still had one flight of stairs to go.

'Alex, wait,' I called.

His hand was on the handle of the door. I saw him grip it for a moment, and then he released it, and turned back to face me. For once, there was no humour in his eyes, only irritation. 'What do you want?'

I came to a halt on the bottom step, suddenly lost for words. I'd expended so much energy getting down that it hadn't occurred to me what I was going to say when I got there.

'I . . .' I began and then stopped. 'I just wanted to say I'm sorry about what happened in there,' I said eventually.

'Why?' He shrugged his large shoulders. 'It's not like you were the one saying all that stuff.'

'Maybe not. But I still thought it was wrong of him.'

'Really?' He cocked his head to one side, studying me through narrowed eyes. 'I'm surprised to hear that. I'd have thought you'd be the first to agree with him. After all, weren't you the one who called me selfish and reckless?'

I winced at that. I suddenly understood why he'd been behaving the way he had. He'd been good to me, and I'd repaid his kindness by criticising him just like his father always did. No wonder he'd gone out of his way to prove me right since then. While I didn't like his behaviour, I could understand it.

I tried to hold his gaze for as long as possible, but I'm sure it wasn't a surprise to either of us that I was the one who looked away first.

'Yeah.' He gave a harsh laugh. 'That's what I thought.'

He turned to leave, and this time I made no effort to stop him. The front door slammed shut behind him, rattling my teeth with the sheer force of the bang.

I stood there for a moment, staring after him. Then I heard someone clearing their throat to make me aware of their presence. I turned to see Duncan. He didn't look happy.

'I'm guessing from what I just heard that you and Alex know each other better than I've been led to believe.'

I dropped my eyes, choosing to study a spot on the ground.

'I understand if you don't want to tell me what's going on. But as you can see from tonight, my youngest son can be difficult. You need to be careful, Nina. I'd hate to see you get hurt.' He paused, letting his words sink in. 'Now,' he said briskly, clearly changing the subject. 'I don't think anyone's in the mood to continue this evening, so I'll get Giles to drive you home.'

We were both subdued on the journey back. I couldn't help worrying about how Alex was going to react to the events of the evening. If his recent behaviour was anything to go by, I could expect another all-night party. The thought was exhausting.

When Giles pulled up outside the apartment block, I thanked him for the lift home. He leaned over, and I assumed he was going to kiss me on the cheek like before, but instead he bent his head and kissed me full on the mouth.

I was so shocked that I didn't react at first. Then my hands came up to his chest and I pushed him away.

Instinctively I looked around, and I knew I was searching for Alex, concerned that he might have spotted us. But fortunately he was nowhere to be seen. Then I turned my attention back to Giles.

'Why on earth did you do that?'

'Why do you think?' He was looking at me as though I was mad.

I blinked. It hadn't occurred to me that Giles felt anything for me other than friendship. His behaviour had seemed almost big-brotherly – nothing else. And as much as I liked and admired him, I didn't feel anything romantic at all. It was a shame. He was hard-working and reliable – the kind of guy I'd always hoped to end up with. But unfortunately it turned out my heart wanted something entirely different.

And to be honest, I wasn't entirely convinced he felt anything for me either. I imagined some perfect Posh Pashmina was more his type than a troubled girl from a rough inner-city council estate. I couldn't help wondering how much of this sudden interest was to do with being competitive with his brother, whether he realised it or not.

'I'm sorry, Giles—' I began.

He swore under his breath, cutting me off. 'You've spent all this time protesting that you don't want anything to do with Alex, but nothing could be further from the truth. At least be honest with yourself.'

I couldn't think of anything to say to that. Clearly Giles didn't deal well with things that didn't go his way, and the best I could do was leave him to nurse his wounded pride. So I got out of the car, and watched as he drove away.

It was nearly two in the morning when I heard movement in the apartment. I had been asleep for almost an hour by then, and the sound of someone moving around in the living room downstairs made me jerk awake.

Lying in the dark, I listened to the heavy footsteps on the stairs, and Alex's bedroom door slamming shut. It sounded like he was alone.

I lay there thinking about what to do. The sensible part of me knew I should go back to sleep, but deep down I had no intention of doing that. After everything that had happened tonight, I needed to see Alex.

Before I could give too much thought to what I was doing, I pushed the duvet back, got out of bed and made my way to his room.

Outside, I paused. I could feel my heart thumping in my chest, and my stomach had that cold, nervous feeling I hated. Before I could change my mind, I knocked on the door.

The hollow sound seemed to reverberate around the high-ceilinged mezzanine. I waited for a long moment, but there was no answer. I debated what to do. It felt like I'd come too far to turn back now, so I knocked again. This time, when there was still no answer, I twisted the handle down and pushed the door open a crack.

'Alex?' I said tentatively into the darkened room. I could just about make out his shape lying fully clothed on top of the covers. All I could hear was the sound of his breathing. 'Alex?' I repeated.

There was silence for a moment, and then, 'What?'

Knowing he was awake emboldened me, so I stepped into the room. From there, I could see him stretched out, one arm thrown over his eyes. 'I just came to check that you were all right.'

'Well, as you can see, I'm fine. Job done. So you can run along.'

I paused for a moment, and then instead of leaving I went over and perched on his bed. He hadn't bothered to close the electronic blinds, so the room wasn't in total darkness, just more of a shadowy gloom. It let me see the way his jaw tightened as he felt my weight press down the mattress. With a sigh, he moved his arm from his eyes, so he was staring up at me.

'It's been a long night, darling.' As he spoke, I could smell the alcohol on his breath. He must have been drinking – heavily – for the rest of the evening, but he was still coherent. 'So why don't you tell me what you want, so we can all get some much needed sleep.'

I didn't bother to answer. Instead, I touched my hand to his cheek, allowing my thumb to gently caress his skin. I watched as he frowned in confusion. Then, a second later, I lowered my mouth to his, in a soft, light kiss.

After a second, I drew away a little to gauge his reaction. He stared up at me with a blank expression on his face, and I noticed his arms were firmly by his sides. It wasn't quite the reaction I'd been expecting, but I could guess what was going through his mind – I'd rejected him so many times. Now, he was going to make me work for it.

I'd never really thought of myself as someone who liked playing games, but suddenly the idea of being in control, of having to seduce him, appealed to me.

'Fair enough,' I murmured. 'If that's the way you want to play it . . .'

I bent my head, and began to kiss him again, harder this time. Once more, he stayed totally still, but this just spurred me on. My lips prised his apart, my tongue moving against his. The more unresponsive he was, the more I wanted to push him. I was hardly aware of what I was doing as I moved so I was kneeling on the bed, straddling his thighs. I grabbed his arms, and pinned his wrists above his head, so I was kissing him furiously, my soft breasts pressing against his hard chest.

That was it. He gave what sounded like a groan of defeat, and his arms closed around me, pulling me to him, and he was kissing me back, his mouth rough and demanding.

He might have made a point of not being engaged at first, but now it seemed he was determined to take control. In one effortless move, he flipped me over onto my back. He pulled his head away briefly, his eyes searching mine in the semi-darkness.

'What the hell's got into you?' he murmured.

'Why?' I have to admit that I was enjoying the look of confusion on his face. 'Are you objecting?'

A smile crossed his face. 'Not at all.'

He bent his head, and his lips found mind again. After a while, I felt him unbuttoning my pyjama top, touching each breast until the nipples hardened. I squirmed a little as his hand trailed down across my stomach, finding its way under the waistband of my pyjama bottoms, and moving lower and lower. And then his fingers found something – so pleasurable that I gasped, my nails digging into his back.

As Alex's touch deepened, my eyes fluttered closed and my whole body tensed and stretched, poised deliciously on the brink of something I'd never felt before.

Right then, I wanted him more than anything in the world. I didn't care if it was just for one night.

But through the haze of good feelings, a nagging voice was telling me that this was a bad idea. The rational side of me was screaming out to put the brakes on. It was all moving so fast. Everything felt like it was getting out of control. This was my first time – did I really want it to be this way? With some guy who would probably have forgotten about me by tomorrow?

Finally I pulled away, struggling to catch my breath.

'We can't do this.'

'Why the hell not?' He was breathing hard, too. His eyes swept mine. He sounded impatient, frustrated, and I didn't blame him. I'd started this, and now I was telling him no. He deserved an explanation.

I just didn't know where to start. There were so many reasons. We were from different worlds. I worked for his family. People I trusted kept warning me to stay away from him . . .

But although those were all good reasons, they weren't the main one. Most of all, it was because my feelings for him scared me. I knew instinctively – had known from the moment I met him – that this was a man I could fall for. And if I let myself, then I was going to fall hard. And when it all ended – as it undoubtedly would – I would be the one who ended up hurt.

He kissed me again, and part of me wanted to give in to all the good feelings, to forget being sensible for one night. But I knew better than that.

'Wait.' I broke away again. It was all going so fast. I'd come because I'd wanted to be with Alex, but now that the moment was there, I felt like I needed to catch my breath, to be really sure of what I was doing and the choice I was making.

'Can we slow down a bit?' I could see him frowning, as if he was wondering what was going on. Knowing what I had to admit to next, I lowered my eyes a little, unable to meet his gaze. 'It's just – well, I've never done this before.'

I hadn't relished the idea of admitting my inexperience to someone as sophisticated as Alex. I sneaked a look up at him, and he seemed to be trying to process the information – to work out exactly what I meant. Then I saw his eyes register surprise. 'What are you saying? That you're a virgin?'

'That's right.' I gave a nervous laugh. 'That's what happens when you've got an alcoholic mother and a younger sister to take care of. It doesn't leave a lot of time for guys.'

For a moment, all I could hear was the sound of our breathing. Alex's expression was unreadable. I bit my lip a little, sensing that all wasn't as it should be.

'Is that okay?' I said in a small voice, one that didn't sound like my own. I was usually so tough – it seemed strange to suddenly feel so vulnerable.

'Yeah, of course. I understand.'

We stared at each other for a long moment. I could tell he was wondering what to do. I guessed it was up to me to get things started again, so I put my hands on his bare shoulders and drew him down to me.

He started kissing me again, but this time I felt his heart wasn't in it. There was an awkwardness and hesitancy that hadn't been there before. His hands weren't roaming my body any more, and he seemed to be trying his hardest not to press any part of himself against me. It was as though he was holding back. I arched against him, trying to let him know that it was all right to touch me, but I felt him stiffen and a second later he pulled away.

'Sorry,' he mumbled. 'This was a mistake.'

Before I could say anything, he rolled off me, hauled himself up, and stumbled from the room.

I lay there half-undressed in his bed, feeling strangely sad, rejected and disappointed. I listened as he made his way downstairs, and put some music on. Once I was sure he wasn't coming back, I buttoned and straightened my pyjamas, and made my way back to my room.

Chapter 18

When I got up the next morning, Alex wasn't there. For the next couple of days our paths didn't cross, and I couldn't help wondering if he was avoiding me. Part of me was glad – I was so embarrassed by what had happened between us that I had no desire to see him again. But then I also knew that I was going to have to face him at some point, and I wanted to get it over with sooner rather than later.

Things with Giles were awkward, too. I saw him a couple of times at the club, and he just nodded curtly in my direction.

On Saturday night, Alex's posse turned up at Destination, but he wasn't with them. I felt unreasonably put out, and spent the evening growling at everyone.

'What's up with you?' Jas asked me eventually, after I'd snapped at her for no reason for the third time that evening.

'Nothing.'

She raised an eyebrow at my short, snappy answer. 'Yeah. Sure seems that way.'

I got back to the apartment that night feeling more drained than normal. I bypassed the kitchen and my usual late-night snack, and went straight to my room. I flopped into the armchair by my bed, pulled off my socks, and began to massage my tired right foot.

I'd just started on the left, when my mobile rang. I snatched it up. It was half three in the morning, so I knew whatever it was about couldn't be good. But when the number that flashed up was our social worker's, I felt my heart-rate speed up.

I wasn't entirely surprised when Maggie Walker informed me that April had run away from her foster home that evening. As she quickly ran through the details of what had happened, I closed my eyes.

Why did you have to do this now, April? I told you to hang on . . .

'Do you have any idea where she might've got to?' Maggie said.

I hesitated before answering. I did, but I didn't want strangers going to find April.

'I've got a few thoughts. Let me make some calls.'

I pulled my shoes back on, and ran downstairs. Once I was outside, I would easily find a cab. The lift pinged just as I reached it, and the doors opened to reveal Alex with his arm slung round Lavinia. He glanced over at me, no doubt about to fire off some mocking remark, but then he looked at me again and the smirk left his face.

'What's happened?' His hand dropped from Lavinia's waist and he stepped towards me.

It was strange – I'd spent the past few days being worried about seeing him again. But now, after the news about April, I found I couldn't care less. All I could think of was her.

'It's my sister.' I was so scared for her that the words just came out, without me considering whether I wanted Alex to know. Right then, I just had to confide in someone. 'She's run away from her foster home. She's only fourteen. I have to find her.'

'Fine.' His voice was clipped, authoritative. 'I'll drive.'

I hesitated for just a split second. Whatever was going on between Alex and me, April took priority. And getting a lift from him was going to be far quicker than taking a cab.

'You're sober?' I couldn't smell any alcohol on him, but I had to make sure. Luckily, he didn't look offended.

'Haven't touched a drop.'

'Then let's go.'

'What about me?'

Alex and I both turned to Lavinia.

'Go to the front desk and they'll order you a cab,' Alex said. 'This takes precedence.'

Lavinia pouted and sulked all the way down in the lift. Once she'd got out at reception, Alex and I headed to the underground car park and his silver Porsche.

'Where're we going?' he asked once we were in the car.

I gave him the address of Hayfield Court. It had been my first instinct – I was almost certain April would go back to our old home.

Alex set off without another word, swinging the car round to take the main road. He sped along, pushing the speed limit, not bothering to make small talk, aware of the urgency of the task and my all-consuming fear.

Fortunately the London streets were pretty much deserted, apart from the odd delivery van or cab, so we had a clean run through. A police car roared up, siren on, and Alex lifted his foot off the accelerator until it passed. I could only wonder where the police car was going to – what if it was to identify the body of a young girl? I pushed the thought away.

Alex glanced over. He seemed to read my mind, because he reached out to give my knee a reassuring squeeze. 'Try not to worry. If she's anything like her big sister, she'll be able to take care of herself.'

It took no time at all to reach East London. As the area got less salubrious, I could sense Alex looking around, getting a sense for where I came from.

Finally we turned into Hayfield Court.

'This is where you lived?' Alex said, frowning.

'Yes.' For a moment, I could see the place through his eyes – the soulless tower blocks and graffiti-covered walls – and felt defensive. 'It's not that bad.'

Alex didn't make any comment.

He pulled up, and I jumped out of the car, saw the *Out of Order* sign was still on the lift, and headed for the stairs. I glanced back, and to my surprise, Alex was right behind me.

'You might not want to leave your car unattended,' I told him.

'You think I give a damn about that?'

I took the stairs two at a time, Alex following behind me. Our flat was on the fifteenth floor, so we were both breathing hard by the time we got there. The front door had been boarded up after the fire, but there was graffiti across it, and the boards were busted where someone had broken in.

I went to go in, but Alex put a restraining arm on me.

'Let me go first.'

I stood back as he pushed the makeshift door open and stepped inside.

It was pretty much how I remembered it from the last time I'd been there, the day after the fire. The carpets were still waterlogged; the walls were stained with ash; and there was still a smell of smoke in the air. No effort had been made to clean up, and it had that feeling of being unlived in.

All the utilities had been cut off, so the only light coming through was from the other flats, making it faintly eerie.

'April?' I called out. 'Sweetheart? It's me. Nina.'

There was just silence, and I wondered if I'd got it wrong and she'd run off somewhere else. But then a moment later I heard a sound from the back of the flat.

'I'm in here.'

I followed the sound of her voice through to her bedroom. Sure enough, April was there, sitting on the floor, wedged in between her bed and the desk where she used to do her homework. She looked up as I walked in, her eyes sad. She still had the cast on her left arm.

Alex appeared, and touched me on the shoulder.

'I'll be in the other room.'

Because April's room was at the back of the flat, it had been less damaged than the living area. I walked over and crouched down by my sister. Her knees were pulled up to her chest, her arms clutched tightly around them.

I had already decided there was no point giving her a lecture. Instead, I just waited for her to speak.

'I hate it there,' she said finally.

'I know you do.'

'Even without Racquel it's awful. I just want everything to be the way it was.'

'Me too.'

She looked up at me then.

'Really? Because I'm worried that your life's better – with me in foster care.'

I was horrified that she'd even consider such a thing. 'Why on earth would you think that?'

'Because for the first time you don't have to worry about me and Mum. You can go off and do what you want, without us being a burden. That's why you didn't come to meet me that time, isn't it? Because you were off having fun.'

'Oh, pet.' My eyes filled with tears. I hated to think that she felt like I'd abandoned her. 'It wasn't like that. I'd just seen Mum, and I wanted to forget everything for one night.'

'Forget me, you mean?' April did nothing to disguise the sadness in her voice.

'No! That's not it at all.' I grasped her arms so she could see how serious I was. 'You mean everything to me. And to Mum, too. I don't know what I'd have done if something had happened to you tonight. And I'm trying to get you back, I promise. I'm sorry if you don't think I'm doing a good job of it. But all I want is for us all to be home together again, I swear—'

My voice cracked then, and I broke down. I could sense how stunned April was. I doubt she'd seen me cry for years. After Dad's death, I'd tried to keep my feelings locked away, and not show any weakness.

Seeing my tears must have given her a jolt. Because she threw her arms around me.

'Oh, Nina, I'm sorry.' Her arms tightened around my neck. 'I didn't mean to upset you. I didn't think about how you'd feel. Please don't cry.'

I closed my eyes and held her to me. It felt good to have her there, and it made me realise once again how much I'd missed her.

We hugged for a long time, until I reluctantly pulled away and gazed at April. Her hair was messed up, and I smoothed it down with my thumb.

'You know there are people out looking for you. I'm going to have to call Maggie Walker and tell her that I've found you.' I bit my lip, worried about what April's reaction to my next words would be. 'I know you don't want to hear this, but you're going to have to go back there – for a little while longer at least.'

'I know.'

I'd expected a fight, but instead my sister seemed resigned to her fate. Obviously seeing how upset I was about the situation had helped her realise that she needed to be more stoical. But there was one last thing I needed to know before sending her back.

'But you have to tell me now – is there a particular reason why you ran away?' I said. 'Because if there's anything going on that shouldn't be, so help me—'

But April was already shaking her head. 'No, it's not like that. They're not beating or abusing me or anything like that.'

'Then what's the problem?'

April shrugged. 'It's just not home. It's not family. I want to be back with you and Mum.'

Her simple explanation made me want to cry all over again. But there was no point.

'I know,' I said instead. 'I get that you want us all back together. I want that, too. And I'm trying to make it happen.'

I hugged my sister again. It was so frustrating. I couldn't help feeling like a failure. April was the one suffering most in this situation, and I should have been the one to protect her. I needed to try harder to get us all back together, that much was clear – even if it meant finding a way to be closer to our mother.

I called Maggie Walker and April's foster mother Denise to let them know that I'd found my sister. Then Alex offered to drive April back to the foster home.

April was impressed by his Porsche, but even more impressed by Alex. I could see her blush as he shook her hand.

'Is that your boyfriend?' she whispered to me as we got into the car.

'No,' I said firmly, aware that he could hear every word she was saying. I hesitated over how to explain who he was. My mother was so against the Noble family – I didn't want her to know that I was having any contact with any of them. 'He's—' I hesitated, unsure how to explain our relationship. 'He's a friend,' I said finally. 'Someone I met through work.'

Unfortunately she wasn't letting it go.

'But he must like you if he drove you around tonight,' she said, once we were out of the car.

I didn't say anything.

'And if he likes you – and you *must* like him – then what's the problem?'

Again, I stayed silent.

'So it's you then?' she said as we got to the front door of the foster home. April stopped, and turned to me. 'Look, I know you've had it hard with Mum. I know you find it hard to trust anyone, because she's always let you down—'

'But you've had all that, too.'

'No. It's different for me. I had you. You always remembered my birthday and helped me with my homework. You were the constant when she wasn't.' I stared at her in disbelief. I'd thought all these years that she hadn't been aware of how much I was doing – or that she'd just accepted it as normal. It was a shock to realise she'd known exactly what was going on. 'I'm just saying don't let that stop you being with this Alex if you want to. I know you think you're protecting yourself if you don't let anyone in, but that's kind of a sad way to go through life. At some point you have to trust someone – even if you risk them hurting you. And deep down you must trust Alex, because you wouldn't have let him help you find me otherwise.'

With those wise words, she turned and knocked on the door.

I'd thought it would be hard dropping her back there. I'd worried that she would break down and beg me to take her with me. But the events of the evening seemed to have calmed her and made her stronger, resigned to the fact that it was going to take a while to resolve the situation. Or maybe having seen how upset I was, she was finally convinced that I was trying my best to sort something out so we could all be back together. And that's why she didn't make a fuss.

Alex drove us back to Knightsbridge in silence. It was still dark, and the events of the night churned through my mind as we sped through the rain-covered streets.

'How are you doing over there?' Alex said finally as we neared the apartment building.

'I just hate leaving her at that place.'

It would have been easy for him to voice meaningless platitudes – to tell me that it would all be fine – but I wasn't in the mood to hear them, and he seemed to sense that.

It was nearly six in the morning by the time we stepped into the lift. Alex pressed the button and then turned to study me. I could tell he had something he wanted to say, but wasn't sure how I would react.

'What is it?' I sounded weary even to my own ears.

'Why don't you hang out for a bit?' He held up his hands defensively, as though already sensing my suspicion. 'No ulterior motive, I promise. It's just I think it would do you good to unwind. You won't sleep for a while after that.'

My instinct was to refuse, but I knew what he said was true. The adrenalin was coursing through me. And I needed to talk the events of the evening over with someone.

I followed him into the flat and through to the kitchen, sitting up at the central island as he made tea.

'I don't take sugar,' I said as he took out a packet. But he ignored me and put two heaped teaspoons in, before placing the mug in front of me.

'It's good for shock.'

I watched him as he made toast and spread it with butter and honey.

He pulled up a stool to sit opposite me and passed me the plate. I shook my head.

'I couldn't eat a thing.'

'Try. It'll do you good.'

I took a tentative bite of the toast, and found I enjoyed it more than I thought I would. Alex took a sip of his tea. There was still an awkwardness between us, and I didn't like it.

I raised my eyes to meet his.

'Look, I wanted to explain about the other night. What you saw . . . me and Giles—'

He held up his hand. 'Don't worry about it. You're right. It's none of my business what you do.'

That floored me. I hadn't expected him to be so dismissive.

I didn't know what else to say. I swallowed down the rest of my tea. 'Well . . . I should get to bed.'

He gave a brief nod. 'Of course.'

I slipped from the stool.

'Nina.'

His voice stopped me. I took a deep breath before turning round, afraid of what he was going to say, and how I would respond. But when I looked at him, his face was impassive – closed off.

'Are you free next Tuesday?' he said, all business.

I nodded. It was my night to see April, but as long as I explained and organised to see her on Monday this time, I was sure she'd be fine with me rearranging.

'Good. I've got a game that I'd like you to work. A big one. Do this, and your debt's cleared.'

Disappointment coursed through me. I wasn't sure what I'd expected him to say, but it wasn't that. I tried to put my confusing feelings to one side, and focus instead on the matter at hand.

'I thought the games were always on Sunday.'

'Tuesday was the only night everyone could do. So,' he said after a moment, 'are you able to make it?'

'I'll be there.' Then I had a thought. 'And the venue?'

I saw him hesitate for a second. 'That's the part you might not like. I wanted to hold it somewhere special – somewhere a bit different. I couldn't think of anywhere at first, but then I had a brainwave.'

'So where's it going to be?'

Somehow I knew what he was going to say. 'At Rexley Manor. My family's country estate.'

And the place where my father died.

Chapter 19

Alex swung the Porsche over onto the outside lane of the motorway and pressed his foot down on the accelerator. I watched the speedometer flicker up towards ninety miles per hour. Rain beat against the windshield, making it hard to see the road ahead. I looked over at Alex. There were no other cars in view, and he seemed focused and in control, but even so I felt nervous. Maybe it was because we were on our way to Rexley Manor, and I couldn't help thinking of my father and the way he'd died.

'Slow down, will you?' My voice sounded shriller than I'd intended.

Alex's eyes flicked over to me, and for a moment I thought he might refuse. But then his gaze shifted to the dashboard, which I was gripping so hard that my knuckles had turned white. A second later he eased off the accelerator, until he was cruising just below the speed limit.

We'd set off in the late afternoon, and the traffic had been surprisingly light as we had managed to hit that magic time between school runs and the evening commute home.

It should have been a ninety-minute drive to Buckinghamshire, but at the speed Alex was going, we made it in under an hour. He finally slowed as we pulled onto the winding country lanes, manoeuvring expertly around the narrow bends, low branches of trees scratching at the paintwork.

We turned onto a private road, and reached the huge wrought-iron gates that guarded the Manor. Alex pulled up to a discreet electronic box, input a security code, and the gates magically eased open.

The sweeping driveway was lined with huge oaks. I'd been here occasionally as a child, and dimly remembered the place, but still I couldn't help gasping as the main house came into view. It was like a fairy-tale castle, a Disney-style elegant sprawl of turrets and towers, encircled by manicured gardens that fanned out into lush woodland. From what I remembered, it had originally been built for a wealthy merchant family during the 1880s, in the neo-Renaissance style of a French *château*. When their fortunes had waned a century later, Duncan Noble had purchased Rexley Manor for his family.

Alex pulled up outside. A middle-aged man and woman were waiting for him – I presumed they were the couple that managed the estate. He gave them a polite nod and introduced me to them – Bill and Sarah Davidson. Then he grabbed our bags from the boot, gave his keys to Bill to park the car, and went into the house. I followed behind.

The entrance hall was exactly as I'd expected – a flagstone floor, dark wood panelling and an array of oil paintings. It was like walking into a little slice of history. Any restoration work had been sensitively carried out, and the sumptuous opulence of the Renaissance style was clear to see. I gazed around in wonder, wanting to linger for a while to drink it all in, but Alex didn't give me a chance. He was already heading for the sweeping staircase that arched up from the hallway.

'I'll show you to your room.'

I had to run to keep up with him. It had been like that between us all week, our conversation limited to no more than polite, impersonal exchanges. I hadn't realised how much I'd miss our banter.

I was staying in the Queen's Suite on the first floor, a beautiful, bright room of ivory teamed with splashes of pale apple-green. The furnishings were lavish – a huge four-poster bed and elegantly upholstered armchairs. But there was every modern convenience, too – a mirror above the fireplace turned out to be a flat-screen TV, and the en suite bathroom came complete with an integrated Bose sound system and rainfall shower as well as a claw-footed tub. It was the perfect combination of classic style and modern amenities.

Once Alex had given me a quick tour, he stood by the doorway, clearly eager to get away. 'Is this all right for you?'

'It's lovely,' I said softly. 'Thank you.'

'Good. Well, you can relax for a couple of hours now. I'll see you at nine for the game.'

Once he'd gone, I looked up at the clock. I had time before I needed to start getting ready. And I knew what I wanted to do.

I pulled on a warm coat, gloves and a hat, and ran back downstairs. There was a stand by the door, filled with huge golfing umbrellas, but luckily it had stopped raining, so I headed out into the early evening darkness, and began to trudge across the estate.

I'd only visited the spot once before – six years earlier, when I was thirteen, the very last time I'd been to the estate – but I knew how to get there. It wasn't exactly something I'd ever forget because it was where my father had his accident, when he'd been driving back to London along that twisting road that led from Rexley Manor, and his car had spun off the road, and smashed straight into a tree.

My mother had taken us there a week later. I could still remember the indent of the car on the trunk.

I cut across the manicured lawns by the driveway, and made for the rougher surrounding grounds that bordered the road. It was a good half an hour's walk, and there was little to illuminate my path – the lights from the house for the first part of the journey, and then I had to use the small torch I'd brought with me.

I passed a neat cottage, which I presumed was where the caretaker couple lived. And then a little while later, I was finally there.

It was as I remembered it. I could see the sharp bend in the road where my father's car had spun out of control. The tree that he'd hit had been removed, though – and the area grassed over. Someone had obviously tried to erase all reminder of what had happened.

I felt an unexpected sadness wash over me, for all the years that we'd missed together. Tears began to spill down my cheek, and I furiously wiped them away.

'Hey.'

The voice made me jump. I whirled round and saw that it was Alex. At first I thought he'd followed me, but it was clear that he was equally surprised to see me.

'What're you doing out here?' I said. It was obvious why I was there – to pay my respects to my dad. But I doubted Alex would particularly want to.

He seemed to hesitate for a second, and then he shrugged.

'Just wanted to clear my head.' He looked around him.

I wondered if he would avoid mentioning my dad – that's what most people did, they were so uncomfortable with death. But then he said, 'You still miss him?'

'Every day.'

We stood there for a moment without speaking. I was pleased the inky blackness stopped him from seeing my face. I didn't want him to know that I'd been crying.

It was Alex who broke the silence. 'We should get back. It's nearly time to get ready.'

We set off towards the house.

'Just think,' Alex said. 'Once tonight is over, you'll be free of me forever.'

For some reason, the thought depressed me, but I did my best not to show it. 'Yes, I guess I will be.'

We did the rest of the walk without a word.

The players – eight of them – were all there by 9.30. The table was set up in the billiard room – which had a distinctly masculine feel, with its wood-panelled walls and huge burgundy-leather sofas. Four of the players were out quickly, but the others went on until the early hours of the morning, in what felt like an endless stalemate.

It was almost three by the time the game wrapped up. The drivers had all waited patiently downstairs in the drawing room – as the players had all elected to return to London that night rather than stay at the Manor.

While Alex went to bid them goodbye, I fixed myself a soft drink and curled up on one of the sofas. I whirled the ice around the tumbler, and allowed myself a second to contemplate the momentousness of the occasion.

This was it. I was finally free of Alex and his illegal poker games.

I expected to feel relief, but there was also something else there – a twinge of regret. I shoved the thought away, and tossed back the rest of my drink.

Part of me knew I should take the opportunity to head up to bed. It would be the easiest way to avoid any awkward conversation. But a large part of me wanted to see Alex.

I was thinking about what to do when he walked back into the room, taking the decision out of my hands.

'Here.' He tossed something onto my lap. I looked down and saw that it was an envelope, a couple of inches thick. Alarm bells went off in my head.

'What's that?'

'Payment. For tonight.'

I opened the envelope and looked inside. It was filled with twenty-pound notes. At a guess, there was about ten thousand pounds in there.

I looked up, my mind turning. Alex was standing at the bar with his back to me, pouring himself a Scotch. 'But tonight was meant to clear my debt with you, nothing more. You shouldn't be giving me this.'

'That's the first time I've known someone to turn down money.' He slugged his drink, before turning to face me. 'Consider it a tip, if you like.'

I knew what he was doing – giving me the money out of pity. And I didn't want to end our relationship with him thinking of me as some charity case.

I got to my feet, walked over to where he was standing and laid the envelope on the bar in front of him. 'I know you mean well, but I don't want money I didn't earn.'

He shook his head in disbelief. 'Are you serious? You're acting like this is an insult, or something. I was trying to do something nice.'

'I know you were—'

'Yeah?' he said bitterly. 'Because it seems like I can't do anything right for you.'

He downed the last of his Scotch, and reached for the bottle to pour another. I put my hand out to stop him.

'Alex—'

He rounded on me. 'What?' His eyes flashed. 'What is it you want from me? Because I'm not Giles, and I never will be. I tried to change, I tried to do my best for you, but it obviously wasn't enough. You made that clear the night of the concert. You'll always see me as bad news, so what's the point of trying to be anything else?'

'That's not true.' I couldn't believe he still thought that. 'I came to you after that to try to show you that I was sorry for judging you. And you were the one that rejected me.'

'Of course I did!' He was looking at me as though I was crazy. 'I was drunk out of my mind and you told me that you were a virgin. It just proves my point. You must have a pretty low opinion of me if you thought I was going to sleep with you then.'

Alex was no more than an inch away from me – so close that I could feel the heat of his breath on my cheeks. The sound of my own heartbeat filled my ears. I knew I should walk away, go to my room, but in that moment I didn't want to move. Lust flooded my belly, and I couldn't stand it a second longer. Before I could think about what I was doing, I grabbed his face and kissed him.

Alex needed no further invitation. His hands went to the small of my back, pulling me to him with a force that made me gasp. My lips parted against his, as my arms snaked round his neck, my fingers burying into his silky dark hair.

For once, there were no thoughts in my head. All I could focus on was the way he was touching me, how he was tugging my shirt from the waistband of my trousers, his cool palms grazing my warm, bare skin. I moaned against his mouth, and our grip tightened on each other, as though we were trying to meld into one another.

Then I felt him tense. His hands were suddenly on my shoulders, and with a willpower I was surprised he possessed, he pushed me away, breaking our kiss. I let out a little mew of protest, looking up at him with a frown, but he held me fast. 'Why?' His eyes searched mine. 'Why are you doing this?'

I thought for a moment. I knew how important the answer was to him. 'Because I want to,' I said finally. 'Because I've wanted to for a long time.' I paused. 'And because I trust you. Because I know you're better than you let people think.'

'And Giles?'

I shook my head. 'There was never anything between us. That kiss – it was him, not me. I set him straight. He knows I don't feel that way about him.' I waited a beat. 'In fact, he's the one who guessed how I felt about you.'

Alex's expression cleared. I tilted my head, wanting him to kiss me again, but he held back. 'No. Not here.'

He took my hand, kissing it briefly, and then led me out of the billiard room and upstairs. He pulled me into what I presumed was his bedroom – a more masculine version of the room I was in. It came complete with four-poster bed, heavy velvet curtains, and a colour palette of magnolia and hunter-green. It was oddly impersonal, not like a childhood bedroom should be – but I had no time to think about that, as he kicked the door shut and then drew me into his arms again.

This time his lips touched mine ever so softly, and I could tell he was deliberately taking it slow. As his kiss deepened, I fell back onto the bed, pulling him down on top of me. I felt the weight of his body stretched across me, and I tugged at his shirt, eager to get on with it. But he stilled my hands.

'Patience,' he whispered, in that low, husky voice of his. 'There's no rush. We've got all night.'

I lay there as he began to undress me, watching as he slowly, carefully unbuttoned my shirt, slipping it from my shoulders in an unhurried way; biting my lip as he unzipped my trousers, easing them over my hips with excruciating slowness, until I was finally in nothing but my underwear. He paused, his eyes drifting over me, drinking me in, and a tremble of anticipation ran through my body. Even with my limited experience I could tell I was in the presence of a master, a connoisseur.

His lips found mine again, his kiss teasingly light, and without me even being aware of it, he was unhooking my bra with a practised expertise, gently lowering the straps. His mouth trailed down my naval, hot and wet against my belly, and I could already feel the throbbing between my legs as he hooked his thumbs into my panties.

He slid the black lace down over my hips. He began to kiss me again as his hand grazed my inner thigh, and I inhaled sharply when his fingers finally moved between my legs. His touch was agonisingly teasing. My back arched and my legs stretched in delicious frustration as his fingers flickered over me, my hands grabbing fistfuls of the duvet, until at last I shuddered against him.

He pulled away from me then, his eyes searching mine as I struggled to catch my breath. 'We can stop now. We don't have to do this tonight.'

In answer, I reached up and began to unbuckle his belt.

When he knelt between my legs, I closed my eyes. I gasped a little as he eased into me. Alex stilled his body, resting his forehead against mine.

'Are you all right?' he whispered.

My eyes flipped open. I nodded, letting him know it was fine to keep going. He kissed me again, and as I began to relax, he started to move slowly inside me. It only hurt for a moment, and then I found myself moving with him, forgetting my apprehension.

It was then that his rhythm became more urgent. He murmured my name under his breath again and again, his hands clutching at my hair as my nails dug into his back, until with a deep, primitive growl, he finally came, his body quivering with the release.

And then he took me in his arms, holding me against his sweat-drenched body as he kissed me over and over again.

Chapter 20

My eyes fluttered open. For a moment, I wasn't sure where I was. Not in London, that was for sure. Instead of the distant rumble of traffic, I could hear birds and the hum of a tractor. The room was half dark, just a chink of light coming through a gap where the heavy velvet curtains weren't fully closed.

That was when the events of the previous night came flooding back to me. I was suddenly aware of my nakedness, and how I was curled into the crook of a warm, male body, a bare arm thrown around my waist.

I stiffened, and felt the arm tighten around me in response.

'You awake?' Alex said.

I murmured my confirmation, unwilling to trust myself to speak. I had no idea how to act in this situation. Everything had happened in the heat of the moment. Now, in what was literally the cold, hard light of day, I didn't know where we stood. Despite the intimacy we'd shared, Alex was still something of an unknown quantity to me.

He propped himself up on one elbow. 'Did you get enough sleep?' He sounded concerned. 'I know we were up late . . .'

'I'm fine.' I wanted to play it cool until I'd worked out what was expected of me. I really wasn't sure of the etiquette. The night before had been a big deal to me, but that didn't mean Alex saw it the same way. He'd had lots of one-night stands. Maybe he was just waiting for me to collect my clothes and go.

'Just fine? Well, that's a blow to my ego.' The flirtation in his voice sounded promising, but I didn't want to make any assumptions, so I kept quiet.

After a moment, Alex gently tugged at me so I rolled over onto my back. I forced myself to look up at him. The bedclothes only covered him up to his waist, and it was hard to ignore his bare, muscular chest.

He cocked his head to one side, and studied me through lidded eyes. 'So are you going to tell me what's going on in that head of yours?'

So much for my plan to keep quiet. Even I couldn't ignore such a direct question.

'I was just thinking about getting ready. You know, to go back to London . . .'

I trailed off. When Alex didn't say anything immediately,

I sneaked a look up at him, preparing myself for rejection. But his eyes were dancing with amusement.

'Don't tell me you're planning to run out on me?' He feigned a look of sorrow. 'What am I – just another notch on your bedpost?'

'Yes . . . no . . . I just wasn't sure what was best . . .' I couldn't believe how lame I sounded. Luckily, Alex didn't seem to care.

'Well . . .' he drawled, bending his head so his lips grazed my shoulder. 'If it's up to me,' he said between kisses, 'I'd rather you stayed here for a little while longer. That is, as long as you're in no rush to get back . . .'

I tried hard not to react, but as his fingers travelled across my bare stomach, I let out an involuntary gasp.

'It all depends on whether you give me a good reason to stay,' I said. And abandoning all pretence at nonchalance, I wrapped my arms around his neck, and pulled him down on top of me.

'Are you hungry?'

An hour later, we were still in bed. Alex was lying on his back, and my head was resting on his chest as he stroked my hair.

'Starving,' I admitted. It hadn't crossed my mind until he said it, but it made me realise I could have really done with some food.

'Let's go down and see what we can find in the fridge.'

'We're expected to make our own breakfast?' I pretended to grumble, as he got out of bed and started to pull on some jeans. 'I thought in a place like this we'd have servants waiting on us hand and foot. What's the point of sleeping with a rich, entitled brat if there aren't at least some perks?'

He laughed. 'They know from experience that I like to be left to my own devices.'

I gave him a cheeky smile. 'Does that mean I can go down naked?'

'If you like. But to be on the safe side, you might want to put on this.' He threw me his T-shirt.

Once I was decent, he grabbed my hand and dragged me out of the room. We were laughing as we ran down the stairs together, him leading with me trailing a little behind.

But at the bottom step he came to a sudden halt. I stopped behind him and peeped over his shoulder to see what was going on. There was a well-groomed, middle-aged man in a dark grey suit standing in the hallway. He was staring at me.

It was Duncan Noble.

The three of us froze – Alex and I at the foot of the staircase, his father on the flagstone floor in the elegant hallway. It didn't take long for the silence to grow uncomfortable.

It was Alex who spoke first.

'Father.' The word was said with a flat hostility. 'What are you doing here?'

'I asked Bill and Sarah to keep an eye out for you.' Duncan's voice was equally cool. 'I was aware that you'd started your little poker games again, and I had a feeling you'd hold one here sooner or later.'

Even though on the surface it seemed Duncan was annoyed about the poker game, I had a feeling there was more to it. Perhaps I was being paranoid, but I got the feeling his anger had more to do with me being there. My hand searched out Alex's. He squeezed my fingers reassuringly, but under his father's stern stare it didn't help ease my fears.

Duncan's eyes shifted to me. I flinched a little under his gaze. He'd been good enough to give me a job and invite me to dinner, and I sensed he was disappointed to see me here with Alex. The only thing I was pleased about was that I hadn't made good on my threat of coming down naked, but with only Alex's T-shirt over my underwear, I still felt very aware of my bare legs. I tried to pull the T-shirt down a little, wishing it covered more of me. Alex wasn't much more dressed, in a pair of jeans and naked from the waist up. Unless Duncan Noble had chosen today to lose all powers of observation, it was pretty obvious what we'd been doing.

At last his gaze moved from me back to his son.

'Alexander. A word, please.' He looked Alex over. 'And for God's sake, put some clothes on.'

With that, he turned and headed towards the rear of the house.

Alex sighed as he turned to me. 'I'd better go and deal with this.'

'Of course.' I was just relieved not to be part of the conversation.

'Won't be long.' He kissed the tip of my nose. 'Hopefully.'

I could have gone through to the kitchen and made myself some breakfast, but I didn't feel comfortable with Duncan Noble around, so I decided to go back to Alex's room to wait.

The house was pretty well soundproofed, but as I walked back up the stairs I could hear the distant sound of raised voices. Maybe I was being paranoid, but it was hard not to shake the feeling that the argument between Alex and his father had something to do with me.

Upstairs, I curled up on one of the armchairs. I expected to be there for just a few minutes before Alex came up, but the time stretched on, and he still hadn't reappeared. At one point, I heard what sounded like the front door slamming. But even then he didn't come back up.

Eventually I began to feel stupid, lying there in my underwear. I got up and dressed. Whatever was going on, it seemed best to get out.

I'd just slipped on my shoes when Alex appeared in the doorway.

'What happened?' I felt relieved to see him. 'Is everything all right?'

He didn't answer but just stood there, staring at me, his face unreadable.

'Alex?' I prompted, as the silence became unnerving.

'Everything's great.' He walked over and flopped down on the bed.

It wasn't the response I'd been expecting. 'Really? Because your father didn't look particularly happy. What did he want?'

'The usual. To ball me out about the poker games.'

'Oh . . . right.'

I waited for more of an explanation, but none was forthcoming. I contemplated joining him on the bed, but something held me back. There was a distinct shift in Alex's mood. All the flirty banter had gone, and he had one arm thrown across his face, so it was impossible to see his eyes. This was the cold, standoffish Alex of the week before. Whatever his father had said to him had obviously had an impact.

He raised himself up on his elbows and regarded me.

'Look, I've got a few things to sort out here. Are you all right getting the train back to London?'

My mouth dropped open. I wanted to ask what had happened to breakfast, but instinct warned me not to. 'Sure,' I said instead. 'The train'll be fine.'

'Good. I'll call you a cab.'

I got my belongings together as he made the call, trying

to ignore the cold, nervous feeling in the pit of my stomach.

'I'm going to take a shower,' he said, once he was off the phone. 'You can see yourself out?'

'Yeah . . . sure.' I didn't know what else to say. Things seemed to have got awkward, and I had no idea why. I was going to leave it, but something stopped me. 'Alex?' I said.

'Hmm?'

'Maybe I'm being paranoid . . . but was your dad angry about us being together?'

But he was busy texting on his phone, and hardly looked up as he said, 'Why would he be?'

I frowned, searching my brain. There was only one thing I could think of – however far-fetched it seemed. 'I don't know . . . Maybe this is a stretch, but you know my mum and him fell out? I wondered if it had anything to do with that . . .'

I'd never been able to get my mum to tell me why she'd ordered him out of the house that night. What could be so awful that it would affect how Duncan Noble viewed my relationship with Alex?

But Alex seemed uninterested in my musings. 'I think you're reading too much into this.' He finally tucked his phone away, and walked over and kissed the tip of my nose. It should have felt like an affectionate gesture, but there was something almost dismissive in it. Or perhaps it was my imagination. 'What can I say? Thanks for a great night. You're the best.'

The whole conversation felt off, but it wasn't anything I could put my finger on. I couldn't keep asking if things were all right. I decided Alex's strange mood undoubtedly had something to do with whatever had transpired between him and his father.

He was already at the door. Somehow I didn't want our conversation to end like that. I searched in desperation for something to say. 'Do you think you'll be back by tonight? Because if so, you could stop by the club.'

He paused, then turned and regarded me for a long moment. 'Yeah,' he said eventually. 'Yeah, you'll see me there.'

'Great.'

The brightness in my voice was forced. I wanted to say something else, but somehow his stance wasn't encouraging me to speak up.

On my way downstairs, I couldn't shift that strange, nagging feeling that something wasn't right. But how could that be? Everything had been perfect between us before he'd talked to his father. But I couldn't imagine that anything Duncan Noble had to say would turn him against me.

Chapter 21

That evening at Destination, I spent the whole time with one eye on the door, looking out for Alex. He never turned up. I texted him during my break, asking where he'd got to, but I received no reply. I thought about trying to call him, but I refused to be that girl.

'What's up with you tonight?' Jas said as we were changing after our shift. She threw her balled-up tunic at me. It caught me on the head and I looked up in surprise.

'What's that?' I hadn't been paying any attention to what was going on around me.

'I was telling you that Hugh has asked me to move in with him, and I wanted your opinion on whether it was a good idea or not.' She stuck her nose in the air and sniffed, feigning hurt. 'But obviously you had more important things on your mind.'

She looked at me expectantly, but I just shrugged. I didn't

want to say anything about Alex just yet. We hadn't talked about what our relationship was, and I didn't want to start running my mouth off.

'There's nothing to tell.'

'Fine.' Jas rolled her eyes. 'Don't tell your best friend then. I don't care.'

She proceeded to rerun her story about moving in with Hugh, and again she asked me for my opinion. That kept us occupied, and she appeared to forget all about wanting to learn my secret.

Jas and I walked out of the club arm-in-arm. The first thing we saw was Hugh parked across the road, waiting for her in his black Bentley. The irony wasn't lost on me. I'd spent so much time telling her that Hugh would let her down, and he was there and Alex wasn't.

Jas grabbed my hand. 'Come on. Hugh'll give you a lift back to Alex's.'

We hurried over to the car. Hugh got out and held the passenger door open for Jas.

'Hey, babe.' She smacked a kiss on his cheek. 'Nina needs a lift home. That all right?'

'Of course.' Hugh made his way to the driver's seat, as I climbed in the back. 'I was going to ask if you wanted to go to the party anyway.' He said it matter-of-factly, as though it was obvious what he was referring to.

'What party?' Jas asked.

Hugh frowned. 'The one at Alex's, of course. I thought that's why you suggested giving Nina a lift . . .' Hugh trailed off as he glanced round at me.

Jas's eyes shifted from one to the other of us. She could clearly sense something was up too, even though she had no idea what it was.

'Well, let's get going, shall we? The sooner we get there the better.'

Jas chattered on during the journey, filling what would otherwise have been a tense and awkward silence. When Hugh parked the car, she suggested they come up with me, and I didn't object. I had a feeling I was going to need all the support I could get.

The moment the lift doors opened I heard the sounds of a party. Music was booming so loud that the walls and floors were shaking, and above the beats I could hear shouts of laughter. The cold feeling I'd had in the pit of my stomach all day – the feeling of foreboding – began to spread, but I forced it back down. Whatever was going on, I needed to face it.

I walked into the living area to find Alex and a dozen of his friends. He was sprawled across the couch, a half-finished bottle of Taittinger in one hand. It looked like it wasn't the first he'd drunk that night.

'Are you all right, babes?' I turned to see Jas looking at me with undisguised concern. Although I hadn't told her about last night, it must have been clear to her that I was more affected by the scene before us than I should have been.

Hugh was standing by her side, frowning, clearly not happy about what we'd walked in on.

'I'm fine,' I said, my voice sounding distant and detached even to me. 'Just – would you mind waiting here for a moment?'

Jas nodded vigorously. 'Of course.'

I left Jas and Hugh huddled together in the doorway, and walked over to where Alex was sitting. I did my best to ignore the scantily clad blonde sitting beside him.

'Alex?' He looked up at me with glazed eyes. 'Can I have a word?'

'You can have anything you want, sweetheart.' Alarm bells were already going off. There was something too mocking in the way he said the words for them to be flirtatious.

I looked pointedly at his friends. 'Can we talk outside?'

'Why would we do that?' He made no attempt to move. Instead, he stretched his arms across the back of the couch, settling further into the cushions. He gave a deliberate glance over the group. 'You can say whatever you want in front of my friends.'

He took a swig from the champagne bottle, and handed it to the blonde next to him. Seeing that, part of me was tempted to walk away. It was obvious he didn't want to know me. But the other part of me wanted to know what had changed. I remembered how sweet he'd been at first in the morning, and how I'd genuinely thought we'd connected. Had all that been in my imagination?

'So?' he yawned. 'What is it you wanted?'

'I just—' I had a feeling I was about to make a fool of myself, but I had to know. 'I just want to understand why you're being like this.'

'Like what?' He looked at me with such a blank expression that I almost began to doubt myself. 'We slept together. That's all. Why're you turning it into a big deal?' He turned to the others, rolling his eyes at them. 'Remind me never to deflower a virgin again. It's more trouble than it's worth.'

I drew in a sharp breath. From behind me, Jas cried, 'Oh, no!' Then as I heard the chorus of titters from around the room, I could feel my cheeks reddening, and I hated myself for showing a reaction.

'You bastard,' I hissed.

'Sticks and stones . . .' He was unperturbed by my name-calling.

I shook my head in disgust, and turned away.

'Funny . . .' His voice stopped me in my tracks. The sheer incongruousness of the word made me turn back to see what he had to say next. He was looking at me with cold eyes, and that faintly mocking smile, which made me want to punch him. 'I thought it would make you happy.'

'Why would it?' I spoke through gritted teeth.

'Because you can congratulate yourself on being right about me all along.'

I stared at him for a long moment. It was hard to believe that this was the same person who'd brushed the hair from my eyes the other night, who'd seemed to care so much. It was like a bad TV show, where he'd been body-snatched and replaced by an alien. Was he really that good an actor? And was I really so stupid that I'd fallen for his performance? I'd thought I was better than that.

I turned away then. If there was one thing I wouldn't do, it was let him see me cry.

Chapter 22

'How're you getting on, babes?'

I looked up to see Jas staring at me sympathetically. It was the same look she'd been giving me since she'd brought me home with her two weeks earlier.

She'd been surprisingly discreet and hadn't pressed me for details about what exactly had gone on between Alex and me, which I was grateful for. Too much of my private life was already public. There'd been enough other witnesses to my final scene with Alex, and word had clearly got around the club – from customers to staff. Conversations now stopped as I walked into the staff changing room, and I could see people looking at me like I was that girl – the one stupid enough to sleep with a louse like Alex Noble.

'Honestly? Not that great,' I said, as Jas slid into the seat opposite me. 'It's tough out there.'

It was Monday morning, and I was sitting at her kitchen table, with my ancient laptop in front of me – looking for another job and a place to live. My mum would be out of rehab in a couple of weeks, and then we'd have a month to get ourselves together before Social Services assessed whether we were fit to care for April. Our social worker's recommendation to the court would determine everything – which meant I needed to find a way to make sure we looked like we could provide a safe, stable home for my sister.

But it was easier said than done. I was desperate to leave Destination – and not just because of Alex. I could handle people staring and whispering about me – I'd had enough of that in the past – but I needed a job with more sociable hours. I'd had an interview the previous week – nothing fancy, just to be a receptionist at a gym in the City.

On paper, the job had been ideal. The pay was all right, and the hours were good – as it was near Liverpool Street Station, in the centre of the banking district, there would be no weekends, and the latest I'd ever be working until was ten at night. But my interview hadn't gone well. The female manager had seemed unimpressed with my reliability, and I winced still at the memory of her questioning.

So why did you only work for three months at the petrol station?

And you've been working at Destination for how long now?

If you don't mind me saying, you haven't stayed in any one job for very long. Is there a reason for that?

And do you have any references?

I'd tried to explain as best I could, but even I had to admit my CV was sketchy. I'd walked out with a distinct feeling of 'Don't call us, we'll call you'. I'd applied for a whole load of other jobs, but if that was anything to go by, I didn't fancy my chances.

'Anyway,' I said, shutting down my laptop. 'I'm seeing that flat at noon. Fingers crossed something comes of that.'

'Yeah, and don't give up on that job just yet. I bet you didn't stuff up as much as you think you did.'

Jas gave me an encouraging smile, and I tried to return it. But I had the distinct feeling that things were just as bad as I believed.

'Now, as you can see, all three bedrooms are well-proportioned.' The estate agent led the way into what I assumed was the main bedroom. Sandra Morgan – or Sandy, as she'd told me to call her – was a hard-faced middle-aged woman, sporting a pillar-box red, 1980s power suit, complete with shoulder pads. She looked like she'd had her hair blow-dried out that morning. I'd been surprised that her waves could fit through the door. 'The rooms can all take double beds, and they each have generous ward-robe space.'

She went on to tell me how the flat was close to all amenities – the Tube and bus stations, and the shopping centre – but really she didn't need to sell it to me. It was absolutely perfect – exactly what I'd been looking for.

It was in Canada Water, across the river from Plaistow where we used to live. The area had begun gentrifying over the past two decades, and boasted upmarket apartment complexes that were now home to young professionals. The building was only about five years old, which meant it had that new-build feel – magnolia walls, cream carpets and small but functional rooms. It was a little impersonal, but at least it felt clean, neat and modern. April would love it, I was sure, and more importantly, I could imagine our social worker Maggie being impressed when she came to visit.

Once we were back in the kitchen, Sandy turned to me with a wide, enthusiastic smile. 'So what do you think?'

The kitchen was a good place to ask the question. Although it was small – or compact, as Sandy called it – it was south-facing, which meant light flooded through the huge window over the sink, hitting the round table in the corner. I could imagine our family gathered round there.

'I'll take it,' I said, and I could see her eyes light up at the news.

'That's wonderful!' She rifled through her leather conference folder, and handed me some papers. 'Here's the application form to fill in. All very standard. We'll just need to check references and clear the deposit, and it'll all be yours.'

I glanced at the form, and something caught my eye. 'The deposit's six weeks' rent? I only thought it'd be four.'

The smile left the estate agent's face. 'Well, it's six. Non-negotiable. Is that going to be a problem?'

It wouldn't have been if I'd taken that cash Alex offered me for the final game. Sometimes I wished I wasn't so principled. My life would certainly be a lot easier.

When I didn't respond immediately, Sandy sighed. 'Look.' She gave a pointed glance at her watch. Her earlier friendliness had been replaced by impatience. 'Sorry to do this, but I have another appointment now.'

With what must have been a practised technique honed over many years, she managed to herd me out of the kitchen and into the hallway. Before I knew it, the front door was open and I was standing outside on the *Welcome* mat.

'You'll let the owner know that I'm interested, though,' I said, aware that the flat was slipping away from me.

'I will. But don't hold your breath. This is a very popular development.'

With that, she closed the door in my face.

When I got back to Jas's flat late that afternoon, I felt very low. It seemed it wasn't going to be as easy as I'd hoped to find a job and a new place. But as I opened the front door, Jas came bounding out to greet me.

'How did things go?' she asked, dancing from one foot to the other.

I'd appreciated how much time Jas had spent with me in the last two weeks – especially as I wasn't much fun to be around. I knew she was dying to move in with Hugh, and could easily have abandoned me, but instead she'd stayed around to try to cheer me up.

'Not great.' I dumped my bag on the floor, and slipped off my trainers. While I loved Jas's spirit, I wasn't in the mood to be jollied along.

'I wouldn't be so sure about that.' She grabbed my hand. 'Come and listen to your messages.'

She pulled me through to the sitting room, and stood over me as I worked the answering machine. I could tell she was struggling to contain her excitement, but even I was shocked as I listened to the first message from the manager at the gym, offering me the job as receptionist, and the second from Sandy, saying that the owner was prepared to accept just four weeks' deposit.

Jas was grinning from ear to ear as I finished listening to the messages for a second time. 'See? What did I say about everything working out?'

Relief flooded through me. It seemed like my fresh start was just around the corner. At this rate, soon we'd have April back, and I'd never have to see Alex Noble again.

*   *   *

'So you're leaving us, then?' Giles said, leaning up against the bar.

It was two days later, and I was in the middle of my shift at Destination. I'd tried to catch up with him earlier to say that I had a new job, but he hadn't been around, so I'd ended up leaving my resignation letter on his desk.

We hadn't really talked since that time I'd rejected him, but I was glad he'd come to find me. He'd been good to me, and I didn't want to leave things on a bad note. It was good to know he felt the same.

'I hope it's not because of, er . . .'

'Alex?' I filled in.

He had the grace to look embarrassed. 'Sorry. I heard a few things. I shouldn't listen to the gossip, but . . .' He shrugged. I knew what he meant, when it was so prolific, it became unavoidable.

'It's nothing like that. I needed something with more normal hours.'

'I'm sure Dad would've found something for you.'

In fact, Duncan Noble had said as much when I'd called him earlier to tell him my news. I'd felt I owed him that courtesy, since he'd helped me out of a hole a few months earlier. His offer had surprised me, given that he'd caught me with Alex at Rexley Manor, and I'd wondered if he'd made it simply because he knew

I'd been rejected by his son. That had been enough to make me turn him down. 'Yeah, well, it's done now, and I'm happy.'

Giles nodded understandingly. 'That's good. I'm glad things are working out for you. And if you need a reference, or anything in the future, just give me a call.'

'Thanks.' I could see he genuinely meant it. 'For everything. You've been really kind to me. You know, not saying anything about the poker.'

As we were talking, I felt someone's eyes on me. I looked up and saw Alex sitting with his group in one of the booths across the room. He was staring directly at us, and for whatever reason, he didn't look happy.

It was the first time I'd seen him since that awful night when he'd humiliated me in front of his friends. Whether he'd been avoiding me, or just hadn't ended up at Destination, I didn't know or care – I'd just been pleased not to have to see him. Until now.

Our eyes held for a moment. Then Alex turned back to Tori, who was sitting next to him, and resumed his conversation.

Giles moved off then, and I went back to my work.

The incident with Alex had taken no more than a few seconds, and I thought nothing of it until later, when I was going on my break. As I walked along the corridor. I heard someone behind me. When I looked round, he was there.

Any irritation I felt at him following me died when I saw the expression on his face. He was furious.

'What's going on with you and Giles?' he demanded.

'Nothing.' I turned, and started to walk away. But he moved in front of me, blocking my way.

'Don't take me for a fool. I saw you two together. Tell me – are you screwing him already?'

I could feel the anger coming off him in waves. I couldn't believe his hypocrisy. He'd slept with me, rejected and humiliated me, and now he had the cheek to – what? What was this even? If I didn't know better, I'd have assumed he was jealous.

I was going to explain that I'd handed in my notice, and we'd just been saying our goodbyes, but then I wondered why I should bother. I didn't need to justify myself to him. If Alex had jumped to conclusions about my relationship with Giles, I wasn't about to set him straight.

'What if I am?' I raised my chin in defiance. 'I don't see what business it is of yours.' I took a step forward, squaring up to him. 'You made it very clear that you wanted nothing to do with me. So why don't you do us both a favour, and leave me alone.'

I turned away, but he grabbed my hand.

'Nina—'

'Don't!' I snatched my hand away. 'I don't know what you're trying to do – whether you want to see if I have so little self-respect that I'll come back to you after you treated me like dirt, just so you can humiliate me again. But if that is it, let me set the record straight – I'm better than that, and I'm better than you. So don't you ever touch me again.'

He stared at me for a long moment. I made sure to hold his gaze. My heart was beating so hard with anger and hurt that I could barely breathe, but I refused to let him see how much he'd affected me. For a second I thought he was going to say something else, but to my relief, he walked away.

I watched him go back inside. Only then could I let out a deep breath.

Something made me follow him and I saw him return to the booth and slip in beside a pretty blonde, his arm snaking round her shoulder as he leaned over to whisper something in her ear. Her eyes lit up. Whatever he'd said must have done the trick, because a second later, the two of them headed for the door.

My eyes blurred with tears, and I quickly wiped them away. There was no point wasting tears over someone like Alex. He had made it very clear he wasn't interested in me. He was a free agent. As far as I was concerned, he could sleep with whoever the hell he wanted.

But seeing him about to do so didn't stop it hurting.

Chapter 23

'Is Sandra around?'

There was only one person in the estate agent's office, a spotty young man who didn't look old enough to shave, wearing a suit that was a size too large for him. I suspected he was on work experience.

'Sorry, she's already left for the day. Can I help at all?'

I hesitated for a second, wondering if I could trust this somewhat nervous, softly spoken young man. But then I decided what the hell. I was only dropping off my signed copy of the lease. If he couldn't process it, I could always come back tomorrow.

In fact, he turned out to be more competent that he looked. He asked me to take a seat, and for the next ten minutes he went over everything in painstaking detail. I'd pretty much tuned out, when I heard him say, 'And we've got the full six weeks' rental deposit paid up front—'

'No, you haven't,' I interrupted.

He looked up in surprise.

'I could only pay four weeks', so Sandra agreed to that.'

He raised an eyebrow. 'That doesn't sound like Sandra.' He flipped through the paperwork. 'No, it's all here. Says paid in full.'

I probably should have let it go there, but something made me want to be clear that everything was all right – I didn't want to assume I had the flat only for it to be taken from me. 'I'm telling you, I only paid four weeks'.'

He frowned. 'Let me check again . . . Yes,' he said after a moment. 'You only paid four weeks', and the other two were paid by a third party. That's where the confusion came from.'

Something in my head clicked. My heart began to beat faster.

'This may sound like an odd question, but what's the name of this "third party"?'

'Uh . . .' I could see him hesitating, likely wondering if there was anything amiss in revealing the information. But then he must have come to the realisation that the money was paid on my behalf – so what would it matter? He scanned the documents again. 'The payment was made by a Mr Noble. Mr Alexander Noble.' He must have seen the shock on my face. 'Oh God. Are you all right? What did I say? Can I get you anything?'

Somehow I managed to assure him I was fine. Feeling like I was in a daze, I collected my bag and stumbled from the office.

As I walked along the street, I thought back to how certain I'd been that I wouldn't get the job or the flat – and then miraculously I'd got both. And I remembered Jas's assurances that things weren't as bad as I thought, and her reaction when I'd found out that everything had fallen into place – she hadn't seemed anywhere near as surprised as I'd been. In fact, it had almost felt like she'd been expecting the news.

'All right, babes?' Jas's voice sang out from the kitchen as I banged the front door shut. 'I was just about to stick the kettle on. Do you fancy a cuppa—'

The last word died on her lips as I appeared in the kitchen doorway. The look on my face no doubt said everything.

'You know, don't you?' I nodded, still too mad to speak. She closed her eyes briefly and swore under her breath.

She looked up at me from her seat at the table, her eyes already swimming with tears. 'Sit down for a minute, will you? Let me explain.'

But I didn't move from the doorway. Instead I folded my arms. I'd had enough of everyone betraying me. I'd been right to keep myself closed off over the years. Any time you trusted someone, they inevitably betrayed you.

'I thought you were my friend, Jas.' My voice was low and controlled as I spoke. It took all my willpower to ignore what seemed to be the genuine anguish on Jas's face. 'I thought you hated him, too.'

'I am! I do!'

'Then why are you helping him? And what's the point of all this? That's what I don't get.' It was the question that had been tormenting me all the way to Jas's flat – and it was the one I couldn't answer. What was Alex's angle here? He'd made it clear that he despised me – that I was nothing to him. So why had he paid part of the deposit so I got the flat I wanted? And what had he done to ensure I got the receptionist post at the gym – because I was almost positive that my being offered the job had something to do with him.

I took a step towards Jas. 'Just tell me what's going on. Is this some other little game to humiliate me? And you decided to be part of it?'

'God, no! It's nothing like that!'

'Then what is this? Because for the life of me, I don't get it.'

Jas's face crumpled. 'Please, babes, don't be mad. There's nothing underhand going on, I swear.' I didn't say anything, and I could see her quaking under my glare. 'Look, Alex came up to me at the club the other week. He asked me how you were doing. I was so angry with him I told him

273

everything – how you were struggling to get a flat and a job, and that it was all his fault. He asked me the details, and, well, I did wonder if he might do something. And then when you said you'd suddenly had these phone calls, I kind of guessed that he was involved somehow. But honestly I thought what's the harm. It was the least he could do after the way he treated you. But we weren't in cahoots, or anything like that . . .'

Her eyes were wide and wet, like a puppy's when it knows it's done wrong and is begging for forgiveness. I was inclined to believe her, but right now, I wasn't in the mood to let her off the hook. 'Maybe you weren't deliberately colluding with him. But you still should've said something.'

She dropped her eyes, her hands fidgeting on the kitchen table. 'I know. And I'm sorry.'

I knew she wanted me to say I forgave her, but I wasn't in the mood. I turned and left the room.

I could hear the scrape of the kitchen chair as Jas followed me out. 'I'm really sorry,' she said as she caught up with me at the front door. 'Please don't be mad at me.'

I sighed. She sounded so distraught that I had to give her something. 'Look, it's not you I'm mad at. It's him.' I spat the last word with all the distaste I could muster.

Jas chewed at her lip. 'I know you are, but . . .'

'What?' I could see her hesitate, wondering if she should say what she wanted to. 'Whatever it is, tell me.'

'Just that if it's any consolation, I got the feeling that he was doing this because he cared about you.'

I didn't bother to acknowledge that. Instead I slammed the door on my way out.

Standing on the crowded street, I gazed up at the glass-and-chrome building that housed Alex's apartment. When I'd left two weeks earlier, I hadn't expected to see it ever again, and I needed a moment to gather my courage. A man in a suit brushed by me, shooting me a dirty look. Obviously the middle of the pavement wasn't the best place to stand. It was nearly eight in the evening, and while the rush hour had died down, Knightsbridge was the kind of area that was always busy. Shoppers were pouring out of Harrods and Harvey Nicks, and the nearby restaurants and hotels were heaving.

Steeling myself, I walked into the marble lobby. Three beautifully turned-out receptionists sat behind a huge oak desk. Four huge guards stood equally spaced across the floor, on the lookout.

I remembered the code for the lift, and could have let myself up. But I wanted to do this properly, formally. So I got one of the receptionists to call the apartment. Alex was there, so she told me to go straight up.

I stood in the lift, watching the floors light up in turn. I was pleased that I was alone. I was like a prize-fighter before a big bout – every part of me was on high alert. I could hear my breathing above the bland lift music; feel my fingers drumming against my right thigh, even through the thick material of my jeans.

Finally, the lift pinged as it reached its destination – the penthouse. The doors slid open, and taking a deep breath, I stepped out into Alex's hallway.

He was standing in the entrance to the living room, a tumbler of what looked like whisky in his hand.

'Good of you to drop by,' he drawled, as I walked towards him. 'Wish you'd let me know, though. I'd have dressed up for the occasion—'

'What the hell do you think you're playing at?' I cut in as I came level with him.

He cocked his head to one side, a smile playing at his lips. 'You might need to be a little more specific, darling. It's been a busy couple of weeks—'

'Oh, stop it with these games. I *know*, Alex.'

The humour left his eyes. He took a sip of whisky before answering. 'You know what exactly?' He was clearly trying to keep the playfulness in his voice, but I could hear the edge there.

'About the deposit for my flat.'

'Oh, that.' Was it my imagination, or did he look relieved? But what else could he have thought I knew about? Wasn't that enough?

With his usual nonchalance, he turned and walked over to the kitchen. I had no choice but to follow him. I watched as he poured himself another glass of whisky. When he held a glass up for me, I didn't bother to even dignify the offer with a response.

'And what about the job at the gym?' I went on. 'Did you have something to do with that, too?'

Alex gave a shrug of his broad shoulders. 'The owner's a friend. I just had a word with him, said I thought you'd be good at the job.'

He leaned against the kitchen counter, trailing an idle finger around the rim of his glass. I somehow resisted the urge to knock the tumbler from his hand. It bugged me that he was acting like this was no big deal, and it was taking all my willpower to keep my emotions in check.

'To be perfectly honest,' he said, stifling a yawn. 'You seem to be blowing this all out of proportion. I helped you out, end of story. What else is there to say?'

'I want you to tell me why.'

He arched an eyebrow. 'Why I helped you?' I gave a nod. 'Does it matter?' I just looked at him, and he sighed, as though the whole conversation was too much trouble for him. He took a sip of whisky. 'I suppose I felt sorry for you,' he said finally. 'Or maybe I felt guilty. It may even have seemed like the quickest way to get you out of my life. Take your pick from those. It's all the same to me.'

I stared at him for a long moment. The look of boredom on his chiselled face was almost enough to make me turn around and leave. But something stopped me. He was being an arsehole; there was no doubt about it. After what he'd just said, I ought to have gone and never looked back. But somehow I sensed that was exactly what he wanted. It was almost as if he was trying too hard to be a dick.

'I don't believe you.' The words were out of my mouth before I could stop myself.

He sighed. 'About what?'

'Any of it.' I refused to let his obvious irritation put me off. Alex might spend a lot of time pretending not to give a damn about anything, but I'd seen that deep down he did care. 'I think you helped me because you still have feelings for me.'

'Seriously?' he scoffed. 'After I hurt and humiliated you in front of my friends, you still think I'm interested in you? Are you delusional or something?'

Maybe I was. Maybe I was making a fool of myself. But some instinct was telling me that wasn't the case. I took a step towards him, refusing to let it go until he finally admitted what was really going on. 'I know you, Alex. You want everyone to think you don't give a damn about anything, but deep down you're a good person. I don't understand what's going on, but there's more to it than you're letting on.'

'Whatever you want to tell yourself,' he said lightly, making it clear he thought I was talking rubbish. He picked up his drink, and turned from me. Maybe I would have given up then, but a split second before he'd looked away, I'd seen tension around his eyes, and I sensed that I was getting to him. So I pressed on. 'I know I sound ridiculous.' He began to pace the room. 'It's not like I've forgotten what you did to me. I remember how you humiliated me in front of your friends. You went out of your way to be cruel—' To my shame, I heard my voice crack. I dug my nails into my palms, trying to stop myself from crying. 'You made me look like a fool. But still I believe in you. Even after all the pain you've caused me—'

'All right! Enough!' He whirled round, his eyes blazing. 'You're right. Is that what you want to hear? That night – blowing you off in front of my friends. I wasn't trying to hurt you. I was trying to protect you.'

Even though I'd been pushing for him to agree that there'd been more going on, the admission left me speechless. 'What do you mean?' I said finally.

He shook his head. 'You know what? For someone so smart, you can be really dense sometimes.' He took a step towards me. 'You want to know why I did that? The real reason? It was because I cared for you. It was because I was falling in love with you.'

279

That was the last thing I'd expected him to say. I was too stunned to speak, so I just let him carry on talking.

'I woke up that morning at Rexley Manor, and I looked over at you, and I realised I'd never felt that way about someone before. All the girls I'd slept with – and you were the only one I'd ever really wanted to spend time with.

'Then my father arrived.' His voice was bitter. 'He asked me what the hell I was doing with you. He said I'd end up hurting you, and that it wasn't fair on you. That you should be with someone kind and hard-working and reliable. Someone exactly the opposite of me. And I knew he was right. I'm not a good guy, Nina. I'm not the right guy for you. So . . .'

'So you decided to prove that by rejecting me in front of everyone?' I didn't bother to keep the disbelief out of my voice.

He closed his eyes for a second, a look of pain crossing his face. 'That's pretty much it. And I've regretted it ever since. Even if I was going to push you away, I should've found a better way to do it.' He gave a wry laugh. 'I suppose that me behaving like a bastard seemed pretty plausible.' He ran a hand through his dark hair. 'These past couple of weeks have been awful for me, too. I asked Jas how you were doing because I genuinely wanted to know. When she told me how bad things were for you . . . Well, I wanted to help out. That's why I made sure you got the flat and the job. Because I wanted you to be happy.' He took another step forward, so I could see the sincerity in his blue eyes. 'So don't ever think that was me rejecting you. I wanted you then. And I still want you now.'

He paused then, letting the words sink in. I stared up at him, not knowing what to say or how to react. He was standing so close to me, well within touching distance. I knew he wanted to reach for me, and was looking for a sign that it was all right to do so. But how could I be sure of him?

My eyes searched his, looking for clues to suggest that he was lying. I couldn't see any – but what did that mean? My voice was no more than a whisper as I said, 'I just don't know what to believe, Alex. After everything you've done, how can I ever trust you?'

'After everything I've said, how can you not?'

We stared at each other. He took a step closer to me. Both of his hands cupped my face, his thumbs stroking my cheeks. I saw him hesitate for a second, his eyes on mine, checking to see if I was going to object. I was suddenly aware that I was holding my breath – terrified that one tiny movement would disturb the fragility of the moment. Then before I could think about whether I wanted to stop him, his mouth bore down on mine, and he was kissing me fiercely, his lips hard and demanding.

I responded instinctively, my arms snaking around his neck, pulling him to me, as though I couldn't get enough of him. After all this time apart, it felt like we didn't have a second to waste. Alex must have felt the same way, because he was ripping my shirt open, sending the buttons clattering across the floor, and yanking my bra straps down. And then his hands were on me, moving over my breasts and stomach, and circling my waist.

Before I knew what was happening, he lifted me onto the kitchen countertop. He pushed up my skirt and eased my panties down. My thighs parted, and I gasped as he touched me.

Unable to stand it a moment longer, I reached for Alex's belt, cursing impatiently as I fumbled with the zip on his jeans, tugging his boxer shorts down.

My legs wrapped around him, drawing him to me, and then he was finally inside me, thrusting deep and hard. His hand twisted round my hair, pulling my head back, as he devoured my neck with hot, hungry kisses.

A shudder ripped through me, my nails digging into his back as I came.

'Nina . . . Oh my god . . .' His grip on me tightened, crushing the air from my lungs, until, with a final cry, he collapsed against me, his head buried against my shoulder.

We stayed locked together, spent and dazed in the

aftermath. The only sound in the room was of us both panting as we struggled to catch our breath. And I knew in that moment that, whatever was between us, there was no turning back from it now.

Chapter 24

A black Mercedes parked on the street wasn't an unusual sight in London. Chauffeur-driven cars like that were standard in the Square Mile, rushing execs to and from meetings.

I wouldn't have thought anything of it as I walked out of the gym at the end of my shift – that is, if I hadn't glimpsed the personalised number plate, which said: *DN1*.

I had to pass the car on my way to the Tube station, and as I did so the tinted window at the back rolled down. Sure enough, it was Duncan Noble inside.

'Do you have a moment?' he asked politely enough, but what was I going to say? I opened the door, and slid into the soft cream-leather seat.

I gave a pointed glance around. 'This is all a bit cloak and dagger, isn't it?'

'Perhaps. But I wanted to talk to you, and I wasn't sure if you'd agree to meet me.'

'So you thought you'd give me no option?'

He smiled at that, and then grew serious. 'Alex tells me that the two of you have renewed your—' He paused, clearly searching for the right word. 'Your acquaintance.'

It was my turn to smile. It was a week since we'd reconciled, and we'd hardly been apart. 'Acquaintance' wasn't quite the word I'd have used. 'If you mean that we're together, then yes, we are.'

He sighed, leaving me in no doubt that he wasn't happy with the news. 'Look, I'll be straight with you, Nina. You're both adults, and it's up to you what you decide to do, however ill-advised I might think it. But—'

He hesitated, and I stared impassively at him, waiting to hear what he had to say.

'All I want to say is, it might be best not to mention that you're seeing him to your mother.'

That was the last thing I'd expected. I shook my head at the sheer ridiculousness of the request. 'Honestly – why not? I know the two of you fell out. But Alex was just sixteen when my dad died. Whatever went on between my mum and you, it wasn't like it had anything to do with him—'

Duncan looked pained. 'I know what you're saying. But I think at the moment, when she's just coming out of rehab, it might be best to keep her stress to a minimum. So maybe just wait a bit before telling her. See how things work out between the two of you.'

285

I looked at him for a long moment. It just didn't feel worth arguing about any longer. 'Fine. I'll think about it.'

'That's all I'm asking.'

I was about to get out of the car, when I turned back to him. There was something nagging at me. 'I just want to know one thing.'

'What?' he said warily.

'What did the two of you argue about all those years ago?'

He sighed deeply. 'Oh, Nina, you don't want to go dredging all that up.'

'That's not an answer.' He just stared at me. I could see I wasn't going to get any more out of him. 'Fine. Have it your way.'

I reached for the door handle. But as I was getting out of the car, Duncan put his arm out to stop me.

'Honestly – trust me when I say it's in your best interests to leave this alone.'

The fierceness in his eyes unnerved me. I swallowed hard. Whatever had gone on, no one was in a hurry to have it out in the open.

On the Tube ride over to Alex's, I couldn't help thinking about that feud between my mum and Duncan Noble. I still had no idea what it was all about. Even now I could remember how he'd been there for our family in the months after the funeral, until that one night when I'd woken to hear my mother screaming at him to get out and saying she wouldn't accept a penny of his money any longer.

It was after that that her drinking began. And we'd eventually lost our house and ended up in Hayfield Court.

What had been so bad that my mother had preferred to lose all our security rather than see Duncan Noble again? I really couldn't imagine.

'It just seems ridiculous, don't you think?' I said to Alex. 'Whatever went on between your dad and my mum, I don't see there's any reason it should affect us.'

It was later that evening, and we were sitting up in his bed, sharing a takeaway pizza.

Alex was quiet for a moment. When he spoke, he didn't meet my eye. 'I hate to say this – but maybe for once my father's right.'

I was about to help myself to another slice of pizza, but I stopped. 'What do you mean by that?'

'Your mum's in a precarious position. I imagine she's got enough to deal with, just staying off the sauce. What's the point of telling her something that's only going to upset her?'

I couldn't believe what I was hearing. Alex was the one who was always so forthright. I hadn't expected him to take his father's side. 'I'm not hiding our relationship away. It makes no sense—'

He reached out and took my hand, stopping my outburst. 'It won't be for long. Just until you get April back and everything's more settled. You don't want to risk upsetting her before your sister's home, do you?'

I bit my lip as I worked through what he'd said. He was right, of course. I didn't want to do anything to jeopardise April's return.

'Maybe you're right,' I said at last. 'I'll wait until things are a bit more settled.' To lighten the tone, I pinched his cheeks playfully. 'Until then, you'll just have to be my dirty little secret.'

He grinned. 'I don't have a problem with that.'

He fell backwards on the bed, pulling me down on top of him, and we started to kiss.

But that night, I woke to find that I was alone in bed. I sat up and saw Alex had pulled up a chair to the window, and was sitting there, staring out into the dark night.

I went over and knelt in front of him, resting my head on the arm of the chair. 'Hey. What's up with you?'

He looked down at me, and tried to smile. 'Nothing.'

I didn't believe him. I thought for a second, trying to work out what the problem could be. 'Does this have something to do with your father?'

Alex looked at me for a long moment before answering. 'I just couldn't sleep.'

His thumbs traced the contours of my face, as though he was trying to memorise what I looked like.

'You worried I'm going to disappear?' I said jokingly.

But he looked deadly serious as he said, 'Maybe.'

I wanted to ask more, but he was looking down at me so sadly that I didn't dare. Instead, I let him draw me up onto his lap. I nestled my head against his chest, and we sat like that for a long time.

His restlessness made me apprehensive. I sensed he was hiding something, but I couldn't think what it was. And he was being so loving towards me, so kind, that I didn't feel like there could possibly be anything sinister to it. So I pushed it to the back of my mind. I already had enough on my plate trying to reunite my family. I didn't want to stir up more problems.

'She seems really committed to trying to making things work this time,' my mum's counsellor said as we waited in the reception area for her.

I made no comment.

It was twelve weeks to the day since my mum had entered the rehab centre. They were meant to work wonders with long-term alcoholics, but I was reserving judgement. I'd been through this too many times before to get my hopes up. For me, the only proof would come from her staying off the booze once she was back home.

She came downstairs five minutes later. Objectively I could see that she looked healthier than she had when she went in – her skin seemed clearer, and there was colour in her cheeks. Twelve weeks off the booze had done her the world of good.

The counsellor stepped forward to hug my mother good-bye, but I hung back a little.

My mother turned to me. I was worried that she might try to hug me, too, but she had the sense to hold back.

'Thank you for coming, Nina. It means a lot.' Her eyes were grave as she spoke, as though she wanted me to know she was taking it seriously. 'I appreciate this hasn't been easy for you. And I know you're fed up of hearing promises that I can't keep, so I won't make any. I'll just say that I'm pleased you're here today.'

The prickle of tears in my eyes took me by surprise. I hadn't expected to get upset. I'd felt sure I was beyond it. But it was so different from her usual speeches – so lacking in bravado – that I found myself getting choked up.

'Yeah, well.' I cleared my throat. 'We should be getting out of here.'

We took the Tube to the flat. My mother asked questions along the way – about my new job and how April was getting on. I gave her short, factual answers.

I enjoyed showing her around the flat I'd rented for us.

The smart new-build was a world away from our flat in Hayfield Court. It was a low-rise block near the river, and now, in the middle of the day, everyone was at work, so the place was beautifully quiet and peaceful. Inside, the flat was bright, clean and neat. I'd already arranged the few belongings I'd managed to save after the fire, so it would feel more like home.

'Oh, Nina.' My mother looked around in frank disbelief, clearly impressed. 'This is lovely. I know it hasn't been easy, but you've done so well.'

It felt good to hear her say that – better than I'd expected.

We cooked dinner together. Mum told me she'd be attending local AA meetings, and that she was also going to try to get a job. I wasn't about to let myself get too excited. We'd been down this road before, and it had led to nothing but disappointment. My main concern was getting April back with us – our social worker visit was due soon.

'Maggie wants to meet up next week,' I said, once we'd finished eating. 'She's coming round here for a home inspection, and to talk to us both to see if we're able to look after April properly.'

My mother listened solemnly.

'We just have to make sure that there's nothing out of place here.' What I meant by that was, we can't have vodka bottles lying around, or my mother doing one of her famous disappearing acts. She looked down at the table, and I could see she understood what I was getting at.

I stood up and started clearing the dinner plates and cutlery. 'I'll wash up.'

I turned towards the sink.

'I'll give you a hand,' my mother said.

I switched the taps on. It helped cover the silence.

I counted to ten and then tried to do up the zip on my skirt again. I wrestled with it for a good minute or so and then finally gave up, muttering a loud curse. Whatever I did, the thing wouldn't budge.

I glanced at my watch, wondering what to do. Our social worker, Maggie Walker, was due round any minute. I'd wanted to look as respectable as possible for our meeting, so I'd ditched my usual jeans and T-shirt, and opted for a grey pencil skirt and white shirt. But at this rate I was going to be meeting her half-dressed.

There was a knock at my bedroom door. 'Everything all right in there?' my mum called through. She must have heard me swearing.

'Yeah,' I answered instinctively. Then I gave a sigh of defeat. 'Well, no. Not really.'

Mum tentatively pushed open the door, and poked her head in. She looked surprisingly conservative in a smart navy coat-dress. She'd also kept her makeup light and had pinned her white-blonde curls back in a neat chignon. Like me, she was determined to make a good impression. 'Anything I can help with?'

I didn't answer, but instead turned my back to her, so she could see the problem.

'Here. Let me.' She came over and fiddled with the zip for a second, pulling out fabric that had caught in it, and then fastened it all the way up. 'There.' She smiled at me in the mirror. 'You look really pretty in that. You should wear skirts more often.'

It was the first time in a long while that she'd done anything for me, and I wasn't quite sure how to respond. Fortunately the doorbell saved me from answering.

Maggie Walker hadn't changed at all over the past few months. She still looked dishevelled and thrown together, like she'd just rolled out of bed. But she wasn't the one being judged. I just hoped she could see that we'd changed – or at least that our situation had.

Maggie made a quick inspection of the flat and seemed impressed. It was just as well, given that my mum and I had spent the previous day cleaning and tidying. Then we all went through to the kitchen. I made tea in a pot, and got out the good china – matching cups and saucers, one of my parents' wedding gifts. Then the three of us sat at the round table, while my mum and I waited to be interrogated.

Maggie asked about my job, and made little notes on her pad as I talked, which made me even more nervous than I already was. I could hear my voice shaking as I spoke. She smiled kindly at me, so it didn't seem like it had gone too badly. I suppose at least she knew I cared.

Then she turned her attention to my mother. Mum spoke in depth about her time in rehab, and the social worker listened attentively. Thankfully, she seemed more impressed by my mother's resolve than I was.

Once my mother had finished her spiel, Maggie had a chance to have her say.

'I know things haven't been easy for your family, and I can see that you've done your best to put things right.' I tensed. I could feel a 'but' coming on, and that worried me. 'But it would be remiss of me to allow April to come back to live with you if I thought for even a moment that she might be put at risk again.'

Hearing that, my heart sank. I opened my mouth to argue our case, but she put her hand up to stop me.

'I've heard everything that I need to hear, and I can see how committed you are to making things work – for April's sake. And so my recommendation is that she can come back and live with you.'

Relief coursed through me. I hadn't even realised I'd been holding my breath until I let out a deep exhale. Without thinking, I found myself turning to my mother.

She looked as relieved and delighted as I felt, and we embraced.

'I can't believe it,' I said as she hugged me to her.

'That's such great news. Such great news.'

Maggie waited until we'd finished, and she had our full attention again. Then, as though she didn't want us to get too overexcited, she gave us her sternest look.

'I will, however, be visiting regularly to check up on you. And if I see any evidence that this isn't a fit place for a minor to be living, I will recommend that April is immediately removed.'

My mother took my hand, in a show of solidarity, I suppose. 'We understand.'

Chapter 25

'That was amazing, Mum.' April pushed her empty plate away, and flopped back in the kitchen chair. 'I'd love to have a third helping, but I couldn't squeeze in another bite.'

She patted the bulge of her stomach to prove her point. I couldn't help smiling. It was my sister's first night back with us, and so far everything was going perfectly. She'd loved the flat and her new room, and Mum had made her favourite dinner, lasagne, to celebrate. But mostly, I think she was just pleased to be back with us again.

For my part, it felt great to have April back. Having her around made the flat feel more like a home. It also forced Mum and me to call a truce.

'Yes, it was one of my better efforts,' my mum said. 'Although I think I could've done with adding a glass of wine to the sauce.'

I shot her a glare that could have cut glass.

'I was only joking!'

Seeing the anxious look on my sister's face, I managed to swallow down my retort. I didn't want to ruin her first evening back.

'I'll make us some tea,' I said instead.

I got up and filled the kettle, leaving April and my mother to catch up. They hadn't seen each other for three months, because Mum hadn't wanted my sister to visit her in rehab. As I waited for the water to boil, I leaned against the countertop, content to watch them together. They looked so alike, and they were both much more girly than me, gossiping about clothes and the latest celebrities.

'So what about boys?' my mother asked. 'Is there anyone nice in your class?'

I rolled my eyes. It was so typical of my mother to ask about boys before schoolwork.

Luckily, April pulled a face. 'No, all the boys are horrible.' I felt pleased that she hadn't turned boy-crazy yet. But then she cast a sly look over to me. 'But Nina has a boyfriend.'

I froze. I hadn't thought to tell April to keep her mouth shut about Alex – mainly because I didn't have a great reason for doing so.

April didn't seem to notice my discomfort, though. She carried on talking, oblivious to my signals to stop.

'He's really good-looking.'

'Oh?' Mum looked absurdly pleased.

'And he's got an amazing car. He must be really rich.'

My mother looked over at me. 'I did wonder about all those secret phone calls you've been making,' she teased. 'So who is the young man, and why haven't I met him yet?'

'It's no one.' I tried to sound dismissive. 'April's got it wrong.'

But April wasn't having any of it. 'That's rubbish, and you know it. He was totally in love with you, and you with him. I could tell when he gave me a lift. Now, what was his name again . . .' She thought for a moment. 'It was something beginning with A,' she mused. I prayed she wouldn't get it, but a moment later she looked up, triumphant. 'I know! It was Alex. Alex Noble. I remember, because I thought it sounded really posh . . .'

The blood began to drain from my mother's face.

I had no idea what to say – or what she was going to make of it. But she obviously didn't want to let on in front of April that anything was wrong, because she turned to her and smiled brightly.

'Now that's enough for now, sweetheart. Let's allow your sister some privacy. Why don't you run along and unpack? I'll bring you your tea.'

She waited until April had left the room, and then she turned grave eyes to me.

'So is April right? You're seeing Alexander Noble?'

'Yes, I am.' I said it almost defiantly. 'What of it?'

Because of what Duncan Noble had said, I expected her to hit the roof, to start ranting and raving. But instead she sighed deeply, looking at me with sad eyes. 'Oh, Nina,' she said, and then stopped, shaking her head at the news. 'How did this happen?'

I quickly explained about having had to approach Duncan Noble for a job. Seeing her mournful expression as I spoke made me finally unleash. 'Seriously – not you, too. Why does everyone have such a problem with us being together?'

My mother studied me for a long moment, as though she was weighing up how to answer. Then at the last minute she surprised me by forcing a smile. 'I don't have a problem with you and Alex being together. I was just surprised, that was all.'

I wasn't sure if I believed my mother. But I didn't care. I was happy with Alex. I didn't give a damn what anyone else thought.

The following night I went over to Alex's place for dinner.

It was a strange period for us. We'd been used to seeing so much of each other when I was working for him and we were living under the same roof. Now it was much more difficult to meet up, especially since I was trying to spend time with my mum and April, and get our lives back to some semblance of a routine.

We'd talked about going out, but ended up ordering pizza again, which we ate curled up under the covers of his bed, watching a DVD. He'd wanted me to stay over, but I'd reluctantly said no. While my mother had been on her best behaviour ever since coming out of rehab, I still didn't trust her alone with April.

'If anything happened to her, and I was over here, I could never forgive myself.'

I still woke up sometimes thinking about how different the outcome of that night of the fire could have been.

Alex said he understood, and when it got to eleven, he drove me home.

I didn't tell him that my mother knew about him until we reached my flat. When he pulled up outside, he leaned over to kiss me, and I let him, wanting to put off revealing the truth to him for as long as possible.

Finally, I pulled away. He reached out and touched my cheek. We were parked under a streetlamp, and the light reflected off his strong jaw and cheekbones.

'I'll wait here until you get to your front door,' he said.

'You could walk me to it, if you want.' I waited a beat. 'Maybe even come in for a bit? I know April is dying to see you again.' I rolled my eyes at that last part. If April had been a few years older, I think I'd have had serious competition for Alex's attention.

Alex raised an eyebrow. 'And how would we explain

that to your mother? Would I have to pretend to be someone else?' I laughed a little. I could tell he was trying to make light of the situation. 'Take on a fake name, a fake identity . . .'

I took a breath. 'You wouldn't have to.'

'How come?'

'Well,' I said carefully, 'as of yesterday, my mother knows all about you – courtesy of my gossip of a little sister – so you might as well come in and meet her.'

It took a moment for him to speak. His face went very still, and his eyes looked away from me, fixing on a point in the distance.

'I don't think that's such a good idea.'

'Why not?' He had no answer. Even though I could tell he didn't want me to, I pressed on. 'Please. Do this for me. It means a lot.' I felt I needed to give more explanation. 'I haven't got on with my mum for years. I'd given up on her, if I'm being honest. But she really seems to be trying this time. You're important to me, and I want her to know you.'

He looked at me for a long moment, and then sighed. 'All right. You win.'

I grinned. 'I usually do!'

He took my hand as we walked up to the front door. I let go briefly to search through my bag and find the keys. But once we were inside, his fingers interlaced with mine again, as though he wanted to be reassured that I was there.

From the small hallway, I could hear the television on in the living room. We walked in to find my mum and April curled up together on the sofa. They both looked up as we came in, and April's face lit up when she saw Alex.

'Alex!' She must have said his name instinctively, without thinking. But then she caught herself, and I could see her blush. My little sister clearly had a crush on my boyfriend, but she was trying hard not to show it. 'It's nice to see you again.'

I bit back a smile at her formality. She was clearly trying to hide how she felt about him.

I'd expected Alex to go over and make a fuss of April, but instead he was very quiet and almost stiff by my side. I glanced over at him and saw that his gaze was elsewhere. I realised then that he was staring at my mother.

I'd been so caught up in my sister's reaction to Alex, I hadn't even thought about my mother. I looked over at her, and saw that her face was very pale.

Daughterly concern took over, and I hurried to her side.

'Are you all right?' I put my hand on her forehead and leaned over, half afraid that I might catch the smell of alcohol on her breath. But there was nothing.

My words had caught April's attention, too. As she saw how drained our mother looked, all thoughts of Alex seemed to disappear.

'Mum!' April scrambled to her knees on the sofa. 'What's wrong? Are you feeling sick or something?'

'No, no.' She waved away our fussing. 'I'm fine. Just a little tired, that's all.' I opened my mouth to contradict her, but she shook her head. 'Honestly. Don't fuss.'

Before I could object, she got to her feet and walked towards Alex, stopping right in front of him. At five foot three and slim, she looked tiny compared to his six foot two, bulked-up frame. But it felt like he was almost the one who shrank back from her.

'So you're Alexander Noble.' Her voice was very neutral, and I couldn't tell if she was pleased to see him or not. Alex must have been worried, too, because I watched as he wet his lips. I was almost holding my breath, waiting to see what would happen.

She stared at him for a long moment, and then to my surprise she put her hands on his shoulders, and stood on tiptoe to kiss him on each cheek. 'It's nice to meet a friend of Nina's.'

I could feel the tension leave my body. She retreated to the couch, and I walked over and took Alex's hand and squeezed it.

'Did you want a cup of tea or something?'

I'd hoped that he might stay and we could all talk, like a real family. But he shook his head.

'Thanks, but I'd better get going.'

I tried to hide my disappointment. 'Right. Yeah, of course.'

He turned to April and gave her a wink. 'Try not to break any boys' hearts.' I could see her squirm and blush under his attention, clearly thrilled. Then he turned to my mother. 'And it was nice to meet you, Mrs Baxter.'

I walked him to the front door, feeling a little down-hearted. It wasn't exactly the great 'meet the family' moment I'd been hoping for. As we lingered in the half-light of the porch, I tilted my mouth up for a kiss. But he just planted his lips quickly on my forehead.

'I'll speak to you tomorrow,' he said. He touched his hand to my cheek in an almost brotherly way.

I didn't have a chance to respond before he headed off.

The following day, I came back after work and headed straight for the kitchen. As I got to the door, I could hear my mother on the phone. I couldn't catch much of the conversation – but I heard her say my name, followed by Alex's.

I didn't want to eavesdrop, so I went in and found my mother sitting at the table. She obviously hadn't heard me come into the flat, and looked up guiltily when she saw me.

Now I was in the kitchen, I could just about hear the voice on the other end of the phone. It was male, and whoever he was, he seemed to be talking animatedly about something.

'Nina's home.' My mother cut the speaker off before I could make out what he was saying. 'I'd better go, but I'll talk to you later.'

As she put the phone down, I walked over to the fruit bowl and selected an apple.

'Who was that?' I bit into the firm skin of the Granny Smith and chewed the bitter fruit slowly, waiting for her response.

'It was my counsellor from the rehab centre, just checking in.'

I stared at her for a long moment. Her counsellor was female, and the voice on the other end had definitely been male. So she was lying – I just had no idea why.

I thought about questioning her, but decided against it. If she wanted to keep her secrets, that was down to her.

'And everything's all right?' I said, playing along.

'Why wouldn't it be?'

I didn't honestly know, but somehow I suspected there was more to this than I was aware of.

I forced a smile. 'No reason.' I waited a beat. 'I'm going to get changed.'

I walked out of the kitchen still eating my apple, as though it was the most important thing in the world to me. But inside my mind was racing. I would let the topic go for now, but the exchange had left me feeling uneasy.

* * *

Now that April was back living with us, we began to get into a routine. She would go to school and I would go to work, and then we'd eat dinner as a family in the evening.

My mother was starting to apply for jobs, too, and seeing some old friends. Luckily she seemed to be staying away from the bad men who used to be in her life. One night, one of them called, and I was proud of her when she told him that she wouldn't see him and that he was not to contact her again. At least she was trying to act sensibly this time.

Because I was trying to bond with my family, I didn't have much time to see Alex. April seemed to be in a clingy mood, and she wanted to be with my mother and me, as though she was worried that our domestic bliss wouldn't last. I was concerned about her not seeing her friends, but I thought I'd leave it for a while before confronting her about it.

Then, one Thursday, a couple of weeks after she'd moved back in, April rushed home full of herself.

'Julie's invited me to sleep at hers tomorrow. Is it all right if I go?'

It was perfect. Finally, I'd get a night to myself. As much as I loved my sister, I was missing being with my boyfriend.

As soon as dinner was finished, I called to tell Alex.

'I've got some good news.'

'Yeah?'

'April's out at a sleepover tomorrow night, so I thought I'd come over and we could have a sleepover of our own.'

He didn't jump at the opportunity like I'd expected. We'd hardly seen each other since April came back, so I'd assumed he'd be dying for me to stay over.

'Of course, if you'd rather not see me, that's fine. I'm sure I can find another young gentleman who'd jump at the chance to invite me over . . .' My tone was teasing, but deep down I taken aback by his attitude.

'There's no need for that.' He was trying to match his tone to mine, but I could detect something of an edge there. 'What time were you thinking?'

'My shift ends at six.'

'Six . . . right . . .' He sounded a bit lost in thought. 'Well, why don't you come round for eight thirty?'

I was surprised he said that. Usually he would tell me to come straight from work, and have a shower and change at his place.

'How come so late?' I couldn't help asking. 'Are you doing something?'

He hesitated for just a split second before answering.

'Hugh asked me to go for a drink tomorrow, straight after he finishes work. I have a feeling he might be planning to pop the question . . .'

The momentary hesitation might have unnerved me, but I was too thrown by the idea that Hugh was thinking of proposing to Jas.

'God . . . wow.' I could barely contemplate the enormity of it. 'I can't wait to hear all about that! Eight thirty it is, then.'

I might not have thought anything more about our conversation. But after hearing him mention Hugh's intentions, I felt an inexplicable urge to talk to Jas. I wasn't going to say anything to her, of course, but I just wanted to hear her voice.

Unfortunately, she sounded busy.

'I can't talk for long,' she said breathlessly. 'We're off to Paris tomorrow, and I'm in the middle of packing.'

Alarm bells sounded in my head. 'When are you going?'

I was praying that she would say the following evening.

'First thing tomorrow, babes. So I'd better . . .' She didn't finish the sentence, but instead made a sound like a car engine.

'Yeah, of course.' It was an effort for me to match her breezy tone, but I just about managed it. 'Call me when you get back.'

After that call, I lay down on my bed, staring up at the ceiling, the phone resting in my hand. A spider had made its web on the light fitting, and I watched as it struggled to make its way to the top, and then fell back down.

I watched the spider climb up and fall down again and again. Losing myself in its struggle was the only way I could stop myself from calling Alex and demanding to know why he'd lied. I hated those paranoid, clingy girls, who were deeply suspicious if their boyfriend wasn't by their side at all times. I wasn't about to turn into one of them.

I had no reason to doubt him. It was probably just a simple mistake, and he'd got the day wrong. We'd probably laugh about it tomorrow night.

So why, despite telling myself that, did I still have a nagging sense of unease?

Luckily, before I had a chance to change my mind, April came in.

'Are you done with the phone? My minutes are all used up, and I want to call Julie to tell her that I can come tomorrow.'

'Yeah. I'm done.'

I got up from the bed and handed her my phone. It was a relief not to have it. That way I couldn't call Alex.

'I won't be long,' April said over her shoulder.

'Take as long as you need.'

She stopped and turned to me, her face animated. 'Really? Brilliant!'

By the time she'd finished almost forty-five minutes later, I'd managed to calm myself down and no longer felt the urge to talk to Alex.

I managed to put the matter from my mind the following day. I woke late and had to rush for work, and then I was kept busy.

I'd planned on going home to change before heading round to Alex's flat for 8.30. But one of the other receptionists was feeling ill, and so I agreed to stay at work a bit longer. That meant staying until the last person was out, so by the time I'd finished, there was no point going home. I knew the code for the lift, and I had clothes with me, so I could shower and change at his place instead. He was obviously going to be out – although I had no idea where – but at least I'd be there when he got back.

I wasn't expecting anyone to be there, but as the lift doors pulled open, I found the lights were all on. It looked like Alex had left them on by mistake.

I was halfway along the hallway when I heard voices from the living room. I was about to call out a greeting, but some deep, innate instinct cautioned me not to speak up. Then I heard a woman say my name.

The voice was familiar. It took a moment to place it, simply because it was so unexpected. It was my mother, and she sounded upset. I frowned. What the hell was she doing there?

I carried on down the hallway, being careful not to make a sound so that I could hear exactly what my mother was saying.

'Don't you think my daughter deserves to know the truth, Alex?' she said, as I reached the door. It was a little bit ajar, so I could hear every word. 'Do you honestly think she'd be with you if she knew what you'd done?'

The words chilled me. What could be so terrible that everyone was scared to tell me what it was? And what could it be that would make me not want to be with Alex? Part of me didn't want to know, didn't want my happiness disturbed. But it was all going to come out at some point. It might as well be now.

I took a deep breath, and pushed open the door. My mother was with Alex and his father. They turned to see who the intruder was – and when they saw it was me, I could see shock then fear cross their faces.

I looked from one to the other.

'I couldn't help overhearing your argument,' I said. 'Now, does someone want to tell me what the hell this is all about?'

Chapter 26

No one spoke for a long moment.

'Well?' I said, still standing, my hands on my hips. 'Is someone going to tell me what this is all about?'

More silence, and then: 'It's about your father.'

It was Duncan Noble who spoke.

'My father?' That was the last thing I'd expected to hear. 'What about him?'

I cast my eyes over the people in the room. None of them looked happy, but it was Alex who looked worst of all. He was so pale, like a corpse in the morgue in one of those crime series. Laughter bubbled up inside me at the comparison, but I swallowed it down. Part of me already sensed how inappropriate it would be.

No one seemed to be rushing to fill in the blanks.

'Seriously – is someone going to start talking? I don't

understand what my relationship with Alex has to do with my father.'

I expected Alex to answer, but he was looking so sadly at me, as though he already sensed that what was about to come out would be the end of us.

Instead, Duncan Noble spoke again. He seemed to be the only one with his emotions under control. 'It's to do with your father's accident. The night he—'

'Died,' I filled in, and watched as everyone around the room winced.

'That night,' Duncan said, carefully avoiding the word 'died'. 'He didn't swerve off the road and crash. There was another car involved.'

It took a moment for the words to sink in, but still I didn't get it. There had never been any mention of another car before.

I frowned. 'I don't understand—'

I stopped as everyone's eyes turned towards Alex. Suddenly it all fell into place.

'You?' I spoke the word disbelievingly. 'You were driving the other car? But you were only – what – sixteen?'

He raised his eyes to meet mine, and I could see the sorrow there.

My mother stepped forward.

'Nina—' she began.

'Don't.' I cut her off. My eyes were focused on Alex. It was him I wanted answers from. I took a step towards him. It was as though it was just the two of us in the room.

'You hadn't even passed your driving test, had you?' The pieces of the puzzle were falling into place as I talked. Alex closed his eyes. 'Let me guess – you'd been drinking that night? Wanted to impress a girl? Probably went joyriding in one of your father's fancy cars—'

'Please, Nina—'

'What?' I demanded. I wasn't about to let him get away with it. 'Am I wrong? Because if so, do put me right.'

Finally he looked up at me. But he didn't attempt to speak. As I'd suspected, there was nothing he could say in his defence.

I looked at my mother. Suddenly it all began to make sense. This was why she had fallen out with Duncan Noble and refused to accept any more help from him – because she'd realised it was blood money. This was the root of her drinking all those years. For the first time in a long while I felt like I understood. She'd been a victim of the Noble family conspiracy – unwillingly caught in a situation she shouldn't have had to deal with.

I would talk this out with her later. Right now, there were more pressing matters to confront.

I turned to Duncan Noble. He'd obviously known. That's why he'd stipulated that I shouldn't tell my mother that we were in touch. Something else occurred to me.

'Is this why you offered me a job?'

'It is.' In fairness to him, he didn't flinch. 'I wanted to help you out in any way I could.'

'You mean you were trying to ease your guilt.'

'Perhaps.'

At least he wasn't trying to deny anything. But there was something still bothering me. 'But why did you send me to Destination? When you knew I was likely to run into Alex?'

'Because I trusted Giles and wanted him to keep an eye on you.'

'So Giles knew, too?' I shook my head in disbelief. 'Anyone else? Because right now it seems like I'm the only one who was kept in the dark.'

Duncan at least had the grace to look ashamed. 'No, that's it.' He took a step towards me. 'Believe me, I knew this wasn't an ideal situation. But I didn't know what to do. So I told Giles to keep an eye on you, and asked Alex to stay away . . .'

He trailed off, and I knew the implication. Alex hadn't stayed away. He'd known exactly who I was, when we first spoke at Destination. What had he said? *You're the chauffeur's daughter, right?* He'd been told who I was – knew that he'd killed my father – and had still gone out of his way to get to know me.

I felt the bile rise in my throat as I turned to Alex.

'But you didn't stay away from me, did you? Quite the opposite in fact.'

He closed his eyes, 'Nina—' he began, but I cut him off.

'How could you do this? How could you let it go this far between us?' How could you let me fall in love with you? That's what I really wanted to know. 'Or was that half the thrill for you? Knowing that you'd seduced the daughter of the man you'd killed?'

He winced at that last word. I heard my mother gasp, and murmur my name, but I didn't care.

'Well?' I demanded. 'What was this – some kind of game to you?'

'Maybe it started off that way.' Alex's voice was surprisingly calm. 'I'd seen you that day in Dad's office. I'd gone over there to meet him, and he told me exactly who you were – and warned me to stay away from you. It made me want to get to know you – just to piss him off.'

'Jesus, Alex,' his father murmured.

But Alex just ignored him. 'I just planned to talk to you a few times – I knew Giles would report it back to my father. But you made it clear from the beginning how little you thought of me, so I gave up on you. Until that night when I saw you play poker. That was when I saw my way in.'

Thinking back over the events made me feel even more

like I was about to throw up. I couldn't get over how calculating Alex had been. 'And you didn't feel any qualms about using me as a pawn in your game with your father? A girl who lost her father because of you?'

'I didn't think of it that way.' He closed his eyes, and when he opened them they were filled with pain. 'All I cared about was getting my own back on my father. But then I got to know you—'

'No.' I was adamant. 'I don't want to hear it.' I wasn't interested in justifications. All I could think about was what he'd done – how he'd killed my father and got away with it.

'Nina, I'm sorry—'

'Sorry? That doesn't bring my father back, does it? Do you know how bad things have been for us over the years? Losing our home . . . my mother's drinking . . . not to mention both me and April growing up without a dad. And that's down to you.' I looked at the face of the man I'd thought I was falling in love with, and all I felt was disgust. 'God, I was right about you from the beginning. You're an irresponsible arsehole, and I was a fool ever to trust you.'

I turned and ran out. I couldn't stand to be in that room another second.

Alex followed me, calling my name. When I wouldn't stop, he moved in front of me, catching me by the shoulders.

'Nina, wait. We need to talk about this.'

I looked up at him. Tears coursed down my cheeks. I made no effort to stop them. Let him see what he'd done – the pain he'd caused.

'You want to *talk*?' I spat out the word. 'Why – what do you want to say? That it was a long time ago? That you were a different person? That you fell in love with me and realised the error of your ways?'

He didn't say anything. Clearly I'd already guessed how he'd planned to argue his case.

'Don't you get it? None of that matters. You killed my dad. You destroyed my family. And then you used me to get back at your own father. Nothing you say can change that. And I never want to speak to you again. Now at least have the decency to leave me alone.'

I broke from his grasp and hurried away. This time, thankfully, he didn't come after me. It was a good thing – because in that moment I never wanted to see him again.

When I got to the Tube station, I realised I wasn't sure where I wanted to go. I needed to be alone, and I wanted to think, and the best way I could do that was by walking.

I set off with no particular aim and in no specific direction. But I found myself crossing London. I walked along Kensington High Street, past groups of tourists and office workers on their Friday night out.

It took me three hours, but eventually I ended up back home. My mother was already there, sitting at the kitchen table in the semi–darkness, waiting for me. I was pleased to see she had a cup of tea in front of her. It had crossed my mind that a night like this might drive her back over the edge. I was going to make some caustic comment about her managing to stay off the sauce, but I didn't bother. It seemed churlish in the circumstances. For once, my mum and I were on the same side.

I slid into the seat opposite her.

'When did you figure it out?' I didn't need to clarify what I was talking about. There was only one thing on our minds tonight.

'It was about six months after his accident. Everything was a blur at first. I missed him so much.' Her eyes filled with tears at the memory. 'But then I started to pull myself together. Duncan Noble had always been a good employer, but there was something off about how much he was help-ing me. He was giving me money every month – thousands of pounds – and something didn't feel right about it. It felt like guilt rather than responsibility.'

'So it was blood money,' I said.

'Something like that.' She smiled ruefully. 'I went to Duncan with my suspicions. To be honest, even then I didn't put two and two together. I thought maybe there was something wrong with the car your father had been driving – that it hadn't been properly serviced or something. But Duncan broke down and told me everything.'

'And that's why you didn't want anything to do with him after that.'

'Yes. I didn't know what else to do. By then, there were no marks on the car. No proof of what had gone on.'

'Which was why you couldn't go to the police, either,' I filled in. I shook my head in disgust.

'It changed everything, you know.' My mother spoke in a low voice. I looked over at her. The moonlight peeked through the window and caught the silver tears on her cheek. 'Once I knew what had really happened . . . and that I couldn't bring it to light . . . I felt like I'd betrayed your father. Like somehow I was part of the conspiracy.'

As she said that, a memory caught hold. Early on, after my father's death, she'd been sad, but she'd still been our mother – she'd still looked after us. But it was six months after his death that she'd fallen apart – and that the drinking had started.

'Is that why you began drinking?'

She gave a rueful smile. 'It was stupid, I know. And it hurt you and April so much. But it was my way of dulling the pain. Just for a little while at least.'

In that moment I began to understand her a bit more. It must have been a terrible burden to carry – knowing that

Beautiful Liar

someone you loved hadn't got the justice they deserved. And then feeling like you'd been given money to cover up the true circumstances of their death. I could only begin to imagine how alone she must have felt.

We sat quietly for a while. It was me who finally broke the silence.

'Well, what do we do now? Do we go to the police?'

She looked at me. 'We could. But Alex would probably go to jail. Do you really want that?'

I thought about it for a moment. I honestly didn't know how I felt. How was it possible to love and hate someone so much? I could go to the police and destroy his life. But would it make me feel any better? And would it bring my father back?

It was funny. I'd always known Alex would break my heart. I just hadn't thought it would be like this.

My mother was studying me closely.

'You love him, don't you?' she said.

'I did.' It was an honest answer.

'And now?'

'How can I after what he's done?'

Tears blurred my eyes. I wasn't even aware of just how hard I was crying until I heard the scrape of my mum's chair. A second later, she was kneeling down next to me, folding me into her arms.

'Oh, poppet,' she said, and I could hear the anguish in her

voice. It matched my own. 'This isn't fair, is it? None of it is fair.'

I was crying too hard to answer. She held me close, stroking my hair and murmuring reassurances as I sobbed against her. It was the first time for years that she'd taken care of me. And right now, I was happy to let her.

Chapter 27

The next couple of days passed in a blur. Jas came back from Paris, and called me to say that she was engaged. That at least Alex hadn't lied about – Hugh had told him that he was thinking of proposing to Jas. Despite my warning her about Hugh, he'd actually decided to make a very formal and very public commitment to her.

I was genuinely pleased for Jas, and I tried not to let her know that anything was wrong, not wanting to ruin her moment. I thought I'd been doing a good job, until she said, 'So out with it.'

'With what?'

'With whatever's going on between you and Alex.' I froze, shocked that she'd seen through me so easily. 'And don't try to pretend there's nothing wrong,' she said quickly, anticipating exactly what I was going to do. 'I know full well that something's up. Every time

I've mentioned his name, you've been conspicuously silent.'

I thought about it for a second, and decided I might as well get it out of the way now. 'We've broken up. And I don't want to talk about it.'

Jas swore under her breath. 'Let me guess – he cheated on you, the rotten bastard.'

It was a fair guess, and I didn't want to deny it and risk her prying further, so I just said, 'It's over. That's all I'm saying.' That left it sufficiently ambiguous for Jas to draw her own conclusions.

'Oh, babes.' Her heartfelt sigh said everything. 'I can't believe it. I know Alex could always be a bit wild, but I genuinely thought he'd changed for you. I guess what they say about a leopard and its spots is right, eh?'

I agreed that it was, and then switched the conversation back to her wedding plans. She seemed to get the message that I wanted to talk about something else, and resumed gushing about dresses and venues and guest lists. I listened carefully, trying to match her enthusiasm, and hoping that it would fill the hollow feeling in my stomach.

'Nina?' I was leaving work the following evening when I heard Alex's voice. I did a double-take when I saw him. He looked terrible – he was pale and unshaven, his eyes red and hollow. He seemed thinner too, his usually strapping body a little hunched, as though he hadn't eaten. He stood a safe distance away from me, as though he wasn't sure how I'd react to him being there. 'Can we talk?'

It was three days since I'd found out. He'd called and left dozens of messages on my phone, none of which I'd returned. But I'd known we'd have to discuss everything at some point. Now seemed as good a time as any.

'Fine,' I said. 'But I don't have long.'

He wanted to go to a coffee shop, but I knew we wouldn't be able to talk properly with people around, so I suggested a place I knew would be empty – a nearby churchyard.

It was the dead of winter, and it was dark and cold there. Even with my gloves on, my fingers were numb. I jammed my hands into my pockets as we perched on a low wall. I could feel the cold brickwork through my jeans, but I refused to show any discomfort. Given the weather, at least our meeting would be brief.

Alex looked exhausted, and I guessed he hadn't slept well since the news had come out. Well, that made two of us.

'So what do you want to say?' I said.

'Just that I'm sorry.' He waited a beat. 'And I miss you.'

I shook my head in disgust, and looked away. I couldn't help noticing how the trees were stripped bare and the leaves were mush on the ground. Patches of green moss had formed on the grey headstones. The place looked as desolate as I felt.

'I just don't understand why you did it,' I said finally.

Alex sighed. 'I didn't realise how drunk I was that night. I knew the roads well. No one else used them. I didn't think—'

'No. I'm not talking about the night of the accident. I'm saying that I don't understand how you could pursue me like that. How you could sleep with me.'

'It's because I fell in love with you.'

'Oh, please.' I scoffed at the answer. 'You've already told me the only reason you went after me was to get revenge on your father.'

'At first, yes. You were this annoying, sanctimonious goody two-shoes, who the father I detested had warned me to stay away from. But then I got to know you. And I fell in love with how strong and self-reliant you were; how you were clever and witty and resourceful; how you were so passionate about saving your sister. You weren't like any girl I'd ever met.'

I couldn't say anything to that. It was everything I'd wanted to hear from a guy – but just not from him, not now after I knew what he'd done.

'Like I told you before, after that night at Rexley, I tried to stay away from you. But it was too late by then. I was already too far gone. I wanted you, and I convinced myself that meant more than everything that had happened in the past. My feelings for you took over any sense of logic.'

I thought about how he'd helped me anonymously with the flat and job. When I'd confronted him, he'd tried to dismiss me at first, but I'd pushed him into admitting his feelings. Still, I wasn't the one who should feel bad here. 'And you think that makes it all right? You think I should just forgive you?'

'No! Of course not. I'm just trying to explain—'

'There's nothing to explain.' I kept my voice deliberately flat and unemotional. Otherwise, I would have broken down. 'You were joyriding drunk in a car that killed my father. What more is there to say?'

He was silent for a moment, and then said, 'Just that I've changed. These past few months, getting to know you, made me want to be a better person. I love you. And I want to put things right between us. Whatever it takes.' He shook his head, as though trying to work out how to prove to me that he was sincere. 'I'll give up drinking. There'll be no more parties. I'll get a proper job.' His voice had taken on a tinge of desperation. 'Whatever it takes to prove to you that you can trust me.'

I hadn't expected the rush of tears, or the tightening of my throat. I'd wanted to stay angry with him, because it was the easiest way to stop myself from feeling so hurt and bereft. The problem was, I still loved him – even the knowledge of what he'd done couldn't take that away. But I also knew there was no way I could ever be with him now.

And I think deep down he knew that, too.

We stared at each other for a long moment, the weight of what we felt for each other hanging between us. Alex must have mistaken my silence for me thawing, because he took a step towards me. He didn't attempt to touch me, but he was so close that I could feel the heat coming from his body.

He looked at me with undisguised hunger.

'I miss you,' he said.

'I miss you, too.'

I genuinely did. Now that my anger had subsided, I could remember how much he meant to me.

'Nina—'

His hand came up to touch my cheek. I could tell he was about to bend his head to kiss me, and part of me wanted to let him. But I still couldn't bring myself to be with him. It would feel like a betrayal of my father – my family. But most of all, of myself. Because whatever he said, there was no way I could ever trust him again.

Maybe I could have forgiven the sixteen-year-old boy who'd recklessly killed my father, but not the twenty-two-year-old man who'd deceived me for all those months – who had made me fall in love with him even though he must have known the truth would come out one day.

I stepped away from Alex, out of his reach. 'I can't do

this. I'm sorry, but I just can't. So please, I'm begging you, let me go. Don't make this any harder than it already is.'

I turned and hurried away. This time, he didn't follow.

My mother was waiting on the sofa for me when I got home. I'd called her briefly to tell her that I was going to talk to Alex, but I'd been too upset after our conversation to let her know how it had gone.

'So you saw him then?' she said.

I nodded.

'How was that?' I shrugged, and she gave a rueful smile. 'That bad, huh?'

She patted the sofa next to her. I went to her without hesitation.

I'd done a lot of thinking in the last couple of days. I knew I needed to put Alex from my mind and move on with my life. At first, I'd felt vengeful. I'd talked again and again about going to the police – always to my mother, because she was the only one who knew what was going on. She didn't tell me not to – she just listened, and said that it was my decision to make.

But now that I'd fully calmed down, I knew I couldn't go through with it. It felt like it would stir up too much unhappiness. It wasn't so much Alex I was protecting as April. She'd made her peace with our father's death. Why start stirring things up now?

'I'm going to let it go,' I told my mother. That was the one good thing to come out of all of this – we were much closer. I finally understood what had driven her to the bottle all these years, and now that she had someone to share the burden of knowledge with, she seemed more content, too.

'And what does that mean for the two of you?'

I frowned. 'Nothing! I couldn't stand to be with him again after that.'

She sighed. 'Nina, I saw the way you two were with each other. It's hard to find someone you feel that way about. You're lucky if that comes along once in your life-time. And try to remember he's a different person now. He isn't the stupid boy he once was. He would never do the same thing again—'

'So that makes it all right? What he did to Dad?'

'I'm not saying that—'

'You honestly think I should forgive him?' There was rank disbelief in my voice. 'How can you even consider that?'

She sighed. 'Because these things are never black and white. You need to have empathy for other people. And forgiveness, too. You don't know what the circumstances were—'

'I can guess. He was drunk and stupid.'

'And very young, don't forget. He's had to live with what he did. That must have been hard.'

'Yeah. So hard that he drank and partied his way through life for the next six years. And then tricked me into going out with him.' The bitterness in my voice took even me by surprise. I shook my head, needing to say what I felt. 'You don't seem to get it. Even if I could get over what he did to Dad six years ago, I can't forgive him for what he's done to me these past few months. He lied to me. He tricked me. And I hate him for that.'

Mum winced. She reached out and covered my hand with her own.

'Try not to be angry, sweetheart. Don't let this ruin any more of your life than it already has. I think you'll feel better if you're able to find a way to forgive Alex, and try to understand this from his point of view. You aren't the only one hurting.'

I could see what she meant. I knew I could be judgemental and unforgiving. I'd held a grudge against my mother for years, but now that I understood why she'd turned to alcohol, I'd been able to forgive her.

But that would never happen with Alex. I couldn't get past what he'd done.

Chapter 28

Six months later . . .

I tried to move on with my life. I concentrated on work and my family. April was doing well at school, and seemed to have put the foster home experience behind her. She asked me a couple of times about what had happened to Alex, but after a while she got the hint that I didn't want to talk about it.

Thankfully I was able to avoid seeing Alex. If I'd still been working at Destination, it would have been painful seeing him regularly. To my surprise, he'd also honoured my wishes, and not tried to contact me. I'd been expecting drunken phone calls, and pleas to take him back, but to my relief I heard nothing.

But I knew inevitably at some point we'd run into each other, especially with the date of Jas and Hugh's wedding coming up. I was chief bridesmaid and he was best man – there was no way we'd be able to avoid each other.

Alarm bells should have started ringing when I tried to plan the hen night. I kept asking Jas what she wanted to do, and she was strangely evasive. Finally, six weeks before the wedding, she took me out to a little coffee shop, and broke it to me that she and Hugh wanted a joint hen and stag night – at Destination, where they'd first met.

'I'll understand if you don't want to come,' she said. 'I know it's not going to be easy, with Alex and everything . . .'

I was touched by her selflessness. She still didn't know the reason why we'd broken up, but she obviously sensed it was something bad enough to still be painful.

'Don't be silly.' I forced a smile. 'Of course I'll be there. I'm going to have to see him at the rehearsal dinner and the wedding anyway. I might as well get it over with.'

To my surprise, Jas didn't look as pleased by my decision as I'd expected her to be. 'That's great.' She dropped a sugar cube into her coffee, and stirred it slowly. 'I'm really pleased you'll be there . . .'

'But?' I prompted.

She sighed, and put down her spoon, pushing her coffee away untouched. 'But I have to warn you about Alex.' She paused for a beat. 'He won't be there alone.'

I let out a harsh laugh. 'That's hardly a surprise. I fully expected him to be there with an entourage of beautiful models, no doubt drunk and high, too. Honestly, Jas – I'm not that naïve!'

But she was shaking her head. 'No, that's not it at all.' She sighed again, and I could tell how difficult she was finding it. 'I mean, at first, after you guys broke up, that's what me and Hugh expected, too. We were waiting for him to go off the rails. But he didn't. Don't get me wrong,' she said quickly. 'He was devastated, spent a lot of time at our place, talking to Hugh. Slept on our couch for a couple of weeks.' She rolled her eyes. 'It kind of got a bit boring, actually. But he held it together – didn't slip back into his old ways.'

This was all news to me. Jas and I had studiously avoided talking about Alex these past months. Of course, I knew she must have been seeing him, through Hugh, but I'd never asked about him. I hadn't wanted to know. Now I did.

'So what are you saying?'

Jas sat back in her chair. 'I'm saying he's cleaned up his act. He's stopped partying and sleeping around, and thrown himself into work. He's setting up his own business. Opening a hotel.'

I didn't say anything at first. I'd fully expected him to have fallen back into his old ways, and I'd prepared myself for that. I wasn't sure how I was supposed to respond to the news. 'Well, that's good, isn't it?' I tried to sound nonchalant. Somehow, from the way Jas was acting, I had a nasty feeling that there was going to be a catch to all this.

'Yes, it is,' she said carefully, avoiding my eyes.

I was trying to work out what she wasn't telling me. Then I got it. 'So who's he bringing along?'

She looked up at me then. 'She's called Helen. She's a lawyer. Very nice and intelligent. They've only been seeing each other for the past couple of months—'

'But for someone who never had a girlfriend before, that's kind of a long time to be monogamous.'

Jas didn't bother to answer. The silence stretched out. 'So,' she said finally. 'I'll understand if you don't want to come.'

I forced a laugh. I hated that she'd obviously been so worried about having this conversation with me. It wasn't fair to ruin any part of Jas's wedding with my drama. 'Don't be silly! Of course I'm still coming. We've got to see each other at some point. It might as well be then.'

Jas looked so relieved I thought she might cry. 'Oh, Nina, that's great news. You can't miss out because of him. You come along, put on something sexy and show him what he's missing out on!'

I shook my head. That was the last thing I'd be doing. It would take me all my time to get through the evening. But it would be worth the pain of seeing Alex if my being there made Jas happy.

When the night of the joint stag and hen night came round, and I was getting ready, I thought about Jas's advice to look my best, and make Alex see what he was missing out on. It wasn't really my style. Instead, I dressed like I normally did, in dark jeans and a tank top, and my biker boots. It was my signature tough-girl look.

April got excited when she heard I was going out to a nightclub in a swanky part of London, and she insisted on doing my hair and make-up. The result was my dark hair hung tousled around my face, and she emphasised my eyes with mascara and eyeliner, and my lips with my favourite black-cherry lipstick. At least it made me look like I'd made some effort.

I walked into Destination and felt immediately out of place. The other girls were all in short, sheath-like dresses and strappy heels. It made me realise that I had never fitted into that world.

I was contemplating turning round and heading back out, but before I could, Jas spotted me. She squealed my name, and ran over and hugged me to her.

'I'm so glad you came.' She pulled away and glanced round the room. 'I haven't seen him yet.' She didn't need to elaborate on who she was talking about.

That should have made me feel relieved, but for some reason I felt disappointed.

If Jas noticed my reaction, she didn't show it. Instead, she grabbed my hand and dragged me towards the bar. 'Come on. Let's get you a drink.'

I wanted a beer, but Jas wouldn't hear of it. Instead, I watched in horror as the bartender poured pink liquid from a cocktail shaker into a martini glass, and handed it to me.

Hugh came up to us as we stood at the bar.

'Thanks for being here, Nina.' He kissed my cheek. 'And sorry to interrupt, but I need to grab my fiancée for a moment.'

'No problem,' I said, and watched as he led Jas away.

I took a sip of my drink and pulled a face. It was far too sweet for me. I really would have preferred a beer, but the bartender had already moved off, and there was too big a crowd to bother waiting to be served.

I moved off and found a corner to lurk in. There was no one around I particularly felt like talking to. The guests were mostly Hugh's friends so far. A group of people who Jas and I had worked with were meant to be turning up later – they had the night off – but until then it was just me and the posh crowd.

I'd been standing there for a few minutes, sipping at my drink, when Alex walked in. For a moment, it felt like I couldn't breathe. It was more of a shock than I'd expected, seeing him after all this time. He looked good – much better than that last time I'd seen him in the churchyard. His dark hair was a little shorter, exposing more of his strong bone structure, and he'd dressed up for the occasion, in a black suit and shirt.

My attention quickly moved from him to the girl on his arm – Helen, the lawyer. She was an attractive woman – model-tall and slim, with poker-straight brown hair hanging to her shoulders. In a tailored black dress and heels, she looked confident and classy. Not like any of the girls I'd seen him with before.

My gaze moved back to Alex. I knew I should stop staring, but I couldn't help it. He must have felt my eyes on him, because he turned. A look of shock crossed his face when he saw me – then a second later he had it under control. I watched him turn to his date, and murmur something. She gave him a quick kiss on the cheek, and walked to the bar.

Then Alex turned in my direction.

I took a big glug of my cocktail as he made his way over, but it did nothing to calm my nerves. I could have probably drunk the bar dry and I'd still be freaking out.

And then he was there, all six foot two of him, a couple of feet away from me. I suspected he wasn't sure what kind of reception he'd get.

'Nina?' His eyes were soft, his voice respectful. 'It's good to see you.'

There was a formality to his words, and I could guess why. Like me, he probably had no desire for us to meet and be reminded of our painful past. But also like me, he probably felt obliged to be there for the sake of his friend. The only reason he'd come over, I thought, was because he wanted to make sure there wasn't going to be a big blow-up to spoil the wedding.

I wanted to show him that I had no intention of creating a scene, so I gave a small nod. 'It's good to see you, too.' My tone matched his own. 'You look well.'

'You too.'

We lapsed into silence then. Feeling impossibly uncomfortable, I took a long sip of my cocktail.

Alex looked at my glass and raised an eyebrow.

'What the hell are you drinking?'

I rolled my eyes. 'Some concoction Jas came up with.' I nodded at a beer bottle on a nearby table. 'Trust me – I would rather be drinking that.'

We both smiled briefly. Then catching ourselves, we looked away.

'I could get you another drink if you like,' Alex said.

'Thanks, but I'm fine.' I tried to think of something to say – so we could have the kind of conversation acquaintances would. 'I heard you're opening a hotel.'

He nodded solemnly. 'Just a boutique. It's been harder than I thought, getting it all sorted out, but I'm enjoying it.'

Thankfully, before I had to come up with any other conversation pieces, his date appeared, carrying two flutes of champagne. Alex made the introductions. Fortunately, Helen didn't seem aware of any awkwardness, and we spent five minutes talking about the upcoming wedding, before I finally made my excuses about needing to go and circulate.

Helen smiled at me. As Jas had said, she did seem lovely. 'Well, it was great to meet you, Nina.' She leaned down and kissed me on both cheeks, then turned to Alex, clearly expecting him to do the same. He hesitated for just a moment and then took a step towards me. I saw his frown and the question in his eyes – he wanted to make sure it was all right with me. I gave an imperceptible nod.

I didn't dare breathe as his hands rested lightly on my shoulders, and I closed my eyes as his lips brushed my cheeks. Then a second later it was over, and he was drawing away. I looked up to see his arm encircling Helen's waist.

As they walked away, I finally exhaled.

Luckily, that was the time my friends who were staff at Destination chose to arrive. I went over to join them, and studiously avoided looking at Alex for the rest of the evening.

I stayed for a polite two hours before saying my goodnights. I was on my way out, heading for the floating glass staircase, when Tori stepped in front of me. She looked stunning as always, in a beautiful sequinned dress and sky-high heels.

'Look, I'm really not in the mood,' I said, pushing past her.

'Wait. Please.' She had to shout to be heard over the music. 'This'll just take a minute.'

Something in her voice made me stop and turn round. 'What is it?' I said in a tone that suggested she ought to make it quick.

She hesitated for a second, and then said, 'I wanted to say that I was really sorry to hear about you and Alex.'

It was pretty much the last thing I'd been expecting to come out of her mouth, but I managed to cover my surprise. 'Really? Well, thanks for the condolences. It means a lot.'

She winced at the sarcasm in my voice, but powered on anyway. 'Can I ask you – why did you break up?'

'I really don't want to talk about it.'

This was clearly a waste of my time, so I turned to go.

'Did it have something to do with a car crash?'

I whipped round. The last thing I needed was what I'd found out being passed around like gossip.

'What do you know about that?'

'Nothing! I swear!' She held up her hands in defence. 'I just overheard Giles and Alex arguing . . .'

I chewed at the inside of my mouth. I didn't want her to start pressing for details.

'Well, it's got nothing to do with you. So don't start interfering where you don't belong.'

I left her open-mouthed at the harshness of my words,

and I hurried towards the exit. Coming here tonight had clearly been a mistake, and one I wasn't about to repeat. Too many memories had been dredged up. I needed to keep as far away from these people as possible.

Chapter 29

Standing in the bedroom of one of Claridge's finest suites, I finished lacing up the bodice of Jas's wedding dress, and stood back to assess my handiwork. The ribbons crisscrossed in perfect symmetry, down to the bow I'd tied at the end. I'd done a good job – which was hardly surprising, given that I'd been forced to practise for hours in the wedding-dress shop until I could get it exactly how Jas wanted. She was determined that everything should be perfect on her wedding day.

Now she twisted impatiently, trying to look over her shoulder to see the result.

'How does it look?' My usually laid-back friend sounded worried.

'See for yourself.' I lifted the full-length, free-standing mirror that the Claridge's wedding planner had helpfully suggested having sent up. Placed directly behind Jas, who was looking into the mirrored wall, it enabled my friend to see what she looked like from all angles.

'Oh!' She clapped her hands to her cheeks as she surveyed the back of the bodice. 'You've done a brilliant job!' She turned to me. 'Well, I guess that's it then. I'm ready to get married!'

With that, her eyes started to water.

'No, no. Don't cry,' I hushed, pushing the mirror to one side and reaching for a tissue. 'You don't want to ruin your make-up.'

I'd never really seen myself as chief-bridesmaid material – especially not for a big society wedding – but I seemed to be doing a better job than I'd imagined.

'There.' I rested my hands on Jas's bare arms. 'No more crying until the church now. We've spent hours getting you to look this good, and I want everyone to see you like this.'

I wasn't lying about how good she looked. Jas really was the perfect fairy-tale bride. She'd said from the beginning that she wanted a traditional wedding, and that's exactly what she'd got. She'd opted for a Cinderella-style dress, made out of the finest ivory silk, and the huge skirt and cinched-in waist gave her the perfect figure. Her beautiful black hair had been styled into big curls, and threaded through with tiny white flowers. Her make-up was subtle and fresh, and everything about her seemed youthful and sparkly – like she was a young woman embarking on a big adventure.

My outfit wasn't too shabby, either. In her desire to keep everything classic, Jas had stuck to a simple colour scheme of whites, creams and a touch of gold. The bridesmaids' dresses were a flattering empire-line, in a pale champagne – pretty enough, while in no danger of outshining the bride's. The soft shade also perfectly complemented my olive skin. My short, dark hair had been blow-dried silky straight, and garlanded with cream roses.

It was set to be the wedding of the year, with over two hundred guests in attendance. If there had been any concern that the occasion might cause a scandal – Hugh Forbes marrying a former stripper – it certainly hadn't been reflected in the planning. This wedding would be on everyone's radar.

We went through to the lounge area of the suite, where the rest of the bridal party were waiting for us.

Jas – being the forgiving soul that she was – had contacted her mother after the engagement. With her mum's boyfriend a thing of the past, they'd reconnected, and now three of her cousins were the other bridesmaids, and her uncle – her mother's older brother – was giving her away. While I wasn't personally convinced that these people were ever going to be there for Jas, she seemed happy that they were there to celebrate with her, so I kept my counsel.

Everyone raved about how beautiful Jas looked, then it was time to leave. A fleet of Rolls-Royce Phantoms had been hired to transport the wedding party. The ceremony was set to take place at St James's Church in Paddington, a short drive away. That had been another surprise to me – that Jas had opted for a church rather than a civil ceremony. But as we pulled up outside St James's, I could see why she'd wanted to be married there. It was exactly as you'd imagine a church to be – with its soaring spire, gnarled wooden door and elegant grey stonework.

When we went in, I was entranced by the beautiful interior – the wooden pews, and the huge stained-glass window above the altar, impossible to miss.

Jas had opted to make her entrance in the traditional way – the bride first on the arm of the person giving her away, followed by her bridesmaids. My heart started beating faster as I walked down the aisle behind her and her uncle. Familiar faces popped out at me from the congregation, and I spotted Tori and then Giles sitting on the groom's side. But it wasn't them I was nervous about seeing again – it was Alex.

Since the joint stag and hen do, I'd run into him a couple of times at meetings about arrangements for the wedding and the wedding rehearsal dinner. Again we'd been scrupulously polite to each other, though I couldn't deny that seeing him had affected me.

I knew that as best man he'd be standing next to the groom, so I kept my eyes on Jas's cascade of hair, carefully avoiding looking at him in case it made me falter in my step. It was only once we were at the front of the church, and I'd taken Jas's bouquet of white avalanche roses from her, and the Vicar had begun his opening remarks welcoming the congregation, that I dared to look at Alex.

He was wearing a traditional morning suit, with a cravat and handkerchief to match the champagne colour of our bridesmaids' dresses. He seemed surprisingly at ease in the formal dress, his broad shoulders carrying off the tailored look. His dark hair was slicked back for the day, and his face was clean-shaven.

He must have felt me staring, because his gaze moved from the Vicar to me. Our eyes met for the briefest of moments, and then I looked away. It took all my willpower to keep my focus on the bride and groom for the remainder of the ceremony.

Jas had opted to hold the reception in Claridge's elegant art deco ballroom, with its marble floors and mirrored walls. I needn't have worried about having to speak to Alex during drinks and dinner – we were both too busy in our respective duties, and always surrounded by other people so we didn't have a chance to be alone.

Coffee and petits fours were served in the reception area while the dinner tables were being cleared, and then we returned to the ballroom, which had been transformed.

The tables had been moved back to make room for a mirrored dance floor. A four-piece orchestra was on a raised dais where the top table had been. As the lights dimmed, all the guests gathered into a circle, and Jas and Hugh took to the floor.

Jas had told me that she was going with a traditional waltz for the first dance. As 'Moon River' started, Hugh took her in his arms and swept her around the dance floor, with an expertise that surprised me – and, from the joyous look of surprise on Jas's face, her too.

I joined in the round of applause like everyone else. Then I felt a tap on my shoulder. I turned to see the photographer's assistant, a young, birdlike brunette, who was super-organised. When I saw Alex standing beside her, I began to get a bad feeling, which wasn't made any better by the apologetic look on his face.

'We need a picture of you two dancing,' she said bluntly.

'Oh, no—' I began, but she held up her hand to cut me off.

'Look.' She nodded towards Alex. 'Lover-boy here has already tried to make excuses. Now, I get that you two have some issue with each other. Bad break-up, right?' She laughed at the astonished looks on our faces. 'Part of being good at this job is being able to read people. All I would say to you both is, you don't have to do this if you don't want to. I'm not going to force you to dance together. But try to remember this day isn't about you. This is for your friends.'

She gave us a moment for her words to sink in, before saying, 'So . . . what's it going to be?'

Alex and I looked at each other. After that little lecture, there was no way either of us could object without feeling childish. Alex held out his arm to me. I hesitated for just a second before taking it. A jolt of electricity passed through me as we touched, and I let out an involuntary gasp. But if Alex noticed my reaction, he chose not to show it.

'Don't worry,' he said, as he led me onto the dance floor. 'Just a couple of minutes and this will all be over.'

Before I could answer, he whirled me round to face him. Then he assumed the classic ballroom dancer's positioning, his left hand enclosing mine, while his right rested just below my shoulder blade, forming a firm frame. Without a word, he began to lead me expertly round the floor, perfectly in time to the music. I'd never waltzed before, but somehow I was moving effortlessly, as though I'd been doing this all my life – the sign of a strong male lead.

I'd planned not to speak during the dance – it had seemed wisest not to. But it was hard not to comment on his skill.

'You know how to waltz?'

A smile touched his lips, probably at the surprise in my voice. 'That's down to Hugh. He insisted on all the grooms-men taking lessons.'

I looked around, and saw that the other groomsmen and bridesmaids were moving expertly across the floor, in a perfect swirl of colours. It looked as coordinated as a scene from a movie.

'It doesn't seem like his style,' I couldn't help saying.

Alex shrugged his large shoulders. 'Maybe not. But he knew Jas would love it, and he wanted this to be her perfect day.'

Even the cynic in me had to admit that it was a nice thing to have done. I'd been wrong about Hugh – he obviously would do anything to make Jas happy.

It was then that I remembered something I'd noticed earlier. 'So where's Helen?'

'Not here.' Alex paused, and I felt my heart speed up. 'We broke up.'

'Oh.' I forced my voice to sound nonchalant. 'That's a shame. She seemed nice.'

'She is.' Alex's eyes flicked over to me. 'But she isn't you.'

The music stopped, which would have been my perfect chance to make my excuses and exit the floor. But I made no move to leave. The orchestra struck up with a slower number, which I recognised as 'What A Wonderful World'. With the change of pace, Alex instinctively dropped the formal ballroom positioning, which required us to keep a distance, and instead drew me closer to him, his left hand trailing down to the small of my back as his right caressed the nape of my neck, taking me into his embrace so I was pressed up against his strong, hard body.

I threaded my arms around his neck, and rested my head against his firm chest. My eyes fluttered closed, and I sighed contentedly against him.

Alex's arms tightened around me, and he buried his face in my hair.

'So help me, I still love you, Nina,' he murmured against my ear.

'I still love you, too.'

I felt him stiffen against me. I don't think he'd been expecting a response like that from me. But the truth was, I did miss him. He meant so much to me. I suppose his betrayal wouldn't have hurt me so deeply otherwise.

The number was coming to an end. I think we both sensed that if we had anything to say, it needed to be said now.

Alex pulled away from me a little and looked directly into my eyes. 'I meant what I said all those months ago. I know I made mistakes in the past, and perhaps they're too big for you to ever forgive me. But I'm trying to change, Nina. I want to change – for you.'

I could see the sincerity in his ice-blue eyes. I'd been adamant that I'd never be able to see a future for us – never be able to trust him again after the way he'd deceived me. But now, six months later, knowing that he was trying to turn his life around, and hadn't fallen back into his old ways, I could see that he wasn't the same boy who'd recklessly killed my father; neither was he the same man who'd set out to use me as a way to spite his father. He'd said that he'd changed – but for the first time ever, I was inclined to believe him.

My heartbeat sped up as I made my decision.

I glanced around the room. 'We can't talk about this here. It's not the time . . .'

'Then say you'll meet me.' He spoke with urgency, as though he knew this might be our last chance to speak privately. 'At half twelve, once this is all over. We can go somewhere . . . just to talk. What do you say?'

'Yes.' I answered without hesitation, and with a breathless quality to my voice that surprised me. 'I'll meet you.'

A smile spread across his features. 'Twelve thirty, then. In the entrance hall.'

Just then, the band played the final chords, and the room burst into applause. Before we could say another word, Hugh's mother appeared by Alex's side, asking for the next dance with him. He squeezed my hand one last time, and then he was spirited away, leaving me by myself on the edge of the dance floor.

I gazed after him, already calculating how long it was until midnight. I was surprised at just how excited I was by the prospect of being alone with him again.

Chapter 30

The rest of the evening seemed to drag. The reception was due to end at midnight, and at a quarter to, exactly on schedule, the bride and groom departed up to their suite. All the guests gathered to watch them go up, Jas pausing on the sweeping stairway to throw her bouquet.

As we all gave the newly-weds one last round of applause, I looked for Alex, but I couldn't see him anywhere. I frowned a little, puzzled by his non-appearance, as I'd assumed he'd have to be there as part of his best-man duties. But I didn't have time to give it much more thought. I was caught up in a flurry of goodbyes, fulfilling the chief-bridesmaid duties Jas had placed on me, making sure to see everyone into taxis and ensuring that any gifts were stored safely for her to see the next morning.

By a quarter past twelve, most people were gone, apart from a few of Hugh's friends, who'd gathered in the bar for a final round of drinks. At twenty-five past, I was standing in the entrance, as Alex had instructed. By twenty to one, he still hadn't turned up, and he didn't appear to be answering his phone. The happiness I'd felt earlier had begun to turn to unease.

'You waiting for someone?'

I looked up and saw Giles.

'It's Alex. He said he'd meet me here ten minutes ago.'

Something in Giles's expression put me on alert.

'What is it?' I could see him hesitating, and guessed he was going to try to evade the question. 'Come on. Tell me. Do you know where Alex is?'

He glanced around, to check who was listening. 'I saw him going upstairs about an hour ago . . .'

'Who with?' The uncomfortable look on Giles's face didn't deter me. 'Giles. Tell me – who was he with?'

'He was with Tori. I think she had some coke with her . . .' I drifted off into a daze. How could he do this to me again? 'Nina? Nina, are you all right? Can I give you a lift somewhere?'

All I wanted right then was to get out of there. 'Yes.' My voice sounded hollow and distant, even to my own ears. 'A lift home would be great, thanks.'

Outside, the valet brought his car around – the dark grey Jaguar. As we got into the car, I gave Giles my address.

He clearly sensed I was in no mood to talk, so we drove along in silence for a while. I stared out of the window, trying to focus on the activity on the streets – anything other than what had just happened. But I couldn't. Something was niggling at me. I couldn't put my finger on it, but something about this just didn't feel right. I didn't care what Giles said – I really didn't believe Alex would stand me up like that. I remembered the way he had held me and spoken to me on the dance floor. The tenderness and yearning I'd felt had been genuine, I was sure of it – there was no way the man who had spoken so convincingly about loving me and wanting to change would have suddenly gone off to get high and get laid. In that moment, I knew without doubt that he wouldn't do that to me.

'I want to go back,' I said suddenly.

Giles's eyes flicked over to me. 'Why?' His voice was guarded. 'Have you forgotten something?'

'No. I just want to speak to Alex – find out what's going on for myself.'

'I really don't think that's a good idea—' Giles began.

As if on cue, my phone started to ring. I opened my bag and looked at the display.

'It's Alex,' I said.

But just as I was about to answer the call, Giles shouted, 'Don't!' Shocked, I looked over at him, and he said in a calmer voice, 'Please, Nina. Don't answer that!'

'Why not?'

'Because I don't want you to.'

Before I could argue back, he snatched the phone from my hand and dropped it on the floor of the car.

'What the hell—?' I stared at Giles in disbelief. 'What's going on?'

He shook his head. 'I'm sorry, Nina. I can't have you talking to Alex at the moment. I just need a little while to sort things out—'

He seemed to be babbling – or at least his words made no sense to me.

'I don't understand. You don't want me talking to Alex? Why not?'

His eyes flashed over to me, and I could see fear there. I took in the way his hands were gripping the steering wheel, so tight that his knuckles had turned white. Something was very, very wrong . . .

I tried to slot the pieces together. Giles had lied about Alex standing me up, and he'd stopped me from talking to his brother too. Whatever was going on, he obviously wanted to keep me away from Alex. But why? What was so important?

Next to me, Giles was still rambling on. 'It was so awful about your father. I lost my mother when I was young, so I know how it feels. That shouldn't have happened to your father, though. It wasn't fair. I did feel for you and your family—'

My father? The turn in the conversation confused me. Why was he talking about my father?

'Giles, what're you saying?' I tried again. 'You're not making any sense.'

But he didn't seem to be listening. 'I shouldn't have taken the car that night. Then none of this would've happened.' He banged his fist against the steering wheel. 'I've ruined your life, and Alex's, too. It's all my fault.'

It took me a second to process that. And then, suddenly, everything started to fall into place.

'Oh God.' I clasped a hand to my mouth, feeling sick.

Giles glanced over at me. 'Nina?' His voice was nervous as he said my name.

'It was you, wasn't it?' My voice sounded hollow, almost disembodied. 'You were the one driving the car that killed my father – not Alex.'

He closed his eyes briefly. 'Yes,' he said finally, and I may have been imagining it, but he almost sounded relieved. 'You're right. I was driving that night. I was the one who killed your father.'

Chapter 31

I looked at Giles. I was still trying hard to digest the fact that he was the one who'd been behind the wheel that night.

'But why does everyone think it was Alex? I don't under-stand.' I'd broken up with Alex; I'd spent time hating him. And he'd just let me. It made no sense. Why hadn't he told anyone the truth? 'What the hell happened that night?' When he didn't answer, I said, 'Giles, please. You need to tell me this. You owe me the truth at least.'

I was aware that Giles had made a U-turn, and we were now driving away from my flat. But I wasn't able to digest the significance. There were far more pressing concerns.

I needed Giles to tell me what had really happened that night.

He sighed heavily, and then said, 'It was the end of the Christmas holidays. I'd just found out I'd got into Oxford, and a few friends invited me out to celebrate.' He ran a hand over his face, and I could tell even now it was painful for him to think about. 'Alex was always breaking rules – the cool kid that everyone looked up to. But I felt I had to be sensible all the time – keep up my marks so I didn't let our father down. I always had something to prove.

'I'd never done anything reckless in my life, but that night I decided I would live on the edge for once. Dad had a collection of amazing cars. Alex would steal them all the time, even though he hadn't passed his driving test. But he always seemed to get away with it. So that night I decided to do the same.'

He glanced over at me, clearly trying to gauge my reaction. I tried to keep my face impassive. I wanted him to tell his story, the whole unvarnished truth.

'When no one was looking, I took one of the cars, and drove to a nearby pub to meet my friends. I didn't usually drink, but that night everyone was encouraging me, and I thought: Why not? I felt I was entitled to enjoy my night – take one evening off from playing by the rules.'

He shook his head, and I could see he still regretted what he'd done. But I hardened my heart to him – after all, it was his irresponsible behaviour that had led to my father's death.

'We started playing drinking games. I have no idea how much I drank. I wasn't even thinking about being over the limit when I drove home.' His eyes were fixed on the road, and I had a feeling he didn't want to look in my direction.

'When the crash happened—' He broke off, choking a little on the words. 'I got out to check on your father. I could see he wasn't in good shape, but I didn't realise he was—'

'Dead?' I filled in.

'Yes.' He closed his eyes briefly. 'But even being injured would have been bad enough. Suddenly I was facing prison instead of university.

'I didn't know what to do. I went straight to Alex's bedroom and woke him up. I was hysterical, saying that my life was over. Alex offered to take the blame. He was only sixteen at the time, whereas I was eighteen. He was younger, so he reckoned that at worst he'd do some time in juvenile detention, but that he wouldn't have a permanent record.

'Alex had already confessed to our father before we learned that the other driver – your dad – was dead. By then it was too late for him to backtrack. Alex was prepared to do the time for me. He didn't intend the crime to go unpunished. What he didn't bank on was that Dad would cover the whole thing up. He felt awful about what happened, but there was nothing he could do about it.'

I tried to take in the enormity of what he'd told me, but it was too much.

'So what you're saying is that Alex was covering for you then, and he's still covering for you – even though it's ruining his life. Even though it's stopping us being together.'

Giles was silent for a long moment, and then he slowly began to nod.

He looked pale and weasel-like, shifting uncomfortably under my gaze. I couldn't believe I'd thought he was attractive. Deep down I didn't think he was a bad person – just a coward. No wonder he'd been so nice to me – I couldn't imagine how he must have felt, being tasked with looking out for me at Destination, the girl whose father's death he'd caused. I must have been a permanent reminder of his sins, which he'd tried to atone for. I thought of how he'd made a pass at me – had he even felt anything for me, or was he just hoping to make up for what had happened? Had he created a romantic fantasy for himself, where we'd fall in love and that would make up for everything? I'm not sure even he would know the answer to that.

'But why didn't you come forward?' I asked. 'Why didn't you set everyone straight?' I couldn't imagine letting anyone take the blame for me like that. Deep down, I'd still know that I'd done wrong. And that would be impossible to live with.

I saw a look of shame cross his face. 'Because I knew Alex would get through it. He was always tougher than me. He'd always dealt so well with our father's abuse. He said to me Dad thinks so little of me anyway, one more incident isn't going to hurt. And God help me—' He let out a sob. 'I went along with it. Because I'd seen the way our father looked at Alex – the constant disappointment – and I couldn't stand the idea of him looking at me like that, too.'

He wiped his hand across his face, trying to rid himself of the tears. I could see his guilt and remorse. He might have let Alex take the blame, but he'd never stopped blaming himself.

'So where's Alex now?' I said quietly, once he seemed to have calmed down a little.

'One of Hugh's cousins drank too much. He's only sixteen, and they had to call an ambulance to take him to hospital to get his stomach pumped. Alex was organising it all, and talking to the police about what happened. He told me he was meeting you, and asked me to ask you to wait five more minutes for him . . .'

'So why didn't you?'

'Because I was worried about what he was going to say to you tonight.'

'He was planning to tell me the truth? That it was you driving the car that night?'

Giles shook his head. 'He said that he wouldn't. He said that he thought the two of you could find a way to get past what you believed had happened, without him having to dob me in.'

Alex was right about that. I'd already made up my mind to try to see beyond it – to recognise that he wasn't that same person who'd caused the accident all those years earlier.

'Then what was the problem?' I said. 'If he was planning to keep your secret, then why did you bother to interfere?'

'Because I couldn't trust him not to say anything. Alex is my brother, and I know he's loyal to me, but I knew that couldn't compete with how he felt about you. If your conversation had gone badly tonight, and he felt he was losing you, I didn't know what he'd say . . .'

'But if that's the case, what was the point of trying to separate us tonight? Wouldn't he just have told me another time?'

Giles frowned. 'I think I was hoping I could reason with him, or we could find a way to tell you together.' Then he shook his head, as though to clear his thoughts. 'Oh, to be honest, I don't know what I was thinking. I just panicked.'

I saw tears in his eyes. 'It was one mistake, Nina. And I'm so sorry that it ever happened. If I could take it back, I would.'

'Oh, save it, will you?' I was growing a little tired of his self-pity. 'How could you be so cowardly? You could have come forward at any time and admitted what you'd done, but instead you preferred to see your brother – your younger brother – suffer for it. You ruined Alex's relationship with his father, and you ruined our relationship, too. You're pathetic.' I gave him a look of disgust. 'Now, can you drop me somewhere, because I really don't want to be anywhere near you right now.'

'Wait, Nina.'

The panic in his voice made me stop, take a deep breath and turn to look at him. He looked pathetic sitting there, his eyes filled with fear.

'What?' I asked.

'I– I just wanted to know what you plan to do. If you're going to go to the police . . .'

I gave a dry laugh. 'You really are unbelievable. I thought you were going to apologise for all the pain you've caused me and my family – and Alex, too. But instead you're still thinking about saving your own skin. I don't know why I expected anything else.' I paused to let my words sink in. 'And now, will you please let me out of the car?'

I expected him to slow down and pull over, but instead the car began to speed up. 'I'm sorry, Nina. But I can't do that.'

It was then that I noticed how fast we were travelling. It was late, so there were few cars on the road, which gave us a clear run. I looked round, trying to get my bearings. We were driving along the Embankment, past Temple Station and coming up to Waterloo Bridge. On the other side of the river, I could see the distinctive Oxo Tower, and the Royal Festival Hall.

'Where are we going?' I looked over nervously at Giles, suddenly concerned about his state of mind. Now the secret that he'd been keeping for years was out, what did he have to lose?

'I want to go to my flat.' I remembered then that he lived in some new development by the water near Battersea. I just wondered what he was going to do when we got there. I'd find out soon, that was for sure – we were already driving by Tate Britain.

It was then that I saw it. In the rear-view mirror I spotted a car gaining on us. It was too far away to see exactly, but I was sure it was a silver sports car of some kind.

Alex.

He must have guessed what was going on, and was coming after us. I felt a surge of hope.

I flicked a look over to Giles. Thankfully, he was too caught up in himself to notice the other car.

I decided to try one last time to reason with him. 'Giles, please, let me out.'

But he shook his head. 'I'm sorry, but I can't do that, Nina. Not until I make you understand that you can't say anything about what you know.'

I wanted to tell him that I wouldn't – it would have been the sensible thing to do. But somehow the lie stuck in my throat. I couldn't betray my father that way – even to save myself.

Giles pressed his foot on the accelerator. The dial on the speedometer flickered up to ninety miles per hour. Ahead,

I could see the pretty lights of Chelsea Bridge, and across the river the looming chimneys of Battersea Power Station. We must have been nearly there, but at the speed he was going I wasn't sure we were going to make it. The car was veering from one side of the road to the other in such an erratic way that I felt a deep fear spread inside my belly.

'Slow down, Giles. Please,' I begged.

As we rounded the corner, I saw a large truck coming for us. It was straddling the middle of the road.

'Watch out!' I cried.

If Giles had been travelling at a normal speed, he could have slowed the car and let the other vehicle pass. But he was going too fast for that. All he could do was try to swerve to the left to avoid a head-on collision. But he must have misjudged the manoeuvre, and instead of pulling back onto the road, the car continued along a diagonal path, cutting straight across the pavement. The low wall that lined the Thames Path should have brought the car to a stop, but the vehicle was going at such a speed that instead we flew straight over it, and towards the dark river below.

In the split second that we sailed through the air, my brain was just about able to process what was about to happen. I clutched at the dashboard, bracing myself for impact, and took a deep breath.

But as the car hit the water, I felt with utter certainty that I was about to die.

Chapter 32

I felt the impact go straight through me, the force rattling my bones.

A moment of relief at still being alive was replaced by a paralysing terror as the full extent of my predicament sunk in. My seat belt had helped hold me in place, so I didn't get knocked out – along with the way I'd braced myself against the dashboard. But as the airbag deflated, I could feel the car was already starting to sink, engine first. Ice-cold water began to fill the compartment, and I sensed I had seconds to get out.

Something clicked in my brain, and I remembered an article I'd read about a woman escaping her car when it went over a bridge and into a river. There'd been one of those breakout boxes, telling you what to do in the event of you ending up the same way. All the details came rushing back. From what I recalled, the window was my best chance of escape, but the electronics would only work for a couple of minutes in the water. I hit the switch, and undid my seat belt, preparing for escape. I gave a quick glance over at Giles, and he seemed to be copying my actions. I had no time to check, as the car became fully submerged. I took a deep breath and slipped out of the window, using all my strength to push upwards through the ice-cold river.

The inky black water seemed endless. It was impossible to see, so I had no sense of whether I was going in the right direction. I could feel panic grip me as my lungs began to fill.

And then I saw them – little pinpricks of light shimmering ahead of me. Relief coursed through me, and I began to swim towards them, my arms and legs powering me along as I found a reserve of strength.

Seconds later I broke the surface, gasping for breath.

As I trod water, I looked around for the shore, feeling disorientated in the dark. My body felt heavy in my sodden clothes, and I wondered how I would muster the strength to swim any further. Then I felt strong arms round my waist.

'I've got you.' It was Alex. His lips were warm against my ear. 'Don't panic. You'll be fine.'

I was too weak to talk. So I relaxed into his hold as he swam with me back to shore.

Arms reached over the side and hauled me upwards and onto the pavement. A crowd had gathered. As someone wrapped me in a blanket, I realised Alex wasn't with me – he was still in the water.

'Where is he?' Alex called up. I knew immediately who he was talking about.

'He's still down there. Giles is still in the car. But Alex, don't! It's too dangerous—'

But he was already swimming off, back to the middle of the river. All I could do was watch helplessly as he dived back down into the deep.

Passers-by were surrounding me, trying to get me to sit down. But I needed to make sure that Alex was all right. My teeth were chattering as I stood by the edge of the river, watching the dark water. Instead of slowing down now that I was safe, my heartbeat was speeding up. If something happened to Alex, I didn't know what I'd do. What was taking so long?

'There!' a man called. 'There's someone in the water!'

I looked in the direction he was pointing. Sure enough, there was a figure, but I couldn't make out who it was. I moved forward, so close to the edge that there were worried murmurs and hands held me back. Then a second later, the swimmer moved into the light, and my whole body relaxed – it was Alex.

He was safe, but alone.

That's when I passed out.

*   *   *

The rhythmic sound of a machine woke me up. My eyes fluttered open and I saw that I was in a hospital bed. There was an IV pumping fluids into my left hand. A heart monitor was beeping steadily – which seemed like a good thing.

I must have been in a side ward, because I had the room to myself. I looked round, and saw Alex sitting in the armchair across from me. He got to his feet and moved towards my bed.

'How are you feeling?' He looked concerned, and reached for the call button. 'I'll get someone in here—'

'No.' My voice was weak, and my throat hurt. I guessed they must have pumped my stomach. 'We need to talk first.'

I patted my bed, so he would sit down near me. I didn't want to strain my voice, given that I could barely speak above a whisper.

'Why didn't you tell me?' I said. 'About Giles.' That's what I hadn't been able to figure out – he would have made his life so much easier if he'd just let everyone know he hadn't done anything wrong.

'It wasn't my secret to tell,' he said simply.

I didn't know what to say or think. I'd said all these awful things to him, and now they'd turned out not to be true. I remembered what my mother had said – that I shouldn't judge him when I didn't know the full story.

'Giles was distraught about what happened – even before he realised how bad the accident was. He'd worked so hard for everything he'd achieved. And he thought he was going to lose it all because of one stupid stunt.

'I was just trying to help by saying it was me. Then, when we found out the driver had died—'

'My father had died,' I couldn't help pointing out.

Alex winced at my clarification. 'Yes. That your father had died. It was impossible to go back and change our story.'

'Let me guess,' I said. 'Giles refused to confess.'

Alex smiled a little, and then grew serious again. 'Our father had done such a good job covering everything up. I was young, and I just went along with it. But as I got older, I regretted ever being a part of it. Someone should have paid for that night, even if it was an accident. But by then it was too late.

'And maybe part of me felt I might as well take the blame. My father seemed so quick to believe the worst of me – that I'd been drink-driving and left the scene of an accident. I suppose I felt that if he thought so little of me, I might as well be the person he believed I was.'

I saw then that Alex was a lot like me – he'd been abandoned, first by his mother and then by his father, with his continued disappointment in him. The drinking, drugs, one-night stands and illegal gambling . . . It was all because he felt no one cared about him, so why should he care about himself?

We fell into silence, as though Alex sensed there was only so much I could discuss right then.

His hair and clothes were still damp. Moonlight filtered through the hospital window, catching his chiselled jaw.

He cleared his throat. 'So what happened tonight? Why didn't you wait for me like you said you would?'

I shook my head. 'Giles came up to me at the hotel. He told me that you'd gone off with Tori to take drugs—'

'And you believed him?' The hurt on Alex's face took me by surprise. I'd expected him to be annoyed at Giles for lying – but I had a feeling he was more disappointed in me for thinking that it was true.

'I'm sorry.' I wrinkled my forehead. 'It just seemed so plausible . . .'

He nodded slowly, but not in a way that reassured me. Somehow this wasn't turning out to be the reunion I'd hoped for.

I cleared my throat. 'So where does this leave us?'

The fact that he didn't answer straight away worried me.

'Look, Nina,' he said eventually. 'I need to think about this for a while. I need some time to process what's gone on. Giles – my brother – he died tonight—'

I winced. 'Oh God.' I buried my head in my hands. 'You blame me, don't you?'

'No,' he said quietly. 'Of course I don't. But I need to be with my father for a while. He hasn't taken this well—'

'Of course. I understand.'

But still Alex didn't move.

'There's more to it, though,' I said. 'Isn't there?'

He sighed. 'I wanted us to be together, Nina. I really did. But considering how easily you believed Giles tonight about me going off the rails – do you honestly think that we have any chance of working?'

I opened my mouth to answer, but couldn't find the words.

He shook his head sadly. 'I thought we could be together. I really did. But now—'

He didn't complete the sentence. He didn't need to.

'Your mum and sister should be here soon,' he said, getting to his feet. 'I only stayed because I didn't want you to be alone.'

Alex was almost at the door, when I called his name. He turned back, and I could see the sorrow in his eyes.

'I still want this to work between us,' I said.

'I know.' He gave me a rueful smile. 'I just don't know if it can.'

Chapter 33

The next week was frantic. I had to give a statement to the police, explaining the events that had taken place on the Embankment, and how they had led to us plunging into the Thames. The detective in charge of the case said that, as Giles was the driver, and he hadn't been drinking, it was likely to be ruled a tragic accident.

The first moment that I had alone with my mother, I told her that it was Giles, not Alex, who'd caused the accident that killed Dad. We discussed what to do, but in the end there seemed to be nothing to be gained from revealing the truth. Giles was dead. And it wasn't as though Alex needed to be exonerated.

As for Alex, I didn't hear from him. I called and left a message every day, but none of them were returned. It seemed he'd made his mind up about us, and I feared there was nothing I could do to change it.

*   *   *

The following month, it was my father's birthday. It fell on a Sunday, and I went with my mother and April to lay flowers on his grave. It was our tradition every year.

Afterwards, the three of us had lunch. When April went off to look at the desserts, my mother turned to me.

'You're not happy.' She nodded down at my plate. I'd scarcely touched my food.

'That's hardly surprising,' I said, deliberately misinterpreting what she'd said. 'We spent the morning at a cemetery.'

She shook her head. 'I don't mean about today.' She waited a beat, and then said, 'You still miss Alex, don't you?'

I studied the table. I didn't say anything, but I didn't need to.

Mum sighed. 'Sweetheart, let me give you some advice. Making yourself miserable isn't helping your dad. I wasted years punishing myself. Don't do the same. He wouldn't have wanted that.'

'Yeah, but . . .' It was hard to put into words. Being with Alex would have made me feel guilty. Somehow it didn't feel right to be happy when my dad wasn't around.

'It's a cliché, but if there's one thing your dad's death taught me, it's that life's too short.' She reached out and grasped my hands in hers, so hard that it almost hurt. 'Don't waste even a second of it.'

April came back then, ending our discussion. But my

mother's words continued to reverberate in my head for the rest of the day.

The next day, I went to see Duncan Noble – to set him straight about who had been driving the car that killed my father. I knew Alex would be too proud to tell him, and I thought it was important that he knew what had really happened – that while his youngest son had his faults, he at least hadn't killed an innocent man.

He agreed to see me early that evening, in his office in Canary Wharf, where I'd met him almost a year earlier. He'd aged exponentially in that time. I no longer looked at him as the man who'd conspired to keep the circumstances of my father's death a secret – all I could see was a parent broken by the death of his child.

Losing a parent was horrible, a terrible sadness, but at least it was the natural order of life. But losing a partner or a child – that was an unimaginable loss to me. And Duncan Noble had endured both.

I quickly outlined what had really happened the night of my father's crash. I didn't want to make things worse – but I felt Duncan Noble needed to know the truth.

He didn't look as surprised as I'd expected.

'You knew?' I said. 'You knew all along that it was Giles?'

'I suspected. I overheard them talking a couple of years ago, put two and two together . . .'

'But why didn't you say anything?' I couldn't believe what I was hearing. 'Do you really hate Alex so much that you were happy for him to take the blame?'

He frowned at me. 'Of course not! But so much time had passed, and I couldn't see the point of opening old wounds. And I don't hate Alex. I never have. I love him. He's my son. It's just that we're very different people. Giles was an extension of me. I knew exactly how he thought, because it was how I did, too. Alex has always been harder for me to understand. But that doesn't mean I don't love him – just as much as I loved Giles.' His brow furrowed, as if he was running through the events of the past in his head. 'Maybe I was harder on Alex, but it was because I cared. I didn't want him screwing up his life, the way his mother had – turning his back on responsibilities. And I think maybe I mistook his partying for being flighty, like she was.' He stopped then, to think the point through. Then his expression cleared, and he gazed directly at me, a softer look on his face. 'But then, in recent months, I've seen the way he's changed, and I realise he's nothing like his mother. He'd do anything for you out of love. He's not the type to walk away; in fact, he's one of the most loyal people I know.' He gave a rueful smile. 'He's a fine young man. And so was Giles. He made a mistake, but it was one he always regretted . . .'

'You should tell him that,' I said. 'You should tell Alex what you just said to me. He needs to hear that.'

Duncan seemed to think this over for a moment. 'Yes,' he said finally. 'He does need to hear that from me. But there's something else he needs more than that.'

'What's that?'

'You,' he said simply. 'He needs you.'

I shook my head. 'He made it plain in the hospital that he didn't want me. That he didn't believe it could work.'

'That's only because he feels that you don't trust him. He needs someone to believe in him. And I think you do. And if I'm right, then you need to let him know that.'

Did I trust Alex? I thought back to the night of Jas's wedding, before I'd found out that he'd been covering for Giles. I'd already made my decision then, hadn't I? I'd already chosen to trust him – to forgive him. And even with what Giles told me, I'd sensed that Alex wouldn't have slipped back into his old ways.

I got to my feet. 'I have to go.'

Duncan smiled a little. I could tell he'd already guessed where.

As I reached the glass doors that led out to the lift, I gave one last look back to Duncan Noble. He was half-turned, so I could only see his profile as he stared out of the window. But I could see a look of contentment had settled over his features. He obviously still had a way to go grieving for Giles, but I think it had made him feel a little better to have helped Alex.

Now I just had to make sure his faith in me, and my ability to make Alex happy, hadn't been misplaced.

Half an hour later, I got off the Tube at Knightsbridge. I emerged from the station into the cool, crisp air. It was autumn now, and the evenings were drawing in.

I crossed the road to Alex's apartment building. Instead of going through reception, and asking to be buzzed up, I went to the underground car park. I wanted this to be a surprise. I got into the lift and put in the code for the top floor.

I drummed my hand against my side as the lift went up. My heart beat harder as I got closer to his floor. It was a risk, of course. He might not be in. Or he might even have another girl there. But there was no turning back now.

The lift pinged, announcing my arrival, and the doors slid open.

I heard rapid footsteps. As the sound grew closer part of me wanted to get back in the lift and disappear. But before I could do that, Alex, barefoot, his hair mussed up in that sexy way I adored, rounded the corner.

I'm not sure who he'd been expecting, but he did a double-take when he saw me.

A look of happiness flitted briefly across his face – his initial, spontaneous reaction. Then he seemed to catch himself, remember how he was meant to act around me, and the smile was replaced with a frown.

'Why're you here, Nina?' His tone was guarded, but I didn't care. I was just happy to hear his voice again. I hadn't realised how much I'd missed that clipped, upper-class drawl.

'I'm here to tell you that you were wrong.'

'About what in particular?' A ghost of a smile crossed his face. 'There's always so much to choose from.'

'About us.' I spoke firmly, refusing to let him put me off. 'You were wrong about us.'

'Oh? I wasn't aware there was an "us" any more.'

I followed him as he turned away and went into the living area. He took a bottle of whisky from the bar and poured himself a drink. I knew he was trying to pretend he didn't care – like he had so many times before. But this time I wasn't going to let him get away with it.

I took a step towards him, my eyes fixed on him, wanting him to know that I wasn't leaving without telling him how I felt.

'You don't believe I'll ever trust you. You said that's why we couldn't be together. But you're wrong.'

'Oh?'

'I did trust you. Even before I found out the truth about Giles.'

As I spoke those words, he went very still. 'What do you mean?'

'At Jas and Hugh's wedding. Remember when you asked me to wait for you so we could talk?'

'Yes, I do remember that.' His voice carried more than a trace of bitterness. 'And from what I recall, my brother told you that I'd gone off to get high, and you believed him.'

I dropped my eyes for a moment, feeling my cheeks flushing at the memory. But then I forced myself to focus on the reason I was there. 'You're right,' I admitted. 'At first I did believe him.' I took another step towards him. 'But then, once we got into the car and he started driving, something kept nagging at me. I knew that something didn't feel right.'

'Oh?' His blues eyes stared at me intently.

'And I suddenly realised that I didn't believe Giles. Deep down, I knew that you would never have done anything like that – that you wouldn't have broken your promise to me. I knew that I could trust you.'

I edged closer until I was standing right in front of him, wanting him to see the sincerity in my eyes, to know that every word I'd spoken was the truth. It was the only way I could convince him to give me – give us – a chance to be together.

I reached out slowly, hesitantly almost, and took his cool hands in mine. 'When I realised something wasn't right, I asked Giles to turn round. I wanted to come back and find you, because I knew you'd still be there, waiting for me.'

I saw surprise cross his face – followed by what looked like a flash of joy. And then it was gone, replaced by what I guessed was dawning horror, as he pieced together what had happened that fateful night. I sensed he was going to draw his hands away, but I held them fast, keeping my eyes locked on his, needing him to stay with me while I got it all out.

'But Giles refused.' My voice was little more than a whisper. 'That's when the truth finally came out.'

In the silence that followed, I felt we were both thinking about how Giles's guilt and remorse had led him to lose control of the car, which had resulted in his death. But that wasn't the point of my confession. Alex had grieved, and would continue to grieve for his brother. And I would always have complicated feelings regarding what had happened to my father and how it had been dealt with by Duncan, Giles and Alex. But that still didn't change the fact that we could be together. I saw that now. I just needed him to see that too.

I dropped his hands then, and reached up to touch his cheek, trying to bring his focus back to me, and the present. 'I know what's happened is awful – for both of our families. But none of that changes the fact that I trusted you that night. Even before I knew the truth about my father's death, I knew I could rely on you. So if you think we can't be together because I don't trust you, then you're wrong. Because I did – and I still do.' I could hear my voice crack with emotion, and it took every bit of strength I had to blink back my tears. 'So if you still want me, then you have to know that I want to be with you.'

I choked on the last word, and I couldn't hold back the tears any longer. As they began to spill down my cheeks, Alex reached up and cupped my face in his large hands, using his thumbs to gently brush the droplets away. 'Of course I want to be with you. You don't know how hard it's been staying away. I only did it because I thought it was the best thing for you. That being away from me would make you happy.'

At that, I laughed through my tears. 'Do I look especially happy to you?'

His eyes swept over me as he pretended to assess my emotional state. Then I saw something change – the first hint of desire appear. 'Not right now, you don't.' A slow smile crept over his face. 'But I'm sure I can do my best to change that.'

Before I could think of a response, he bent his head and kissed me.

Afterwards, we lay together in his bed in that comfortable, sleepy way lovers do. Alex was propped up against a mound of pillows, one arm wrapped casually around my shoulders while he played with my hair. I leaned against his bare chest, tracing his muscles with my fingertips.

'So what made you come round here today?' he said eventually. 'After all this time, there must have been a reason . . .'

I thought back to my conversation with Duncan Noble and smiled to myself. It would do Alex good to know that I wasn't the only person who had faith in him. 'It wasn't "what" – it was "who",' I told him.

'Huh?'

I sat up a little and turned so I was facing him. 'I mean, you should be asking *who* made me come round today. But it's kind of a long story, and right now I'm starving. So if we can go to your kitchen and find some ice cream, I promise to tell you all about it.'

Chapter 34

Three months later . . .

My mother bent down and removed a tray from the oven. The rich aroma of roast beef floated over to where I sat at the kitchen table, with Alex by my side.

Juices sizzled as she set the tray on the worktop. Her new boyfriend, Jeff, stepped forward and began to carve the joint, while she and April started to put roast potatoes and vegetables into serving dishes, and carry them over to the table.

'Can I help at all?' Alex asked, as my sister set down a bowl of crisp green beans.

'You're a guest. There's no need.'

It was hard to miss the flush on my sister's cheeks, or the breathlessness of her voice. Her crush on my boyfriend clearly hadn't diminished. But it was harmless enough, and I had a feeling it would dissipate soon. She'd started mentioning a boy in her maths class at increasingly regular intervals . . .

Alex's hand scrunched the back of my neck, turning my face towards him. 'So I get that I'm not helping because of my status as a guest. But what's your excuse?'

'I'm just lazy.' I raised my eyebrows suggestively. 'In the kitchen, at least,' I said, low enough for no one else in the kitchen to hear.

'Hmm . . .' He nuzzled his nose against mine. 'So I'm guessing that means no home-cooked meals? I think I should've found that out before I asked you to move in with me.'

'It's always worth reading the small print,' I agreed solemnly, and then lightly kissed him on the lips.

The truth was, I was happy to watch them dish up. I'd already offered to help once, and been told that everything was under control. That was good enough for me. I sat back in my chair and surveyed the busy kitchen, feeling an unexpected sense of contentment wash over me. Sunday lunch with roast beef and all the trimmings. You didn't get much more of a traditional English family ritual than that.

My father had loved Sunday roasts, and after he'd died, my mother had refused to cook them – it was too painful for her. So it had surprised me that she'd been the one to suggest it. Perhaps she was feeling nostalgic. I was officially moving in with Alex that day, and he'd come round to pick up the last of my stuff. I'd been worried my mother might break down, but she'd genuinely seemed to enjoy cooking – giving April little lessons, the way a mother should. I could see Sunday roast becoming a regular thing.

Once the plates of meat and Yorkshire pudding were ready, my mother and Jeff came to sit down. Alex poured glasses of water from a jug – the one element missing from the meal was wine, something we'd forgone for my mother's sake. April was the last to join us. She placed a jug of gravy on the table and slipped into her seat.

'Did you tell Nina about Paris?' my sister said as she helped herself to potatoes. Although her focus was on the food, it was clear she was talking to my mum.

I'd been about to cut into a slice of perfectly cooked beef, but now I set my knife and fork down. 'No,' I answered before my mother could. 'It's the first Nina's heard of anything about Paris.'

'We're going there in the school holidays. On Eurostar. For five nights.'

April couldn't keep the excitement out of her voice – and I didn't blame her. It would be her first time abroad. But I couldn't quite share her enthusiasm for the imminent trip.

'So who's going?' I asked as casually as I could. My eyes moved from April to my mum and then settled pointedly on Jeff. 'The three of you?'

It was true that my mum was doing a lot better lately. She'd worked as an accounts assistant before having me, and she'd managed to get a job doing just that at a local architect's. It had been hard for her at first, having not worked for so long, but now that she'd got the hang of it, I think she genuinely enjoyed the little challenges and triumphs of a daily job. I had a feeling it had helped her stay sober, too – to have something to occupy her time.

She'd met Jeff through work, too. He was a structural engineer, who freelanced for her boss, and he would come into the office once or twice a week. They'd gone on their first date two months ago, and so far he seemed like a good guy – amicably divorced, with two boys of his own, aged eight and eleven. But while I had tentatively given Jeff my seal of approval, it was still early days in their relationship. I wanted to get to know him better before he started becoming a permanent part of April's life. I didn't want my mother making the same mistake she often had – plunging straight into a relationship and forgetting everything else. If things didn't work out, then she risked going straight back to the bottle, which we all wanted to avoid.

But to my relief, she shook her head.

'No, Jeff's not coming. It's just going to be me and April.' She reached out and placed her hand over my sister's, and squeezed. 'A girly holiday, with lots of sight-seeing and croissants, and maybe a bit of shopping.'

As April squealed with delight, I opened my mouth to suggest that perhaps I should come along, too. But before I could speak, I felt Alex's hand move to my knee, and give it a squeeze. I knew what the gesture meant – he'd obviously guessed what I was about to say, and this was his way of stopping me. We'd talked a lot about this – how I needed to find a way to let go, and trust my mother to take care of April, and concentrate on myself instead. It was funny how it was easier said than done.

I looked around the table, surprised once again at how well my once-fractured family were doing. That's why, when Alex had asked me to move in with him, I'd had no hesitation in agreeing. He was about to open up his hotel, which took up a lot of his time, and while he still liked to go out when he could, the self-destructive behaviour hadn't returned. He'd even started to get on better with his father – the loss of Giles having made them call an unspoken truce, and make an effort to get on. While they'd never be twin souls, they could at least start to appreciate each other for the people that they were.

So Alex had started seeing his father for dinner once a week. I had no objection to him going, but I hadn't been able to bring myself to join them. I understood Duncan had concealed the circumstances of my father's death for his family's sake, but I couldn't forgive his actions quite yet. As he was Alex's father, I knew I'd have to find a way to be around him at some point, but that was for the future. There was only so much growing I could do at one time. Right now, I wanted to enjoy the present.

I raised my water glass. 'Well, here's to Paris.'

'No, we can't toast that,' my mother said. 'It's the day you're moving out of home. There has to be something more appropriate.'

'How about – to new adventures?' Alex suggested.

'That's good,' April agreed.

We all raised our glasses, and clinked as we chorused, 'To new adventures!'

'That's the last of them.' Alex dumped the box down on the floor of the bedroom, and then straightened and rubbed his back theatrically. 'And by the way, you owe me a massage later. I thought you said you didn't have much stuff?'

It was early evening. After Sunday lunch, we'd all gone for a long walk to work off the roast and the apple crumble that had followed. Now, we were finally back at Alex's flat.

'Hmm . . .' I looked up from the suitcase of clothes I was unpacking, and glanced around the room. 'Yeah, there's more than I'd imagined there'd be.'

Alex glanced at his watch. 'If we do this quickly, we might still manage a movie tonight. So where do you want me to start?'

I nodded over at one of the boxes labelled: *Schoolwork*.

'How about that one?'

'Sure. I'll take it to the study.'

He lifted the box, and carried it down the hallway to the third and smallest bedroom – which was also going to serve as my study.

I'd enrolled at a nearby sixth form college, so I could go back and take my A levels. So far, I was loving every moment of it. The only downside was my lack of free time. It was an intensive course, where the usual two years' worth of material were crammed into one. What with my job as well – I worked twenty hours at the gym still, whenever I didn't have classes – I was kept busy.

Alex had told me not to worry about working, and that he'd give me any money I needed – after all, I only had to earn enough to cover my own living expenses now, as my mum was able to support herself and April. But I'd insisted on keeping my job. While I'd come a long way in opening up to him, it was still important to me to maintain my independence and pay my own way. If nothing else, I thought it was a good example to set April. I wanted her to learn to stand on her own two feet.

Five minutes must have passed, when I heard him walking back towards our bedroom. I looked up just as he appeared in the doorway. He was frowning.

'What're these?'

It took me a second to realise what he was holding up, but when I did so, I closed my eyes briefly. I'd hoped we could put off this conversation for a little while longer.

'University prospectuses,' I admitted. I got to my feet, brushing off the dust from my jeans, and walked over to take them from his hand. There were three in total – for Nottingham, Manchester and Exeter. The closest of them was a two-hour train journey away from London. Driving would take longer. 'I'm thinking of applying to study law.'

Of course I could apply to a London university, but instinct told me not to. Although it would be lovely to be near Alex, it would be far too easy to be lazy about making new friends. What would be the point of going to university if I didn't embrace the experience?

His eyes swept mine. 'And why didn't you tell me about it?'

I sighed. After twelve weeks of bliss, was our honeymoon period about to end? I felt knots forming in my stomach just at the thought of it.

'I suppose I didn't want to bring it up until I had to.' I ran a hand through my hair. 'The problem is, it'll mean I'll have to move away from here. We might not see each other much during term time. And I didn't know how you'd react.' I frowned. 'We've only just got together. It seems like a bad idea to put obstacles in our path when our relationship's barely even begun—'

'No, it isn't.' Alex interrupted me mid-flow. His blue eyes were soft and sincere as he cupped my face in his hands. 'If you want to apply to university, then that's what you should do. Even if it means us having a long-distance relationship for a while. You'll just have to trust that we'll find a way to make it work.'

As he bent his head to kiss me, I realised that I did.

Acknowledgements

I'd like to thank the following:

My agent, Darley Anderson, for his unshakable support, wisdom and kindness. He really is the best at what he does! Also at the agency, Andrea Messent, who provided a wonderful set of insightful comments after reading an early draft of this novel.

My UK publishers, Simon & Schuster, particularly the eternally charming and patient Suzanne Baboneau, my long-suffering editor, Clare Hey, for her perceptive sugges- tions, which improved the novel immensely, as well as for her ongoing hand-holding of a very nervous author, and above all for her witty company at lunch. Emma Capron at The Hot Bed, who I'm having the pleasure of getting to know. At Atria in the US, Judith Carr and Sarah Durand.

After a long period of misdiagnosis, my mother was finally told she had colon cancer on 23 August 2013. By then, the disease was terminal. She'd always been my biggest supporter, and her greatest wish was that she'd be alive to see *Beautiful Liar* published. Sadly, that wasn't to be, as she died less than six months after diagnosis, on 6 February 2014.

My mum was born in Ireland, and only moved to England in 1962. She never lost her lovely Irish accent, or her easy, outgoing nature. She was the kind of person who woke up happy in the morning, and always had a smile on her face. She had such enthusiasm for life, and people who met her were always shocked to learn her age, because she seemed a decade younger than she was. I miss her so much, as does my father, John James Hyland, and my husband, Tom Beevers (her Tomsy-womsy). This novel is for my lovely mummy, as there's nothing else I can do for her now.

Turn the page for an exclusive sneak peek of

SWEET DECEPTION
by
TARA BOND

Coming soon in eBook and paperback

Chapter One

Present Day

I burrowed further under my duvet, trying to block out the incessant ringing. I wasn't sure where the shrill sound was coming from, but it was the last thing I needed after the tequila shots I'd downed the previous night. All I could think about right now was the incessant throbbing pain hitting me right between my eyes, beating away like a pulse. I just wanted the noise to stop, so I could fall back to sleep, and hopefully wake up hangover free in a few hours.

It was only when I heard my flatmate, Lindsay, throw open her bedroom door and stomp across the hallway, that I finally figured out the source of the noise – it was our intercom. That was when the pieces fell into place.

It was *him*, of course; the bane of my existence – here to ruin my day.

As Lindsay answered the intercom, I closed my eyes and

willed her to pretend that I wasn't in. She knew how much I hated these occasions, and had been known to lie on my behalf more than once. But it was too much to hope for today, I realised as I heard her tell him to come up. Lindsay was a good friend, but she didn't like to get up before midday, and I knew she'd hold me responsible for today's early morning call. This was her revenge.

She didn't bother waiting for him to climb the five flights of stairs up to our top floor flat. Instead, I heard her leave the door on the latch, and then on the way back to her room, she threw something against my door, to make sure I was awake – from the thud it sounded like a shoe.

'Charlie? Mr No Fun's here,' she called out. I winced at the volume. 'You might want to make yourself decent. If that's even possible . . .'

I heard her bedroom door slam shut, as she headed back to sleep. Lucky her.

As though I didn't have enough problems already, the mattress next to me shifted, and I froze as a warm, hairy leg brushed against my bare skin. I came out from behind the pillow, peeled my crusted eyes opened and saw a man lying next to me, naked apart from a sheet pulled over his middle, mercifully preserving his modesty. My alcohol-addled brain couldn't exactly place him right now, but he was an attractive guy, if you liked that rough, rock band look. His hair was way too long; his nose and lip were pierced, and both arms were covered in tattoos. He was entirely my type.

I couldn't remember much about last night, but it didn't take a genius to figure out what had happened. I worked behind the bar at a pub in Camden, and he was typical of our clientele. No doubt I'd served him, we'd got talking, and then after my shift we'd headed on somewhere to continue drinking. Before one thing led to another. It wasn't the first time something like this had happened – in fact, it was kind of a weekly event for me. I was just surprised I'd let him stay over. Most of the time, I kicked them out straight after the deed was done. It was the best way to avoid that awkward morning-after moment, where the guy felt obliged to pretend he was going to call, and I felt obliged to pretend I wanted him to.

But I didn't have time to worry about getting rid of my unwanted guest right now. I had far more pressing problems with my other male visitor, who I'd just heard coming into the flat.

I'd just about managed to sit up and pull on my black kimono dressing gown when the door to my bedroom door was thrown open by my self-appointed protector – and gigantic pain in my butt – Richard Davenport.

Even at this time in the morning, Richard was the epitome of a young, successful businessman. Tall and tanned, no doubt from Saturday mornings on the tennis court, he was, as always, impeccably turned out in chinos and a blue button-down shirt. He never seemed to step out of the house looking anything less than perfect, and today was no exception – his dark hair was short and neat, his strong jaw clean-shaven, and I could smell the fresh scent of his shower gel from where I sat hunched over on the side of the bed, reeking of my own signature aroma of fags and booze.

I'd known Richard for most of my life. He'd gone to the same boarding school as my older brother, Kit, and they'd been best friends since they were eleven. We'd never had much to do with each other growing up. After all, I was five years younger than him, and a girl – he'd barely seemed to notice me. But when I'd moved to London seven years ago, that had all changed. I guess out of some sense of duty to my brother, he'd taken it upon himself to keep an eye on me, which entailed phoning every few weeks to check up on me, and making sure that I attended the obligatory family get-togethers. Which would explain his presence in my flat today.

Of course, his interference irritated me no end. At twenty-five years old, it wasn't like I needed a babysitter. I wasn't sure why he couldn't just mind his own business.

It was hard to believe he was only thirty, a mere five years older than me. The contrast between us couldn't have been greater. I didn't need a mirror to tell me how I looked – I'd had enough mornings like these to know that I had mascara and eyeliner smeared round my eyes, and my bleached hair was sticking up all over the place. I no doubt resembled something even the cat wouldn't bother dragging in.

With a strength I was surprised I could muster, I forced myself off the bed and stood to face him, my arms folded across my chest. 'You could've knocked.'

Irritation at being woken, and the pounding in my head, put me on the defensive. But if I was hoping he might apologise, I clearly had no chance. He looked just as furious as I felt.

'And you could have answered the door. I've been ringing that wretched intercom for twenty minutes.'

'Yeah?' I affected a bored look. 'Well maybe you should've taken the hint and left.'

'Oh, no, Charlotte.' I winced at his use of my full name – only he and my family ever called me that these days. To everyone else, I was Charlie. 'Not today. It's your parents' thirtieth wedding anniversary party. You're going, even if I have to drag you there, kicking and screaming.'

I didn't doubt that he would, so I wisely kept my mouth shut. I felt too fragile to be getting into one of our arguments this early in the day.

Richard cast a quick glance around my room. I could sense his disapproval, and I felt a twinge of guilt at the state of the place. Lindsay and I were lucky enough to live in a top-floor warehouse conversion in the heart of Shoreditch.

Even though the area's relentless gentrification meant it was no longer considered cutting-edge, it was still a decent enough area for going out, with lots of good bars and clubs. Our flat was pretty impressive, too – it had double-height ceilings, exposed brickwork and original iron beams – way out of our price range. A school friend of Lindsey's owned the place, and when his lucrative banking job took him to Hong Kong, he'd let us stay here for a fraction of the market price – I suspected because he had a crush on my friend. We'd repaid his generosity by completely trashing the place.

My room was by far the worst. Dirty plates and mugs were scattered across every surface; it was impossible to see the polished concrete floor with all the clothes strewn over the floor; and there were two used condoms on the bedside table. Oh, well – at least Richard should give me points for practicing safe sex. It always amazed me, my instinctive sense of self-preservation – no matter how drunk I was, I always managed to insist on that.

Richard's eyes finally settled on the naked man in my bed – taking in his long, greasy hair, the piercings and tattoos.

'And who might this be?' Richard made no effort to disguise his distaste. It didn't bother me in the slightest. I'd never made any attempt to hide how I lived my life, and while this might be the first time he'd been so directly confronted with it, I didn't give a damn if he had a problem with it. If anything, I hoped this might make him stop coming round. It wasn't that I didn't like Richard, I just resented his interference in my life. It had become a game, whenever we saw each other I'd try to push his buttons, being deliberately rude and ungrateful, and he'd do his best to ignore me. One day I was sure I'd find his Achilles' heel and get him out of my life for good. Until then, I'd just have fun goading him as best I could.

I followed his gaze to my unwanted bedfellow and shrugged. 'Your guess is as good as mine.'

Richard's nose wrinkled at that, which was exactly the reaction I'd been trying to elicit. In fact, I knew exactly who the tattooed guy in my bed was. It had come back to me now – his name was Gavin – he was the lead singer in a band who'd played at the bar a few times. But it amused me to try to shock calm, unflappable Richard.

My bed-mate was by now wide awake and struggling to sit up. His eyes were wide with apology and fixed firmly on Richard. 'Aw, shit. I didn't realise she had a boyfriend, mate.'

'He's not my boyfriend,' I said automatically.

'And if I was, you wouldn't still be in that bed. Trust me. Mate.'

Richard's silky smooth voice belied the threat behind his words. I could see Mr Rock Band swallow, hard, and I bit back a smile. Richard might act and dress all corporate, but at six foot three and 180 pounds of pure muscle, it was clear he wasn't someone to pick a fight with. Even if you didn't know he had a black belt in Taekwondo, it was obvious from the cold, ruthless look in his eyes that he was entirely capable of taking care of himself.

He turned his attention back to me, his eyes sweeping over my kimono and dishevelled appearance. 'I take it you're not intending to attend lunch looking like that?'

'Of course not. Give me fifteen minutes to have a shower and get ready.'

'You have five. We're already late.'

He didn't need to bother adding that it was my fault we were in that predicament. Earlier that week, when he'd phoned to arrange picking me up, we'd agreed that I'd be outside, ready and waiting when he arrived. Personally I thought he should have known better than to expect me to be so willing.

'Fine.' I wasn't about to argue with him, but I had no problem teaching him a lesson for being so inflexible. 'If that's how you want it . . .'

Before he could figure out what I was about to do, I loosened the tie on my kimono and slipped it from my shoulders, letting it drop to the floor so I was standing there stark naked.

Perhaps it wouldn't have been such a statement if I had the kind of boyish figure that fashion models possess. But instead I had Jessica Rabbit curves, which I'd given up trying to hide a long time ago. Even Richard, the master of self-control, couldn't help letting his eyes linger on my 34C breasts a second longer than he should have. I watched his jaw tighten, which was pretty much the biggest reaction I ever got from Richard, and then he averted his eyes.

I crossed the room, walking deliberately by him, and started hunting in my drawer for underwear.

'Jesus, Charlotte,' he muttered.

I turned back to him, affecting an innocent look. 'What? I'm just getting ready, like you asked.'

His scowl deepened. 'I'm not in the mood for your games today. I'll wait downstairs in the car for you. Be there in five minutes, or I'll come back up and drag you out. Like the child that you are.'

He swept from the room before I had a chance to reply.

Once he was gone, Gavin let out a long sigh of relief. I started at the sound – I'd almost forgotten he was there.

'Wow.' He shook his head. 'That's one tightly wound asshole.'

'Tell me about it.' I turned back to my underwear drawer, selecting the only clean bra and panties left in there. I put them on with my back to Gavin, but he didn't seem to get the hint that I just wanted him to shut up and quietly disappear from my life.

'Well . . .' I rolled my eyes as he drawled the word. Why was it that men felt obliged to make conversation with their one-night stands? I blamed all those movies that suggested women got upset if a guy didn't automatically propose after they slept together. I forced myself to face him. Gavin had on what I presumed was the most polite expression he could manage. He scratched his head a little, looking beyond awkward. 'I guess I should get your number or something. Maybe we could hang out sometime.'

'Yeah.' I spoke with exaggerated seriousness. 'We should totally do that. Maybe go for dinner and a movie. We could hold hands and everything.'

'Huh?'

It took all my willpower not to laugh at his obvious confusion. It was clearly his looks rather than his quick wit that had attracted me last night.

'Look,' I said, as I wriggled into a denim miniskirt and pulled on the cleanest white tank top I could find. 'Let's not pretend last night was anything other than what it was. We got drunk, I invited you back here and we shagged. To be perfectly honest, I can't remember much about the whole evening, but I'm guessing that we both got what we wanted out of it. So, as far as I see it, that's pretty much the end of our involvement.'

I couldn't help enjoying the look of astonishment on his face. He obviously wasn't used to the women he bedded behaving this way.

'So, you're saying you're happy with what went on last night. You don't want anything else?'

Ten out of ten for catching on so quickly. I'd obviously picked up the equivalent of a dumb blonde.

'That's exactly what I'm saying,' I said with exaggerated patience.

He looked at me with the kind of undisguised admiration that should be saved for whoever cures cancer. 'You know something? You're a really cool girl.'

'Yeah? My parents will be so proud.'

I reached for my biker boots, my footwear of choice, but then noted the sun streaming through the Velux windows that lined the ceiling. It was late September, but it looked more like mid-summer, and so I slipped on a slightly grubby pair of cream pumps instead. I dug through the pockets of the jeans I'd had on last night, found my purse and keys, and chucked them into the busted up, faux leather bag I took everywhere.

'Help yourself to tea, coffee, and whatever we have in the fridge,' I said, as I made my way out the door. It was meant to be a good exit line, but it seemed to throw Gavin even further.

'What? You mean, you don't mind me staying here once you've gone? That's a bit trusting of you.'

'Not really. If you even think about disturbing my flat-mate, she'll stab you in the eye, and—' I gave a pointed glance round the room— 'if you can find something worth stealing in here, then you're more than welcome to it.'

The intercom sounded then, Richard's way of letting me

know that my five minutes were up. I popped briefly into the bathroom, deciding he'd rather I took the time to brush my teeth and gargle some mouthwash than have me breathing stale alcohol fumes all over him for the two hour drive.

Once I'd finished, I made the mistake of looking in the mirror above the sink. Panda eyes stared back at me. Why couldn't I ever remember to take my makeup off? I ran a hand through my bleached hair. I was still getting used to it. I changed the colour every few weeks – I'd been everything from bright pink to ebony black. Platinum blonde wouldn't have been my choice, but I'd told Lindsay to surprise me, and she had. If my skin had been more tanned, maybe it would have looked tartier – but the white blonde against my Casper-the-friendly-ghost colouring gave me an Emo, edgy look, and made my eyes look an even more unnatural cornflower blue than usual.

A wave of exhaustion washed over me, which had nothing to do with how little sleep I'd got last night. I so wasn't prepared for this day – lunch with my parents and one hundred of their closest colleagues and friends. I can just imagine my mother's face when she sees me – her trouble-making youngest daughter, the university dropout who works in a bar – turning up hung-over and in a ridiculously tiny mini-skirt, amongst a sea of overachievers in floral dresses and suits. Ah, being the black sheep of the family was always a fun role to play.

I took a deep breath, mentally shaking myself out of my moment of self-pity. Then I grabbed face wipes and stuffed them in my bag, sprayed on a liberal amount of deodorant that I feared still wouldn't mask the smell of fags and booze, and headed downstairs to see what the dreaded day would bring.

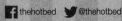